Rave Reviews for the Works of

SHANNON DRAKE

"Drake is an expert storyteller who keeps the reader enthralled with a fast-paced story peopled with wonderful characters."
—*Romantic Times BOOKclub* on *Reckless*

"Shannon Drake lures [readers] into a spellbinding romance tinged with a gothic twist."
—*Romantic Times BOOKclub* on *Wicked*

"Drake weaves an intricate plot into a delicious romance, which makes for captivating, adventurous and wonderfully wicked reading."
—*Romantic Times BOOKclub* on *When We Touch*

"Bringing back the terrific heroes and heroines from her previous titles, Drake gives *The Awakening* an extra-special touch. Her expert craftsmanship and true mastery of the eerie shine through!"
—*Romantic Times BOOKclub*

"Well-researched and thoroughly entertaining."
—*Publishers Weekly* on *Knight Triumphant*

"Captures readers' hearts with her own special brand of magic."
—*Affaire de Coeur* on *No Other Woman*

"Shannon Drake continues to produce addicting romances."
—*Publishers Weekly* on *No Other Woman*

Other historicals written under the pseudonym Shannon Drake

Wicked
Tomorrow the Glory
Blue Heaven, Black Night
Ondine
Damsel in Distress
Bride of the Wind
Lie Down in Roses
Emerald Embrace
Branded Hearts
No Other Man
No Other Woman
No Other Love
Princess of Fire
Knight of Fire
The King's Pleasure
Come the Morning
Conquer the Night
Seize the Dawn
Knight Triumphant
The Lion in Glory
When We Touch

SHANNON DRAKE

Reckless

HQN™

ISBN 0-373-77130-4

RECKLESS

This edition published by arrangement with Harlequin Books S.A.

www.HQNBooks.com

Printed in U.S.A.

To Jeanne Havens Beem,
with deepest thanks for the love she always gave Vickie,
and the encouragement she has always given me.

Reckless

Chapter 1

"DEAR LORD! HE'S GONE into the water!"

Katherine Adair—Kat to her friends and beloved family—gasped and leapt to her feet. Just seconds before, she'd been sitting on the deck of her father's vessel—sadly misnamed *The Promise*—reading and indulging in dreams. The day had been like many other Sundays she had spent throughout the years with her small family aboard the boat on the Thames. Often, as they'd watched the elite in their far more magical vessels, she had smiled as her sister, Eliza, mimicked the upper-crust accents, then joined her in singing old sea chanties—all the while looking to see if their father was about before adding a few of the more risqué lyrics.

But there were times, of course, when she did nothing but indulge in dreaming…about the very fellow whom a wave had just swept from the deck of the far finer leisure yacht *The Inner Sanctum!*

David. David Turnberry, youngest son of Baron Rothchild Turnberry, brilliant student at Oxford and avid sailor and adventurer.

"Kat! Do sit down! You'll rock this old scow and we'll be in the drink, too," Eliza chastised. "Don't worry. One of those Oxford chaps will dish him out!" she said with a sniff.

But none of them did. The river was wicked that day—fine for Kat's father, who used the turbulence in his work—but a poor time for entertainment. The young swains who had accompanied David on the sail were clinging to the rigging, looking into the water, shouting…but *not* jumping in and attempting a rescue! She recognized one—Robert Stewart, handsome, landed and charming, as well, David's best friend. Why wasn't he in the water? And there was another of his chums…she couldn't remember his name…Allan…something…

Oh, the fools! They hadn't even thrown in a life preserver, and David was so far from her own vessel that any attempt on her part to do so would be useless.

They shouldn't have been out on a day like today. They imagined themselves to be such sailors, and they were still so young, so raw. The river was far too rough, only for fishermen and fools. And, she thought ruefully, her father.

But now they'd lost David! And still, there was no one aboard heroic enough to dive in for the dear man's salvation.

Indeed, the waves were high, and she could understand their trepidation. But her heart cried otherwise. He was beautiful, magnificent. No fellow in all of England or surely even beyond had such a smile. Nor had she ever heard a fellow of his social position speak so kindly to those who were hard put to earn their meager living from the sea. She had watched him so often.

"They're not going for him!" she cried.

"They will."

"But he will drown!" Kat looked around quickly. Her father had brought in their own sails; the scow was merely riding the waves now.

In fact, her dear father was not working or paying the least attention to her. Lady Daws had come with them today; and she was laughing—the sound something like that of a sea-witch cackling, Kat thought sadly, something her father simply didn't hear—and that completely enraptured the hardworking man upon whom she had set her sights.

Kat looked back anxiously at the river. Maybe what had seemed like an eternity to her had been nothing more than a few seconds. Maybe the fellows had needed a moment to draw on their reserves of courage. But no...time ticked away, and none of those young swains aboard the richer vessel had made the slightest attempt to effect a rescue.

"Kat! Don't look so perplexed. Come, come...he can probably swim. The beaches are still all the rage with his crowd, even though the poor can now reach our beaches by train. Of course, the elite, they say, prefer to frolic in the Mediterranean."

Though Eliza spoke of the rich with disdain, in these moments with the sailing almost done for the day and the afternoon near its end, she always had her nose thrust into the pages of *Godey's Lady's Book*. She did love her fashion. And she could sew delightfully, creating fantastic designs from such bizarre materials as cast-off sails and canvas.

Kat paid her sister little attention. Her heart seemed to have lodged in her throat. She couldn't even see the young man's head bobbing in the waves.

Ah, there! And far from his own sleek vessel.

"The sea is too rough!" she exclaimed in a whisper. "He will die!"

"There is nothing *you* can do. You'll but kill yourself," Eliza warned fiercely.

"Ah, but I *would* die for him. I would sell my very soul for him!" Kat returned.

"Kat, what...?" Eliza began in horror.

Too late.

Being poor sometimes had its advantages. Kat shed her heavy, solid and sensible shoes and slid her cotton skirt down her hips to the floorboards. In seconds, she had also shed her secondhand jacket. She had no corset, no bustle, no darling little hat to discard, and so, despite her sister's protests, she leapt into the filthy water in her shift.

The chill hit her viciously.

And the waves were mercilessly rough.

But she had spent her life nearly as one with the sea. So she took a big lungful of air, plunged beneath the surface and swam hard.

She bobbed up first near the sleek yacht. She could hear the fellows on deck shouting, their voices sounding desperate.

"Can you see him?"

"His head... He's down again. Oh, God! He's going to drown... Bring her around, bring her around, we've got to find David!"

"I can't see him anymore!"

Kat took another deep breath and plunged beneath the surface again. She kept her eyes open, straining to see through the murky depths. And there...

There she saw him. To the right and a few feet below her.

Dead?

Oh, Lord, no! She prayed as fervently as she sought to reach the man. David. David the beautiful, the magnificent. Eyes closed...body sinking...

She grasped him, as her father had taught her to grasp a fisherman fallen overboard, catching him beneath the chin with the palm of her hand, allowing her to draw his head to the surface, while leaving her torso, legs and the solid strength of one arm to draw him toward shore.

Ah! The distance.

She could not make it!

But it seemed that both the luxury yacht and her father's fishing vessel were ever farther out to sea. What other vessels were at sail or anchored seemed at even greater distances. She had to make the shore.

She kicked, trying to stay calm, to remember that she mustn't lose her strength by using it to fight the rough water—that she must go with it, let the tempest take her until it drove her toward the shore.

She tried hard to keep David's head above the water, tried harder to keep breathing and moving herself against the waves, white-tipped, gray and brown, like living, breathing, beings anxious to suck her into their depths. How slender the river could seem at times, but...how great its span!

And yet, chilled and desperate as she was, it occurred to her...

He was in her arms. Oh, God! He could die in her arms.

As she would gladly die in his.

"GOOD LORD! WILL YOU LOOK at those young fools!" Hunter MacDonald stared at the young swains who raced around their yacht like simpletons. They'd lost one of their number, yet none was doing a damn thing about it.

He cursed them roundly, then called out to Ethan Grayson—his mate at sea, manservant and his friend. "Bring her in! I'm going for the boy."

"Sir Hunter!" Ethan, weathered and strong and far too sensible a fellow not to have risen far, protested strongly. "You'll but go down yourself!"

"No, Ethan, I'll not." Hastily removing shoes, jacket and trousers, he offered Ethan a grimace. "My good man, I've escaped crocodiles in the Nile. I shall be fine in this bit of English weather."

And so, stripped down to his drawers and shirt, he dove neatly overboard in the direction where he had last espied the young fellow's bobbing head. As he did, he could hear Ethan scolding him angrily: "Being a 'sir' does not give a fellow common sense, no, it does not! He survives famine, war and the evil in the hearts of men, but then drowns himself like the young idiot he would save!"

Too late! thought Hunter. The Thames closed around him as he cut through the waves, swimming with strong exertion to bring the heat of movement to his person.

The water was bitterly cold.

It had been easier to swim in the Nile with crocodiles, he ruefully admitted to himself.

AT LAST! KAT AND HER BURDEN had nearly reached the embankment.

She was far from the docks, closer to Richmond now than the City of London. A mist of rain was falling as she struggled through the remaining few yards of water, hitting mud beneath her feet at last, mud and God knew what else, some broken crockery that cut into her sole. She barely felt it, however, for she had him to land at last. Exhausted, near crawling at the end, she dragged David's dead weight up onto muddy sod and scraggly grasses, but not far from the road; homes and businesses and even ships at dock were visible nearby. She fell to his side at first, breathing, ah, doing nothing at all but breathing! Then as her lungs filled, she looked at his face and was roused to fear. She jerked up, then leaned on his chest, hard, pushing, determined to expel the water from his lungs. He choked, and water dribbled from his blue lips. Then he coughed and coughed...

And finally fell silent, other than the slow rasp of his breath.

She stared down at him, shaking. He lived. "Thank you, God!" she whispered fervently. And then, seeing his long lashes sweeping the contours of his noble face, she added, "You are so beautiful!"

His amber eyes opened. He stared up at her.

And she was horrified, for she was far from looking her best. Her hair was, as a rule, rich and long, if a bit glaringly red, but now it hung in sodden ropes. Her eyes—normally the oddest shade of green and hazel, sometimes almost the color of grass and at others almost gold—must be quite pinkened. And her lips were surely as blue as his. Her linen shift clung wetly to her body, and she was shaking uncontrollably. That he should see her so, when she still lived in a world of dreams, when society did not allow for the daughter of a humble, struggling artist, an Irish one at that, to so much as dare imagine a life among the elite, was the worst thing she could have imagined.

His hand moved. Fingers touched her face. For a moment, his own was dark and troubled, as if he sought an answer as to where he was, and why. "We were with the wind, listening...laughing...for there were songs on the air, as if the Sirens called to us, and then...pushed!" he murmured. "By God, I swear I was pushed! Why..."

Then his eyes focused on her. And a smile flitted over his lips. "Yes, yes, I felt hands against my back, pushing...but who the devil...and then...the cold...and the darkness. Then...you! Am I seeing things? You're an angel!" he whispered. "A sea angel...an angel, and I love you!" Then he laughed. "No! A mermaid, and thus I am alive!"

His fingers—on her face!

And the words he had said!

Ah, she could have died then and drifted to heaven in pure bliss.

His eyes closed. Panic seized her. But she could see him breathing, his chest rising and falling, and she could feel his warmth.

Voices suddenly sounded. Looking up, she saw a group coming from the gravel road that led down to the embankment. She jumped to her feet, aware of her near-naked state, her shift plastered to her body, providing not the least bit of modesty. And she was very chilled, of course, making that immodesty all the more apparent. She wrapped bare arms around herself.

"Oh, they're searching for him...but I saw...something!" The voice was feminine, sweet and touched with the sound of a sob.

"Now, now, our boy can swim, Margaret!" returned a male voice. "He'll be just fine."

Kat now saw a very pretty woman, slim and elegant in a late-summer day dress, a jaunty little hat sitting at an angle on her head, a parasol in her hands, her bustle twitching as she walked on dainty heels. Her hair was a soft ashen blond, and her eyes were as blue as the sea. Beside her was an older gentleman in a resplendent suit, cape and top hat, and they were coming closer and closer.

Kat's heart seemed to stop. In her mind's eye, she saw only the contrast between the elegant lady and herself, and she knew she had to escape. Quickly.

As she turned to run back into the water, a man rose from the waves not twenty yards away.

He was tall, lean and sinewy, his musculature quite evident, for he, too, but for an open shirt, was stripped down to his unmentionables. His dark hair was plastered to his head, and his classically sculpted face was frowning.

"Miss!" he called.

And that was it. She cried out softly, sprinted the few feet back to the muddy water's edge and plunged in, diving beneath the surface as soon as she could and swimming harder than she had ever done in her life, unaware now of the cold and the aching in her lungs and limbs.

She surfaced, she knew not where, just as the rain began.

"MARGARET!"

David blinked, staring up through the mist of rain. And there she was, Lord Avery's fair daughter, the very lovely and rich Lady Margaret, on her cheeks tears of a greater substance than the rain, staring down at him. Heedless of the mud, she sat on the embankment, his head cradled in her lap.

His heart leapt. Although she often appeared to care for him deeply, in fact, in the race for her hand, he had thought both Robert Stewart and Allan Beckensdale to be far ahead of him.

And yet now...how sweet to see her face!

For a moment, he was puzzled. There had been a fleeting moment when...he had thought he'd seen someone else. A different face. Fair and comely, with eyes a strange green fire and hair a searing flame-red. An angel? Had he come so close to death? No, then perhaps a mermaid, a sprite from the sea, or rather the river?

Had he imagined her?

And had he imagined, too, in the bluster of the day and the roll of the yacht, the hands at his back, pushing him, forcing him into the river?

"David! David, please, speak to me again, are you all right?" Margaret demanded anxiously.

"I…oh, dear, dear Margaret! Yes, I…I'm fine!" Not true. In fact, he was quite cold, but that mattered not in the least, not when this much-sought, beautiful lady was so gently tending to him.

Those eyes, so brilliantly blue, so studded with tears!

But…

"You saved me," he said, still confused.

"Well," she murmured, "I did drag you up the bank, hold you here, so dearly, in my lap."

"He will live!" These words, dry, rough and impatient. And a spray of icy water falling on him.

"Sir Hunter?" David gasped, looking toward the voice. And, indeed, he was there, the renowned sailor, soldier, excavator and all-round adventurer; the toast of London society, standing above him, furious and frowning.

And dripping.

"He's safely in your hands now, Lord Avery," Hunter said dryly to Margaret's father, who stood, David saw then, anxiously watching just a few feet away. "I must find the girl."

"The girl?" David echoed, blinking again.

"The one who saved your life," Sir Hunter said curtly, and David could hear the unspoken "You fool."

"Good God, Sir Hunter, you cannot mean to plunge back in—" Lord Avery began.

"Oh, but I do," Hunter said. "Lest she drown."

"You'll drown yourself!" Lord Avery argued. "If there is a girl out there, the boatsmen or fishermen will find her surely."

Lord Avery's protests were apparently insufficient for Hunter turned and strode back into the water.

"Father, he'll be all right!" Margaret called, adding with a touch of admiration that sent a pang through David's heart, "Sir Hunter MacDonald can withstand any hardship."

Sir Hunter, David thought, ever the hero, strong and brave and invincible. And I myself here on the muddy shore, gasping, barely alive…

But in her *arms!*

"I hope you're right, my dear," Lord Avery said, kneeling down beside David as well and, slipping his fine jacket from his shoulders, placed it around David. "Thank God you survived, my boy! Can you rise? We'll get you to the road and then to the town house before you catch your death of cold."

David, trying to fathom what was real and what lay in the soul of his imagination asked, "There really was a girl?" He looked at Margaret.

"Yes…that or, truly, a sea creature!" Margaret said.

"We'll see that she's rewarded for the act, assuming that Sir Hunter can indeed find her. How very odd that she ran back into the river. She must be quite mad. Or perhaps she's a lady of some fine family, afraid to be seen!" Lord Avery said gruffly. "One can only speculate, however, David. Right now, we must get you warm. That blasted river! Rarely is it anything less than wretched!"

"Yes, of course," David murmured, "Thank you. But if there was a girl...a strong girl, rich or poor, we must indeed see that she is rewarded."

Again he remembered—imagined?—being pushed into the river. It had been an act of pure malice and evil intent.

Whoever had done it had meant for him to die.

But why?

Margaret? To eliminate the competition for her hand?

Or was it something else entirely?

Suddenly he was afraid, deeply afraid, though he dared not show it. The thoughts tore through his mind. He and his friends had simply gone out for a day of sport and fun. Alfred Daws, Robert Stewart, Allan Beckensdale, Sydney Myers, all fellows he knew well. He'd studied with them, played cricket with them, trusted them....

He had to be mistaken!

And yet, if it hadn't been for the girl who'd—

"David?"

His name was said with such anxiety! And Margaret smelled of roses, so delicious, and her arms were around him as she helped him to his feet.

"The girl saved your life," Margaret agreed. "Your precious life."

He forgot Lord Avery, forgot his fear regarding his friends, everything, as he stared into the sky-blue of her eyes. He needed his future secured. As the son-in-law of Lord Avery, it would be.

"Ah, but we know the real truth! *You* saved my life," he declared. "You, with your gentle caring. You have brought me back. Even here, upon this shore, I might have died. Indeed, I would have died had I not opened my eyes to see your beautiful face!"

Her cheeks turned a delightful shade of pink, and he dared to mouth "I love you so!"

She did not reply, but the pink suffused to a darker shade as she reminded him softly, "My father, David!"

Yes, he thought, Margaret was indeed beautiful. And sweet. And very rich. For him, she would be the perfect wife.

He vowed then and there that he would be her husband.

SAVING THE OBJECT OF HER deepest desire had been difficult, but never in the long, cold struggle to bring him to shore had Kat feared for her own life.

Now, suddenly, she did so.

What a fool she had been to plunge back into the water! True, her sad state of undress might have brought about a few snickers and she'd certainly be considered rather scandalous. But what was scandalous compared to being dead!

Tired, cold and disoriented, she fought to retain her strength, to rise enough within the growing fury of the river to find either the shore or one of the vessels—fine or misbegotten—that braved the Thames no matter the weather. But though the rain had not come in heavy sheets as the sky had seemed to warn, it had formed a thick, blinding mist atop the churning waves. She was adrift in a cold sea of gray in which she seemed entirely alone.

She treaded water, turning this way and that, trying to see something through the haze. She knew she had to keep moving, lest the chill enshroud her. The euphoria she had felt after her rescue had faded completely, along with her strength. She was not sorry she had saved him—was his life not worth far more than her own?—but only sorry that she had been so foolish to run—or swim!—away. She struggled to give herself the impetus to go forward. She was her father's daughter, after all. A creature of the sea, a part of this wet, murky world.

At last, she calmed herself and rolled onto her back, then frog-kicked sideways into the current. But as she relaxed, a new fear—that of the darkness, of knowing that the Thames was little more than a sewer pit, seized her as she saw something move. Ridiculous notions shot into her mind. Snakes! No, none in the waters here, surely. Serpents—just as silly. Sharks—in from the sea? Here? In the Thames? Heavens, no, but still... Oh, God, there was something in the water!

She let out a scream, then choked on water from the wave that splashed over her, gagged. Desperate, choking, barely able to breathe, she started her frog kick again.

Something touched her!

Something...against her bare leg, and then on her hip. She kicked harder, to propel herself away. Then she felt it again. Something smooth, strong, slippery...

"No!" she shrieked. She would not die so—definitely not on the day he had told her he loved her! She would not die in the water. Water was her home, it was what she knew, and she would not, could not, give in.

When the thing rose near her, she lashed out with a fist as hard as she could.

"Good God, girl! What on earth ails you? I am doing my best to save your life."

It was a man. Just a man. She could make out little of him against the waves, but his voice was deep and rich and commanding. And then she remembered that a man had come out of the water when she'd been at David's side, that his appearance, along with that of the elegant young woman, had been the impetus to send her back into the dreadful river.

"Save my life! You're the reason that I'm threatened with the end of it!" she shouted back.

"Child, my craft is but a hundred yards south!"

A wave crested and washed over her. She had not been prepared, and she chocked in water, coughing, gasping.

And he was there, a wall of steel, an arm coming beneath her breasts, sliding most immodestly against her. She struggled.

"Damn you, be still! How on earth will I save you?"

"I don't need to be saved!"

"Indeed, you do!"

"If you'd cease trying to drown me, I'd be doing quite well!"

But she was lying, she realized. She was truly spent. Staying on the surface and fighting the waves was becoming ever more difficult.

Naturally, however, as she cried out her accusation, he released her.

And just as naturally, another wave smacked over her just as she was still recovering from the last. And she went under.

A mighty kick brought her back to the surface and into his arms.

"Be still!" he snapped. "Else I shall slap you into unconsciousness so that I can save your wretched life!" The sting of his words was far worse than a slap.

"I'm telling you—"

"Don't tell me!"

"But—"

"Dear God, woman, will you shut up!"

She had to then, for once again her mouth filled with river water, and she choked. She felt that steely power wind around her again, and despite the cold, his arms were warm, and despite her fury, exhaustion was winning. She felt a blackness creeping over the gray and brown of the day and the river, and suddenly it seemed right to close her eyes, give in....

His strength was great, for she was no longer moving on her own, yet felt as if she had been lifted, as if she were skimming over the water. Her head and nose remained above the surface.

Then there were voices, men's voices, and she realized that they had come to a sailing vessel, a very fine one.

"Ethan!"

The shout startled her and she jerked violently away. Her head slammed against the bow of the yacht, making her gasp with pain.

Stars burst brilliantly before her eyes.

And then...blackness.

"SWEET MARY!" ETHAN exclaimed, his powerful arms capturing the slender being Hunter had salvaged from the sea, lifting her as if she were no more than a toy. And holding her tenderly, he stared at Hunter for the briefest moment before hurrying with his bundle down to the cabin.

The yacht yawed, and Hunter stumbled to the helm, grasping control as the wind ripped around them. Ignoring the fact that he was soaking wet and chilled to the bone, he swore as he struggled with a wicked shift in the wind, furled the sails on his own and brought the craft around. Ah, well, he was a sportsman, was he not? Still, he had not intended such sport today.

Ethan returned topside bringing a blanket and a cup of warm brandy. With a nod of thanks, Hunter took the latter first, drained it and felt the heat seep back into his body. He took the blanket, wrapping it around his shoulders, while Ethan took the helm.

"She's all right?" Hunter asked, shouting to be heard.

"Nasty crack on her head!" Ethan shouted back. "But she opened her eyes. I've wrapped her in several blankets and given her a sip of brandy. She'll be warm enough, and well enough, I imagine, while we make for shore. Where do we take her? To hospital?"

Hunter frowned and shook his head. "They say such places are improving, but I'd not take even a dog there. We'll go to the town house. You're sure she's all right? She fought me like an insane woman...."

"Begging your pardon, Sir Hunter, but when you reached the yacht, I believe her head might have struck the hull."

Ethan had seen a number of injuries, since he'd served alongside Hunter in battle and across several continents. He was a fine man when it came to setting bones, and he was equally adept at dispensing medications. He knew a mortal injury when he saw one, and this one certainly didn't qualify.

"Who is she?" he demanded.

"I haven't the faintest notion," Hunter replied. "She apparently dived in to save young David, but from where, I do not know." He paused, thinking. Had he seen her before? She was not among last season's display of coming-of-age young society beauties, of that he was certain. He would have remembered her. Even wet and bedraggled, she was striking.

She had the abilities of a fish in water, so it seemed, and had been quite positive she didn't need rescuing. Her hair...what color! Even wet, it was like fire. And her eyes, when opened, flashed fire to match that hair.

Then, of course, only a blind man could miss the perfection of her form. She was no hothouse flower, but all lean muscle and sinew, long legs, trim hips and...beautiful breasts. Firm, full, straining against the taut fabric.

He winced at his lascivious thoughts. But he wasn't a blind man. He couldn't have missed them.

"Brave little thing!" Ethan said. "Diving in when none of his fine, hearty companions could manage to do so."

That, too, was true.

But then again, Hunter had seen the way she had looked at David on the embankment. Utterly rapt. She hadn't dived in for someone who was a stranger to her. There had been something about that look, something that any man or woman living seldom achieved, yet might crave with all the heart. Indeed, she would have gladly given her life for David.

She's in love, he thought.

"You think she's a friend of the chap?" Ethan asked now.

"I've never seen her before," Hunter said. "But then, I'm certainly not privy to all of young David's acquaintances. Indeed, I've only come to know him because he is due to take part in the upcoming excavations along the Nile. And because, of course, his father is interested in financing such work."

"Good Lord! You don't think she's a..."

"Doxy?" Hunter cocked his head, musing. "No," he said after a moment. "She hasn't the look. No hardness in her eyes. Not yet, anyway. But whoever she is, she will be a bit richer than she was, for Lord Avery is determined she be rewarded. Meanwhile, let's just see to her welfare, eh?"

In another thirty minutes, the yacht was in and duly berthed. Hunter held the girl in his arms, wrapped warmly in the blankets Ethan had provided her, while Ethan brought round the carriage. Though the area at the docks had been much busier early in the day, the fair-weather sailors had come to realize that such a day was not for sport. Now there was no one about.

Certainly not young David, or any of his party. Though Hunter knew that Lord Avery would be true to his word and reward the girl, the man would not be overly concerned about her welfare. David would be his first concern.

And, of course, Margaret.

Ethan reined in the handsome carriage horses, and the two stood still, awaiting their burden. Hunter entered the carriage with the girl in his arms, needing little assistance.

"Home then, and quickly," Ethan said, closing the doors and climbing up top to take the reins.

And as they rode, Hunter looked down at her face. It was truly beautiful. Skin, though ever so slightly tanned, as smooth as alabaster. Straight nose, lips perhaps a bit too wide and full for the current accepted state of fashion. Her cheekbones were high, her eyes large, lashes long and dark.

She stirred. Frowned.

A smile creased her lips, so sweetly.

She seemed to doze and to dream, and whatever she dreamed, it was sweet.

The dark lashes twitched and then rose.

Her eyes focused upon his, and she frowned.

"You're with us," he said softly.

Her lips moved. She seemed to have lost her voice.

"What?" he coaxed.

Something about her at that moment awoke a deep tenderness in him. He wanted to protect her. To bring all that was warm and gentle around her.

Her lips moved again.

He leaned close to catch the least whisper.

"You!" she breathed.

He heard the intense dismay. He clenched his teeth, forced a smile. And remembered the way she had looked at young David.

"Indeed, dear girl, 'tis I. And I do apologize. I should have left you in the water!"

Her eyes closed again. Apparently she still hadn't realized where she was.

He was tempted to throw her off his lap, but he held his temper. Even in his most wretched moments, he had never been that bad a scoundrel.

"All right, then, who are you? And when we return you safely to your home, just where would that be?"

Once again, her eyes flew open and assessed him with what appeared to be anger. By all the gods, they were truly magnificent eyes, blazing with their unusual color. At this close range, he could truly inspect them. Blue-green along the outer rims, fading to green, then to gold. Extraordinary. Hmm, she was definitely a redhead, but it wasn't a carroty color, rather like a deep, rich flame. And those dark lashes...

Wherever she came from, she was probably pure temper, and some poor father, brother or lover might well be glad of a holiday from her tongue!

She continued to stare at him, her expression becoming perplexed.

"Well? Who are you?" he demanded.

Her lashes fell. "I..."

"Good God, answer me!"

"I don't know!" she snapped.

And so saying, she pushed from his hold, righting herself most regally—until she realized that she'd lost her blankets. She flushed, cast him a furious glance, and dragged the blankets back up to sit in noble silence.

Chapter 2

HUNTER EYED HER LONG AND carefully, then a slow smile crept onto his lips.

"You're a liar," he told her quietly.

"How dare you!" she accused.

He shook his head. "I simply do not believe you struck your head that hard."

She turned to gaze out the carriage window as the busy streets of London passed by. Then she lowered her eyes, the wealth of lashes concealing her thoughts. Her hands, which showed small signs of hard work, were resting on the fine upholstery of the carriage seat and he could see that she was enjoying the soft feel of the fabric.

"My head pains me a great deal!" she snapped, and her gaze returned to his.

Again, he had to smile. "But you are alive," he said.

"I was doing quite well without you."

He didn't bother to respond.

Her frown deepened and she eyed him warily, drawing the blankets more tightly to her throat. "Who are you?" she demanded.

"Hunter MacDonald." He inclined his head in an ironic gesture. "At your service."

He thought that he saw her eyes widen just a bit; she was quick to hide any sign that she might have recognized his name, if indeed, she had done so. Had she? His exploits were frequently in the papers, he knew, something about which he seldom gave a thought. He was equally referenced in the society pages, usually with a gleeful note—readers loved a touch of scandal.

Frankly, and certainly as of late, he did not deserve most of the more scandalous items of gossip, but he had long ago determined that no matter what one did, it was impossible to live up to the high standards set for a man such as he. He was able to be quite entertained, fortunately, by what fabrications might come along.

His passenger didn't appear at all frightened to be in the company of such an ill-reputed fellow. Indeed, she seemed to be scheming within her own mind.

"Where are we going?" she demanded.

"Why, my town house, of course," he told her.

At that, he was pleased to witness the slightest bit of alarm pass briefly over her countenance.

"I may not know who I am," she said, "but I'm quite certain that I..." Her voice trailed off as if the right words failed her.

"That you what?" he offered helpfully.

She lowered her head. "If you would just return me to the sea, I believe I might recognize something...someone."

"The sea?"

She flushed. "The area by the river."

He appraised her with both his mind and his libido, ever more fascinated. She spoke well, extremely well, as if she had been decently educated. But he suspected that, nevertheless, she belonged to the poor area of the river.

And a class of Victorian society from which she might never hope to encounter her precious David except under unusual circumstances.

He found himself looking away, feeling the oddest little ache, as if he wished that *he* were the object of that deep affection she most obviously felt for the youngest son of the Baron Turnberry. It didn't matter that David would not inherit his father's title—there wasn't just one or two male siblings above him in line, but five!—he was surely something of a shining, glittering star to this girl.

And if she felt such an affection for himself?

Ah, well. Some of his reputation was deserved. But never had he tarried with a member of the fairer sex who was truly young and innocent, and tender of heart, as well.

Then, again, what made him believe that she was truly innocent? She had plunged into the Thames nearly naked. For a man.

"I believe that he's about to become engaged," Hunter said harshly.

She was good at her charade.

"Who?"

"David Turnberry, my dear."

"And why should that concern me?"

"I beg your pardon, I forgot. You do not know yourself, so how would you know of Mr. Turnberry?"

She looked at him, red tendrils of hair, drier now, falling softly across her face. "How would you happen to know about the relationships of...this man to whom you refer?" she asked.

"We run in the same circles," he responded. "In fact, the man you saved—I'm sure you must remember dragging a man out of the water?—is due to leave shortly for a season working the excavations in ancient Egypt. When he returns, I believe he will be married."

"Is he officially engaged?"

"No," Hunter admitted. "But he has been a contender in the quest for the hand of Lady Margaret for some time, and I believe that today, after such high drama and fear for his life, she may have decided that he's the one she'll choose to marry."

She turned away quickly, as if she felt distressed and would prefer he not see it. Then she lowered her head and murmured, "Please...if you would take me back to the river, I would be most grateful. I'm sure I shall find out who I am and where I belong."

He leaned forward, absently setting a hand on her knee as he spoke. "But, dear girl, Mr. Turnberry is anxious to thank you for his life. We must allow him to do so."

She visibly winced. "As I am? I would deeply appreciate a return to the sea."

"River."

"River!" she snapped.

She moved. He realized that his hand touched her still—and that it was far more disturbing to him than to her. He withdrew.

"We are nearly at my town house. My sister often spends time there—I'm quite sure we will find something appropriate for you to wear."

"Sir! I cannot go with you to your town house alone."

"Fear not," he said, smiling. "I have the most proper housekeeper one might ever hope to have. You'll be in the best of hands."

They came at last to the town house with its elegant wrought-iron gates and handsomely manicured lawn. He wondered if she had not caught his attention before because, in a very strange way, she reminded him of himself. In his younger years, he'd seen what he was and what he was not. And he'd realized he must improve his own lot, which he had managed to do quite nicely, first in the military, then by charming the queen, and then with his very real fascination for all things Egyptian. He had written a number of books on his experiences, and therefore earned a fair penny from his publishers, and if his own efforts had not seen him to financial success, the death of his beloved and landed godmother had increased his position most pleasantly. The boon had not been expected, because the old girl, who had been a true adventurer herself and had always engaged him in tart conversation, had always pretended poverty and gratefully accepted his many gifts.

The carriage passed through the gates to the porte cochere at the side door. It opened as Hunter jumped down from the carriage, reaching back to assist his unwilling guest. She hesitated, but at last accepted his hand, apparently deciding that it would be churlish to refuse it.

"Dear me, dear me!" This from Mrs. Emma Johnson, his housekeeper. She gave Hunter a scathing look, as if he had committed a crime. "Sir Hunter! What in heaven's name? Dear child, do come in and I will see to you! Do your parents know where you are? Hunter, did you take this young lady sailing on such a day and lose her in the river? Oh, child, thank the Lord you're all right. I shall see to you immediately." She slipped an arm around his red-haired sea vixen, staring him down. "Now, Hunter, it's none of my business, but—"

"No, Emma, it's not!" he said, but smiled. She was very dear to him. When he was quite young and struggling, she had even suffered many a week without pay, assuring him that he could pay her when…well, when he could. He had done his best to reward her for those days of service when her work had been based on loyalty alone.

She narrowed her gray eyes in a severe warning, and again he had to smile. "Emma, I did nothing terrible, I assure you. She was drowning—"

"It was not until he tried to help me that I was drowning!" the girl protested.

"It's amazing what you *do* seem to remember," Hunter murmured.

"Good heavens! What did happen?" Emma demanded.

"I suppose we must let the young woman explain," Hunter said.

"Young woman? What is your name, dear?" Emma asked.

"Yes, dear, what is your name?" Hunter repeated. He watched her face heat with color. "Ah! Dear me, how could I forget so quickly? She suffered a bump on the head and has forgotten everything. Can you imagine, Emma?"

The housekeeper looked horrified. "Hunter, what did you do?"

"I'm innocent, I swear!" he said.

"Aye, mum, he's innocent this time, I can vouch for that," Ethan said, coming round from having led the horses and conveyance on to the carriage house and the groom. "Sir Hunter saw a friend swept clean off the deck of another yacht, and he dived to rescue the fellow. Seems that, wherever she came from, the girl had the same idea."

Emma stared her. "Child! You went into the Thames? Why, 'tis filthy with the rot of thousands, no matter what they say has been done for sanitation in the reign of our good Queen Victoria!"

"I've been in it before," the girl murmured. She flushed again, catching Hunter's glance, "I...uh...think I've been in it before! I mean...perhaps I've been in water quite frequently... at least, I believe that I have...."

Emma glared at Hunter once more. "Well, and look at you, in just your drawers and a blanket! Humph!" She wagged a finger at Hunter. "You, sir, have your reputation, but it shall not sully mine. I'll see to it that our poor dear guest has a bath and is set right up. Ethan! You must go for the doctor immediately—"

"Doctor!" the girl protested.

"Of course! You've lost your memory. And with the master of the house around, dear, we wouldn't want to add to that the fact that you've lost your senses! No, no, this must be handled in all proper haste!"

"Emma, I'm hardly likely to seduce the girl beneath my own roof," Hunter murmured wryly.

"Indeed, hardly likely," the girl muttered.

"In fact, Ethan will help me out of this river sop I wear, Emma, and you see to the young lady here. They'll be wanting to know about this at Lord Avery's manor—it was David Turnberry who went into the drink, and he'll want to thank our mystery girl properly. I'll give a call to the manor—assuming the blasted telephone decides to work—let them know that I've got the girl."

"But I do think we should have the doctor—" Emma began to protest.

"I'm fine!" the girl assured her.

"Humph!" Emma said.

"Let's see...perhaps we should give her until the morning, see how she is faring then. Emma, I'm sure you will have a delightful room ready somewhere in this place?" Hunter said.

"A bath...and a bit of rest. Alone. If I may. That would be lovely," the girl said. "And if I feel at all ill in the morning, I swear I'll see a doctor!"

"All right, then, Hunter, be gone up the stairs. Young woman, I'll get a good deep bath going, and you'll be warm and cozy in no time. Now, Hunter, you must stay away."

"Good Lord, trust me, I intend to!" he assured Emma. He couldn't help winking at his less-than-gracious guest before he passed her by. His fine deck shoes squeaked and he was beginning to feel more than a chill, despite the blanket around his shoulders.

Ethan followed him to his room, dragging out the hip bath, ready to be of service. "Stop, my friend," said Hunter. "I'll heat my own bath. See to it that there are coins left on the dresser in the blue room—which is surely where Emma will take our guest. Oh, and see that there are enough coins for transport in the pocket of whatever piece of clothing Emma chooses for our guest."

Ethan arched a brow.

"Believe me, my friend," said Hunter. "It is for the girl's benefit."

"You want her to run away?"

"She's going to run back to the river. You mark my words. Besides, don't worry. I intend to run after her. Ah, Ethan! Please, just do as I say!"

Ethan grunted but left to do as bidden.

KAT, HER MEMORY QUITE INTACT, found being and talking with Mrs. Johnson—Emma, as she preferred to be called—easy and comfortable. The woman was so warm and caring! Kat didn't think that she'd ever had such a delightful bath, the water so deliciously warm. The house and furnishings were exquisite. Kat had never been in such luxury!

Emma chatted about the neighborhood—charming, she adored it, they'd been there almost a decade. Then there was the amazing way one could now get about—on a train in a tube underground! "Oh, that it had been there when I was a young girl!" she declared. She mostly talked about Sir Hunter MacDonald, the love of her life, it seemed.

Kat wished desperately that she'd been taken to the home of David Turnberry, instead, for she was certain that there she'd have heard from *his* housekeeper and might have learned all kinds of delicious little nuggets about *his* life. But it wasn't to be. She had to remember where she was. And why.

And remember to be grateful. So she listened. Sir Hunter had been an impressive soldier, and it had been for his gallant service to his country that he had been knighted. Why, Emma gushed, he was called upon often to play the diplomat for the queen! And, well, of course, he did have his reputation, but only because there were so many widows and even a few divorcées who did not understand mourning as did their dear queen. And Americans! Well...they were a breed of their own, adventurers-adventuresses, all. And then, of course, there was his obsession with Egyptian antiquities. Yes, there had been quite a hullabaloo at the museum just a year ago. Dastardly going-ons, but all settled in the end, the evil ones out of the picture, and those involved would be sailing off again, learning more and more, and adding to the grandeur of the British Empire!

Yes, yes, yes, Kat thought. But how much could a girl listen to, especially about a fellow who had almost drowned her? All right, it was true that that had not been his intention, and he *had* made her a guest in his very beautiful home. So she held her tongue while his housekeeper worked her hair with sweet-smelling suds and prattled on. She didn't have much of a choice.

"But, of course, you've read about him, I'm certain," Emma continued. "He has been the idol of the country many a time. Oh, I forgot! Poor thing. Your memory is gone. But if anything stirs in the darkness, let me assure you, despite his wretched reputation as a ladies' man, Sir Hunter is a gentleman, a *true* gentleman." Emma seemed determined that Kat should understand that.

The woman added ruefully, "I'm certain that many of the rumors are fact, I'm sorry to say, but as I told you, tarries only with divorcées and widows, women who are quite adult and mature, and responsible for their own actions. I don't believe he frequents houses of ill repute—well, not the lower sort, anyway. But surely, you must be aware that he has a kind heart. And courage! Why, he has fought again and again in the queen's service, held his own, even when he didn't think we had the right to be where we were— Good Lord, child, you mustn't ever repeat that! He is a loyal subject of our good queen, right down to the toes! And then, of course, there is his constant hunt for Egyptian antiquities."

"Do you mean treasures?"

Emma Johnson sniffed. "Treasures? Not as we think of them, dear. Treasures to Sir Hunter are relics of the past, the older, and so it seems, the nastier, the better! But then again, it is such a thing among almost *all* of the British aristocracy and elite these days. That, and mesmerism!" she said with a snort. "Still, he might have chosen a season by the Riviera or in Italy. Oh, he enjoys his stops in Rome and such, but it's Egypt he goes for, Egypt he loves. He works with the museum, you know. And he always manages to wrangle the best dig for himself or be granted the best location, through our own embassies and the Egyptians, who are in charge. Well, we say that Egyptians are in charge, but it's still our influence that guides it all. And glad they are of English intervention."

"English money, I would think," Kat murmured softly.

Emma laughed delightedly. "Well, now, and there's the truth. But the Turks were there for a quite a long time, as well, and the Egyptians are glad of our protection, you mark my words. And, of course, the French are forever around. But...I do so wish Sir Hunter would settle for an autumn in a lovely European city!"

"But...it sounds fascinating. Really." Kat leaned back. "I've only ever dreamed of Ancient Egypt!" She jerked back up. "David Turnberry is going for this season in Egypt, as well, isn't he?"

"Many go, as I said. And you must understand, this is when the season for archeology begins—summer is far too hot! Fall into winter...well, they're all about to set sail for the mysteries of the past as it is...next week!"

A week! Kat thought. *A week. A week in this country, and then...*

David Turnberry would go to Egypt. When he returned, he would marry?

Kat sighed softly. It was insane to think, just because he looked up at her after she had saved his life and said *I love you,* that anything in the world could bring her to his true attention. He was about to become engaged to be married. To an elegant creature of his own class.

He can't love his presumed fiancée! Not when he said those words to me!

But she had panicked and run away. In part because of Hunter MacDonald. But now…he meant to introduce her to the man. She would have a formal introduction to David Turnberry.

"All right, step out now, child," Emma was saying. "I've a fine set of clothing for you. The Lady Francesca—she's Sir Hunter's sister, married Lord Hathaway—leaves ample here, and she'll be more than pleased that she could help out with a girl pulled from the river, one willing to risk her own life to save another!"

Kat suddenly felt terribly uncomfortable, hearing the words of praise. She had to wonder if she would have attempted the rescue if it had been anyone other than David Turnberry. The thought troubled her, and she barely noticed the silk of the drawers she stepped into, or the simple elegance of the gown Emma slipped over her head, with exquisite lace on the bodice.

"And, oh dear! If a night's sleep doesn't help your memory, we must do something," Emma said suddenly. "There is bound to be some young fellow somewhere, terribly worried about you. No ring on your finger, though."

Kat's heart seemed to stop in her chest. No, there was no young fellow worried about her. But her father would be. And her sister, and so many dear friends…

How far had she come? How was she going to get back? If she had to walk...

She lowered her head, biting her lower lip. Surely, a man such as Hunter MacDonald would have left a few coins somewhere about. She would not steal! She would see that they were returned. Public transport was getting very good indeed, and she knew London well.

Like the poor man's daughter, the urchin, that she was!

"Yes, indeed," she managed to say somberly. "By tomorrow, I'm sure I shall be fine. I do believe that when I wake up, everything will rush back," she lied. Then she yawned. "Forgive me. I'm exhausted." She lifted her hands with her words, then let them fall. She heard a soft tinkle within the folds of the dress. Her fingers moved dexterously over the pockets. The relief that swept through her almost caused her to faint in reality. *Coins!*

"As well you might be after such a day! Now, just sit before the fire while I brush out your hair. I'll have you upstairs napping in no time."

Kat could barely sit still while the kindly woman dried her hair before the fire, brushing all the snarls from the long tresses. When she was done, her hair was as soft as silk, far softer than it had ever been. But she was so riddled with guilt about the hasty departure she planned that she had to force herself to stop fretting long enough to voice a sincere thank-you for the housekeeper's help.

That same guilt made it difficult for her to appreciate the subdued elegance of the house or the little touches that made it so uniquely Sir Hunter MacDonald's residence—the relics sitting atop the newel posts, the hieroglyphs that adorned the walls. The fine oil paintings, some of English country sites and some of ancient Egypt. One was of the Sphinx at sunset, and it was so breathtaking that her steps did falter.

"I can show you more of the house, dear," Emma offered.

"Thank you, I shall so enjoy that…later. But I beg of you, I must have a few hours of undisturbed rest."

"Of course!"

And so she was led up the grand staircase to a room. It was planned for female guests, or so it appeared, for the furniture was a light and lovely wood, and the canopy and spread of the four-poster bed were blue and white, enhanced by the shades of an Oriental rug.

"Rest well, my dear. I will see to it that you're not disturbed," Emma vowed.

"Thank you again, ever so much!"

The door closed. Kat moved to the bed and lay atop the spread, keeping herself still for several long seconds.

Then she rose. She started for the door, then noticed the coins sitting on the dresser. She placed them in her pocket with the others and took the time to look in the lovely little Oriental bedside table for paper and a pen.

"I will return the dress and the coins," she wrote. The words looked cold and rude. She hesitated, then added, "Thank you ever so much." No, it wasn't enough. But time was ticking away. She sketched herself as a Sphinx, with a smiling face, and as the caricaturists did, she added a little balloon at the side of the lips, writing in, "I do thank you!"

Enough. She had to leave, make her way home, then return here before anyone was the wiser and be ready to allow David Turnberry to thank her for his life.

She hurried for the door and out into the hall. There, she listened. There was no sound other than that of the ticking of the grandfather clock in the foyer.

She fled down the stairway to the front entry. There was no lock on the front door. Not now. What would she do when she returned? Perhaps it would be locked by then; dusk would surely be coming on.

Well, that was a worry she would have to contend with when she returned. Right now, she had to go to her father and sister.

And worry that she would be able to return at all!

On the street and down the block, she paused to draw a breath.

She was out. She had gotten out very easily.

Now the great problem—was she going to be able to get back in?

"THE BIRD HAS FLOWN!" Hunter noted.

He sat astride Alexander, his riding mount, hidden against a small field of trees in the narrow side yard of the town house. Ethan, at his side on Anthony, glanced his way, his features wrinkling in a silent question.

"We shall follow," Hunter said.

She obviously knew where she was going. She quickly made her way through the streets by Hyde Park, finding a station for the omnibus.

There, she boarded.

Following the bus, which was pulled by heavy draft horses, was quite easy. The streets were busy, and the pedestrians often careless, so the going was somewhat slow.

His redhead changed vehicles and headed, as he had suspected, for the river. And, there, of course, his concealing themselves became a bit more difficult. Hunter dismounted, handing Alexander's reins to Ethan, and bidding the man to wait with the horses.

"I don't know what either of you is about!" Ethan grumbled.

Hunter laughed. "I'm not at all sure I know myself!"

He hurried then, for once the girl had departed the vehicle, she began to move quickly through the streets, the rows of tightly packed houses, the people milling in the walkways and alleys. He assessed the neighborhood.

It wasn't the poorest section of the city, but rather the old City of London itself, where some of the architecture of the late sixteen hundreds remained, simple homes built soon after the Great Fire had ravished the city. Most of the inhabitants were hardworking tradesmen, though the area attracted students, musicians and artists. The streets, if not grand, were clean.

"Why, core and blimey!" an old woman who'd been sweeping called out. "It's Kat!"

"Shh, Mrs. Mahoney, please!" the girl cried, and she raced past the woman. "Is Papa in the house?"

"Frettin'and wailin', he is!" the woman said. "Why, he has some of his friends in the police out looking for you, child! There was a rumor that you had been rescued from the water, but...well, no one knew just who had done the rescuing and where you'd gotten to!"

"Oh, no!" the girl cried.

"And what is that you be wearing, Mistress Kat?" the woman demanded.

"I must see Papa," the girl said, and rushed by the woman, heading into a small house that was painted and finely detailed with new gingerbread trim. The place surely dated back to the days of the Flemish weavers, Hunter thought.

Determined to avoid a conversation with the old woman, Hunter slid quickly against a wall. There was a narrow alley leading to a rear courtyard, and he sidled down the length of it. He did not need to go far.

An open window and drawn draperies allowed him an excellent view of the show within. There she was, the girl whom the old woman had called Kat, wrapped tightly in the arms of a tall, bewhiskered fellow. Another girl, also red-haired, though of a lighter shade, stood by. She embraced Kat next, then stepped away as the dignified older fellow wrapped Kat in his arms again.

When at last the embracing ended, the second girl—her sister?—demanded, "Katherine Mary! What on earth are you wearing? Goodness! Where did you get such an elegant dress?"

"I shall explain," Kat said.

"Indeed, you shall!" the old fellow responded gruffly. "I have been out of my head with fear and grief. Eliza told me of this insane thing you felt you must do, and I was left to convince myself that you would return, that you had not gone down to the bottom of the Thames! There are police officers out looking for you, young woman. Eliza, send Maggie to inform the police that my child has been found, that we will not need to dredge the river!"

The man was truly furious, and yet obviously greatly relieved. Hunter felt guilty, as he knew the girl must. She appeared stricken, as if she had not realized till now just how painfully her absence had been experienced.

The girl Eliza hurried from the room to summon this Maggie—a servant of some sort, Hunter assumed—despite the fact that this household seemed rather poor—but was very quickly back, not about to miss an instant of what was going on.

"Papa," Kat said, apparently in an effort to soothe. "Poor Papa, I am so sorry, I hadn't imagined such a fuss. Why would you send the police after me? You know that I swim better than a fish."

"Aye, that I know," her father said proudly. "But you'd gone after a university bloke, and then disappeared from sight! What will I do with you, what will I do? If only your dear sainted mother were still alive!"

"Kat, where did you get the dress?" her sister demanded again.

"It is borrowed... Papa, please, all will be well. You see, I was helped by another gentleman after I helped the first gentleman. I have been at a safe and truly gentle place, I swear it! You see, I am to meet with David Turnberry, the first gentleman, who is soon to be affianced to Lord Avery's daughter, and I must—"

"Lord Avery!" Eliza exclaimed. She looked across the room. "Papa, she will get a reward. A good reward!"

"I needed no reward," Kat said.

"Well, I'd be happy for it!" Eliza exclaimed. "Scrimping and saving for something other than fish on the table."

"Eliza!" the father said sadly, shaking his head.

Eliza apologized quickly. "Papa, Papa, you do so well, I am truly sorry for my words of complaint. But...Kat! That gown! It's exquisite—where did it come from? Oh, my God! I should get dressed. I must go back with you and—"

"No," the man said firmly. "No one is going anywhere."

"But we must give this serious consideration," Eliza pleaded.

"Katherine Mary, you are my child. My daughter. And you'll

not go off among young men, whether they're poor as paupers or rich as Midas, without proper escort. Without me!" he bellowed.

"Oh, Papa, please! I must go to Lord Avery's on my own. I swear to you, I am safe. There is a wonderful woman named Emma Johnson, and she is like my guardian angel."

"You were at the grand house of a woman?" her father inquired. "Why have these people not escorted you home?"

"Papa...forgive me, but I'm pretending to have lost my memory. I've told them I don't know who I am."

The man sank into a chair. "You are ashamed," he said softly.

"Oh, Papa, never!" she cried.

He looked up at her sadly. "We do not need the charity of others. I work hard, we work hard. And we earn our living. Meager, that it is. But I'm an honest man, and I do an honest day's work. You will take no reward."

"Papa!" Eliza protested. "Papa, in truth, you are a great artist! You are simply too quick to work for those who promise to pay, but cannot pay."

"They are the interesting subjects," the father murmured.

"And then, when there is a rich man about, you refuse to charge what your work is worth! I would say that many a rich man owes you. And if the truth of your service were ever known, you, Papa, would be knighted! Therefore, nothing coming our way would be charity, but rather your due," Eliza stated.

He shook his head again. "A man's life is far greater than any sum of money. Kat will take no reward."

Eliza groaned, turning away.

Kat lowered herself to her knees, setting her hands upon her father's knees. "Papa, I will take no reward. But may I go back to Mrs. Johnson just to meet these people? I swear to you, I shall refuse the reward. But I would like… I would dearly love…just this time…to meet these people, to let them thank me. Oh, please, Papa!"

"It is a hard world out there, lass! We haven't money, but again, we've pride. And you've no great dowry, but again, lass, you have your virtue."

"It is not at stake, Papa," she vowed levelly, not offended, her promise earnest.

"I fear to let you from my sight!" he said.

"She is in lo—" Eliza began, but Kat flew to her feet and whirled on her sister.

"Perhaps, since it is a castoff, Papa will allow me to keep the dress, and *you* may have it!" she said, her eyes offering both a plea and a warning.

"What kind of a father would I be to let you go?"

"A kind and trusting one?" Kat suggested.

"No!"

"Oh, Papa, please! It's just a dream, a silly dream, to have one chance to be thanked and feted. And I know the streets, the way of people, rich and poor. You've taught us well. You used what you worked so hard to attain to see that Eliza and I had an education. You taught us to know right from wrong. Please…trust in me, Papa!" The last plea seemed to touch his heart, for he rose and took her hands in his.

"I do trust in you. But I'm deeply sorry that you may not have your moment of glory. I am a poor man, but I will not sell my pride, nor my responsibility."

"But, Papa—"

"Hate me, child, rail against me. I will not let you go."

"Papa, I can never hate you!" She was in his arms again, cherished, but dismayed.

Hunter, from his position outside the window, could see her face as she held on tight to her father. She loved him, but she was stubborn. Reckless. And she was plotting. She had come upon a dead end, and she would discover a way around it.

What would it be? Hunter wondered. He realized that, listening, he had caught and held his breath. He released it slowly, thinking.

He wondered if the wicked little redheaded vixen knew that she already had far more than money, a title, or half of the silly things considered important by members of the so-called elite, the place her beloved David inhabited.

Her father drew away. "The dress, lass, must be returned. Where did you acquire it?"

"It belongs to Francesca, Lady Hathaway," Kat said unhappily.

"But she lives far from London!" the father said.

"Her brother's town house is not so far."

Eliza gasped. "You were at the town house of...Sir Hunter MacDonald?"

"Hunter MacDonald!" Papa roared.

Hunter winced. It appeared he was well known.

"Papa!" Eliza said, apparently shocked by her father's response. "The man is a favorite of the *queen!*"

"Yes, and it's because the man has a reputation for outlandish adventure, always riding into the fray. I daresay that the queen enjoys the stories of his escapades—and the flattery he doubtless showers on her."

"But they say that he's brilliant!" Eliza said excitedly. "And oh! Far more than charming. Why, there have been rumors of his affairs with ladies of the highest strata!"

Both her sister and father were staring at her in horror.

"No, please," Eliza persisted. "He has sullied no reputations, he has merely…well…goodness! How do I put it delicately? Played among players?"

Hunter shook his head. Things were only getting worse. And though he hadn't really the least idea of what he was about, he decided that the time had come to knock on the door.

He was just heading for the door when Kat spoke.

"Sir Hunter is not so much, I assure you, Father," she said. "I promise you, there is not the least worry regarding my virtue as far as he is concerned. But…I might have met Lord Avery, Father."

"And her precious David!" Eliza murmured.

"What?" their father demanded with a frown.

"Oh, she might have had a lovely dinner, Father, that is all," Eliza said. "You know, Papa, rubbed elbows with the truly elite!"

"There is no sense in it," the man said softly. "No sense at all, and you must believe me, and accept this regret rather than one far greater. Do you understand, Katherine Mary?"

Kat looked down. "I bow to your wisdom, Papa," she replied. Then she gave a massive yawn. "Papa, I am to bed."

"'Tis best, my girl," he said gently. "Tomorrow, we will return the dress."

"Tomorrow," she agreed.

She started for the narrow stairway. Then she turned. "I love you, Papa," she said.

"Aye, child, and I love you."

Kat smiled, hesitated and went on up the stairs.

Outside and unseen, Hunter leaned thoughtfully against the wall. Then he looked through the window again, and a frown creased his forehead. He realized that he knew of the girl's father. His frown dissipated, to be replaced by a small smile.

At last he moved away, certain of the need to hurry home. Kat, he knew, would soon be on the road again.

Chapter 3

A NOTE HAD BEEN DELIVERED to the house in Hunter's absence. Lord Avery begged pardon; the excitement of the day had been too much, and he wished to retire early that evening. He requested, however, an audience the following morning, and asked if Hunter would bring the young lady to the manor, or if they might call upon the town house.

He could have tried calling on the telephone, but Lord Avery never seemed to hear what was said, so Hunter sent Ethan off with the reply, requesting Lord Avery and his party to attend a late breakfast at his town house the following morning.

He went upstairs, obviously intent on entering the Blue Room, despite the fact that Emma pleaded he not do so. "She doesn't want to be disturbed!" Emma said firmly.

Hunter laughed. "A quid says she isn't in there!"

"*Quid!* Street language, Hunter," Emma warned with a sniff.

"Bet me?"

"Good heavens, Hunter, a respectable matron doesn't gamble!"

"Good thing—because the girl isn't in there!" Hunter said, and pushed open the door. Emma frowned, looking in.

"But she was so very exhausted!"

"Well, she's awakened now," Hunter murmured.

Emma squared her shoulders, a frown furrowing her brow. "Has she run away?"

"I think she just needed…a little air," Hunter said.

"I do hope she returns. Such an exquisite little creature. Why, Hunter, in all my life, I've never seen such eyes as hers. And she's ever so polite. A true joy. Not that it's my place to say, but compared to a few of the women you've had here… Oh, sorry. And I've worked so hard on a lovely supper… Oh, not that I don't want you to enjoy a lovely supper, but—"

"Emma, I do believe she'll be right back," Hunter said. "You go tend to the supper."

When Emma was gone, he saw the note on the dresser. As he read it, he was surprised by the little stirring of emotion that seized him.

And then there was the sketch. A marvelous reproduction of the Sphinx.

Her father.

Not that it had been such a natural thing that he should have realized the man's identity by peeping through his window. But oddly enough, it had just been the week before that he had been out in the country at the home of his friends, the Earl and Countess of Carlyle, that he had first seen one of the stirring seascapes painted by William Adair. Brian hadn't really known anything about the artist. He had simply fallen in love with the wild natural turbulence, the sense of the sea, of the wind, in the painting. "A local fellow, I was told, though the gallery owner didn't know much about the artist personally, for he had acquired the work through an agent. I must, soon, find out where he does live.

The piece is quite magnificent, but I bought it at a steal from a fellow down on Sloane Street."

Hunter had been entranced and had studied the oil at his leisure. The signature had been small but firm, and entirely legible. William Adair. And once he had followed Kat, peeped in through the window and seen the pieces hanging within the small abode, he had realized that oils of such power and emotion could have only been created by the same artist.

And so his mermaid was the man's daughter. And her little sketch gave proof of an amazing, if untapped and untrained, talent, as well.

He replaced the note as it had been left and slipped out of the room, leaving all as if he had never entered it.

Then he waited in the yard, determined to catch his guest in the act of trying to return undetected. He wondered how long she waited to depart her home unnoticed. It would have taken her a bit of time, since she would have had to convince her sister to be part of her subterfuge. In Kat's mind, all she would have to do was elude her father for the evening. Her one magical evening. She couldn't know as yet that there would be no way to see Lord Avery—or David—tonight.

At last, he saw her. Behind a pillar on the porch, he watched as she made her way down the street. She slowed before reaching the house, and must have been dismayed to realize that he was outside. She hovered by a mulberry bush, certain that he must give up soon and go into the house.

He did not.

At last she wandered by, twirling a piece of impossibly brilliant hair between her fingers. "Sir Hunter!" she said, sounding politely surprised.

"My dear girl," he replied just as pleasantly. "Wherever have you been?"

"Oh, not far," she lied sweetly. "I just slipped out for...some air."

"Ah. And did the air help any?" he inquired.

"Help with what?"

"The return of your memory, of course!"

"Oh! Well, no...I'm so sorry. Yes, yes, of course, I had thought that a walk might bring much more to mind regarding my identity, but...alas, I'm afraid that it hasn't been so."

"Oh, dear," Hunter sympathized.

"Will...will I be seeing Lord Avery and David Turnberry this evening?" she asked.

"I'm afraid not."

"Oh?" She sounded startled, certainly. And, actually, quite cross.

Understandable, given her circumstances.

He smiled. "Lord Avery has an old ticker, my dear. Heart, that is. He must rest tonight. He will come tomorrow."

"I see." She lowered her head quickly, hiding her disappointment. And trying to come up with a new plan, he imagined.

"I'm so sorry that you're disappointed. However, we've a lovely dinner awaiting us, at your convenience."

"How very kind of you. I... Would it be possible to dine in my room? I do believe the excitement of the day has made me quite tired."

"But have you been out walking so very long? I was under the impression that you'd had a nice long nap this afternoon after we returned."

"Well, I did, yes, of course, but near drowning can be so very tiring!"

"Mrs. Johnson has a meal prepared. We were only waiting for you to wake up. Imagine! We didn't want to disturb you, but you were already awake and wandering about."

"Right. Imagine," she murmured. "But I am so very exhausted…"

"You must join me for a meal."

She lifted her hand, smiled—her teeth grating beneath the facade, surely—but not at all certain how to escape his insistence. "As you wish."

"As *you* wish," he returned, but his tone gave evidence that they would, indeed, dine together. He walked to the door, opened it and indicated that she precede him. She did so, the sweet smell of rosewater drifting to his nostrils.

He followed her, showing her the elegant dining room to the right of the main entry, adjacent to the kitchen. A fire burned brightly and the table was beautifully set. He pulled out her chair, seating her with all propriety. Her head was lowered. When he took his own chair, she looked up and murmured, "This is all quite lovely. Thank you."

He noted that she was looking at the clock on the mantel. Was her intent to slip back to her own home this evening? Or had she thought that she could sleep the night and be back before her father noticed her bed empty in the morning?

He waved a hand negligently. "Emma loves to cook. She doesn't get the opportunity all that often."

"You don't eat?" she inquired with fake courtesy.

"I'm usually at my club, arguing with someone," he admitted. "When I am in London."

"Ah, yes. You are seldom in the country."

"You knew that?" he asked.

"Of course. Your name is quite often in the papers."

"Ah. So you remember reading the newspapers."

She flushed but rebounded admirably. "Indeed, I do."

Emma swept in then, bearing a large silver tray with delicate slices of beef and pheasant, generous servings of au gratin potatoes and greens. Ethan—handsomely attired in livery—was at her side, ready to serve.

Hunter noted that his guest sat up, savoring the aromas. He wondered then when she had last eaten.

"Child?" Emma said. "Oh, this is so difficult! We must call you something!"

"Mmm, true," Hunter murmured. "It does seem rude to keep referring to you as 'girl' or 'child.'" He watched as they were both served, and thanked both Emma and Ethan, then sat back in his chair, surveying his guest.

"Ah, well, soon enough, we must discover your real name!" he said. He smiled up at Emma. "But for the moment, well..."

"Perhaps she is a Jane," Emma suggested.

"Possibly. Or Eleanor," Hunter said.

Ethan poured glasses of wine, then looked up. "Anne, perhaps. It's a popular name."

"A lovely name," he agreed, lifting his glass, and politely waiting as the girl realized that she must lift hers, as well. She did so; he took a sip of wine, and mused once again. "A name...a name...Adriana, for she so comes from the sea! But then again, into the sea, out of the sea...like a creature with many lives. I know—Kat!"

As he had expected, she choked on her sip of wine.

But then again, she recovered splendidly.

"Kat?" she inquired. She stared straight at him. "Why, sir, how amazing. It does have a most familiar ring."

"Kat?" Emma said.

"Kat, Kathy...Katherine," Hunter said. "At any rate, my dear, you will always be our little Kat, then. And like the creature, the cat, may you have nine lives!"

She lifted her glass, coolly observing him.

"Cat!" he repeated. "Ah, yes, the most clever of creatures. Yet one known for the danger of its curiosity. And, hmm, cat...a sweet lovely creature that curls on the sofa at night, and then again, the kind of creature that prowls the jungle, ever searching for prey."

The coolness in her eyes turned to fire. How they blazed at him!

"Mistress Kat," Emma murmured. "Will that be all right, my dear? Until we learn otherwise?"

"It will be lovely," Kat assured her.

Emma nodded, pleased, and absented herself from the dining room with a swish of her petticoats. Ethan shrugged and followed in her wake.

"Lovely," Hunter murmured, ready to address his meal.

"Lovely!" she repeated, her voice low, sweetly dangerous. And he looked up to see that her expression was one of fury. "You wretched—bastard!" she cried.

"Good heavens!" Hunter's eyes widened in mock horror. "What language from such a gentle maiden."

"You should rot in hell," she declared heatedly. "You followed me!"

"I did," he informed her flatly.

"You'd no right!" she cried in dismay.

"Indeed, I had every night. I might well have been nurturing a viper at my bosom."

She started to rise. "Sir Hunter, I'm sure you've nurtured many a viper at your bosom, and with the greatest pleasure! I did not ask you to 'rescue' me from the sea—you chose to do so. You'll remember that I awoke in your carriage and that it was you who caused me to bump my head! And now it will be you who…who…"

She seemed at a loss for words.

"Who what?" he demanded, suddenly angry. "Who will betray you? No, what I need to know for myself is not necessarily information I will share. Play your little charade tomorrow for Lord Avery and your precious David Turnberry. I'll not give you away."

"Why not?" she asked warily, still tense, half risen, half seated.

"Sit down, Kat. That is what they call you, correct?"

"Kat…Katherine. I'm sure your hearing is excellent," she muttered.

"Sit down. Emma worked hard on this meal. For her sake, you will enjoy it."

Rigidly, she took her position once again.

Then she winced. "You will really let me meet with David and Lord Avery as if…as if I were…"

"Their equal?" he suggested. "Oh, indeed. Since you feel you must."

A flush betrayed the edge of shame she was feeling. "My father is a fine man."

"Of that, I'm quite certain. And a talented one."

"He *is* talented! Don't you dare mock him!"

"I am not mocking him."

"Then don't patronize me. You don't know anything about him."

"Oddly enough, I do know a bit. I sincerely believe that he is an incredibly talented artist and that his light, as they say, has been hidden under a bushel for too long. And it was quite evident that he cares for you a great deal. He is a good man. And there is nothing wrong with your home or with your father's being an artist. So why this charade?"

She was instantly defensive. "Everyone must lead a slightly different life at times."

"If you say so."

"Well, you do!"

"Do I?"

"Traveling the globe, gadding about," she said. "Digging into other peoples' live! Ancient lives."

"There's a difference."

"There is not."

"I do it as myself."

"Well...you, sir, have more opportunity than most," she argued weakly.

He shook his head. "Who are you trying to be? And why? You're playing a dangerous game, Kat."

She shook her head. "I'm not! I just want—"

He sighed. "Good God, do you think that silly boy, your dear David, will see you and simply forget his very rich and titled lady? Do you really believe that you two will somehow live happily ever after?"

She did not reply but sat back stubbornly silent. He shook his head. "The man leaves for Egypt in a week. I suppose there is no harm in seeing that you are somehow properly introduced."

She let out a soft sigh.

"Thank you," she said with amazing dignity.

She toyed with the meat on her plate, then ate in earnest, then apparently feared that she was eating too quickly and slowed down. She caught his eye, and her fork froze in mid-position. "Tell me," she inquired. "Will David's lady be going to Egypt with him? Does Mrs. Johnson accompany you?"

"Cairo can be a delightful place and many women do come. But the digs are hard, most difficult on women, and few do attend, though there are those who are remarkable scholars and eager for the digs. They are equally willing to accept the rugged accommodations one must abide in the desert. I believe that Lady Margaret will make the trip, but not that she'll attend the dig. There's a wonderful hotel the English frequent each season. Shepheard's. We all start off there before heading off in various directions. Arthur Doyle is heading down, if he's not there already. His wife is ailing. The dry climate down there is excellent for her condition."

"Arthur Doyle?" she repeated.

"Indeed. The writer."

"You know him?"

Hunter arched a brow. "I've written quite a bit myself, and so have spent some time in literary circles."

She didn't seem at all impressed. "The man who gave us Sherlock Holmes?" she inquired.

"Yes."

"And then killed off his hero?" she demanded.

He laughed. "Look, the last time he wrote, it was to complain about the way people are so disturbed over Holmes—who is nothing but a product of his imagination—when his dear wife is fighting for her life. The hotel, as I said, is wonderful. So while your David digs in the desert sands, Lady Margaret will comfortably await him. And the others, and her father, of course."

"And so many people go every year!" she murmured. "What about Mrs. Johnson?"

"Emma prefers London," he explained. "Or the coast of France. Sometimes she comes, but usually she begs out."

Kat sighed again. "I'm really not at all in that world," she murmured. And for a moment, there was no guile in her eyes, no cunning, and her hair, catching the light from the fire, shimmered, and she was so beautiful, yet so lost and forlorn, that he longed to touch her, was tempted to rise and go put a reassuring arm around her shoulders.

But this cat, he knew, had claws.

However, she rose once again to her feet, this time with impeccable dignity. "Since you followed me and are well aware of my home and family, you'll understand that I must return tonight. I had hoped that tonight... Well, it wasn't to be. I will go home and give my father no more reason for concern. I can find my own way, but would be grateful if you would have your man escort me."

"I'll see to it," he assured her.

"Thank you."

"Perhaps..." he began, then paused, for he wondered why he was willing to go to any trouble to see that this urchin met the object of her ridiculous desire.

He inhaled and exhaled. "Perhaps there is still something that I can do."

"You don't know my father, sir." Her shoulders squared. "Though he possesses great talent, he...well, we are usually behind in our rent. Oh, he is a good parent, but...he loves the sea, and so we keep something of an excuse for a boat. He does wondrous oils, but he sells those for almost nothing and makes a living doing portraits. More often than not, he finds an old woman sitting on a step to be intriguing and...well, those works simply haven't sold. Still, he is fiercely proud, and he will allow for no reward. As perhaps you're aware, his family was a good one, and as a strong believer in education, he saw to it that my sister and I were schooled. But he will not allow me out tomorrow morning, for he believes that it is a disgrace to reward someone for saving a life, since human life is precious, not something to be bought or sold."

Hunter was again moved in a way that made him long to touch her. He shrugged instead. In her simple pride and honesty, she had a rare appeal.

"Still...well, we shall see."

A flush rose to her cheeks. And hope flickered in her eyes.

"Thank you," she said, and the words sounded sincere. Then a rueful smile curled her lips. "Why are you being so kind?"

He nodded gravely. "Perhaps I am doing you no favor," he said.

"But you are."

"Icarus wanted to fly...and the sun melted his wings," he reminded her. "It's a hard crash back to earth," he said.

"I do not intend to crash land," she assured him.

He kept staring at her as he reached for the bell at the side of the table and rang it lightly. A moment later, Ethan was there. "This young woman needs a ride home, my friend."

"Yes, Sir Hunter," Ethan said, his expression impassive.

"Thank you very much," Kat said to Ethan, then she turned back to Hunter. "Good night, Sir Hunter." Her smile deepened, became soft, tender and whimsical. "And whatever may come, thank you. Truly. From the bottom of my heart."

She turned and moved gracefully from the room, and he felt his breath catch.

Ethan stared at Hunter, waiting. Hunter gave a nod and Ethan disappeared after the girl.

Hunter's every muscle seemed to twitch and burn.

Insane!

He rose, took a small cigar from the cedar-lined box on the mantel, and lit it.

Good Lord, he was Hunter MacDonald, not some besotted young twit.

He lit the cigar and paced the room. *Let it go,* he told himself. She would be safely back with her family. There was no need for her to see with her own eyes that what she craved would never be. And yet…

She appealed to him on such a strange level! In many ways, she seemed so naive, and in many other ways, she was as clever as a fox. When she meant no seduction or sensuality, her eyes spoke otherwise.

And, he reminded himself ruefully, she found him so…well, so *nothing!*

He grinned at the fire, shaking his head, and he knew what had so intrigued him. *She was a lot like him*. An adventurer, willing to take chances, centered on a quest. She was fresh and bright and so different from any other woman he knew.

And so…

He realized that he was now the one plotting.

He glanced at the clock, ticking away in the corner. The hour was growing late. Still, he strode through the house, anxious to saddle Alexander and ride out into the night.

No help for the hour.

Lord Avery would have to understand. And he would. He was a good fellow.

ETHAN HAD NO DIFFICULTY understanding that Kat was sneaking back into her own home. "I shall be watching for your safety, miss, and that is all."

She smiled at him from the street. "Thank you. But I'm afraid your carriage will be quite evident here, in this street."

He nodded somberly. "Then, miss, you should hurry." He nodded his head toward the east. "It wasn't so long ago that Jack the Ripper was at work, and his haunts are not so terribly far from here, and Lord knows, they never did catch that bloke, not that anyone will admit, so...please get on in, miss. I'll not be leaving until you do so."

"Thank you again, Ethan!" she said, and waving, hurried around to the side of the house and the trellis she could climb to her upstairs room. As she did so, she feared that she would emerge through her window into her room to find her father waiting in fury.

She crawled through the window into the darkened room and then nearly screamed as a form rose from the bed.

"Kat!"

"Eliza!"

Kat grasped her throat, then exhaled in a rush. Her heart was beating loudly enough to wake the dead, she thought. It slowed as her eyes adjusted to the lack of light. Eliza was sitting up now, staring at her, wide-eyed, excited and full of questions.

"Did you see him? Lord Avery?" she demanded.

Kat shook her head, sitting on the bed next to her sister. "I'm afraid not. The day's excitement was far too much for him." She sighed deeply and hopelessly. "At least I wasn't discovered sneaking out of the house. And as for Lord Avery—and David—I would have met them both tomorrow."

"Where have you been, then?"

"Oh. Sir Hunter had a meal laid out," she said with a dismissive wave of her hand.

"Sir Hunter! You had a private dinner with the fellow? A tête-a-tête?"

"No! I ate, and that is all. It was...I suppose...a lovely meal. His housekeeper enjoys cooking."

Eliza climbed off the bed and danced elegantly around the room. "A private dinner—with Sir Hunter MacDonald!"

"There was nothing all that private about it!" Kat protested.

"But...well, the man is exceptionally fine looking!"

"He is?"

Eliza paused, staring at her. "Are you daft, Kat? I've seen the sketches of him—and the photographs that have been in the journals. Furthermore, he is...pure legend! On the queen's business in India! Cruising down the Nile, joining up with his old military friends on some great excursion! Sailing in one race or another and taking the cup! Oh, Kat!"

"Eliza, stop! Oh, he's been quite decent, it's just that I had to listen to his housekeeper rave on and on about him all day, and...don't you see? In my heart, my mind, David is the perfect man," Kat said. She looked woefully at her sister. "And now I never will meet him properly. Unless I can think of...something." Her expression changed. "Papa really has no idea that I slipped out of the house?"

"None," Eliza said a little sharply.

"What's wrong?"

Eliza wrinkled her nose. "Lady Daws was here again! I was very afraid for a few minutes that you would be caught, because the wretched woman was insisting that she see you and give you a piece of her mind. Be warned—according to her, you are the basest of creatures, causing such a commotion, bringing the police out and, of course, worrying poor Papa. Luckily, he was firm when he insisted that you be allowed to rest. Why, I could hear her! The woman was actually halfway up the stairs when our father stopped her!"

"A close call indeed," Kat murmured. "But...she didn't come up. And I thank you, Eliza, for keeping my secret."

Eliza laughed, "Little sister, it's as if it's the two of us against the world, at times. With that wretched woman to make life ever more miserable."

"Well," Kat said, "she does bring him a certain happiness."

This time, Eliza let out an incredibly unladylike snort. "She flatters him! Then she takes his work and he gets a few shillings, and—"

"And what?" Kat said.

"She's after him," Eliza said.

"After him? Papa is a poor artist."

"And a very handsome man. An extremely talented one, as we both know...but so often, artists are long dead before their genius is realized. Kat, I don't know what it is, but I don't trust the woman. She did not come with us once we moored the boat today, but then she returned tonight—acting as if she were so concerned about you! I stayed up here, of course, eavesdropping and pretending that we had both gone straight to sleep. I think she really wants the two of us out of the way! I'm telling you, she is looking to marry him."

"That truly makes no sense," Kat said. "She is, after all, Lady Daws. And Papa is a poor artist. A great one, but a poor one."

"Sometimes men of great artistic talent do become known during their lives and are rewarded for it," Eliza said. "And I can guarantee you that Lady Daws sees that in Papa, and the fact that she is Lady Daws does not mean that she is not in need of support. I think she only *pretends* that she has money of her own."

"I've thought sometimes that she must make much more selling Papa's art than what she gives to him," Kat said worriedly. "She tells him, of course, that she works for a pittance, a small commission...."

"My thought exactly. She has been robbing him blind."

"She cannot be in such sorry shape. I mean, she *is* Lady Daws. And she was married to Lord Daws."

"But Lord Daws had a son by his first wife. The son inherited, and I think he probably despises his stepmother. I would!"

"Do you know that to be true?" Kat asked.

"No, I'm just willing to wager that it's true. The son, Byron Daws, goes to university with your young swain, you know."

"Does he, now."

"Yes. But I never see him out sailing," Eliza mused.

"Maybe he hates the water."

"Maybe. Or has other interests," Eliza said, shrugging. "There's just so much about that woman that's...well, frightening. It didn't matter at first. At first, it seemed she was only being kind. At first, we all saw her as someone admirable. But then...well, to me, her designs on Papa became all the more evident. And, do you know what I heard?"

"No, what?"

"That there was some scandal in her past. That Lord Daws himself was nearly cast out of the family when he married her. But his father died before he could be cut out of the will."

"Where did you hear this?"

"In one of the fabric shops," Eliza said.

"Gossip!" Kat protested.

"Ah, but where there is smoke..."

"My dear sister, I think we must face the fact that we don't like her, she doesn't like us, but that we must all pretend that everything is fine—for Papa. And whatever the past, she is not an artist herself, but knows art. She finds and sells the work of others," Kat said. "She makes a living, and we are doing better now than we were when Papa had to go out and sell his work himself."

"I do not believe she is satisfied with what she is making. She will rob unknown artists like Papa blind," Eliza said.

"Well," Kat said very practically, "I don't care much for her, either. But we're both grown. And soon enough, we'll both be gone, either to find a means of support ourselves or to be married. So even if we don't trust her and don't like her, if she makes Papa happy..."

"She's evil," Eliza insisted.

"Evil!" Kat said with a laugh.

"Yes, evil." Eliza was truly upset. "Papa will not recognize his own talent. He will not go out and insist that the galleries recognize his work...but she makes him believe that only she can turn him into a true artist. Which is utter nonsense. Furthermore she is ever on about how he can afford to send us to schools elsewhere...in France, in Germany. Places where the daughters of men such as himself can work to earn their tutors and their board. Kat, quite honestly, I believe that she wants to be rid of the both of us. Just tonight, she was talking about a school for young women in Switzerland where Papa could afford to send you because the students earn their keep by cleaning and scrubbing and so forth! She hates us both, I think, but you more, for I have always been the more dutiful one. Quieter, less likely to make a fuss. You must be careful, Kat, because she wants you gone." Eliza sighed. "If only..."

"If only I were far more pleasant and pliable with her—or about to marry a man of her choosing?" Kat asked dryly. She sighed, as well, and shook her head. "It's only a dream if and when…never mind. And never fear. I'm not afraid of Lady Daws. She will not get her hands on me! And as to the other…I'll just keep dreaming," Kat said. Eliza still stared at her with such concern that she fiercely hugged her sister. "I'm all right. But now, truly exhausted. Let's go to sleep, shall we?"

"But, Kat, don't you see?" Eliza said. "Tonight, your dream was shattered. Papa is furious. We don't live in the same world as the David Turnberrys."

Kat sniffed. "Lady Daws borders on it!"

"Not in a good way, I don't believe," Eliza murmured. "Ah, dear sister! You're still dreaming away while I…" She laughed. "I would have lived a dream already, having had dinner with such an eminent fellow as Hunter MacDonald!"

"Eminent also in scandal!"

"In a way, but he does nothing underhand. He isn't secretive, unless he is protecting the honor of a woman. While Lady Daws—"

"We all see and hear, and even believe, what we choose," Kat said sadly. "Anyway, it is time to go to sleep. And I'm sure you'll get to go with Papa to return this dress. I mean, you must go with Papa! I don't think that Hunter would betray me, but…you need to be there to protect me regarding this little episode tonight, and that is all there is to it."

Eliza laughed. "Well, indeed! I will meet the man of such intrigue and fascination!"

"And I will…stay home. And dream some more," Kat said.

"Will you?" Eliza said. "If I know you, you will be thinking up another way to get close to your David!"

"Such a dream is hardly likely. We must go to sleep!"

But trying to sleep and actually falling asleep were two different things.

First, Kat allowed herself a few silent tears into her pillow. She'd come so close…

And then, she tossed over, staring at the ceiling.

Eliza was right. She knew her well. She could not just forget.

She wouldn't be beaten. She simply wouldn't be beaten. David was going to take a ship and go on a long, long journey, and then spend a season in the ancient sands of the Sahara. His dainty fiancée would not be around *all* the time. He wouldn't be married until he returned.

Scores of things could happen before then!

When she slept at last, she had determined that, come what may, when David left England, she would not be far behind.

Chapter 4

KAT WAS AWARE OF DISCOMFORT and did not know why. As she opened her eyes, blinking from sleep, the room was first a blur. It came into focus and then she knew why the discomfort.

Isabella, Lady Daws, was staring down at her.

"You are an incredibly cruel and uncaring young woman, Katherine Adair!" Lady Daws stated, her voice low and ever cultured, but carrying with it such malice that Kat was chilled. She was shamed, thinking that she had so worried her father. But it was not this woman's concern.

"Why, good morning, Lady Daws." She sat up, keeping the coverlet hugged close to her bosom. She looked around. "How strange, dear lady, for this does appear to be my bedroom. My private quarters within our home, however humble."

"Get up, Kat!" There was now a snap to her voice.

"I've discussed my actions yesterday with my father, Lady Daws. And I expressed my sorrow for the anxiety I caused him. I owe you no explanations."

The woman smiled. "Of course not, dear." Her smile was icy. "Not yet," she added sweetly. Then she lowered her face close to Kat's. "But I do find your behavior totally reprehensible. In my opinion, you should be sent far away, to a school where they teach girls like you how to obey and to be grateful—and to learn your place in life."

"*My* place is in this house," Kat returned lightly.

Lady Daws straightened and crossed her arms. Kat was certain that, beneath her skirts, her foot was tapping furiously.

"Ah, but you were rather anxious to leave it yesterday, weren't you?"

Kat stared at her. To be quite honest, the woman *was* attractive. Her face was narrow and fine-featured, and her eyes were large and deep brown, a color that matched the thick waves of her hair. Her bearing was so upright and regal that Kat liked to imagine she wore a broomstick beneath her petticoats.

"Dear Lady Daws, please, say whatever it is you wish to say. And then, if you'd be so kind to allow me the privacy of my own room, I will be happy to rise."

"Yes, you'll rise, and you'll rise quickly. We've company."

"*We've* company?"

Either Isabella Daws ignored the bite in Kat's query or simply couldn't even entertain the notion that Kat didn't consider the place also *her* home.

"Your mad dash into the sea has made the papers. Apparently, Sir Hunter extolled your...brave deed to a reporter and now your poor dear papa is both proud and concerned."

"I made the papers?" Kat repeated, and mentally she realized that she had to thank Sir Hunter once again, no matter how difficult and condescending the man might be. "And Papa is...pleased? Who is it that is here?"

She started to rise. To her amazement, Isabella pushed her back.

"Not so fast."

Kat let out a sound of irritation. "You were just telling me to get up!"

"Careful, girl. I may hold your future in my hands."

Kat stared at her warily, eyes narrowing. Perhaps the woman truly *was* evil. Regardless, it was certainly true that she held great sway with her father.

"Really?" she queried carefully.

Isabella gave her a tight smile. "I personally think that you should be sent to a strict school, a very strict school—"

"Yes, Lady Daws, I know all about it. Eliza told me of your concern for us both last night."

"Further education in such a place would do you very well. There's no place for a young woman such as yourself other than in gainful employment or as the wife of a working man. But to be quite honest, you are a terrible drain on your poor father. You exhaust him, drain his talent."

"I beg your pardon—"

"I am not finished."

"I am!" Kat started to rise.

But this time, Lady Daws stopped her with words.

"Then you'll never properly meet Lord Avery—or young David Turnberry."

Startled, Kat went still.

Again, Isabella Daws lowered her face to Kat's. "Sir Hunter MacDonald has come to your father with an offer from Lord Avery. The man will fund and provide a chaperone for you if you accompany his group as an art student and assistant to Sir Hunter on his expedition to Egypt next week. Apparently, you doodled some of your silly sketches when you were at Sir Hunter's house. After Sir Hunter convinced the man that your father would not allow you to accept a monetary reward, Lord Avery was anxious that at least something be done. And he agreed that your sketch showed promise. There is no accounting for taste."

Kat controlled her temper and said nothing.

"Your father is against the idea. One word from me, and he will refuse, no matter how eloquent Sir Hunter may be. And yet, one word from me, and...well, you just may be allowed to go."

Kat stared at her then, chagrined, and in silence.

"And there we have it. Plain and simple. Let's see. I do believe the 'cat' has now got your tongue."

She thought she was so clever! Still, Kat did hold her tongue.

"Well, my dear?" Lady Daws demanded.

"Why would you help me?" Kat asked.

"Because you'll have just so long on that excursion, Kat. And perhaps, just perhaps, you will gain something of what you're seeking—though I doubt it. You see, I know that crowd. My stepson is one of those foolish youths, and they are so arrogant that they believe that those not within their elite circles exist merely for their amusement. I believe that you will no longer see them through such rose-tinted spectacles once you know them. And so, you will discover the truth of who and what you are."

"I've nothing against either who or what I am, Lady Daws," Kat said tautly.

"Really?" Lady Daws hiked an elegant brow. "Then it's quite amazing how you disappeared...and then reappeared. Sir Hunter surely would have seen you home immediately, had he known where your home was. But the truth is you didn't want to show him."

"I had a nasty blow to the head—"

"Oh, Kat, lie to others. I know what you are."

"How dare—"

"Spare me the indignity. You didn't want your background known. As it has happened, your father's talent is an unexpected asset in this little farce of yours. But here it is, on the line. You will go. You will have just the months while you are gone...and then, when you return, you will not stay. You'll go away to school. The school of my choice. You will be sent away. And you will agree to this."

Kat gritted her teeth. She'd had no idea just how much Lady Daws wanted her gone. Eliza was right.

"You're not afraid for me?" Kat asked sweetly.

"Well, you are going into the desert, aren't you? And there's always a measure of danger on an expedition. Gold and riches tend to make men covetous. Are you afraid for yourself?"

Kat felt the slightest chill. She remembered David's disjointed words when he had come to consciousness on the embankment. He thought he had been pushed into the river....

But if he had been in danger, that danger had been here, right here, in London. And afraid or not, she could not miss this incredible opportunity.

"I am not afraid at all," she said coolly.

"If you get into trouble, my dear," Isabella warned, "I will see to it that you are dealt with most seriously. In fact, your lovely face will never so much as be seen around here. Do you understand? Besides, I will have friends aboard the ship, and on the expedition, and I will know about your progress—or lack thereof—day after day!"

Now Kat was afraid. But then, once she was gone, Lady Daws couldn't really touch her. The woman might bear the title "Lady," but she was not at all on a social par with men as noble as Baron Turnberry and Lord Avery—nor, even, with men of renown such as Sir Hunter MacDonald.

Still...

For a moment, she wavered. She'd be leaving her father and Eliza.

Her head was suddenly spinning. The offer was astounding.

Eliza would be with their father, and though she hadn't Kat's spine—or sharpness of tongue—she was not in the least a weakling. She would be safe until she returned, and that was what mattered.

Nor could she prevent Papa from...forming whatever liaison he chose to form with this woman. Her mother had been gone since she'd been a child. If Papa craved feminine attention, even from this wretched woman, there was little she could do. No one could choose where another would look to find affection and solace.

Certainly, she knew all that herself.

She lifted her chin. Somehow, Lady Daws knew about her obsession with David Turnberry. Yet Kat had only ever spoken of it to Eliza, and her sister would have never betrayed her.

She must have given herself away, she thought. And it was true, coveting David was like coveting a star in the heavens.

And yet...

If only he had time to be with her, time to get to know her! Stranger marriages had come about. They were living in an enlightened age, and—

"What will it be, Kat?" Isabella asked.

Kat felt as if she were selling her soul.

"I would love to go on the season's expedition," she said pleasantly.

Isabella smiled smugly. "You will remember our bargain," she said softly.

"Oh, yes. Though I feel I've signed my soul to the devil," Kat said.

"There will be no more comments like that!"

"Of course not, Lady Daws."

"Then I will leave, and you must arise. We are all invited to breakfast at Sir Hunter's."

With that, Lady Daws swept out of the room.

And for a panicked moment, Kat thought that she really *had* sold her soul to the devil.

AS KAT CAME DOWN THE STAIRS, Hunter wondered if he hadn't somehow lost his mind. Just what was it that he was doing?

I should have just let it all go.

She was no longer wearing his sister's day dress, but she was every bit as beautifully attired, perhaps even more so. The neckline had a most unusual design that rose fashionably against the neck, yet had a small, flattering V right at the throat. The skirt was in elegant layers. With the bustle in serious decline, there was just a small rise at the rear, and the skirts seemed to flow grandly with her every movement. The color was also something that must have been selected with her in mind, for it was an amber color that made her hair seem even more like fire, her eyes more the color of gold. That hair today was respectably pinned in a loose chignon in the back, allowing small tendrils to escape.

When her eyes touched his, they were alight with a question. He knew she was wondering why he was doing this for her.

He offered her the slightest grin, and a shrug. *I haven't the foggiest notion!* he might have responded.

Or maybe he did. Was it just petty annoyance that such a young woman would so blindly covet such a young fool as David Turnberry? Was he annoyed that her fixation was not on him? Ridiculous, of course, because she might not be from his customary social circles, but neither was she a woman to be taken lightly. He didn't dare take a closer look at his emotions.

"Good morning, Katherine," he said. He realized that her father was staring at her with a strange look in his eyes, a mix of worry, concern. Lady Daws had a look of annoyance. Eliza gazed at her sister with anxiety, as well. Was she, too, seeking something from all this?

"Good morning," Katherine replied, and her eyes moved to light upon her father. Was he concerned that their home had been thus invaded? He must know everything that Lady Daws had said to her.

William Adair stretched his hands out. Kat, her head at a curious angle, a small smile curling her lips, took his hands as she reached the landing. "My princess of the sea," William murmured softly as she stood in front of him. He turned to look at Hunter. "A man's riches, you see, Sir Hunter, are not in gold or coin. My daughters are my treasure."

Hunter decided that he not only liked the man, but admired him greatly. But he felt a slight ripple of unease. His intentions, if not entirely honorable, were at the least to teach his "treasure" a sad lesson in life—that such men as David Turnberry were not worth the seeking. And he felt a strange excitement, as well, because he had discovered a treasure himself. Those who had seen William Adair's work referred to him as the "king of the sea," for his paintings of great ships at sail were exquisite.

That he made most of his income doing individual and family portraits was not a waste, for he was excellent at such work, as well; it was evident in the oils he had done of his daughters, framing either side of the firelight. Just as he caught the wind and the fury of the waves in his seascapes, he had caught something special in his subjects in his portraits. There, in Eliza, was the pride, and in Kat's face the recklessness in the eyes, the dreams in the slight upturn of the lips.

And, of course, it was true, absolutely, that his daughter showed hints of his talent in her quickly dashed-off sketch.

"My dear, Sir Hunter has come to ask the family to breakfast. It seems that Lord Avery is most insistent on meeting you, and seeing that you receive his patronage, as well. I have explained that no thanks of any kind is necessary, but it seems that Sir Hunter and Lord Avery wish what they consider a favor from me in return."

"A favor?" Kat said. She smiled, but her eyes narrowed slightly, letting Hunter know that she was wary of this "favor."

"I'm a tremendous fan of your father's work," Hunter said.

"Yes, and..." William began, still looking a bit uncertain.

"Oh, Father!" Eliza cried. "You mustn't be so stunned." Eliza spun on Kat with a brilliant smile. "Sir Hunter, did you know, is close friends with the Earl of Carlyle—who has one of Papa's paintings on his walls at his castle! So Sir Hunter knew who Papa was when they met, and he wants to commission several oils from Papa, and...and he thinks you show equal promise! Mr. Thomas Atworthy, one of the finest tutors from the college, will be accompanying the group with which Sir Hunter is associated on their dig this season, and he wants to take you on as a pupil, and in return, of course, you will be at the excavations, serving as an assistant for Sir Hunter, helping in many ways—sketching and keeping notes. Papa has assured him that you can act in the capacity of secretary with diligence and capability!"

He watched Kat spin around, look at her father, and then at Lady Daws.

Hunter had been afraid that his entire scheme—though rather clever, he thought—might still be far too overwhelming for William Adair.

But he'd discovered that he had an ally.

Lady Daws.

He'd never been overly fond of the woman himself, not that he knew her well. He had seen her on occasion at various social events. Since the death of her husband, perhaps five or six years past, she had been into a number of strange enterprises. He'd heard that her husband's son had completely alienated himself from his stepmother, and that she had therefore been left scrambling to make a living. A sad state of affairs. Except, there *had* been rumor that she had married the old fellow in the hopes that he would make a quick exit from the world of the living.

Apparently, she had sometime ago befriended William Adair. Hunter knew that she had put herself forward to him as something of an art expert and had been busy selling his work.

He had a strong suspicion that her commissions were well above the artist's take.

But at the moment, he was certain, the woman was eager to assist him. Perhaps she didn't care for competition from the man's rather extraordinary daughters.

Kat looked at him then, her hazel eyes burning with excitement. "So...this is all true. I would accompany your group on the voyage and during the entire season in Egypt?"

"Yes, of course," he said pleasantly. "I know that I am asking a great deal to tear you away from your home and your family." His sarcasm was certainly audible only to her. "And there are long days at sea. A few stops along the way...perhaps a week spent in Rome. And you will have to work, I'm afraid, but in return, you'll have time most days with a man considered to be one of the finest art tutors in our country. Of course," he lied, "I haven't the least idea if such an arrangement appeals to you. You—and your father—must give the concept grave consideration."

She glanced immediately at her father.

Lady Daws was also looking at him. He still appeared uncertain.

"Yes, well, please, think on it," Hunter said. "In the meantime, I entreat all of you to come for breakfast at my town house. And there, Mr. Adair, should you have more questions or concerns, you can speak with Lord Avery himself. So, please, do come."

"Oh, yes!" Eliza answered for them all.

"Papa?" Kat said.

"Sir Hunter, thank you for your kindness. It would be churlish of me, I suppose, to refuse such an invitation," William Adair said. "But if Kat accompanies you, she will fulfill all the tasks that you have for her. I do stress that there will be no reward given or accepted."

"I will make your wishes known to Lord Avery," Hunter assured him. "My carriage awaits," he reminded them.

"But we're an entire household!" Eliza pointed out.

"I'm returning now, on my own. I rode my horse behind the carriage. I think that the four of you will find you've plenty of room."

Kat's eyes were on his again, alive with speculation. He inclined his head slightly in her direction, bid them all farewell and departed.

They would, he was certain, follow.

ELIZA, KAT KNEW, WAS NERVOUS about meeting the great Lord Avery. But she herself was in a similar state about another momentous meeting.

With David, of course. It did occur to her that Lord Avery's lovely daughter might be there, as well. But she had watched David Turnberry from afar for so long, and she was certain in her heart that Margaret could not really love him. In fact, surely, she was being pressured into the marriage but was doubtless in love with someone else. Kat had convinced herself that if she could somehow make David fall in love with her and end his relationship with Margaret, the young woman would be entirely grateful.

The carriage pulled up under the porte cochere.

"The house is magnificent, isn't it, Papa?" Eliza said. To Kat she whispered, "Ah, and so is Sir Hunter!"

Kat looked up. As they exited their host's carriage, the man himself was there. Kat had to acknowledge that Hunter made quite a striking picture. He wore a gray suit, cut admirably to his lean and muscled form, a brocade waistcoat, white shirt beneath. His stance was nonchalant, yet still tall and imposing. His eyes were filled with humor, and Kat found herself resentful despite his largesse—this was all a game to him. She had amused him, and he would be further amused to watch her as the weeks wore on. Was he hoping that she would fail? Did he mock her quest, find it ridiculous?

Yes, well, the majority of the sane world would, an inner voice warned.

And yet what did it matter? He mocked her, yes, maybe was even betting with his friends on when she would realize her position in life. And whatever that might be, it wasn't among these elite.

Still, her father could prosper from Sir Hunter's patronage. And if Lord Avery were impressed with her father's work, a truly decent living could be found.

Moments later, they were all inside, and Hunter was leading the way to the drawing room. Kat hadn't realized that there were already visitors within and was at a disadvantage when Hunter instantly said, "David! I've brought your mermaid. Lord Avery, Margaret, may I present Miss Katherine Mary Adair, her father, William, sister, Eliza, and I believe you've met Lady Daws."

Whatever other introductions went round, Kat did not know. She was completely unaware of all else, because David Turnberry was standing and looking at her, his smile deep and full of admiration. He walked to her, taking her hands—touching her!—and she was aware of nothing but the force of his eyes.

"I cannot convey what a pleasure this is," he said, and his voice was such a tremulous tenor, so full of emotion, she was afraid that her knees would give up. "You saved my life. And I am eternally grateful."

Perhaps her adoration, despite the fact that she had been quite certain she could hide it, was far more apparent than she would have wished, because he quickly stepped back, releasing her hand. "You risked your own life. Truly, I will never thank you enough."

She, who was usually so quick with words, found herself speechless.

"My God, and what a beautiful mermaid from the sea!" Another voice extolled, and then a second man, tall, lean and dark with deep blue eyes, stepped between her and David. She recognized him as one of David's regular companions. "Robert Stewart, at your service. And may I say, should I ever so sadly fall into the drink, as well, Miss Adair, that you would be there to do me like service?"

"Miss Adair!" And now, it was Margaret who spoke, her voice as soft as the touch of her hand. "I'm Margaret Avery, and I, too, must express my deepest appreciation. Were it not for you being there, being so capable, brave, poor David might not… Oh, how easily he might have drowned!"

Kat felt her cheeks color; the young woman sounded so sincere, so sweet and so very admiring. The praise was beginning to make her uncomfortable. She had thought that she would revel in this moment, glory in it, and instead, she felt the need to protest.

"Please…it was… I swim very well," she said simply.

She felt a touch on her shoulder. Hunter was behind her. She longed to shake him off, but he murmured, "Ah, but the thing of it is, you did not save just any life. You saved David's! So here, we are all grateful—as would be the friends and loved ones of any man's—or woman's—life that was saved."

Then Kat realized that Hunter was directing her toward an older man. "Miss Katherine Mary Adair, Lord Avery," Hunter said.

She managed to offer her hand. "My Lord."

"Jagger to my friends, my dear," the fellow said, smiling. She liked him instantly. He was tall and gaunt, white-haired, and with a gentle smile that reminded her of his daughter's. She felt her cheeks flame slightly as she realized that both these people, who were being so kind to her, would be appalled if they were aware that her humble sights were set on David.

Who would be affianced to Lady Margaret.

And still…

They were rich. Titled. The world was theirs. They could have anything.

She wanted only one thing in the world.

And she could not give up her quest.

"It's a pleasure meeting you…Jagger," Kat said softly.

"No, no, my dear, the pleasure is mine. In so many ways! We were eager to offer a reward, but it seems, according to Sir Hunter, that none will be accepted. And it is not, I'm afraid, with any thought of reward that I have championed Hunter's suggestion that you must accompany us, both to work and to learn. We would have had to find an assistant somewhere, and Professor Atworthy will be pleased to have a student such as you. And I am quite in awe to meet your father. Mr. Adair!" he said, addressing William. "Your ships at sea entrance me. There is one on the wall in a castle belonging to a good friend, and I have long coveted it. He did not know where the artist was to be found. And now, I have made your acquaintance!" He chuckled. "The Earl of Carlyle has not yet had that pleasure, so I have one-upped the man, you see."

Her father looked rather flushed, as she was sure she herself was. But he did stand straight and proud, as well. "Lord Avery, I must tell you, I am not a man who needs or feeds on flattery. You need not feel that you must purchase any of my pieces because of what has occurred. Your words are kind. And your sponsorship of my daughter is an incredible piece of fortune for her."

"The apple does not fall far from the tree, dear fellow. I try to think of myself as a patron of the arts. She is so young… Sir Hunter showed me the little sketch that she did and I was instantly enchanted. Mr. Adair, you are doing *us* the favor."

Lord Avery could not be judged as anything other than sincere. William Adair ceased any protest. "Lord Avery, I thank you."

Emma appeared at the entryway. "Breakfast is served," she said cheerfully.

Kat was still in pure bliss as they filed into the dining room.

Hunter, however, had made the seating arrangements, and she found herself not beside David, but between Lord Avery and his daughter. Lady Daws was between David and Robert Stewart—good heavens, she had managed to completely forget the woman!—and Eliza was seated next to David's other close friend, Allan…Allan something. He was fair-haired and pleasant, and he smiled with approval when he looked at her, and naturally, she smiled when she looked back.

"What a lovely breakfast, Emma!" Margaret said cheerfully, helping herself to a slice of ham as the plate went round the table. "Ah, muffins, eggs, ham…bacon! And soon we'll be on a ship, and off to foreign parts—we'll miss your cooking, Emma!"

Emma nodded, pleased with the compliment, but said, "My lady, there will be fine fare aboard the ship, and in the company of such prestigious folk, I daresay, none of us will suffer."

"But nothing will be so fine as your creations," Robert Stewart said, and catching Kat's eye, he winked.

Margaret shivered. "This is such an adventure for all of you! I'm not at all sure why we can't remain right here where we are, in London. After all, London is the heart of civilization!"

Margaret's words made Kat forget any sense of shyness, or that she was not among the company she usually kept. "But London is the heart of civilization because we English have explored so vastly, in such faraway places!"

"Bravo, Miss Adair!" David said, delighting Kat.

Margaret did not seem to take offense. She laughed. "That's because you haven't been wretchedly seasick for days on end. Or felt the desert sands in your mouth when you breathe! You'll see."

"I've never gotten seasick," Kat murmured.

"Because you're a mermaid!" Robert Stewart teased.

"No, because she has a sense of adventure," Hunter murmured.

Lord Avery cleared his throat. "Indeed, a joie de vivre. We've forgotten, Hunter, I believe. I am, dear friend, sorry that I neglected to mention that we owe you a debt, as well. You, too, went diving in for David and wound up rescuing the rescuer."

"Oh, but you see, she didn't really need rescuing," Hunter said, looking at Kat. Then he looked at her father apologetically. "In my fear that she should drown, I believe I caused her injury."

"But 'all's well that ends well!'" Eliza quoted cheerfully.

"Indeed," Lady Daws said, staring at Kat with narrowed eyes. "Yes, now the dear girl will have excellent opportunities, and, gentlemen," she added, her gaze sliding from Sir Hunter to Lord Avery, "you will have works of sheer passion and genius to hang on your walls."

"Here, here!" Lord Avery said. "When will we see some of your work, Mr. Adair?" he added.

"I...I..."

"There is a great deal of it hanging in my apartments," Lady Daws said. "After breakfast, perhaps, we will all take a very small expedition and go see them."

"Oh, I'm afraid not," Hunter said. "I'm due at the museum to tie up a few loose ends with Brian. And Miss Adair must accompany me."

"But dear Lord Avery!" Lady Daws persisted. "There is so little time left before you leave the country!"

"Hunter, you and Miss Adair go on to the museum," Lord Avery said. "If you will forgive me, Hunter, the rest of us will go on Lady Daws's art expedition! She is quite right. Time is a precious commodity right now."

"Indeed, Lord Avery, I wouldn't deny you such a pleasure."

"I should accompany the crowd," Kat murmured. "I know my father's work so well—"

"But I shall be there! And you must learn your duties, Katherine," Lady Daws said.

"I will be there, as well," Eliza said firmly.

"Yes, you do need to become aware of what the future will bring," Hunter said, staring at her. His eyes were hard. She didn't know if he was referring to all that she needed to know regarding ancient Egypt—or if she needed to learn that, despite the charm and camaraderie they were all enjoying today, her place among them was slightly below the rest.

"But surely," Kat murmured, "one afternoon will not matter so much?"

"One afternoon matters greatly when so few are left," Hunter said.

"I insist you accompany us!" Robert Stewart protested gallantly.

"She must not," Lady Daws said firmly. "Such an excellent offer for learning does not come to every...young woman."

Kat bit her tongue, wondering just what adjectives Lady Daws really intended to use.

She looked at her father, who was smiling at her with assurance. She realized that he believed her protests were because she was worried about him. "It's all right, Kat. If you need to see the museum, then you must do so."

"We are agreed, then," Hunter said, rising. Kat refrained from giving him a baleful stare and rose, as well, politely excusing herself.

"You do ride?" Hunter said. "I will send Ethan and the carriage with your family."

"Of course I ride," Kat lied. She could, indeed, swim like a fish. She'd grown up, however, in the City of London where public transportation was excellent and there was no need to ride a horse.

She saw her father frown.

He, like the other men, had risen when she had.

Forgetting David for one moment as she saw her father's concerned face, she turned to Lord Avery. "Truly, my lord, my father is a genius," she said proudly. "As you will see."

"I have seen!" Lord Avery assured her. He turned to her and clasped her hands in his. "All will be well, my child. You will see."

She thanked him.

Hunter was at her side. His hand was on her elbow. She bid the others farewell.

"Oh, but it isn't goodbye! We will have a lovely time together for weeks and weeks...months!" Lady Margaret assured her.

Guilt rippled through Kat. She smiled. "Of course. And thank you."

"Good heavens, this is more like an Italian goodbye," Hunter said impatiently. "We are merely headed in opposite directions for the afternoon."

"I shall call you this evening," Lord Avery told Hunter, "if the blasted telephone works."

"Now and then," Hunter agreed wryly. "If not, we'll talk soon enough."

Kat looked back as they departed the room. She thought that David was studying her pensively.

And with admiration.

Her heart thundered.

But soon they were at the carriage entrance to the house. Ethan was there with Hunter's massive mount and a smaller animal—one fitted out with a sidesaddle.

"You *don't* ride, do you?" Hunter said, studying her face.

She shot him a glance filled with the venom that had been growing in her heart. "I will, never worry," she said shortly, and moved toward the animal. Her skirts were cumbersome, but she was determined to get on the beast and ride.

Ethan, holding the reins, started to move forward. Hunter was there before him, his hands on her waist as he lifted her. She felt his touch as he adjusted her limbs and thrust her feet into the stirrups. The length of her burned with outrage.

"You'll be all right," he said. "We're not going far."

"Yes, it's quite amazing that we're going, isn't it?"

He looked up at her where she sat. "And what does that mean?"

She leaned down, cheeks burning, not caring to have this argument with Ethan so near. "It's amazing that it's truly *nec-*

essary that I begin learning the volumes regarding Egyptology this very afternoon."

He studied her gravely. "Do you wish to discard the entire idea?"

"Of going to the museum?" she said hopefully.

"Of going to Egypt."

She fell silent, staring at him, biting her lower lip. He left her side, thanking Ethan, taking the reins to his own mount. He leapt onto the beast with the agility of one who had ridden since birth. To her horror, she wavered tenuously as her own horse followed his.

Dear heaven, she thought. Would that this afternoon soon be over!

Chapter 5

ELIZA DIDN'T REALIZE THAT she'd been holding her breath until Lord Avery said, "I *must* have this series."

The man had been studying one of her father's finest collections, a set of five oils on canvas featuring different sailing vessels in different hues. *Morning,* with brilliant golds, yellows and oranges. *Evening,* with silver and shades of mauve and gray. *Storm,* with colors as tempestuous and moody as the title. *Calm,* with the softest butternuts and pinks. And finally, *Against the Wind,* with bright and deep blues and the whites of swirling clouds that seemed to race overhead, even in the stillness of the artwork.

Her head was spinning. This was all too good to be true.

And all because Kat was headstrong and had plunged into the Thames!

And now Kat was also going to get to go on the expedition and follow David off into the desert...

Along with Lady Margaret.

"Jagger," Robert Stewart said, standing by the man, "I am in serious envy. I can feel the sea, looking at these. I can feel the wind, the spray of the water." He turned to William. "Mr. Adair, I am quite seriously in awe."

Her father appeared tongue-tied. Lady Daws was not. "Ah, then let's pray that the awe being felt translates to serious business, shall we?"

She linked arms with Lord Avery. Eliza felt that she must protect her father, because for whatever reason, the woman frankly scared her. What would Kat do in such a circumstance?

"Oh, Lady Daws! No business just now!" Eliza was surprised at how firm she could make her voice. "Papa can talk with Lord Avery at another time. Naturally, his art is his living, but it is also a thing of beauty, just to be enjoyed, and I do know my father. He is so delighted to see you appreciate his work. Let's savor this moment, shall we?"

Lord Avery actually appeared impressed with her.

Lady Daws, of course, looked furious.

Eliza couldn't help a smile of triumph.

"Mr. Adair," Allan said, "it's a true pity you will not be accompanying our group to Egypt. What you could do with the pyramids at sunset!"

"I'm sorry, there is no way for me to accompany you," William said.

"And why is that?" Lord Avery asked, frowning.

William looked sheepish. "I'm afraid, Lord Avery, that when I'm not topside, I become wretchedly ill—seasick."

"Ah, but we'll have the next best thing—Katherine!" David declared.

"Indeed...but her art is a bit different, isn't it?" Robert Stewart demanded. "She could be a great caricaturist—there's a touch of the satirical in her work."

Margaret laughed. "Robert! We've seen but one piece."

"You mark my words. Her work could actually be dangerous," Robert said teasingly, coming close to the beautiful Margaret with mock menace.

"Dangerous! Artwork!" Margaret protested.

"If she really sketches all that she sees," David murmured. He looked from Robert to Allan and back again. His expression seemed odd, Eliza thought.

Then Robert clapped him on the back. "Good heavens, Davie, I was but teasing. Mr. Adair, your daughter has your talent. And I believe you'll be delighted with the growth in her work once we've returned."

"If Hunter, the tyrant, gives her time with Professor Atworthy," Allan warned.

"Hunter is not a tyrant!" Margaret protested.

"She has a crush on the fellow," Allan said, putting himself between Robert and Eliza and rolling his eyes.

"Will you all please act like respectable adults?" Lord Avery demanded. "You're frightening Mr. Adair. Sir Hunter is a man who is very serious about his work, but not at all a tyrant, I assure you, Mr. Adair. All will be well!"

Allan winked at Eliza. "And what of you, Miss Elizabeth? Do you draw or paint, as well?"

"Rather poorly, I'm afraid," she said.

"I can't believe that," Allan said. "Creativity runs in families!"

"She designs," William said proudly.

Eliza heard a choking sound. The evil Lady Daws, she was convinced.

"Clothing," Eliza explained.

"The dress she wears, and the one her sister was wearing," William said.

She looked at her father and smiled. Bless him. What a wonderful, dear man. Always showing them equal love, concern and pride.

"How wonderful!" Margaret exclaimed. "Oh, Miss Adair! You must design something for me."

"Why—" Eliza was left almost speechless "—I would love to, Lady Margaret." Oh, the day was going so very well! If it were not for the presence of Lady Daws...

And the strange way David Turnberry looked at his friends.

"Now, there," David said suddenly, pointing to the painting *Storm*. "That's how I remember the water when I fell in! It was the oddest thing, almost as if the wind were there, riding the waves, right along with us. As if it had arms and legs, and was boxing us! I swear, it felt as if the wind picked me up and pushed me right off the ship. Oh, did you know, Lady Daws, that your stepson was with us that day?"

Eliza was delighted to see the woman stiffen like steel. But she recovered quickly. "No, I did not. But I believe that Mr. Adair and Lord Avery would agree with me—none of you young men should have been out in that weather."

"Mr. Adair was out in it," David pointed out politely.

"He may become seasick in closed quarters, but my father is an excellent sailor," Eliza said. She had been glad to see Isabella Daws discomfited, but something dark seemed to have fallen over her beautiful afternoon. "But I must say," she added with a deep smile, having had no intent to hurt with her words, "that perhaps our dear Father above had something to do with David's accident, for it has been the greatest pleasure to be able to meet you."

"Of course. The silver lining on the cloud," Lord Avery said.

"Soft blue…soft blue with deeper shades," Lady Margaret said, turning to Eliza again. "You planned your sister's attire to match her coloring, did you not? You must do the same for me. I'm right to think blue, do you not agree?"

"Indeed, with your eyes…blue," Eliza said, feeling a suffusion of warmth once again. Lady Margaret was lovely, kind, without being condescending.

Inwardly, Eliza winced. This was the woman most likely to become the bride of the man her sister cherished!

And yet…

It was a lovely day. Incredibly so. And it was all thanks to Kat's impetuosity and recklessness. She had to thank Kat!

And pray, of course, that her day was just as lovely.

"YOU'LL BE RIDING IN THE desert," Hunter said pleasantly.

"And I will do so," she replied. She thought there was amusement in his eyes, and the glance he gave her was incredibly irritating.

He had the most unusual eyes. She had thought that they were brown, in fact, so deep a shade of brown that they appeared black. But they weren't brown at all, rather a deep shade of blue. And he had such a way of using them! He could look at one with such contempt it made the flesh burn. And yet sometimes his amusement seemed addressed at himself more than others. Now, as he looked at her, she thought that he was enjoying her discomfort far too much.

"Indeed, I will ride with assurance," she added sharply. Oh! At that moment, she longed to slap his face.

"Nearly there," he said.

"Really? I should have enjoyed this for hours more!"

"I could make such an arrangement, if you wish."

"You could, but you would not. You've business, I believe."

He shrugged, turning, leading the way. His horse broke into a trot. Her mount did the same. Her entire frame was jarred, and she tried very hard to sit without popping up and down like a jack-in-the-box.

He intended to let her suffer, she realized.

The streets had been fairly quiet in the morning, but as they neared the area of the museum, it seemed that more people were out and about, strolling, riding, hurrying toward various destinations. They passed cabs and omnibuses—still trotting along at the wretched gait.

Kat managed to draw abreast of Hunter.

"Is this why you have shown me such largesse?" she demanded. "You are entertained by torturing me?"

He raised a brow. "Going to the museum is torture?"

She looked ahead. "I don't believe I will have any teeth left by the time we arrive."

He smiled slightly. "I should have taken you to the park for riding lessons today. But the truth is, I do have business. I have a meeting with the Earl of Carlyle. Contrary to what lies in your mind, my life and timetables do not exist around you, nor do I wake every morning since our meeting desperately conniving on how to make you suffer!"

She felt a blush cover her cheeks, but then realized what he had said. "You are to meet the Earl of Carlyle? Now?"

"Naturally, his involvement in antiquities is the major impetus now of all that happens. The man comes by his love of archeology naturally. He inherited it."

She stared at Hunter. "His parents were murdered. There was a huge to-do. It was in all the papers—I remember."

"Yes, but justice was served, and his energy and his resources are tantamount in all that we do."

"He married a commoner!"

Hunter gave her a long look that she couldn't quite read. Then he sighed. "Perhaps I have truly done you a disservice," he murmured.

She was startled to feel the sting of tears in her eyes. "You have done me no disservice. Whatever comes, you have brought my father's work to the attention of those who can do him justice. I am in your debt."

He reined in sharply, turning back to her. "No. You are not in my debt. And you may dream whatever dreams you wish in that silly little head of yours, but a bargain has been made here."

"Meaning?" she asked, startled by the way he looked at her.

And by the sudden realization that he was very much a man—imposing, charismatic and with a will of steel.

"I am not...Sir Hunter, I will not...I mean...you mustn't think that I'm willing to trade...anything...for this opportunity!" she warbled awkwardly.

His gaze was chilling then. And those eyes of his! As dark as an abyss.

And contemptuous.

"I have taken you on as an assistant, Miss Adair," he informed her. "That is what I am saying. And as my assistant, you will work. In your free time you may moon over a man you will never have—and wouldn't want, should you acquire him! But if you're not prepared to seriously work at your art *and* more mundane tasks, then we should part ways here and now. You have now made the acquaintance of David Turnberry and Lord Avery, and it was a pleasure and a privilege to meet your father, because I had seen his work. To be sadly crass, my dear, if I were seeking a certain companionship myself, I assure you, I'd not have to go to nearly as much trouble!"

Her cheeks flamed, but she wouldn't allow her eyes to fall from his.

"Then we are agreed," she said.

"As you wish."

"As *you* wish. After all, you are the legendary Sir Hunter MacDonald!" And with that, she nudged her horse, planning on a smooth and dignified movement to take the lead.

Unfortunately, the wretched horse decided to rear!

"Whoa!" Hunter cried, catching the mare's bridle. "You're lucky you kept your seat!"

She didn't look at him. "You see, I will ride, and will ride well. I swear it. And I will be an excellent assistant, I promise. Now, may we proceed?"

She clung desperately to her dignity. Hunter moved forward again.

Moments later, she was off the mare and feeling as if her muscles and bones weren't particularly well put together anymore. She forced herself to walk without the slightest limp.

"We will have to get you a habit, riding trousers," he murmured, his hand on her back as he ushered her ahead up the massive steps. "Riding astride is far more natural than sidesaddle."

He was striding through the ground floor exhibits as he spoke, heading for another flight of stairs. She kept up with his brisk pace, looking around as she did so. She had been to the museum before, naturally. Her father had taken Eliza and her several times—it had been determined years ago that the museum was not just for the elite, but for all the people of England. She had not particularly liked the Egyptian exhibits, not being fond of mummies. There was something eerie about peering at the sad visages of what had once been living men and women with their dreams of their preserved bodies being of use in the afterlife.

She kept this thought to herself as she hurried up the stairs, following him through a door labeled No Visitors. They came upon a room with a huge desk that was more like a table. No one sat at it.

There was, however, a woman seated on the floor, poring over pages of manuscript that were spread out before her.

She was in a simple skirt and embroidered blouse, the sleeves of which were rolled up. Her hair was slipping from its pins. She looked up, and her face was quite beautiful and radiant. "Hunter! You're here. I'm delighted. You've got to take a look at the translations I've made and the mapping I've done. I'm almost positive that the tomb you were seeking is here, just in the cliffs at the edge of the temple. I'm certain, and so very excited. But, of course, I am going by texts and papers and translations, and you have actually been on so many digs...you'll be a better judge of my determinations!" She had been speaking quickly, and she suddenly paused, aware that Hunter was not alone. She smiled sheepishly. "Hello."

"Camille, this is Kat—Katherine Adair. Kat, may I introduce Camille, Countess of Carlyle."

The woman rose, offering Kat a grimace and a smile. "Welcome," she said. "I'm afraid you've caught me in a bit of a dither. We're leaving so soon...and this is my dream. I've studied Egyptology most of my life and never been on an expedition." She kept her smile steady for Kat, but her glance toward Hunter was certainly one with a question.

Who is this woman and why is she here?

"How do you do," Kat murmured.

"Kat is going to be my assistant," Hunter said.

"Oh, I see." But did she? She seemed perplexed. "Are you an Egyptologist?"

"No, I'm afraid not."

"Ah."

"Miss Adair is an excellent artist," Hunter said.

"How wonderful."

"Where is Sir John?"

Camille laughed softly. "Taking time off! He said that I must have the run of the place and see that all goes well until we leave. He does not want to get in my way. Actually, I think that he is afraid he'd go quite insane with me here at this moment, running his smooth organization straight into the ground!"

"Ah, well, the fellow should have a holiday," Hunter said.

"Sir John?" Kat asked.

"The true head of the department," Camille explained.

"Is Brian about?" Hunter asked.

"Um, yes. He just went down the hall. He should be right back."

"I'll take a quick look," Hunter said.

And he left Kat there, alone with this woman who was gazing at her with such perplexity—and who suddenly exclaimed, "Ah, Katherine Adair! Goodness! You're the young woman who pulled David Turnberry from the Thames."

Kat blushed. She'd forgotten that she had been written up in the papers. "Yes," she murmured.

"What a heroic thing to do!"

"Not really. I'm not an Egyptologist, but I am an excellent swimmer, you see," Kat explained. "And...I'm not sure I'd realized it myself, but something of an artist. Because," she added quickly, "my father is really an excellent artist. It's rather a long story, but—"

"But you're to come with us on the expedition. Bravo! It will be delightful to have you along."

"Thank you." Could this woman be serious? But, of course, Kat had read all about Camille, Countess of Carlyle, as well. She had been a commoner, a woman working at the museum, and there had been some terrible horror going on at the time, Kat couldn't quite remember the details, but Camille and the earl had solved all the mysteries and married, and not even the most vile of the gossip journals could find a single negative thing to say about the woman.

"Are you ready for a few hardships?" Camille asked.

"Will you actually work the digs?" Kat cross-queried.

"Indeed! I wouldn't miss a minute. But you see… Here, come round and I will show you!"

The map she had on the floor beneath the various parchments and papers displayed the lower half of Italy and the northern region of Africa. "First, you see, we take a ship to the coast of France. Then we're on a train, and we'll travel through Paris, ever southward, and here go through Italy, perhaps with a bit of time in Rome, then over to Brindisi, and we're on a ship again. The journey itself promises excitement. The ship we board in Brindisi takes us to Alexandria, and from there, we go by train down to Cairo. The hotel there is lovely. But here! Here is where I am most anxious to be. I'm certain that everything I've read points to this little area here."

"It's the tomb of a pharaoh?" Kat queried.

"Better! The tomb of a high priest. He served Ramses II—the Great. And what a life that one led! Biblically, he was pharaoh during the exodus Moses led from Egypt. But he became pharaoh at a young age and rode out to be a great warrior-leader. He had a queen, of course, but quite a harem of wives, and hundreds of children. His oldest—groomed to follow his father—died at a young age. How is still in question. Oh, there are theories. But the tomb we're looking for belongs to that of one of his high priests. A fellow who was supposed to have had incredible influence over the pharaoh—like a mesmerist, even! Therefore, he gained great power and tremendous wealth, and had his own tomb dug out of the cliffs here, near the temple where he kept people cowed and in awe! To find his tomb, and all that may be within, may help to prove—or disprove—many theories regarding Ramses and his life. It might clarify fact from fiction and myth. Oh dear, I *am* going on. I do hope I'm not boring you."

"No, not at all," Kat replied honestly.

"It will be boring, some of it. There will be days of just sifting through sand...but I do hope you'll come to love it."

"So...there is a new person on our team, I hear."

Kat was kneeling on the floor when the Earl of Carlyle made his appearance. He was a very tall man, maybe half an inch more than Hunter's imposing height, with a scarred cheek that might have lent him an air of danger, had he not had such a pleasant smile and such merry eyes.

She struggled to stand; he raised a hand. "Please, don't get up. I believe Hunter and I will be joining you on the floor. My wife is eager for Hunter to agree with her. I've learned that not only did you salvage a student from the sea, but brought to our attention a man we were seeking—your father."

Her eyes widened. "You really do think so much of his work, then?"

"When you come to the castle, you will see," he assured her.

"Hunter, please, will you get down here and look at my calculations?" Camille demanded. "The painting is in the den, and it is fabulous," she added, waiting for Hunter to lower himself to her side. He hunkered down, and she looked at him anxiously as he gave her work his most serious attention. There was a protractor on the ground and he made note of her translations and certain sites, then swept arcs on the map. "There... or...there," he said at last.

"Aha!" she cried with delight.

"Nothing is exact, Camille," Hunter warned. "If it were, we'd not be digging endlessly. The sands have shifted over time. What appears simple may not be so."

"Oh, but we will make a great discovery, I know it," Camille said with pleasure.

"We may discover sand and rubble," he cautioned.

"Whatever we discover, it will be my first dig," she reminded him. "I have waited all my life for such an opportunity!"

"I thought you'd waited all your life for me," the earl said.

She laughed, "Well, that, too, of course!"

Watching them, Kat felt a poignant tearing at her heart, a wistful longing, such as she had never known before. Their feelings for each other were so evident, in words, in their laughter. Every time their eyes met.

She knew what it was like to hunger for someone...but not what it was like to be so tenderly regarded in return.

When she looked away, she realized that Hunter was watching her. His eyes were strangely grave, and she looked away quickly, determined that the man would not pity her.

Nor would she fail him in any way.

"What do these mean?" she asked, pointing to some of the hieroglyphs.

"Ah, basically, they mean that he is a man who talks to the gods, and whom the gods honor," Hunter replied. "He is the right hand of the pharaoh."

"And here, it says that as such, he rests near those who are great builders, men who will touch the sun," Camille continued.

Hunter was looking at Kat again as he asked, "Do you have that book, Camille? The one by Professor Lornette?"

"I do. In the desk. I'll get it."

"We have some logistics to go over, don't we?" the earl asked Hunter.

Hunter nodded. "We'll set Miss Adair to some learning, and I'll be right with you."

Camille rose to go into the desk and produce the book. "It's the best, the most accurate and comprehensive, that I've read. I hope you'll enjoy it."

"I hope you'll learn it," Hunter murmured, and his eyes were on Kat again.

"I shall set out to do so," she said. He was always challenging her, and warning her, she thought somewhat resentfully. But then her mind began to spin again. She had been seated on the floor with a *countess.* She'd shared a meal with Lord Avery. And with David.

She was about to embark on a fantasy that was so far removed it had never so much as entered into the realm of her dreams.

She would be polite. And good at the work he wanted.

"Hunter?" the earl said.

"Whenever you're ready, Brian," Hunter said.

"We're right down the hall in the old workroom. There have been a few renovations round here lately."

"If you need anything..." Hunter said.

"Go away. I'm here," Camille said cheerfully, waving her hand in the air. When the men were gone, Camille asked Kat, "Is there anything that you need?"

"I'm fine. Happy as can be. I shall just sit and study, unless I can be of any assistance to you. Then just tell me, please."

"Read away. And I will go back to some of my translations, see if there is more to verify all that I've found!"

They settled into an amazingly comfortable silence. To her surprise, Kat found the symbols and representations fascinating. Learning to put them all together was a bit difficult as first, quite different from translating, for instance, French to English. But after a while, it became easier to insert the implied meaning, and symbols began to run together more smoothly, making sense to her.

"Kat?"

She looked up, startled. Apparently, the Countess of Carlyle had been standing there for some minutes, looking at her. Not in annoyance, however.

"You're hooked," she said, smiling.

"I beg your pardon?"

"Hooked on ancient Egypt!" Camille said happily. "Be careful, it can become an obsession. I'm taking a break. Would you like to come along? There's a place here for tea...not open much longer."

Kat would have loved to go. But she didn't dare. Hunter might return at any minute.

"Thank you so very much. But I've little time and a great deal to learn," she said.

"As you wish. I can bring you back a scone or the like."

"I had breakfast, thank you."

Lady Carlyle left. Kat returned to the book, then looked up and gazed round. She was in some sort of main office, but where people worked, not where they greeted the public. This room was large, with the desk, filing cabinets and a few glass exhibit cases. She got up and walked to one, stared at it, frowning, for several seconds, then felt a shudder seize her.

The exhibit was of a pair of hands. Mummy hands. Broken at the wrists.

"Ugh!"

Kat stepped back. She glanced at the door, unnerved, hoping someone would return. But seconds later, she realized that her curiosity was greater than her fear and she began to walk around the room again. Another case offered a far prettier sight. Shimmering gold jewelry.

She found that jewelry had changed little over time. There were beautiful pieces there, thousands of years old, that might just as easily grace the fingers, wrists or throat of any wealthy woman today. Fascinated, she moved on. There were a few pieces of jewelry that held symbols she had just learned. "Ever in care of great Horus!" she read aloud with pleasure.

A moment later, she finished with the cases. There were two doors in the room. She stared at them, hesitating. She was just a guest here.

Ah, but one about to sail away—and work!—with a group of Egyptologists, amateur and professional. She walked resolutely toward the first door and opened it, stepping in. There was another desk in here, more filing cabinets, framed ancient maps on the walls and a few more exhibits.

On the desk sat a stuffed crocodile with gaping jaws. She noted the stationery on the desk, saw the emblazoned initials HSM.

Hunter's office?

Most likely. No, most definitely. There were several swords on the walls, some with plaques that described just how and when they had been received, gift of such and such a ruler. There was also a long, elegantly carved stick on the desk. She realized that it was a blowgun. Oh, yes, this was all Hunter's!

"Charming, I'm sure!" Kat murmured.

She stepped out, found herself still alone and opened the door to the second room. Hands clasped behind her back, she wandered in. Camille worked here, she thought. Astonishing. The woman had married an earl, yet kept working at the museum. This desk was so evidently hers! Papers in just a bit of disarray on it, but there were items on the desk of pure beauty—a gold and enameled scarab, little pieces that appeared to represent various gods...

Suddenly there was a sound from beyond the room, in the main office. Kat felt a moment's panic. It had to be Lady Carlyle returning...or Hunter. And she didn't want either catching her snooping about in areas to which she had not been invited.

Still, she was ready to burst out the door when she heard a whispered voice. "No one is here!"

"Well, do you see it?" Another voice, just as hushed, demanded.

"No, we've got to go in and find it. Quickly."

"Quickly? We've made a mistake, a major mistake. There are far too many people working here today. We've got to get out."

Kat couldn't make out the next words. But they ended with "...else we shall be to pay for it! And if the truth is known...better off dead!"

Then something and "...we missed the other day."

"Fool!" Again, words she couldn't make out. "Ah, well, there will be more chances! A long journey, a dark desert." Something totally uncomprehensible, and then "...dead is the only answer."

Kat gasped, then clamped her hand over her mouth. She was alone here at the moment, and these people, whoever they were...

"There's someone coming."

At that whisper, Kat found courage. She burst out of Camille's private office, certain that she would confront the intruders, and Hunter and the Earl of Carlyle would be coming in from the hallway.

But she burst out into an empty room. Surprise stopped her for a moment, then she strode across the room to the door that opened to the hall, throwing it open.

Again, there was no one.

And to her distress, as she stood in the hall, the door closed. She turned to enter again, but the door was now locked.

She swore softly. Words that might have distressed her father, but here, there was no one to hear them. At least, not at first.

As she tugged at the handle, she heard footsteps. Alarmed, she looked up.

Now Hunter was coming. "What's the problem, Miss Adair?"

"Rather apparent, I believe. I'm locked out."

"Ah." He stopped in the hallway, staring at her. "The question is, Kat, what are you doing on this side of the door? I thought you were working."

"I *was* working."

"Ah...well, there's little fresh air to be had in the halls here. Were you exploring?"

"No!" she protested.

"Then…?"

"I heard whispering," she said.

He sighed, looking weary and amused. "Miss Adair, mummies do not come back to life and walk the halls of the museum. They don't whisper, and they don't run around in their wrappings. And their mouths are wrapped shut, so the idea that they—"

"Hunter MacDonald!" came the soft, teasing voice of Lady Carlyle. She was approaching from the opposite direction. "Don't let him taunt you, Miss Adair. The man has been known to wear mummy wrappings himself!"

Kat was amazed to see Hunter flush. "Camille, at the time, I was afraid for your life!" he said.

"Yes, you were." She caught his arm and squeezed it, smiling with affection. "But be kind! This is all new to Miss Adair."

"Kat, please," she murmured.

"Only if I am Camille, and not all this 'Lady' here and there with every sentence! So what's going on?"

"Kat heard whisperers and decided to investigate," Hunter said. "And thus locked herself out of the office."

Camille looked at Kat, smoothing back a stray lock of her hair. "There's really no one else about."

"But there was!" Kat insisted.

"Perhaps some of the students?" Camille suggested to Hunter.

"I've not seen any of the fellows."

"Neither have I. Are you sure you heard something? The place is cavernous—voices can echo about."

"I heard people whispering," she said stubbornly.

"Men or women?" Hunter asked.

"I don't know."

"You were reading at the desk when I left you…and you heard something from outside?" Camille asked.

Kat opened and closed her mouth. *No, actually, I was snooping about in your private office, and the whispers came from just outside that door!*

She shook her head. "Never mind."

"Now you're angry," Hunter said.

"And maybe you're in danger!" she snapped back.

He smiled, looking at Camille again. "Everyone did read about all that happened here, I suppose," he said.

Kat, frowning, looked from one of them to the other. They both seemed amused, doubtless certain that she had let her imagination get the best of her.

"As I said, never mind!" she said to Hunter. "I think I've done quite well with your book this afternoon, and I believe I've learned a great deal."

"Take the poor girl home, Hunter!" Camille said. "There's always tomorrow, you know. And if you and Brian finished up with the budget, we're actually ahead of ourselves. Oh, you know you must be ready to sail on Saturday, Miss Adair." She gave Hunter a fierce look. "Arrangements have been made?"

"Emma is coming to look after the girls," Hunter said.

"I don't need looking after," Kat murmured.

"Girls?" Camille said.

"Lady Margaret has decided to go along. As far as Shepheard's Hotel."

Camille laughed. "Emma will not be happy."

"Oh, she seems in a jolly enough mood about it all. She seems to have acquired quite a fondness for Miss Adair." *Why? I can't begin to imagine!* Kat thought he implied.

"She'll be whining and complaining all the way," Camille warned.

"Well, Lord Avery gets along swimmingly with Emma, and he's been through several housekeepers in the past few months. And since his world rises and sets in Margaret, and Margaret loves Emma, as well, that's the way it must be."

"Good enough, then. I believe my husband is eager to head home now, and it's a bit of a ride. Kat Adair, delighted to meet you and to have you with us. Hunter, good night!"

She kissed him lightly on the cheek. He nodded, watching her for a moment as she departed. There was a very deep friendship between the two, Kat decided. Almost like brother and sister. She couldn't imagine such a thing herself. Especially since he seemed to have a talent for irritating her mercilessly.

He studied her, then, in the hallway for a long moment. "It is growing late. I shall see you home."

"I've been waiting all day for the pleasure of riding again," she told him.

"You'll get used to it. But we need only ride to the town house. Ethan will have the carriage there, and he'll take you on to your father's house."

There was no help for it; she had to allow him to help her back into the saddle. She was annoyed that she should feel his touch so keenly, as if her flesh burned beneath her clothing where his hands had been.

He was silent, pensive, as they rode. She chose not to break that silence. Still, she wondered if she should have been more persistent, made Hunter and Camille pay attention...tried to remember all that those whispering voices had said, word for word.

Now, as they rode out in the evening, the streets busy here and there with coaches, omnibuses and people on foot, the whispers seemed quite unreal.

And if she tried to bring up the subject again, he would simply be derisive once again!

At the town house, he lifted her from the saddle. She was very aware of the power in his arms as he lifted her so easily, then equally aware of the length of his body as he set her down. Where his strong hands had gripped her waist simply burned...

There was no time to think about that. He turned away, calling for Ethan, who, as usual, seemed to be at his master's beck and call.

"Miss Adair is anxious to get home."

"Yes, Sir Hunter."

He turned back to Kat. "Be ready at nine o'clock sharp tomorrow morning."

"Ready for what?" she queried.

"Just be ready!" he commanded.

Then he entered the house and she couldn't persist with *ready for what* because the door had already slammed closed.

"Miss Adair? The carriage is just down the drive." This from Ethan.

In the carriage, she silently cursed Hunter MacDonald. She considered telling him the next day that he and Lord Avery were ever so kind, but they were welcome to take their offer and...drop it in the sea!

After all, her father had probably sold some of his work that day, and at a fair price.

Because of Hunter and Lord Avery!

And if she told Hunter such a thing, she would not go on the expedition, and she would not be near David, subtly seducing him.

She frowned, realizing that she had given David little or no thought since she had arrived at the museum.

Incredible disloyalty!

Something had happened to her there at the museum. She had tapped into something in her own heart and mind. She still wanted to go on the expedition because of David…but she was fascinated. In love with the call to adventure, with the sights and sounds promised by all that she had seen and read today.

Bits of the whispered words came back to her.

"…a long journey…"

"…a dark desert…"

"We missed the other day…"

"…better off dead…"

She sat up in the carriage, shivering.

Had they been referring to David?

Fear shuddered through her. What if someone had pushed him, for some reason, off the sailboat? What if that same person…or persons meant to keep trying?

Outlandish! She assured herself. And yet…

She'd be watching. Now she'd be watching.

She felt a fearful, trembling sensation again. She would watch over him…and she could only pray that someone would watch over her.

Chapter 6

EVERYONE WAS HAPPY, Kat discovered.

Everyone, as a matter of fact, couldn't seem happier. And she couldn't help but feel a bit disgruntled.

Her father swept her into his arms the minute she came through the door. He was shaking with excitement. "Katherine! Ah, dear child! In a thousand years, I'd not have had you risk your life, but you did. I swore there would be no rewards for such a deed, but what you've given me is far greater than any cache of pounds sterling! These men...respected men, collectors! They have said that I am a good artist."

"Oh, they said much more than that!" Eliza cried, also rushing to the door to greet Kat. "They think Papa is one of the most talented artists they have ever seen. And, Kat! I am to design clothing for Lady Margaret!"

Kat had barely disentangled herself from her father's loving embrace before she found herself nearly crushed by her sister.

"That's...wonderful!" she gasped.

"I shall be busy as a bee all week. I must have a few garments ready for her before she sails. Oh, Kat! I will give the work my most fastidious attention, and perhaps other ladies will envy what she is wearing, and I will become known as a designer!"

"I'm so glad. I…had hoped you might manage a few pieces for me before I left," she murmured.

Eliza waved a hand in the air. "There are dozens of pieces of clothing I have done for you—you'll be all set, you'll see."

"Kat, how did you do at the museum?" her father asked. "Do you think that you will enjoy the work? Is it what you truly want? I swear, child, I'd not gain a thing from the pain of either of my daughters. I was still quite concerned today, but I have been assured by Lord Avery that you will be chaperoned as carefully as his own daughter."

"The work…I can't wait."

"You will learn so much with Sir Hunter!" Eliza extolled.

"Oh, yes. I'm sure I will."

"Are you tired?" Eliza asked her, frowning. "You don't seem at all happy."

"Oh, I am. Happy as a lark." She forced a smile.

"Maggie has our dinner about set," her father said. "I'll see if she needs help."

William Adair headed for their small kitchen. Eliza grabbed her sister again, her eyes wide with excitement. "Oh, Kat! I dared not say so in front of Papa, but…now I think *I* am in love!"

"With David? Goodness, his would-be harem is growing!"

Eliza frowned. "With David? Good heavens, no! It is Allan! Allan Beckensdale. Kat, he was ever so kind. We talked…oh, how we talked. Don't worry—I didn't desert Papa. I watched him. Isabella was there, ready to step in front of Papa and sell his work, but I managed to put money matters off! But then…Papa was so concerned about you, and he was deep in conversation with Lord Avery. Well, and Isabella—I couldn't quite make her disappear. But I had this delightful time with Allan in the sitting room, waiting until the others were all set and ready for tea. He's going to be a doctor, Kat. And...well, he's not so landed and rich, you know. A trust from his grandfather has put him through school, but he must then make his own way. And he was so lovely, talking about the roles of men and women and how he longed for a family, but that he wanted a wife with a mind of her own and talents to match. And then we talked books and plays and... Kat! It was wonderful."

"He's leaving in a week, as well, Eliza," Kat warned.

"But he will come back. And he has promised to write to me throughout the journey!"

"Well, that is lovely," Kat said.

Eliza frowned again. "Kat, I'm so sorry."

"Why?"

"I just realized...we're all so happy, almost living a dream. And I'm afraid that you've sold your soul for all this largesse. And that—"

"And that what?" Kat asked a little sharply.

"I'm sorry to say, I do believe that Lady Margaret, Lord Avery and David all intend that one day...that your David is the one for Lady Margaret."

"I don't believe that she's in love with him," Kat said stubbornly.

"How can you say that?" Eliza studied her sadly. "You've spent no real time with them," she reminded gently.

"I will be aboard a ship with them for a long journey," Kat said. "And in the desert. There's a long time before we return home."

"Kat," Eliza said worriedly, "you wouldn't try…well, you wouldn't let yourself…You really can't trap a man of his standing," she said.

Kat stiffened, staring at her sister. "I wouldn't want to trap anyone," she assured her. Furious—even though Lady Margaret had what she did not, a fortune and a title—she stepped around her sister, heading for the stairs.

"Kat!" Eliza called.

She paused.

"I don't mean to hurt you. I'm amazingly grateful. But you're my sister and I love you. The world is opening for all of us, and…I wouldn't want to see you throw your life away."

"I'll not throw my life away."

"It's just that you can be so…reckless. And you are so…*obsessed* with David."

"Our father has decided to trust me. You should, too."

"Papa is unaware of your infatuation."

"It has not made me a raving idiot. Eliza, I must wash for dinner."

She escaped up the stairs, surprised to find that she was shaking and ready to cry. She loved her father, no, adored him. He'd been the most gentle parent. And her sister was her best friend in the world. But they were all so happy, and she was just tired. Egyptian symbols now seemed to swim before her eyes. And her muscles ached from the ridiculous way she'd had to sit on the horse.

The trotting horse.

And she was certain, of course, that Hunter MacDonald had been determined to trot the whole way in order to cause her pain!

She washed her face, cooled somewhat by the water.

But downstairs, even Maggie, who had stayed with them after her mother's death, eschewing her own pay at times to see that the family ran well, was in the highest spirits that night, going on and on about the wonder of such men as Lord Avery.

Kat couldn't wait to go to bed.

But when she did, she dreamed. The mummy hands from the exhibit case were free, hopping about in a black fog, and it seemed that the hands were whispering to each other.

She awoke with a start.

She realized that she had because of a knocking at the front door.

Frowning, she leapt up in her cotton nightgown and ran down the stairs, anxious to reach the door before anyone else was awakened. It was surely a delivery of dairy goods.

But it was not. It was Hunter, looking impatient.

"Come, come, girl, we've got work to do."

"But…you said nine o'clock!"

He drew out his pocket watch. "It is ten minutes before the hour."

She was tempted to slam the door in his face. She refrained. "Then I have ten minutes."

"I had hoped you might be ready early."

"Yes, well, since you are here, I shall hurry. What is the work? Are we going back to the museum?"

"My dear child, we are heading to the park. Riding lessons." He produced a package for her. "You won't have to waste your ten minutes redressing. Come along now, I do have other engagements this afternoon. But don't worry. We'll have three hours."

"Three hours. On a horse. What fun. Don't fear, I shall prepare in all haste!"

This was not a household that rose early, Hunter determined wryly as he waited. The housekeeper, Maggie—a lovely woman with an Irish brogue so thick he had to mentally translate as he listened—appeared as he waited, wanting to know if he desired coffee or tea. He thanked her and assured her that no, he was fine. William Adair came out and began thanking him, and Hunter, discomfited by so much gratitude, told him that *he* was the lucky one, for he'd be known as the man who discovered William Adair.

Eliza came flying down the stairs, eager to greet him, as well. Therefore, when Kat came down the stairs, clad in Francesca's old riding habit, her entire small family was there, beaming.

He was disturbed, too. The riding attire became her, as all else did. A light beige skirt fell over the pants of the ensemble, so that it appeared the outfit consisted of a tailed jacket, shirt, vest and skirt. Beneath, however, were pants allowing a woman to ride astride while the sham of a shirt was slit to fall handsomely over the legs once a woman was seated. The accompanying hat sat nicely atop her head. The beige, and the tailored, businesslike cut of the habit sat marvelously on her lean but curved shape.

Then again, she had appeared quite the beauty in her flowing cotton nightgown, as well, hair tumbled about her face in waves of fire.

It was at that moment, standing there, surrounded by her loving family, that he realized, in his heart, just what was driving him.

He was fascinated by her. Stirred and aroused, both physically and mentally. She was young, she was naive. She was filled with courage, reckless bravado, and beneath the devil-may-care attitude, she loved those who surrounded her. She was willing to dream, to explore. She longed for the world. She longed for what she couldn't have. Nothing was going to stop her.

And here he was, wanting her, with her father just steps away.

"Sir!" William Adair turned to him with such a frown that Hunter feared that he was aware of the very carnal desire arising in his heart. But the man was not. He was perturbed about the outfit! "That habit is of the finest quality. We cannot accept—"

"Mr. Adair, pray forgive me. But the habit is my sister's, and she would be delighted to know that your daughter was wearing it."

"It must not be a gift," William said.

Hunter inclined his head. "Then it is only on loan."

"Which is so kind," Kat murmured, the tone of sarcasm with which she spoke so low that her father did not realize it. "Sir Hunter has seen how avidly I have taken to the sport of riding."

"Not a sport on an expedition," Hunter corrected her. "A necessity."

William nodded gravely. "It fits you well, daughter. And suits you," he noted.

"Thank you, Papa," she murmured, walking to him, kissing his cheek.

"Such a clever design," Eliza murmured.

"I'm sure you'll be able to take from it and create something even better," Kat said. "Well...I believe we're off?" She looked at Hunter, irritation lingering just beneath her polite query.

"Indeed, we're off," Hunter agreed. "Mr. Adair, Miss Adair, good morning."

"Be careful!" Eliza warned.

"I'd never let harm befall her," Hunter assured them both.

"I feel that she is indeed safe in your hands, Sir Hunter," William said gravely.

Hunter ground his teeth together as they departed. If the good man only knew! But, indeed, yes, she was safe with him.

"Come," he told Kat, leading her to the mare Giselle, having led the animal through the streets as he rode Alexander. The pair did well together. She was not the first woman to have been taken riding on Giselle.

She walked to the horse, obviously ready to attempt to mount on her own. He set a hand on her shoulder, stopping her. "Always mount from the left," he began.

"I know that much!"

"Put your hand here," he directed. "Hold the reins—always have the reins. My horses are not hacks, and they might spook. Being dragged through the streets of London is not an adventure you'd want to experience."

"I'm assuming that I do need to learn to mount the animal myself. I doubt that you will be at the constant beck and call of your secretary," she said.

"Correct, but I shall help you right now."

He didn't allow the next protest to leave her lips; he was certain she argued at times just for the sake of argument. Catching her firmly about the waist, he set her on Giselle and looked up at her. "Sit easily, comfortably, in the saddle. Heels down at all times. That is of the utmost importance. Heels down at all times. If you are ever thrown, it is far better to leave the horse than be trapped beneath it."

She nodded. He walked away and quickly mounted Alexander. "We'll head for the park," he told her.

"Indeed, Sir Hunter. It seems that my time is yours. Wherever you wish."

The workday streets were busy as ever. Vendors hawked fruit and pastries. People bustled about, walking with purpose. Delivery vehicles were making their stops. Omnibuses and hacks made their respective way. Here and there, becoming more frequent and not quite so much objects of curiosity, were horseless carriages, huffing, puffing, making noise, and causing some fear among the draft and riding horses that plodded alongside them. Despite the bizarre horns and the fellow whose engine suddenly sputtered and spewed before them, Kat was able to keep control of the mare, and she and Hunter moved along briskly.

Inside the park at last, they were some distance from the mayhem of city life. The greatest distraction was a nanny here or there, strolling with a pram.

"You're doing well. Are you any more comfortable astride?" he asked her.

"Yes," she admitted. She hesitated. "Do we ride from the time we reach Egypt?"

He smiled, shaking his head. "There's a train from Alexandria to Cairo. When we leave the hotel for the excavation site, we'll ride."

"And the site that we'll go to is the same one where the Countess of Carlyle is working?"

He nodded again. "Yes. So that meets with your approval."

"I like her very much," Kat said.

"Ah, because she was a commoner who married an earl?"

She narrowed her eyes. "Because I like her."

"She is quite amazing," he said.

"Do you know her…very well?" Kat asked. It seemed a pleasant enough question, but there was also an insinuation to it. He could have done a great deal of explaining. He chose not to.

"Yes, I know her very well."

"And her husband, of course."

"Yes. We were in the queen's army together, and during the last year, renewed our former acquaintance."

"I'm trying to remember," Kat said. "There was such a stir in the papers. Lord Carlyle's parents were killed, and he had hidden out, and everyone thought that he was a beast, but he had been trying to learn the truth of what happened. And there was a gentleman, Sir something—I have forgotten his name—and he was nearly killed, but I believe that the earl saved the fellow's life and caught the real culprit and…your name was mentioned in several of the stories!"

"That was the past, and this, my dear, is now. Brian has his parents' legacy, and is anxious to go on this expedition. He's disturbed that so much leaves the country illegally, and anxious that more of the treasures discovered in Egypt remain in Egypt."

"If he wants them to remain in Egypt, why is he so eager to find them?" Kat demanded.

Hunter arched a brow. "It's the knowledge, the discovery, the understanding of a people who could create such great monuments…it's what they've left for today, what we can learn from them, that's so important. And the desert is so vast! There are endless discoveries to be made. And as far as the treasures go, the point is this. There are those that can be legally obtained and are not one-of-a-kind pieces. There are fantastic monuments that belong here. At the Cairo museum. There is a small fortune to be made in the relics, even when all is legal and right. Museums across the world covet fine Egyptian mummies and artifacts—they draw people. People eat in the cafés, they purchase books and trinkets, all based on what they see. So while the entry to a museum may be free and the museum may get financial support from the government, as we do, great exhibits such as those provided by fresh discoveries are of the utmost importance to an institution's growth. Some exhibits come on loan. And some pieces, as I said, are legally obtained. But...again, it's the discovery that is so significant. Seeking information, solving puzzles, finding that you have followed ancient clues correctly—there lies real treasure."

He ceased to speak, realizing that she was watching him with serious contemplation, the slightest smile curling her lips.

"This is amusing?" he asked.

Her smile deepened. "No, Sir Hunter. Actually, I am impressed with your passion. And I am truly sorry I do not know more about this subject that so enthralls you. But I promise, I will do my best to serve your needs." She blushed, realizing the awkwardness of her words. "To be a good secretary. Taking notes...working."

There had been many times in his life when he would have followed such a statement with teasing repartee, often to make an older, less attractive woman feel that she was comely and appealing. Banter and sexual innuendo had been his specialty. But at the moment, he had no such urge.

"I have the strangest feeling that you will do whatever you have set out to do," he told her. "Let's move on to a faster gait, shall we?"

He kicked Alexander's flanks with his heels, that day refraining from spending too much time at a trot, teaching Kat to move into a smooth lope straight from a walk.

She was an excellent student.

When asked about her comfort, she did not tell him that she was in pain, or that she was doing fine. "I am learning, and I believe I shall do quite well."

"Yes, I am sure you will."

And so, at last, he led her through the streets, and they wended their way back to Kat's home. But no matter what her words, he was certain that her limbs were sore. After he dismounted Alexander, he lifted her from her saddle.

She was ever so slightly shaky. Her hands fell on his shoulders, seeking support. He felt the pressure of her fingers as he set her down.

And there were seconds there when she clung to him, finding her feet. He smelled the subtle scent of her perfume, felt the warmth of her body and the slim strength of her midriff. He held her, waiting, until she balanced on her own, and let go her hold on his shoulders.

"Sore?" he asked, annoyed at the huskiness of his voice.

She looked up, still so close to him. "I will be fine," she said firmly.

"I suggest a very warm bath."

"Thank you." Her eyes touched his without faltering. "I'll give it consideration."

He smiled, stepped back. "Tomorrow, then."

"Will we go back to the museum?"

"Yes. Be ready by nine," he said, striding back to Alexander.

"You're a dictator, you know!" she called after him.

"Nine," he added, annoyed now that his voice was curt, and that he was oddly eager to be away.

He didn't look back, but led Alexander with the mare in tow. The scents of the city rose around him. Horses, food being sold by hawkers, refuse...

But underlying all that was the subtle and unique scent that was hers. And it seemed to follow him all the way home.

AGONY! SHE WAS IN AGONY, Kat decided.

Eliza wasn't home, as she had gone off to buy fabric, filled with excitement over the task of designing for Lady Margaret.

Her father, too, was gone. He was somewhere with Lady Daws, something to do with the sale of his art. According to Maggie, he, too, was in high spirits.

She must have looked a little lost because Maggie made clucking sounds, wound her arms around her and said, "Poor thing! All that riding. But we'll get you into a hot tub and all will be well. Why, that Sir Hunter! The fellow isn't at all what I expected, but a hard taskmaster. Handsome man, he is. Adventurer, explorer! Not at all indecent, such as I expected. But 'tis hard for you, darlin', being the one to pay for all the good that's come!"

"Maggie, I'm not paying for anything, really. I'm a bit sore, that's all."

"Well, we be fixing that. Ah, with all the good fortune, Lady Daws is still about, playing the grand dame! Well, your father be a fine and smart-enough fellow, but he does believe that she's been behind him, that she's the one got his work out where it's been seen, and he's still listening to the witch! And don't you go telling him what I call the woman, though like as not he will be marrying her, and I'll be the one to get the boot!"

"Maggie, never!" Kat assured her. "Why, my father might be a bit under the witch's spell, but he knows that you cared for Mother, and that you've been a pillar of strength to all us, indeed staying on when your pay wasn't coming! Papa will not forget that."

"Ah, well, strange it may be, but true, when folks are in love, they do strange things," Maggie said sagely. "They do...ah, well, they may do anything, risk all!"

Kat offered her a weak smile. Was she herself willing to do anything for love? So far, it seemed that she had indeed sold her soul!

And the worst of it was that it seemed the rest of her world so easily saw David, while she had always to chafe at the bit, so to speak, to be at the fellow's side!

"Soak, moppet," Maggie told her. "Soak in the hot water and you'll feel better, I swear it!"

They did have fairly modern plumbing and a decent-enough bathtub, and so she was left upstairs. But when the water began to cool, Maggie added more that she had heated herself over the open flame in the girls' room. When the doorbell rang, Maggie bustled off to get it.

She returned excitedly to the bathroom several minutes later. "Up, child! 'Tis David Turnberry downstairs, anxious to take you out for a spot of tea. He says he has photographs of his father's expedition a decade ago, and he'd like you to see what you're up against!"

Kat was so surprised and pleased she feared that she'd give away her absolute infatuation for the man.

"David Turnberry?" she managed to say casually. "And...is he with the Lady Margaret?"

Maggie shook her head, frowning and then tsking again. "He's alone. Perhaps I'd best go back down and tell him that you're not to be going off with any man alone, even for so much as a spot of afternoon tea!"

"No!"

She was out of the bath in the wink of an eye, grabbing a towel, already wondering what she would wear. "Um...he's a most decent young man, Maggie. And tea! Surely, there's no harm in my accompanying the fellow. He's trying to be kind, of course."

"I don't know...I don't know. Such a thing has never occurred before!" Maggie said worriedly. "Oh, I should have sent him packing!"

"Good heavens, Maggie! We are living in the eighteen-nineties!" Kat decided to wheedle. "Oh, please! If he came for Eliza in order that she might purchase some fabrics, you'd think nothing of it. And, Maggie, I sat upon that stupid animal, and on the floor in the museum, working, learning. Surely a brief spot of pleasure would not be an ill thing!"

"Perhaps your father will return while you're dressing," Maggie murmured.

Perhaps he would. Kat meant to be ready in seconds. "Please, Maggie, don't let David leave. Please go and entertain him while I dress."

Maggie, still uncertain, left her. Kat nearly flew from the bathroom and all but tore the wardrobe apart in her effort to quickly find the right clothing.

He's come for me! He does care for me. He looked up at me with such adoration when I saved him. He just needed to be reminded of it...

Perfect. A slim skirt with the slightest bustle, a chemise and overblouse, decorous, almost prim, and a little jacket over the skirt. Perfectly presentable and respectable.

She fought with her thick red hair, seeking to pin the wild tresses with the same respectable appeal. But she thrust the last pin in with a certain defiance; she had to leave. Her father could return.

Worse. He could return with Lady Daws.

She raced down the stairs. And there he was, amusement and appreciation in his eyes, casual but elegant in his gray waistcoat and deerstalker cap. He was listening to Maggie's chastisements, and his bright eyes rolled as they met Kat's.

"Miss Adair," David said, bowing slightly. "I have been warned that we must stay on main streets, and that I may have you out for no more than two hours."

"Thank you, Maggie," Kat said, frowning slightly. In David's house, she was certain, the servants were servants. Maggie was much more than a servant.

"Tea, David, how lovely of you to think to come to offer me some refreshment. I've had a busy morning, learning to ride."

"Ah, Sir Hunter!" David said, his eyes sparkling so that she remembered exactly why she had fallen so head over heels for the man, even from a distance. "Well, he can be a tough fellow, eh? Soldier and all, wounded, knighted, ever at the front! Don't be dismayed—he will be as hard on every student who joins the expedition. Hands in the dirt, and delicately so, and there will be so much done per hour and a quota of work to be met by nightfall. We'll all suffer from his rigid schedule, I'm afraid. But then, we'll learn much, eh? Shall we go? Maggie, dear woman, thank you for allowing Miss Adair to go out with me for tea, and I will return her within the allotted time, I do so swear!"

Maggie arched a brow in warning, and Kat again offered her a frown, slipping to the door ahead of David.

Maggie was quickly forgotten.

"Are we to... Oh!" Kat said. No, they weren't to ride, or to walk, or to take public transportation. An elegant carriage awaited them.

"To the Tarlington Club, please!" David told the driver, who was waiting to help them up the steps to the body of the vehicle, emblazoned with the illustrious coat of arms of David's family.

She was seated across from him, quite appropriately. But as he joined her, his knees brushed with hers. And when he sat across from her, he took her hands in his.

"I'm delighted that you will be joining us in Egypt!" he said passionately.

"Thank you. I'm delighted to be going."

She thought that, strangely, he shivered slightly. "Sad to say, you are something of my champion, my lady in shining armor!" he teased.

"Please, David," she said, relishing the sound of his given name, spoken to him, on her lips. "I swim well, and I'm sorry to say, it was not such a heroic gesture. As my father says, it was merely an act of human decency."

"Yes, but..." Sadly, she thought, he released her hands and sat back, looking out the window of the carriage. "But I was there with all those strapping fellows." He stared at her again. "Alfred, Lord Daws was there, as well, you know."

"Alfred, Lord Daws?" she repeated.

"Mmm. The stepson of Lady Daws," he said, as if she didn't know.

"I don't believe that they are...close," she said carefully.

David was not so careful. He let out a brief laugh. "To say the least! I was quite startled to realize that Lady Daws was a part of your household."

"She is not a part of my household!" Kat said.

Again, David laughed, eyes warm as they touched hers. "Such passion, Kat! So lovely, and you are a fierce lady in shining armor, ready to do battle for all those weaker around you."

It was her turn to look out the window. "My father is not weak," she said a bit curtly.

"Dear, dear Katherine! I've offended you. I did not mean to do so. All men can be...weak. She's an enchantress, I think." He leaned forward again, and he was so close to her that she longed to reach out and touch his dear face! "Alfred—Lord Daws—is not so kind or careful when he speaks of the woman. And yet...he says that he knows why his father was so bewitched! She's not much older than Alfred and I, you know. Around Sir Hunter's age, actually. She was far too young for Alfred's father, and that is, of course, the rub. Alfred is quite convinced that she married the old fellow for his money, and he can only be grateful that half the family riches came from his mother's side, and therefore, all was in trust for him, and his father's widow could not wrest his inheritance from him. Oh, dear, Maggie would be wretchedly distressed. I'm hardly being proper."

"Maggie isn't here," Kat reminded him. And she was grateful! She never wanted the ride to end. He was confiding in her. Taking a risk, curious, perhaps, to see what she knew about Lady Daws and the situation, but whatever he was actually seeking, she didn't care. Their knees touched, he held her hands in his earnestness, and his face was so near...

"It's quite all right. Since we're being woefully improper, I can only say that she is a friend of my father's, and not, I repeat, not a part of my household."

"But lovely to look at," David said.

"I suppose."

He laughed again, truly enjoying their time together, and perhaps even the curtness of her tongue.

"Not," he said, and his words were husky, "not at all as you are lovely. She has an appeal, of course, which she has used, but...you are like the beauty of a wild fire! Truly, Kat. And I find that I am fascinated, as man is fascinated by fire, drawn ever closer to the flames, red, orange, blazing, ever tempting..."

So close...the two of them. She could feel him, feel the sweet rush of his breath, his lips, almost upon her own, and she knew that she wasn't breathing. She was waiting, and it was truly and ridiculously improper....

The carriage came to a halt; the door swung open. They jerked apart.

"We have arrived," the driver said.

"Indeed! Well, time for tea," David announced.

Then he appeared flushed and a bit uneasy. As if he had been lured by a spell himself and been awakened. He jumped up, hitting his head on the roof of the carriage. He managed the few steps down, reaching back to assist Kat himself.

"The afternoon tea is quite lovely here," he said. "I pray you'll enjoy it."

"You needn't pray," she said lightly. "I promise you, I shall."

And on his arm, she entered the elegant tea room.

"TELL ME MORE OF THE STORY about your little fire goddess!" Camille said, sitting back in her chair in the outer office.

He had been quite serious, discussing business. Camille, at the moment, was not interested in the subject that was usually dearest to her heart.

They were awaiting Brian's arrival to go over a few of the last of the packing details. There was much that could be hired or purchased once they reached Cairo, but since Camille, though a splendid Egyptologist, had as yet to go on an actual dig, they were doing their best to assure her that everything was set just as it should be.

Hunter waved a hand in the air. "Camille, there is nothing else to tell. The story is simple. When others were fools, she was actually a bigger fool, risking her life for the lad. Her father is a very proud man—"

"An amazing artist," Camille interjected.

"Yes, a truly amazing artist, and it's quite incredible that his work hadn't come to be properly appreciated."

Camille arched a delicate brow. "Not so difficult to see, since Isabella Daws has apparently been using her 'influence' and 'managing' his work."

"Oh, I've heard her explain how she has sold pieces—then seen them appear in the homes of men with greater incomes. She does have a certain charm, and she's been able to talk her way out of every question put her way. She also pretends to be greatly enthused that he has now come to the attention of members of the aristocracy. I believe that she's been selling his work for a great deal more than she's told him."

"That's likely. You know, in the past year, she's tried to sell several pieces of her husband's Egyptian collection to the museum."

"Oh? I thought that Alfred inherited the estate."

"He did," Camille said. "But apparently, a number of his personal effects were left in her hands. She is extravagant, and in need of an income constantly. Actually, she was in the museum not long ago. On a day when Alfred happened to be in, as well, filling out papers, since he is part of the expedition. I saw them run into each other by the Rosetta Stone."

"And no blood was drawn?" Hunter asked.

Camille laughed softly. "No, they appeared to be quite civil. I remember everyone's shock when Lord Daws married her. Rumors flew fast and furious. His first wife had been ill for quite some time, so I didn't believe the whispers that suggested Isabella had murdered him. Of course, I didn't really know them at the time. I knew that Lord Daws did some work with the museum, and contributed some artifacts. Apparently, however, he had known Isabella years and years before." Camille sighed. "Well, she must be a happy woman now. Apparently, she has had a relationship with William Adair for some time."

"She would never marry a poor artist, but a rich one makes possible marriage material?" Hunter asked dryly.

"Precisely," Camille agreed. "So, I must say, however you managed it, I'm delighted that William's daughter will be along. What a quick study she is! I gave her a book, and she learned to read so many hieroglyphs in such a short time I barely believed it." Then Camille shook her head and a frown furled her brow. "Things are a bit chaotic right now, what with benefactors and students about, but I have seldom had so much trouble keeping track of all the maps and itineraries. They're on a desk one minute and disappear the next. In fact, I've lost any number of papers lately."

"Lost?"

She shrugged. "As I said, maps and itineraries, also calculations. Nothing truly valuable has disappeared. Don't look so fierce. There haven't been any break-ins, nothing so dire. Still, it's good to know that someone as clever as Kat, as quick to capture images and learn their meanings, will be with us. How did you manage to secure her services as an assistant?"

Hunter hesitated, then said, "To be honest, she is so ridiculously enamored with David Turnberry and the world he lives in I thought that if she spent time with him and his peers, she would see how shallow and unworthy he and his world are. I knew she was entranced by the idea of our voyage to Cairo, so I arranged with Lord Avery, who believes she must somehow be rewarded, that she accompany us."

"So you intend to work her to pieces."

"She wishes to come. That is what we do."

"Ah! But you wish to work her—or punish her?" Camille asked softly.

"Punish her! Camille, whatever for? She showed extraordinary courage."

"Or, as you said, foolishness."

He waved a hand in the air, frowning, concerned. "At this point, that particular question is moot. She did dive in and she did save the poor fool's life. He is the dearly beloved son of Turnberry, and Avery and Turnberry are the best of friends. So. She sits on a pedestal. Sadly, without a rich inheritance, one cannot live upon a pedestal. Her father will accept no charity."

"But as we both know, her father could become a wealthy man."

"True enough."

"Money can be acquired many ways—heavens, far too often, people are born with it. But talent, now, talent cannot be bought."

"She is very talented herself," Hunter said.

"And you are a benefactor of the arts!" Camille teased.

"What are you trying to say, dear Camille?" he inquired.

"I've never seen you act so strangely, that is all," she said innocently.

"I am not behaving strangely."

"But you are. And you must be careful."

"Oh?"

"Good heavens, Hunter, why don't you simply express your feelings and your intentions, and court the girl?"

"What?"

"No, she isn't Lady-so-and-so, nor is she a rich widow…a gay divorcée…but, quite seriously, Hunter, as one who knows and loves you dearly, I do feel inclined to pry. And advise."

"Camille, I don't need advice."

She laughed. "Personally, I believe she's perfect for you."

"*You* were perfect for me. You do recall that I once asked you to marry me," he reminded her.

"But you didn't really love me, Hunter. It was simply the proper gesture. Now, with this girl…"

"Camille, I am just trying to look out for her."

"You? That's rich!"

"Yes, well, thank you."

"Oh, Hunter! Believe me, I know that you are far more ethical than you will ever admit. After all, you were willing to marry me because you thought that I was in trouble, in over my head."

"Camille, you are a gorgeous woman."

"Ah, and you are a flatterer! As I said, you cared about me, but you were never in love with me," she said.

"I'm not in love with the girl. Don't be ridiculous."

"Fine. As you wish. So, where is the lovely girl today?" Camille asked.

"Home, I believe. We had a riding lesson. She is unfamiliar with horses, and she will have to be comfortable riding in the desert. Sadly, I'm afraid she must be in some pain."

"In pain?" Brian Stirling, the Earl of Carlyle, asked, walking into the office. "Hardly. Your lass is at the Tarlington Club with David Turnberry. I noticed their table as I was leaving." He grinned, moving behind his wife's chair, looking at Hunter. "I believe she is causing a few whispers, since she is quite a glorious young woman. And hardly unnoticeable, with that brilliant hair. I do believe a few heads are turning. And with her father's growing reputation, she'll soon be the toast of the town. Ah, yes! Tongues will wag."

Hunter stared at Brian, startled. *She's with David Turnberry, the object of her obsession. And yes, she's beautiful, and she will indeed be drawing attention,* he thought.

What are David's intentions?

"So," Brian continued, "shall we go over the lists?"

Hunter barely heard him as he strode for the door.

"Hunter!" Brian called. "Where are you going?"

"I believe he's heading out for tea, dear," Camille said.

Hunter barely heard either of them.

David Turnberry would never turn away from a marriage to Lady Margaret. But he is young.

And he is tempted.

And good God, the silly little mermaid will never be able to resist him.

Chapter 7

KAT CARED NOT THAT WHISPERS flew around them.

The Tarlington Club was exquisite. Great sheets of stained glass covered the windows, blocking the view of the inner sanctum from the streets of London beyond. Only the most elite of London's society strode through the doors—the cost of membership was very high.

Chairs were of the finest leather. The scent of tobacco smoke was everywhere, even in the tea room, slipping in from the bar beyond the elegant tables. The silver was polished and gleaming, and the teacups were the most delicate. And those sitting at the tables munching on tiny, elegant sandwiches were dressed in the latest fashions.

Kat was barely aware of the stylish extravagance around her, so focused was she on the young man before her. She was laughing. Now and then, because they were at tea, she would nibble on a sandwich. Mostly, however, she just watched David, listened to his stories about life at school. Listened to tales about his friends, including Alfred Daws, Allan Beckensdale and Robert Stewart.

She had seldom felt so intimate with another human being, and her heart was racing. She felt beautiful, truly beautiful. She knew that she had drawn the appreciative stares of many a man in the room. And she knew that David was proud to be in her company. It was exhilarating. She might have been soaring in the clouds. The way that he looked at her—

"Ah, David! And this must be the incredible Miss Adair!"

Kat looked up to see a tall, striking young man standing by their table. He had dark eyes, his light hair an arresting contrast. His build was lean and wiry.

There was something familiar about him.

"Why, Alfred!" David stood and extended his hand. As they shook, the fellow looked at her with keen interest.

"Sorry," David said. "Miss Adair, Lord Alfred Daws. Alfred, Miss Katherine Adair."

Alfred Daws took her hand, met her gaze, then made an elaborate show of planting a light kiss on her flesh. "How do you do? This is a pleasure I hadn't begun to imagine for the afternoon." His smile did not reach his eyes. "I understand that you are acquainted with my father's widow."

Kat realized then why he looked familiar—she had seen his picture in the social pages of the newspaper. And it was evident that he didn't care for Isabella Daws. She noticed that he didn't refer to her as his stepmother, but rather as his father's widow. She also recalled Eliza's telling her that they didn't get along.

"How do you do," she murmured. "And, yes, I am acquainted with...your father's widow," she said, answering in kind.

His smile warmed. "May I?" he asked David, indicating one of the other chairs at the table.

"I suppose," David replied less than graciously.

But Alfred Daws ignored the hint. He sat, his eyes on Kat. "How very strange, Miss Adair, that you should be the one to fish old David from the sea. You leave us all humbled! We were running about, thinking to get the small boat and search…but you! You dived straight in. Then to discover that your father is the mysterious artist whose magnificent pieces good old Isabella has been flogging…well, 'tis extraordinary!"

"It's a small world," David murmured.

"Apparently," Kat said. It had never seemed so before!

"Will you have tea, Alfred?" David asked.

Alfred waved a hand in the air. "Tea? I'd say it's time for sherry. Or champagne. David, where are you manners? We must have champagne to salute this heroine."

"No, no, please…" Kat protested.

"Kat is made quite uncomfortable by too much ado," David said.

"Then you must join David and me for champagne simply to be social," Alfred said. His gaze swung to David. "We're school chums, you know, and I'm afraid that we're students who sometimes distress our professors. Living a bit on the wild side. Yet I hardly think it would be out of line to order champagne now?"

Their waiter, seeing the young swain who had joined the table, moved closer. Alfred looked at him. "Why, it's Humphrey!" he said.

"Lord Daws," Humphrey acknowledged.

"Champagne, I think. Something very fine for Miss Adair."

"As you wish."

"So, tell me, how well do you know Isabella?" he demanded.

Kat shrugged. *Well enough to know that she is a witch!* she longed to say. But despite her loathing for the woman, she was uneasy. She didn't know this man.

And sadly, he had interrupted the incredible magic of this precious time she'd had with David!

"As you said, she is acquainted with my father," Kat allowed.

"Egad, but that is kind!" Alfred said with a derisive laugh.

"Alfred!" David warned. "Your title does not make up for your lack of manners!"

But Alfred was undaunted. His smiled deepened. "Miss Adair is not some aging battle-ax!" he protested. "And she knows my dear old stepmum! And ah, here's the champagne."

Humphrey had uncorked the bubbly brew. Alfred took a taste and nodded. "Delicious. Dry, smooth, lovely. Please, Humphrey, do pour."

Humphrey handed Kat a delicate flute and she thanked him. She sipped it, thinking it rather awful herself. But then, she'd never had champagne before.

"To you, Miss Adair!" Alfred said.

She lowered her head in acknowledgment. "Thank you," she murmured.

"So! You are to accompany us to the desert," Alfred said.

"Yes, I will be working for Sir Hunter."

"Ah, the dear girl has been sold into slavery!" Alfred said, chuckling.

"We're all sold into slavery for the expedition," David said.

"True enough." Alfred swallowed down his glass. "Drink up, my friends. May I call you my friend, Miss Adair?"

"Certainly," she murmured.

"How is it that you've escaped this afternoon?" Alfred demanded.

"I'm not sure," she replied.

He tapped her glass again. "Drink up, Miss Adair." He leaned closer. "I dare say, you might as well! Every nasty matron in the town is watching this table."

"They're wondering that I am here," Kat said simply.

"Ah! Indeed, they're gossiping disgracefully, and why? The daughter of the artist is far more beautiful than their debutante daughters! Well, we should let them envy you, and talk their evil little hearts out!"

He was outrageous, but Kat liked him.

And she was probably able to excuse his devil-may-care attitude because they certainly did have one thing in common—an acute dislike for Isabella Daws!

She swallowed more champagne, realizing that the more she drank, the better it tasted. It also made her feel very lightheaded.

"I am embarrassing you. I'm sorry," Alfred said.

"I'm fine," she murmured.

"I'm not!" David said irritably. "Alfred, you've got the entire place looking at us!"

"You honestly think that they weren't looking before?" Alfred demanded, refilling their glasses from the bottle that rested in ice at a stand by the table.

"You should lower your voice," David pleaded.

"Are you afraid that your presence will be noted?" Alfred demanded, winking at Kat.

"Heavens, no!" David snapped back. But something in his voice suggested that he might have grown uneasy.

"We could leave," Alfred said.

"Yes, I should go home," Kat said, heartily sorry.

"I didn't say that you should go home. In fact, you *shouldn't* go home. But we should leave. We must finish up this champagne—it's frightfully expensive and not to be wasted—and leave, letting all their tongues wag!"

David swallowed down his champagne and glanced at Kat. She did the same. David appeared anxious now to leave, and she wanted to make him happy.

"Humphrey, please add all this to my bill," Alfred called cheerfully, then he rose, pulling out Kat's chair so that she could rise, as well.

She did so.

The world wobbled slightly, but she quickly gained her balance. She felt like smiling. Yes, there were people in the room frowning at them. She didn't care. Lord Daws had a prestigious title. And he didn't care about the silly scowls of the matrons he called battle-axes! And David…

David had her arm. He was touching her. And he seemed to be aware that being on her feet was a bit difficult for her.

He led her from the tea room. Out front on the sidewalk, in the growing darkness, he looked around, then turned to Alfred.

"My carriage is gone."

"Of course, I sent it away. We'll travel in mine."

Despite the slightly askew world around her, Kat knew that the hour was getting late. "I do need to get home," she said softly.

"Of course," David replied gently.

She could not have drunk so much of the champagne! But when the second man came to her other side and offered a supporting arm, it seemed quite natural. And moments later, barely aware of exactly how she had gotten there, she found herself in an elegant carriage. Now she did smile.

For David was sitting next to her, a dream come true. In fact life was a dream now, as sweet as anyone could hope. Except, of course, when she was with Hunter. But Hunter wasn't around right now, and both young men were so handsome and attentive.

"Miss Adair, forgive me for staring," Alfred said. "But you are truly and exquisitely beautiful."

"Thank you," she murmured, her face heating. She felt David move closer to her. A protective gesture, she thought, warmed.

"And you will accompany us to Egypt! It is a marvel," Alfred continued.

"Alfred," David said a little sharply.

Alfred gave him a strange look. He lifted his hands. "David, dear friend...I am on your side, you know."

Kat glanced out the window. "Pardon me, but I believe that we should have taken that turn."

Alfred leaned forward. "We can turn around immediately, of course. But I thought that perhaps I might show you some of the Egyptian treasures in my apartment in Kew Gardens."

"I'm afraid that I really need to go home. If my father has returned, he will be worried," Kat said.

"I believe," David said, sounding slightly uneasy, "that your father will be occupied until late."

"Oh?" Kat said, startled.

"Oh, yes, he's with Lord Avery and my father's widow," Alfred said. He stared at her. "Lord Avery, did you know, has commissioned him to do a painting of Lady Margaret. He was most impressed by those portraits William has done of you and your sister."

"Ah. But I really must go home."

"Please, Kat," David said at her side. "We might have a few minutes away from the stares of others if we take a trip to Alfred's lodgings. And it's also true that Alfred has been on expedition before and can show you more of what to expect. Perhaps a brief exploration of his maps, books and study will help you."

"I've worked with Sir Hunter," Alfred explained. "And he is indeed a slave driver!"

"Well... You're certain my father will be some time?" she asked worriedly.

"Quite certain." Her hand lay on her lap, and now David's covered it. It suddenly occurred to her that the encounter with Alfred had been planned. David had only pretended to resent Alfred's intrusion at the club. He had no lodgings of his own here in London; he was staying with Lord Avery. But Alfred Daws had his own apartments. A place for them...

It was wrong. She was taking a terrible chance.

But she couldn't resist. She needed to make David fall in love with her. So in love that he would forget Lady Margaret. Before it was too late. Before their engagement was official.

"I would cherish any bit of time with you," David said, looking at her.

She sat up straighter and stared at Alfred across the carriage. "I cannot stay long. But since we are headed toward your residence, I suppose it would do no harm to spend a few moments there."

"Splendid!" Alfred said. Then his eyes fell on David, and she felt a slight ripple of unease. David squeezed her hand reassuringly.

She glanced out the window again. They had come down an elegant street, and the carriage was turning into an entrance heavily guarded by foliage, bushes that rose high on either side of the drive. They reached an arbor covered thickly with vines, and there they stopped. Alfred exited first, and David helped Kat from the carriage.

A few steps took them to the house, where Alfred used a key to open the door. The entry brought them into an elegant entryway, where Alfred offered to take Kat's jacket.

"I cannot stay long, thank you. I will keep it."

"Well, then, come into the parlor," Alfred invited, and with David's hand at the small of her back she followed him down a hallway. By the time they reached the parlor, she thought that Isabella must have been angry indeed that all this wealth had gone to Alfred and not herself. Every stick of furniture gleamed, the lamps were elegantly shaded, fine artwork graced the walls. Alfred hadn't lied about his Egyptian treasures, either, for across the room, artistically placed by the side of a sofa, was an inner sarcophagus. It was elaborately painted, and thanks to her hours at the museum, she could read some of what was written on it.

"Nasheeba," she said aloud. "Wife of the great pharaoh, mother of Thutmos, prince of the temple."

"You do know what you're doing!" Alfred exclaimed.

"Not really. I've simply learned a few symbols."

"Beautiful. Ah, well, I think I should make us all some Egyptian tea!" Alfred said. "Excuse me. I shall leave the two of you alone for a few minutes."

He walked out of the elegant parlor, leaving her there, facing David.

"Katherine..." David said softly, then stepped forward.

She was so surprised that she hadn't the least idea of what he was doing at first. Before she knew it, he had taken her into his arms.

His eyes seemed to pour into hers, and he said her name again. "Katherine…the beautiful, the magnificent, the brave!"

And then he kissed her.

She felt his lips, soft on her own, ever so slightly awkward. His hands, planted on her back, pressed her hard against him.

It was her dream, she thought. David. Wanting her. Kissing her.

But something was not quite right. His kiss wasn't how she had imagined it. She wanted it, yes…

But not this way.

She placed her hands on his chest and pushed. He seemed to take her action as merely a token protest and held her more tightly, his lips growing harder against hers.

She twisted her face from his. "David!"

"What?" he whispered huskily. "Oh, Kat, I need you. You're truly what I need…what I want. When I saw you…you had saved my life. And you were gone…and then you were back. And more beautiful, more desirable… I dream about you breathing, about your eyes, about the way you looked. And I know you care about me, I know it."

"Yes, I do, but…"

"But?"

"This isn't right…being here."

"But, Kat, where else could we be? We'd be seen. Alfred is my friend. He would protect us. Kat, we could steal hours and hours here."

David had relaxed his hold. He stroked her face gently, looking into her eyes. There was an honesty in his words. Pain, craving. He cared about her, wanted her.

The world should have been on fire.

She felt a chill.

"Why should we *steal* hours?" she asked.

He groaned, pulling her against him again. "Oh, Kat! If only you had remained but a poor waif! But now your father might well become famous and wealthy.... But then, artists are Bohemian, avant garde.... No, he still wouldn't understand. You...you wouldn't want him to know. And then, of course, there's Lord Avery. And Margaret."

She stiffened. Her mouth wouldn't quite work correctly. "You want me...to be your mistress."

He looked at her in apparent puzzlement. "Kat, I would always care for you!"

"But you wouldn't marry me," she said.

"Kat, I'm the son of Baron Rothchild Turnberry!"

She had never felt so cold in her life. "Younger son," she reminded him.

"Yes, yes, but, Kat, I truly love you."

"And Margaret?"

"Well, of course, there is a difference. You must understand. You are not so naive not to know the way of the world. Please, don't stare at me so. You've wanted this. I thought you'd must know that...we'd have to be secret."

His fingers were still moving over her face. Knuckles stroking her chin. His expression now was that of a kindly tutor explaining a piece of learning that every child should know. Then he bent to kiss her again. His lips were more forceful this time, trying to wedge open her lips. And his hands upon her were stronger, moving, creeping around her ribs, rising to her breasts.

She made a sound of protest and pushed hard against his chest. She was ice now, but love died hard.

He broke from her again. "Kat, I must have you!" His whisper was frantic. "You are such fire! And...and my intended bride is ice! You are the passion, Kat. A man needs passion in his life."

He wasn't letting go of her, and he pushed her suddenly, so that she fell backward onto a sofa. And then he was on top of her. "Kat...you must understand."

She shoved hard, but he was too heavy to dislodge. She twisted her head, and he caught her chin between his thumb and fingers. "Kat, I love you!" he said, and the words were real, as if torn from his heart. His lips found hers again.

Kat, I love you!

For a moment, the words were a sweet echo in her heart. And the feel of his kiss was not painful, but bittersweet, less than stirring, perhaps, but searching and sweet, his quest, a dream perhaps, similar to her own and yet...crucially different.

Then truth sliced bitterly into her heart. He wanted her. And she was made for desire, carnal, a woman to be a mistress, but never a wife for so high born a person.

She ripped her mouth away. "Get off me, David, please."

He went still. He stared at her, then frowned, and she could see that his temper was growing. "You have teased like the worst, cheapest whore in the East End!" he said hoarsely.

She stared at him, stunned, gaping. "Get off me. Now."

"Kat!" The anger faded from his features. "You don't understand. God, I am so sorry! You see, I must have you!" he repeated.

"Let me go!" she enunciated.

"You're not listening. I really love you!" Again, the whisper was so heartfelt, the look in his eyes so earnest, that her heart skipped a beat. She forgot the base cruelty of his earlier words.

"I love you!" he whispered.

She stared at him. "Love is not enough," she said softly.

"Kat!" He still did not release her. He buried his head against her. She struggled to free herself from his hold, but he was like a dead weight. She considered her options. Screaming, scratching, kicking.

"David, you must get off!" she tried again, and shoved him with all her might. This time she succeeded in dislodging him and she struggled to her feet. She would have stayed there, but he caught her dress and pulled her back down. Now, however, she was on top of him.

And that was when Hunter barged into the room.

"What the devil...?" David demanded.

"Let go of her," Hunter snapped. "Now!"

Instantly, David grasped her, arms around her, manner protective. He struggled awkwardly to rise with Kat in his arms.

He didn't have much time. Hunter was across the room. He caught Kat around the midriff and lifted her, disentangling David's hold at the same time. For several seconds, Kat found herself dangling in Hunter's arms like an errant schoolchild.

"Get up, David," Hunter said, his voice low and threatening.

Kat was entirely indignant. "Sir Hunter, please put me down."

"Hunter!" David protested, rising as told. "We are both of age!"

"She has a father who is worried sick about her," Hunter said.

"Could you please put me down!" Kat said again.

"How dare you, sir!" David protested, and he flushed with a dark discomfort. "You have scores of mistresses!"

"I do not prey on the innocent, filling them with champagne and taking a detour to a friend's house where the servants have mysteriously disappeared for the day," Hunter thundered back.

"She wants to be with me!" David protested. "Kat, tell him!"

"Would you please put me down!" Kat again said to Hunter.

And he did. Naturally, she staggered, and he put his hand out to steady her, a hand that remained hard on her arm. He glared at her with such sharp anger and disappointment that she was left speechless.

"She wants to be with me!" David repeated.

Hunter's eyes raked over her in a way that was almost physically painful. And then his hand fell from her arm and he stepped back.

"You and Alfred tricked her into coming here," Hunter accused.

"She wants to be with me," David said once again.

"I see. So it was her idea to come here."

"She wanted to see me again, alone, and I knew it!" David protested.

Kat's cheeks flamed, for what he said was true. She *had* wanted to be alone with him. But things shouldn't have gone so quickly. He should have spent days seeing her, falling in love. Needing the sound of her voice, as she had come to yearn for his. Needing the look in her eyes, the sound of her laughter. And then, somewhere, there should have been the lightest touches. And at last...a kiss. For which he should have apologized, and...

And then, of course, he should have said that he loved her—in a way that defied all else. That he loved her and wanted to marry her. He would forsake all others. He would defy his father, if need be! For that was love.

"Were you tricked into coming here?" Hunter asked Kat. "Or," he asked pointedly, "was this your intention?"

She gasped, far more ready to slap him than David. Tears threatened. She had no intention of spilling them before either man. She would not, however, dignify Hunter's question with an answer.

She straightened to the most regal height she could manage. "I'll see myself home, thank you, gentlemen!"

Head high, she started out of the room.

But at that moment, Alfred Daws came racing in, making a beeline for Hunter, in an apparent fury, ready to tackle him.

She was amazed at the deftness with which Hunter sidestepped his opponent. Alfred crashed onto the couch, rose again and turned. Hunter raised a fist, caught Alfred in the jaw, and the man went down.

Kat stared at Hunter. "You are all truly animals," she said very softly. And she walked from the room and out of the entrance they'd come in.

She realized that the pins were cascading from her hair and that her neat and proper attire was scarcely together. She tried to catch the escaping strands of her hair, but the effort was fruitless, and so, still hidden behind the high bushes on Lord Daws's property, she tried to straighten her skirt.

She didn't hear Hunter's approach, but somehow he was there, right behind her, a hand on her back. "Let's go."

"I'm not going anywhere with you!" she cried.

"Indeed, you are."

"I am not—"

"Your father is frantic."

She went still, no longer angry, but dismayed. "It can't be so late!"

"Lord Avery tried to reach David at the club. He was to bring you back to his, Lord Avery's, house. But you all were not at the club, and you were not at home. I had a fair idea of where you might be when I discovered that Alfred Daws had joined you. Luckily, I followed, and you may feel free to thank me at any time."

"Thank you?"

"So you *did* intend to let him bed you?" Hunter demanded coldly.

She stared at him, choking with fury. Then she found action. She drew back her arm, ready to slap him for all she was worth. He caught her wrist before the blow could find its mark.

"No, Miss Adair, because I don't deserve that. Not the way that I found you."

"I didn't intend to let him bed me," she said icily, "but neither did I need you to rescue me! I could have taken care of myself."

He arched a brow. "Ah! So that's what I saw." His tone was dry.

She wrenched her arm free of his grasp. "I was trying to rise!"

"You were not doing very well."

"I didn't have time!"

She was stunned when he suddenly let out an oath and gripped her shoulders. "You little fool. Do you really think that a pair of arrogant college boys, who think themselves superior to others, would have hesitated to rape you?"

She swallowed hard and shook her head. "I don't believe... I *won't* believe...that he wouldn't have accepted my refusal!"

His fingers tightened on her flesh. "You are far too pathetically naive to be on the streets!" he informed her. He released her, stepping back, shaking his head angrily. "Fix yourself," he suggested, his tone so soft it was menacing. "You're going to see your father."

She tried to muster what dignity she could to adjust her clothing, difficult with his eyes on her with such condemnation. But he turned away before she was done, heading out to the street where Ethan and his carriage awaited. Ethan, ever polite, offered her an encouraging smile when she emerged. "Good evening, Miss Adair."

"Evening, Ethan," she returned, and managed a smile. She accepted his help into the carriage. A moment later, Hunter climbed in.

She couldn't see a thing out of the window. The light from the street lamps seemed to swim before her, and all else was a haze. She continued to look out the window, anyway.

He didn't speak. She felt heated in his presence, as if she sat near the burning coals of a chestnut dealer. His arms were folded over his chest. As his team of horses clopped through the streets, she knew that his eyes remained on her. He didn't touch her. His knees didn't brush hers.

They'd been riding some time before he said, "You might want to do something with your hair."

Self-consciously, she tried to capture and restrain the escaping tendrils as best she could. He crossed over to the seat beside her.

"Turn," he ordered, and she did so, her back and shoulders stiff as he first collected pins, then straightened the wild tendrils and repinned them with an expertise that could only have come from practice.

The brush of his fingers sent tremors along her spine. She was painfully aware of his slightest movement.

But he didn't stay by her side. He shifted back to the seat opposite the minute he was done.

"Unless you are truly willing to become the man's mistress and nothing more, I might suggest that you keep your distance from the Right Honorable David Turnberry for the time being," he suggested from the darkness within the carriage.

"He would have listened to me," she said.

Hunter snorted derisively. "It did not so appear."

"Well, we'll never know, will we?"

"A thank-you for the rescue," he said next, "might be a courteous gesture," he said again.

"Once again, Sir Hunter, I don't believe that I needed to be rescued! And...did you have to resort to such violence with Alfred?"

"No. I could have let him beat me to a pulp."

She lowered her head, feeling the urge to burst into tears again.

"Will there be repercussions?" she asked him after a moment.

"For what?"

"For...what you did to Alfred?"

"I'm rather certain neither of the young men will ever mention what happened there. Though you are convinced otherwise, you were a victim tonight. And it could have been far worse."

"But..."

"But what?"

She looked out the window again, very hurt.

Dreams, she realized, died hard.

"Are your intentions so much more honorable?" she asked.

She wished she had never spoken. She could feel his anger sweep off him in waves.

He leaned forward, still not touching her. "I have been accused of many things, Miss Adair. And of some, I was guilty. But seduction and rape of an innocent? That is one sin that does not sit upon my conscience."

She was startled when the door of the carriage suddenly opened. He had so held her attention that she hadn't realized the carriage had come to a halt outside Lord Avery's.

She exhaled, aware that Ethan, courteous as ever, was waiting to assist her from the carriage.

Aware she had been holding her breath.

Aware…that she was sorry, and that she might well have been in trouble. Though she would never really know.

"Miss Adair?"

She accepted Ethan's hand and stepped down from the carriage. Hunter followed. She swallowed hard, knowing that she had been wrong and that the pain in her heart had refused to allow her to admit it.

She turned, ready to offer Hunter an apology.

But he was sweeping by her. The door to the house had opened, and Margaret came rushing down the steps.

She paused by Hunter, smiling, rising on tiptoe, kissing his cheek, then turning to Kat.

"Ah, there you are! Hunter, you found our missing Kat. Ah, dear Kat! Come in, come in! You must see what your father has done! Come, come!"

As she dragged her into the house, Kat looked back.

He was watching her. And for some strange reason, the disappointment in his eyes seem to tear at her, like salt upon the abrasion that was her heart.

I'm sorry, truly sorry!

But she could no longer say the words. And she was afraid, very afraid, that a door had closed that might never open again.

Chapter 8

THE EVENING SEEMED unendurably long to Hunter. Margaret was as ever gracious and welcoming to everyone. While they awaited dinner, she and Lord Avery showed Kat the work that William Adair had done during the day, and, seeing the sketches for the portrait he would do of Lady Margaret, Hunter could only marvel that the man's talent had not been discovered before. The essence of the young woman had been caught. The sheer blond beauty, gentleness, kindness and warmth.

It was intriguing to watch Kat study the works. There were a few minutes in which her heart seemed painfully evident; she liked Margaret, admired her and was grateful to her. It must have been something of a conflict for Kat to so adore a man who was intended for this young woman. Where he might have been prone to sympathy at some point, he felt only the rise of his temper. How on earth could she be so certain that if she had said that she could not be David's mistress, that would be the end of it? It was sheer lunacy.

Did she really believe it? Or had she just been trying to convince him, Hunter?

David's friends, Robert Stewart and Allan Beckensdale, were at the house. Both were courteous in the extreme to

Lady Margaret, and yet both were smitten by Eliza Adair. When the work had been viewed and wine served—the glass offered to Kat politely refused—Lord Avery grew anxious.

"Margaret, where is that young man of yours and his friend? The hour grows late, my stomach is growling, and I don't think we'll wait for them much longer!" he said impatiently.

He, of course, looked at Kat, as did Lady Margaret.

"Um...I believe they had something to do at the home of Lord Daws," Kat murmured.

"I'm sure they'll be right along," Hunter said.

Kat didn't look at him. Her cheeks reddened as she stared at the fire.

"Call the house, Father," Margaret suggested.

"Oh, blast! I hate that gadget!" Lord Avery complained.

"I'll call," Hunter offered, but as he approached the phone, Lord Avery's butler appeared, announcing that the Right Honorable David Turnberry and Lord Alfred Daws had arrived.

The two young men entered the room. David appeared fine. Alfred was sporting a serious bruise on his jaw.

"David!" With her customary graciousness, Margaret welcomed the one man first, then turned to the second. "And Alfred. Welcome."

They both greeted their hostess. David looked at Hunter with serious trepidation and shook his hand gravely. Alfred, too, approached him sheepishly. Hunter said nothing, only inclined his head, curious to see how the two would greet Kat.

They did so with gallantry. Kat, too, kept silent.

"Well, then, dinner," Lord Avery said.

Hunter found himself seated between Eliza and Margaret that evening. He chafed.

Kat was not next to David, but she was beside Alfred. Frequently during the meal, he would see their heads come close together, their words spoken only for each other.

He caught Eliza Adair studying him gravely at one point. She flushed when he met her gaze.

"What is it?" he asked her. She hadn't Kat's fire, but she did have a sweet nature and her own brand of dignity.

"You're concerned about my sister," she said softly.

"Am I?" he asked.

"Yes, and I am, also."

"Oh?"

"It seems we're all blind at times. Father doesn't see the evil in Lady Daws, and yet to so many others, she is transparent. Kat doesn't see that David Turnberry is often petulant, and that he thinks himself above everyone else—of course, his father's holdings are vast.... Perhaps it's true that we see only what we choose to see."

He smiled at her. "You are an astute young woman."

"In her way, you know, Kat listens to you," Eliza told him.

He laughed softly. "No, I'm afraid not."

"Oh, she would never admit such a thing!" Eliza said. "But she does. Perhaps you might use your influence to make her drop her blinders where David is concerned. I know that you will see that her art is encouraged."

Eliza spoke with sincerity, her gaze intense.

"There's really not much I can do, you know."

"Sir Hunter," Eliza said with a laugh, "you hardly seem the type to underestimate yourself! She will be working for you, after all."

He glanced across the table. He still could not hear the words being said between Kat and Alfred, but he was certain that Alfred was doing his best to apologize. At one point, he saw Kat smile.

"Where is Lady Daws this evening?" he asked Eliza.

"About on business. That is all I've been told."

"Do you know when this business came up?"

Eliza offered him a grin. "When she heard that David's good college chum, Lord Alfred, would be present."

"I see," he murmured.

At last, dinner came to an end, the men excused themselves for brandy and cheroots, and Hunter found himself in the smoking parlor with Lord Avery, William Adair and the two young men. Both, he knew, were extremely uncomfortable with him, and he was glad. They still needed to exchange words, and the occasion presented itself when Lord Avery, who had grown very fond of William Adair, insisted on showing him a Rembrandt he had in an upstairs salon.

When they were gone, a moment of silence ensued. Then both young men began to speak at once.

"Sir Hunter, I don't know what I was doing...." Alfred began.

"There was no evil intent, I swear!" David avowed.

"It hadn't seemed so unlikely, sir!" Alfred said. "Lord knows what the young lady in question has done in the past, and David truly believed that...that..."

Hunter shook his head, stopping them both with a look. "She is a young woman of good family. Which you've seen."

"But—" David said.

"She is not to be any man's mistress," Hunter said flatly.

"My father would never agree to a marriage," David said miserably.

"Well, it is a new world. If you really love the young woman, you can defy your father and marry her," Hunter pointed out.

David flushed. "Sir, and then what?"

"Well, you are a student."

"And you think that I might make an income at the law?" David said, his tone incredulous.

"Sir, you nearly broke my jaw," Alfred reminded him. "Please believe, you have made your point. But please believe, too, that we were all a little hotheaded at the time. After all, sir, you barged into my house."

"Better me than her father," Hunter said. "Someone might have died. At any rate, lives would have been ruined."

"There could be a way..." David murmured.

"A way for what?" Hunter demanded sharply.

"I do love her!" David said defiantly.

"If that's the case, perhaps you should discuss the situation with Lord Avery now, and the young woman's father afterward."

"I can't do that!" David said.

"Then may I suggest that you stay away from her, far away."

"You, Sir Hunter, have seen to it that she will be on the expedition."

"At my side," Hunter assured him.

"I would not have hurt her!" David swore again.

Footsteps sounded from the hallway.

"See that you don't," Hunter warned very softly. "There will be much more than a bruised jaw to pay in the future."

"ARE YOU PACKED AND READY to go?" Margaret asked Kat, sipping tea and looking at her with interest and kindness.

Guilt ran deep within her. In fact, the entire day had been a misery. Kat forced a smile, aware of her sister, and aware that her sister knew so much about her.

Eliza, thankfully, knew nothing about the afternoon.

"I'm afraid I'm not ready at all," Kat said.

Margaret laughed, setting down her cup."Well, if you should lack anything, I will surely have it! I have been preparing for this trip for some time. At first, I didn't know if I would go or not. But if I didn't go...well, I would be here. I'd be off to more lessons in...something. And it's so sad. I can't play a piano or sing, and Father is convinced that with enough teachers, I will learn to do so admirably."

Her smile was beautiful. Contagious. Kat felt even worse.

"I, too, am certain that you can learn to do both admirably," she said.

"Oh, no! It's like...well, art. Perhaps classes and instructors can teach design, layout, color...but if a person has no innate talent, all the lessons in the world will not produce a masterpiece! But then, you see," she said a bit sadly, "I'm not really expected to do anything other than become a model wife and mother, dedicated to my family, after the example set by the queen! My father is very old-fashioned."

"Well...there's not much wrong with being a model wife and mother," Kat said.

"Nor in knowing that the rent will be paid, and there will be food on the table," Eliza added.

"Oh, dear! I sounded so petty!" Margaret said."Forgive me! It just seems that there is so much excitement going about. I would like to be useful."

"Oh, but you will be useful, I'm sure," Kat said.

Margaret shook her head. "Sir Hunter has told Father that your grasp of Egyptology, from no more than a few hours' learning on your own, is quite incredible. So you will be a part of all that goes on. And, to be honest, I do like my creature comforts and...well, I shall probably spend most of my days in the bazaars, having tea at Shepheard's and waiting. I'd be bored silly digging for hours and painstakingly removing sand from an object hour after hour with a tiny brush! Nevertheless, I'll enjoy being there for the excitement. Father says that every man with a love for the ancient and a desire for treasure and adventure is there! The English come, the French come… Why, did you know that the Romans traveled to see the pyramids and temples of Egypt on *their* holidays? We are talking about a tourism with incredible history! Besides, Father is funding much of the expedition, along with the Earl of Carlyle, so I really should be there."

"You could, of course, remain in England," Eliza suggested.

Margaret laughed. "That is not, to me, an option!" She sighed. "My father so wants to see me married. He is afraid that he started his own family at too advanced an age, and he wants a grandchild before he dies, so…I have promised him that I will marry by the summer."

Kat felt as if she were choking. Luckily, Eliza spoke. "Pardon me if I am prying. Have you decided who you will marry?"

Margaret had dimples. They showed so beautifully when she smiled. "Most likely, David. But then again…well, perhaps that is why it is so important I go. I had thought Allan to be madly in love with me, as well, but…have you noticed the way he looks at you, Miss Adair?"

She was staring at Eliza. Eliza gasped, as red as a beet.

"Oh, but…I mean, he is charming, but he is only being nice to the poor daughter of a struggling artist."

Margaret shook her head. "Fear not, I have no interest in a man who does not love me and only me. If only you were going with us, as well!"

"I need to be here," Eliza said, "to look after our father."

"Is Lady Daws truly so evil, then?" Margaret demanded, leaning forward, eager for gossip.

Eliza glanced at Kat. "It is the word I use."

"Alfred so loathes her!" Margaret said with a shudder.

"And yet..." Kat began.

Margaret looked at her gravely. "And yet people open their doors to her? Indeed, well, she is the widow of Lord Daws. Alfred says that she despises him, as well. As you've noticed, she is not about tonight."

"Perhaps we should have Alfred around more often," Eliza said lightly.

"Perhaps!" Margaret agreed.

Margaret and Eliza began to chat more about clothes. Kat pretended to pay attention. But her head was throbbing.

At last, the men rejoined them. William said that he and Eliza would be back the following day to work again, and he thanked their host sincerely for his kindness. Lord Avery was gruff, telling him that he was most welcome.

When he said goodbye, David Turnberry held Kat's hand several seconds too long. His eyes met hers. And in them was sorrow and a plea for forgiveness. Her heart flipped. And yet...

It was different. She *felt* different, somehow.

Still, they had all gotten through the evening. Eliza might be suspicious, but William seemed oblivious to anything being amiss.

And Hunter...

He was no different. He took them home in his carriage, and his voice was harsh when he reminded Kat, "Nine o'clock. We will ride first and work at the museum after. You will be busy the entire day."

She simply nodded, then walked up the stairs while he bid her father and sister good-night.

KAT WAS READY IN THE morning. He did not even have to go to the door. She was outside waiting when he arrived, leading the mare.

He started to dismount to help her.

"Please. I believe I can do this myself, and I must learn," she said. And it seemed she had already learned, for she easily put her foot in the stirrup and swung astride. She didn't seem particularly proud of her accomplishment, and merely looked at Hunter when she was seated, asking, "Was that acceptable?"

"Yes."

She was subdued, silent.

After a moment, he asked, "Do you still wish to go on this expedition?"

"Indeed, yes," she replied gravely.

He considered his next words carefully. "I would have thought that you might have realized by now that the object of your obsession will not be, indeed, *cannot* be what you want."

She cast a gaze at him then, her head cocked. "Cannot, Sir Hunter?"

"His father would not allow it."

"Perhaps he will defy his father."

Hunter trotted on ahead. She followed, at his gait, holding her seat well. They rode on to the park, where he loped, walked, trotted and had her mount and dismount several times. She did all with excellence.

Finally, he called a halt to the exercise.

"And now?" she asked.

"We will return to your house. You may change. I'll send the carriage for you."

"And then...?"

"To the museum. Ethan will have already taken me there."

She nodded. "As you wish."

Hunter was startled when she stopped him as they neared the house. "Sir Hunter?"

Impatient, he looked back. "Yes?"

Her cheeks were pink, and not from exertion. "I...want to apologize."

He watched her gravely. "So...you realize that you were in danger?"

She smiled, shaking her head. "Sir Hunter, I believe that you underestimate me. And that you too easily condemn David. And Alfred. But you seriously believed that I was in danger and came to my aid. So I'm sorry for causing you concern, and I thank you for acting on it."

Hunter felt grateful for the apology, such as it was, then continued on toward the house.

CAMILLE, AS ALWAYS, WAS buried in a mountain of charts, maps and texts. She looked up when Hunter entered. "Good morning. Is all well?"

"Yes."

"You found David Turnberry and Miss Adair without difficulty?"

He hesitated. "I found them. Miss Adair should be here shortly. I will leave her under your supervision today. Is that all right?"

"I'll be delighted to have her," Camille assured him.

"Then I'll head to the basement and start with the loading sheets for the supplies," he said.

"Excellent!" Camille said. She looked back at the work on her desk, frowning.

"What is it?"

"I still haven't been able to find the maps and things that disappeared. How could I have been so careless, Hunter? You know what this means to me. And I may well be new at being Lady Carlyle, but I have been with the museum a long time, and I was always excellent at my work!"

"Do you want my help?" he asked. "Should I plow through some files or desks?"

"I've already looked everywhere," she said. Then she shook her head. "No, Hunter, please, there are all kinds of picks and brushes that must be packed for shipping, some texts. If you'll see to that, I'd be most grateful!"

"Camille, you're not worried about the expedition, are you?"

She shook her head again, but a little cloud seemed to pass over her eyes. "No. I mean…there was trouble, we had tremendous troubles, but…it's over. Still, I suppose…well, there are always those who covet gold enough to steal?"

"One must always be careful on a dig, of course," Hunter said. "Anytime gold is involved, men can be blinded."

"Of course. But…"

"Camille, I'm thrilled to be heading out again. I have no apprehensions."

She smiled. "Good. I will let my excitement return, then, and let it rule my every moment. We leave so very soon!"

"Indeed we do," he said. Then he left her to make his way through the museum to the stairs that led to the workrooms and storage rooms.

The museum was busy, odd during the week. But then, the coming expedition had been well covered in the newspapers, and people had been encouraged to come in and see what was there now so that they might ogle the new when it arrived.

He pulled his set of keys from his pocket, heading for the workroom. When he opened the door, he sought the switch for the light—the entire museum had been wired for electricity a few years back.

The light did not come on.

He was about to turn back and find a lantern when he heard a noise from within. He stood very still, waiting. The noise did not come again. But when he started out once more, he heard a definite thud.

"Who's there?" he called out sharply.

No answer.

He was as good as blind in the dark, of course, yet determined not to leave until he knew what was going on. He purposely walked in, closed the door, hunkered down and waited for his eyes to adapt to the lack of light. After several seconds, he thought that he heard the sound of someone breathing from across the room.

And so, trying not to make any sound himself, he began to inch in that direction. As he came around a set of shelves, one was suddenly cast down in front of him. It fell with a loud thud against the next shelf, which in turn fell, hitting the next.

The wall stopped a total collapse, but he was trapped.

Then he heard more sounds. Footsteps, flying across the floor.

He crawled over the shelves with all the haste he could manage in an attempt to follow the intruder. When he reached the door, it was open. And the culprit was gone.

Swearing, he moved through the museum, searching for anyone who looked in the least suspicious. He saw no one.

Upstairs, he found Brian Stirling, Earl of Carlyle, digging through files with his wife.

"There is something going on," Hunter said.

They both stared at him. "There's white powdery stuff in your hair," Camille said. "What happened?"

"There was someone in the workroom, though God knows why—there's nothing in there but tools."

"Are you certain someone was in there?" Brian asked. Hunter arched a brow. "Sorry, old boy, just checking. I'll go downstairs with you, see what repair we can manage," Brian said. "Curious. Really curious."

"Has anyone else been about?" Hunter asked.

Camille shook her head. "No, but there *are* those missing papers of mine. Though they're really rather worthless, except to me and the expedition." She frowned. "Brian, you don't believe anyone would want to sabotage the expedition, do you?"

Brian shook his head. "Why would anyone?"

Camille looked at Hunter. "Miss Adair thought that she heard voices whispering in here the other day. Perhaps we shouldn't have dismissed what she said."

Hunter groaned. "Camille, don't go making a mystery out of this, please!"

"But, Hunter, someone was in the storage room. You have said so yourself."

"Most probably one of the students, and why he ran, I will never understand. There is nothing in there, nothing of importance. Brian, if you don't mind, let's go back there together."

They went through the museum to the stairs. Hunter didn't realize that he was studying everyone in the museum again until Brian said, "You said you thought that it was just an errant student."

"I did."

"Then…"

"I didn't say that I wasn't anxious to know which student!" Hunter informed him.

STANDING ON THE FRONT STEPS, Kat realized that she loved the museum. It was so grand and housed so many treasures. For several moments, she forgot all else and simply stared at the magnificent building. Then she looked about, pleased to see the very different people who enjoyed the exhibits. Some wore work clothing and had perhaps just left jobs for the day. Some were more elegantly attired. Some were children, led by a parent or perhaps a teacher. She was startled to feel a real sense of pride about being asked to be a part of an expedition that was associated with so fine an establishment.

She hurried to the staff room, where she found Camille at the desk. The Countess of Carlyle once again greeted her with a smile and welcoming words. "Ah, Kat! I'm so glad to have you here. It's not my usual way of being, but I'm afraid I'm a bit scattered. Would you take the book and the text over there—" she indicated a papyrus that was framed by glass "—and see what you can make of it? Thank God you learn so quickly!"

"I don't know if I'm that capable, but I'll certainly try," Kat said. She was surprised that Hunter was nowhere to be seen. And she was equally surprised at her disappointment.

She had stayed up most of the night, going over every second of what had happened, and she had realized that she had to be far more intelligent about what she did. Still, though her dream had become tarnished, it hadn't quite died.

She looked up at Camille and tried to sound casual. "Is Sir Hunter about?"

Camille, engrossed again in her work, lifted a hand but did not look up. "He's down in storage room with Brian. They're working on everything that must be on the ship with us."

"Oh. Well, I shall get to work, then."

"Use my office—there's space on the desk."

"Thank you."

She went into Camille's office and looked around. As she sat at the desk, she felt a chill. She had not forgotten the whispers she had heard the last time she'd been in this room. She frowned, trying to remember what she had heard.

There had been two people, of that she was certain. They had been looking for something, and they hadn't wanted to get caught. *We shall have to pay for it*...she'd heard, along with *a long journey, a dark desert...better off dead...*

She started to rise, to go out and remind Camille of what she had heard. But she sat down again. She had tried to tell them what had happened. They had waved away her fears. She simply needed to get to work.

She found paper and a pencil in Camille's top drawer and painstakingly began looking up each symbol in the book. As she did so, she quickly became as engrossed in her work as Camille had been in hers. The papyrus told a story.

Hathsheth, he who talks to the gods, who hears their words of wisdom and delivers them to all men. He who will sit among them, and great will be his reward. He will need all that was his in life; and he will be rewarded with gold, for golden was the knowledge he shared ever with Pharaoh, and golden was all that he lived. Worshiped he will be in the new life. He will lie by kings. He will take precedence over wives, even sons. For like Pharaoh, he will rise to the gods. But like the ancients, he will rest. He will lie in the gentle shade of those who built the kingdom; he will take with him servants and servers. Ever will he lie protected, by those who came before, by the sun, by the shade, on the left bank of the great and mighty Nile.

She looked up, her fingers cramping, her neck stiff, and gave a start. She hadn't heard him. Hunter had come in. She wondered how long he had been watching her.

"May I?" he asked, coming to the desk.

"I believe you may do whatever you wish," she murmured.

"Ah, if only that were true!" he responded, but his eyes weren't on her; he had picked up her translation and read it aloud.

He reached for the framed papyrus, twisting it to see the symbols himself. Then he did look at her.

"This is excellent."

"Thank you."

"Who would have guessed...?"

Camille came in then. "You've finished?" she inquired.

"Nearly," Kat said.

Camille, too, picked up her translation. She smiled. "Hunter, you see?" She was triumphant. "He is not in the Valley of the Kings! He is protected by the ancients.... Don't you think this must be that he is near the great pyramids at Giza?"

"Yes. I think your calculations on where to search have been extremely well done. I just hate to see you get so excited and then suffer even greater disappointment if we're wrong." He was smiling worriedly at her, his affection for her apparent.

"Hunter, please don't concern yourself so. I know there will be disappointments. But this will be *our* particular dig, and I'm ever so excited." She frowned suddenly. "And I don't intend to share it!"

Hunter laughed. "We won't share the dig, Camille."

"There is a bit more, if you would like me to finish," Kat murmured.

"Yes, yes, of course. No, it's late!" Camille said. "Brian is waiting for me, and the museum is closing."

"I won't take long," Kat said. "Truly, I'd like to finish."

"I have to lock up below," Hunter said. He kissed Camille on her cheek. "Go, meet your husband. Ethan is waiting. He'll see Kat and me home."

"All right." Camille smiled at Kat. "Not much longer though. That is work we can take with us. And you wouldn't want to turn into one of those people who squint all their lives, from reading too much."

Kat smiled vaguely. "Good night, then."

"Good night."

"Kat, there are keys on the desk," Hunter said, just before walking Camille to the main door of the museum. "Finish up and meet me at the main door. Be sure that this door is locked."

She nodded and went back to work.

After a few minutes she was disappointed. It seemed that the rest of the writing did nothing more than continue to extol the virtues of Hathsheth. There were hints to his power in the words. *He who looks one in the eyes, and sees what lies there. He who speaks, and the ground trembles. He who holds sway over man and beast.*

She looked over her work and shivered. If she was translating and understanding correctly, Hathsheth had condemned many wives to death, for they were apparently buried with him. Alive, she could only assume.

Thanking God she lived in the modern England during Victoria's long and prosperous reign, she rose at last, closed the desk, left the frame and paper neatly aligned and went out. The keys were on the outer desk and she carefully locked the door behind her.

In the hall, she paused.

The museum was empty. And now it seemed huge and cavernous. Her footsteps seemed to echo like thunder in the hall.

Well, I shall not be sneaking up on anyone! she thought, trying to find some humor in the emptiness.

But she failed. She still felt eerily uncomfortable.

She left through the exhibits. Giant statues, jewelry. A row of glass casements that showed mummies in various stages, some still in their inner coffins, some in wrappings, some in stages of being unwrapped. Long-dead, contorted faces seemed to stare at her.

She hurried her steps.

Then she heard something from upstairs. She had locked the door, hadn't she? But...

She gritted her teeth. She was letting her imagination run away with her. And yet... Sighing, she turned. She averted her eyes, not wanting to see the pinched brown faces of the mummies. At the top of the stairs, she hurried toward the door to the offices.

Only night-lights illuminated the hallway now. As she started toward the door, her heart seemed to leap to her throat.

There was something on the ground in front of the door.

Something. Or someone.

Not moving.

For a moment, she froze. Then she burst into action, dashing forward. Someone, yes, a body, crumpled in front of the locked door.

She hunkered down, her heart still in her throat.

And when she saw who it was, she began to scream.

Chapter 9

THERE IT WAS AGAIN, Hunter thought, that deep, heart-wrenching concern. And the sight that now seemed to cut him to the core was that of Kat bending over an obviously stricken David Turnberry.

He had been at the main door when her scream had sent him flying up the stairs at a record pace. And when he had arrived, she had been on the floor, David's head held tenderly in her lap as she dabbed at a cut on his forehead with material ripped from a panel of her petticoat.

Swallowing his gall, he rushed forward with a true concern for the life of the young man. David was rousing now, groaning softly.

"Move back!" he told Kat a bit too harshly.

She did so, and as he hunkered down, David's eyes blinked open. For a moment they were wild. Then they focused on him. "Sir Hunter…"

"Stay still a minute," Hunter said, dabbing the cut with the piece of Kat's petticoat. The wound was superficial, he quickly realized, bleeding so because head wounds always tended to bleed a lot. After a minute, he had stanched the flow.

"All right, now, sit up carefully," Hunter said.

Still groaning, David allowed himself to be helped up. Then he leaned against the wall.

"What happened?" Hunter demanded.

"Are you all right, David? Hunter, will he be all right?" Kat asked anxiously.

"Yes, he'll be fine," Hunter said. "David, what happened?"

David shook his head. "I was coming to see you," he told Hunter. "I had called the museum…Lady Carlyle said that you were here, working with Lord Carlyle. So I thought that perhaps I would still find you here. I came in just at the closing, but the guard knows me, of course, and he said you were still here. I was on my way up to the office and then—"

"My God," Hunter interjected. "How did you manage to miss me as I walked Camille to the door? We must have—"

"And then?" Kat interrupted Hunter to demand the rest of the story.

"Uh, I think…I think…"

"Yes?"

"I think I…tripped into the door and slammed my head into the nameplate," David finished.

"You tripped right in front of the door and hit the nameplate?" Hunter repeated incredulously.

"I *must* have!" David said a little desperately.

There was a mat in front of the door. It was possible that someone not paying attention could trip. But it was most unlikely.

"David, that's preposterous!" Hunter said.

David let out a little grunt of agreement. "But I'm afraid it must be true. What else could have happened? There's no one else in the museum." He looked up at Kat, his smile weak, his eyes wistful. "You didn't decide I needed a knock on the head, did you?"

"Of course not!" Then she looked at Hunter. "There *is* no one else here."

"We'll make sure." Hunter rose.

"Where are you going?" David asked with apparent alarm.

"I'm going to get the guards to search the place."

"But I'm fine. Surely—" David began.

"It seems there are pranksters afoot," Hunter said. "I want to know that the museum is secure when we leave this evening."

Just in principle, he was not fond of the idea of leaving Kat alone with David, but he was also sorely disturbed by the incident and beginning to wonder himself what was really going on. He moved quickly down the stairway, calling out for the guards. There were only a few remaining, but his voice echoed in the halls and they quickly came running. He explained the situation, and the men went off.

They weren't going to find anything, though, he was certain.

The museum was huge. And if someone knew it at all well, he would be able to find any number of nooks and crannies, offices, maintenance closets and more in which to hide.

Had someone struck David Turnberry? Or was this just a ploy on the part of the young man?

He returned up the stairs. "The guards are searching the museum," he said. Naturally, David was leaning against Kat, and naturally, Kat still had that tender look in her eyes.

"Shall we go to the police or get a doctor?" he asked.

David slowly shook his head. "There's nothing to tell the police. I believe I fell. And I don't think I need a doctor. I mean…I don't think I even blacked out for more than a second or two."

"All right. Let's get you down the stairs."

"I'll help you up," Kat said.

"No, let me," Hunter said impatiently. "I'm far stronger."

He didn't exactly push her out of the way, but he did press himself between the two. David, however, was fairly capable of standing on his own.

"I'm all right," he insisted.

"Yes, but we don't want you tumbling down the stairs, especially as you're so prone to tripping," Hunter said dryly. "How did you get to the museum?"

"I rode my horse."

"Then Ethan will take you in the carriage—you shouldn't ride after a head injury—and I will ride behind on your horse," Hunter said, trying to tamp down his growing temper. It irritated him no end to think of the two of them alone together in his carriage. And it was at *his* insistence!

But it seemed there was little else he could do.

Ethan was waiting just outside the main doors. He gave David and Kat over to his keeping, then returned to talk to the main night guard. They had found nothing thus far, but the man assured Hunter they would keep a sharp eye out during the night.

When he came out, he searched the street for David's horse. He found the animal and mounted it in an extremely foul mood.

IT WAS STRANGE. Here she was in a carriage again with David, and this time, completely alone with him.

And his face, despite the cut, was still beautiful, and his eyes were filled with painful adoration. But her mind was somewhere other than on his feelings for her.

"David," she asked, allowing him to rest his head on her lap. "Are you sure? Are you quite certain that you tripped?"

He smiled. "I must have."

She shook her head. "But, David, when I fished you out of the water, you said something that has bothered me since."

"Oh?" he said carefully.

"You said that you were pushed."

His eyes closed, beautiful lashes sweeping his cheeks. He opened his eyes again, then shook his head slightly, his smile rueful. "I must have been babbling. I think I also believed that you were an angel or a mermaid."

"David, you went off a sailing ship."

"On a day when I shouldn't have been out. The tossing of the craft was wretched, and I possibly—"

"There is a cut on your head."

He reached up to touch her face. "Actually, you are an angel. Still so concerned for me. And I…oh, Kat!"

She caught his hand and pulled it back down, frowning. "David, are you not concerned?"

"I feel foolish," he muttered. "Off a ship, and then down on a floor. Quite frankly, I am embarrassed."

He was lying, she thought. He was afraid. But of what, or of whom? And if he was afraid, why wouldn't he admit it?

"It is ridiculous to be embarrassed," she told him. "Especially if you are afraid."

"I'm not afraid!" he claimed, and sat up.

She sighed, looking out the carriage window. "Well, then," she said softly, "allow me to be afraid for you."

"Kat! You'd never be afraid of anything, would you?" he asked, and she was startled. Her gaze flew to his, for there had been the slightest hint of bitterness in his voice.

But he was smiling at her, and the look in his eyes was that look again, so pained, yet adoring. As if he were saying, *I love you so! And you are hurting me, denying me....*

"Perhaps you shouldn't be going on this expedition," she told him.

"No, I have to go."

"Why?"

"I have to," he repeated. "I just have to go!" he repeated.

"To prove that you can?" she inquired softly.

He stiffened, his father's son, almost literally looking down his nose at her. "Anyone can go to Egypt. I am part of a legacy. I will be part of discovery, of riches found. And you needn't be so afraid for me. Really. I am an excellent rider. I'm even a good sailor. I handle a gun with accuracy." He inhaled and exhaled. "I am a man of courage."

"Of course you are. I did not suggest anything else! But even the bravest man may be a victim!" Kat said in protest.

Again, he smiled at her. And he reached out his hand to smooth back a tendril of hair from her forehead.

"I would never need be afraid, ever, would I, with you by my side?" he asked softly.

She stared back at him, not pulling away and yet, strangely, not touched by the tender look in his eyes. "But I can't be by your side, can I?" she said.

The carriage had come to a halt. The door was opened with force.

Hunter was there. "Ethan will see you in, David," he said curtly, and offered a hand. David looked at Kat.

"Thank you," he said quietly.

And that was all. He accepted Hunter's assistance from the carriage, and Ethan helped him to the house. Then Hunter entered the carriage.

He said nothing but stared at her while they waited. In the shadows, it seemed that his look was menacing.

"What?" she whispered, annoyed that the word sounded a little desperate. "I did nothing."

"I did not suggest that you did."

Again, he was silent. And she could not bear it.

"He is in danger, I believe," she said.

"What?"

"David is in danger," she said firmly.

Hunter let out a sound of impatience and looked toward the house, anxious to be on his way.

He looked back at her suddenly, angry. "You would create a drama where there is none in order to justify your continued obsession."

She felt as if she had been slapped. She braced herself against the carriage wall, staring at him. "I am creating nothing. When I dragged him from the sea, he looked up and said something about being pushed."

"Strange, he never mentioned such a thing to anyone else."

"I know. He pretends he does not remember now."

"Perhaps he does not remember because it did not happen."

"All right, Sir Hunter, you tell me how he managed that cut on his forehead tonight! By tripping into the door? That is ludicrous!"

"Did you see or hear anyone else about?" he demanded.

"No," she admitted. She sat up. "But I told you...the last time I was at the museum, I did hear whispering."

He sighed, looking away again.

"Hunter, I am telling you, it's the truth. I heard whispering. I wasn't exactly…forthcoming because I was so nervous. You see, I had gone…exploring a bit. I looked at your office, and at Lady Carlyle's. And it was then that someone slipped into the outer office."

He was staring at her intently. The interior of the carriage was in shadow, but she could feel the rapier sharpness of his eyes. "Many people come in and out of the office."

"No, but this was…furtive. They were whispering about finding something. And about…the desert being dark, I swear. I believe that David is in danger."

Ethan had returned. The carriage jerked into motion again. It was so sudden and unexpected that Kat was thrown to the opposite seat, landing right on top of Hunter.

She felt the instant grip of his hands on her, steadying her. She felt the rush of his breath on her face, the searing heat of his body.

He didn't release her as he said, "You silly girl! I think that you would say or do anything to follow David about, to remain close!"

He still didn't release her. And she felt as if she'd been glued where she was, unable to break his hold, unable, even, to look away. She was crushed against his chest, between the spread of his thighs, and there was something about the awkward position that seemed to light a fire in her, equal to that he seemed to emit.

Finally, his hold eased ever so slightly. His thumb traced a path over her cheek, down to her lips, treading over them lightly, ending at her chin. She couldn't breathe.

"No," she whispered. "It's truly that—"

"He's not what you want," Hunter interrupted.

"I can handle myself, I know it," she whispered.

He shook his head. "Can you? Maybe, because you are playing with nothing but a callow youth? If he were suddenly to cast the world aside to claim you legally and before the masses, you would be sorry, can't you see that?"

She could not respond, for suddenly, he kissed her. And it was far different from that kiss she had experienced just the night before. Hunter's lips were firm and possessive from the second they touched hers, creating a thunder of a heartbeat within her chest. They were not light, they did not tease, they were not awkward. His mouth molded to her mouth, created a passionate fusion, and his tongue pushed between her lips, and with liquid fire to it, something intimate and stirring, rousing, liquid, molten. His tongue demanded, sought, and she was startled to feel an immediate response inside her, a desire to allow the demand. There was a hunger in his kiss, vitality, strength, a force of life that seemed to quicken the very soul. She should have been fighting him. She should have been pulling away. But she could not move, in fact, did not wish to move, for she was eager to know more of this ever greater warmth, his hands upon her now, touching her…

Then his mouth lifted from hers. His subsequent words cut deeply into her, stilling the rise of fire.

"Oh, yes. I see that you can handle yourself in the midst of assault!"

"Oh!"

That did it! She shoved hard against his chest, then slammed her hands on his knees to rise, to thrust herself back into the opposite seat. One of her hands slipped, however, landed high on his thigh; touched—

"Oh!" she cried again, struggling for balance. She would have touched him anywhere then, just to escape.

But by then, his hands were on her waist, cleanly lifting her and setting her firmly back in her seat, well away from him.

And at last, blessedly, the carriage came to a halt. Trembling, she wiped the back of her hand over her face. He didn't notice, for he was already out of the carriage. She shrank back when he reached for her, but he would have none of it. She needn't have feared. He was obviously anxious to be done with her for the night, lifting her out, setting her down in one rapid motion.

She spun away, still quite speechless, and nearly ran for her front door. It opened, and Maggie was there. Kat tried to still the wild beating of her heart, fearful of betraying the storm of sensation and emotion he had created.

"Good night, Sir Hunter!" Maggie called cheerfully from the door.

She didn't know if Hunter responded.

In fact, she didn't even know if Maggie spoke again or closed the door. She raced for the stairs.

"Kat!" Maggie called. "Will y'not be having your dinner?"

"Oh, Maggie, bless you...but no. I'm...um...exhausted, not hungry, thank you."

"Child! Your father will want to see you!"

"Oh, Maggie, please, beg Papa to understand...I'm just too exhausted!"

And she ran on to her room, still shaking.

Tired, oh, God, yes, she was tired! But could she sleep?

She tried, but tossed and turned all night, still feeling the burn. And something far worse. How could Hunter's touch have caused this tempest, when David's had not?

HUNTER DID NOT HAVE TIME to assess his own eddy of emotions because there was a carriage in front of his house when he returned.

Lord Avery had arrived.

He frowned, thinking that he had barely left David Turnberry at the man's house.

He entered through the side, frowning when he saw Emma Johnson preparing a silver tray with a glass of whiskey.

She shrugged. "His Lordship arrived just a few minutes ago. Would you like a whiskey, too?"

"A very large one," Hunter said, nodding his thanks and striding through to the parlor.

"Lord Avery," he said.

The man was agitated, pacing before the fireplace. Emma entered almost right behind Hunter, carrying her tray.

"My thanks, good woman," Lord Avery said, taking a glass. Emma gave Hunter another look that indicated the man had given her no reason for his arrival, and when Hunter had taken his glass from the tray, she quickly took herself out of the room.

"What is it?" Hunter asked.

"I am torn," Lord Avery said. "Sorely torn."

"Mmm, so am I this evening," Hunter murmured.

"I beg your pardon?"

"No, 'tis nothing. What is your dilemma, Lord Avery?"

The older man swallowed down his whiskey, as Hunter had already done so. They stared at each other with empty glasses.

Lord Avery opened his mouth, then shut it again. He let out a sigh.

"Dear Lord Avery, what is it?"

"I don't believe that we can bring the girl," Lord Avery said at last.

"Pardon?"

Lord Avery began pacing again. "Lord knows, Margaret will not make up her mind about anything! So this is surely as much her fault."

"This...what?" He frowned. Had David Turnberry been in any way sincere? Had he told them tonight that he was in love with the artist's daughter?

"Hunter, I feel like the most wretched excuse for a peer of Her Majesty's realm! There is nothing specific, really. Are you blind, my good fellow? That little waif is not just exquisite, she's like a lava flow! Her every movement, her smile, her eyes... Oh, don't get me wrong, I don't believe she's a tart in any way. She's just...dangerous."

"Dangerous?" Hunter echoed.

He'd thought the same thing himself on occasion. In fact, tonight, on the ride back to his house...

"You're saying that she's done nothing," Hunter said. "But she's dangerous."

"I see the way they look at her."

"They?"

"All those young fellows." He waved a hand wildly again. "All those fellows Margaret refuses to choose between!"

"Ah."

"But if I renege, what will her father think? And he is a fine man, a truly fine man. I would dare say that I call him a friend now! Ah, would that the lass who saved the boy's life have been the sister! Sweet, gentle and more like...well, a little more like a mouse."

"Is Margaret anxious that Katherine Adair not accompany us?" Hunter asked.

"Margaret adores the girl! She is eager to have her as a companion."

"Is there really nothing specific that has happened?" Hunter asked.

Lord Avery hesitated. Sighed for at least the tenth time. "Young David. When he came in tonight, he said that she found him on the floor when he had apparently hurt himself. And the way he spoke of her…forgive me for being a father, but that's what I am. I will not have such competition for my Margaret, and that is that."

"I see," Hunter said. And he did. And he had wondered several times himself if there had been a way to ground Kat. When it had all begun, he had thought himself the one in control. He had certainly considered himself to be in control of himself, if nothing else.

But he wasn't. He was as smitten, or at least as much in lust as every one of the young swains around her were!

So. That was it. Lord Avery had decided. He did not need to be an ogre himself!

And yet…

"You're forgetting that you did promise her father she would be tutored in art."

"There must be another tutor."

"You don't trust me to look out for her?" Hunter grated his teeth, wondering what the hell he was doing. Did he want to be able to say, without lying, that he had tried his hardest?

No. He wanted to see her. Wanted to touch her, wanted to have her, wanted to quell the fierce desire that shook him to the core. He wanted to believe that she was just a woman, like so many others who had come through his life.

"Sir Hunter! If the woman were your mistress and those chaps knew it, none of them would be brave enough to so much as kiss her cheek! But I know and you must know, she is too young and innocent, as well too well protected by her father, to be a man's mistress. Hunter, I have so agonized over this!"

"She is also an excellent assistant," Hunter mused aloud. "She is uncanny with her ability to learn. She can translate intricate pages already."

Lord Avery paced again. "Can you call Emma for another whiskey?" he demanded.

"Of course," Hunter said.

And he strode out to the kitchen to find Emma, who was, of course, attempting to eavesdrop.

"Will you bring another round of drinks, please?" he said.

"What? Oh, yes, surely, Sir Hunter!" Emma said.

"You'll be able to hear us better while you're doing that, too," he said, a quirk of humor stirring within him.

"Sir Hunter!" she protested. But then she came to him and whispered indignantly, "You can't let him do this! Why that lass...she risked her life and asked nothing for it!"

"Mmm," he said noncommittally.

"Hunter, she is lovely and polite and charming and...you mustn't let him do this!"

"Thank you, Emma, I'll bear your thoughts in mind. He is, however, Lord Avery."

"And he has no expedition without you!"

"I beg to differ. He will have Brian Stirling, Earl of Carlyle, and his countess, and they are both excellent Egyptologists."

"You are the best! You are the most knowing, you have fought the queen's wars, you speak the language, you…you know everyone in Cairo."

"Thank you, Emma. Could you get the drinks, please?"

He strode back into the parlor. He didn't know how Emma managed to pour the drinks so quickly, but she was right behind him again.

Lord Avery took his. Hunter did the same.

They looked at each other and swallowed them down in a gulp.

They were replaced on the tray.

Emma frowned. "Lord Avery, will you be having another?"

"No, thank you. That's it. I've said what I've come to say."

Emma stared balefully at Hunter.

"That's all, Emma, thank you," he said.

With a whish of skirts, she departed. Slowly.

"Lord Avery, let me ponder the situation tonight," Hunter said.

Lord Avery frowned, but then he nodded. "I do not jest when I say that I am worried. Why…I am worried now for her father! I take responsibility for that girl when we sail. As I would expect the man to look after *my* child."

"Sadly, neither are children, Lord Avery."

"Precisely!"

"Let me think about the right thing to do," Hunter said.

"Am I a fool?" Lord Avery asked. "I thought it all such a fine idea! And the man, the father, what a true talent! They are innocents, all of them. I'd not hurt them. But I'd also not cause a tear to fall from my daughter's eyes!"

"I don't believe that Lady Margaret will be at all upset," Hunter offered.

"I don't know," Lord Avery said. He shook his head. "Perhaps I am blowing this situation all out of proportion… You're right. A night's sleep. A night's sleep may well make sanity of it. Thank you, Hunter, for the suggestion."

He smiled a brittle smile. "I will take my leave, then. I will talk to you in the morning."

"Call me at your convenience, Lord Avery."

"Bah! I hate those gadgets. We'll talk."

"We've two days before we leave. There's much still to be done."

"We'll talk," Lord Avery said with assurance, and he turned to depart by the front door.

"Good night, then, my lord," Hunter said.

And so Lord Avery donned his hat and cape and departed. Hunter took a seat on the crimson sofa.

Emma made an immediate appearance.

"You mustn't let that poor child be cast out of this!" Emma said.

"Hardly a poor *child,*" he murmured.

"Sir Hunter!"

"I'll have another whiskey, Emma."

"Humph!"

"In fact, just bring the bottle."

"Sir Hunter!"

"I'm thinking, Emma."

"Humph!"

She went to the kitchen, returned with the bottle and another clean glass. His tray, however, did not hold only whiskey. She had seen to it that, despite the hour, he was given a hot supper.

"Sir Hunter, you must eat."

"Fine!"

And she walked out.

He picked up the bottle and swigged straight from it. The whiskey burned down his throat and into his gullet.

He drank more.

HE BECAME AWARE OF A pounding on his door, and it felt as if someone had taken a hammer to his head.

He groaned and thundered out, "Go away!"

"Sir Hunter!" It was Emma.

"Is there a fire?"

"A fire? No."

"Then go away!"

For a moment, he thought that he had been left in peace. Then the door to his room opened. He opened an eye slowly. It wasn't like Emma to just walk in. He slept in nothing but his flesh, and there was no guarantee that the covers would be in a proper position.

But it wasn't Emma. It was Kat!

Her hair was down, a luxurious fall over her shoulders. She was wearing one of her sister's perfect concoctions, something with a bodice that enhanced the breasts and made the waist minuscule. For once, her eyes were a soft hazel, guileless, and he knew that she was nervous, that it had taken her a great deal to come into the room.

He groaned, turning into his pillow, offering her the expanse of his back.

"Sir Hunter, please!" she said.

He rolled back, wishing he had forgone the whiskey. And why the whiskey?

Her!

"What?" he demanded.

"You have to help me."

"No, I don't."

She inhaled a deep breath. "Eliza is worried. She said that Lord Avery was very upset when David came in last night, that for some reason it seemed that he was angry with me! I can't imagine why."

He stared at her then, at the length of her, at the perfection of her form, the classic beauty of her face, and the wildfire of her hair.

"Nor can I," he said sarcastically.

"He seems to think that I'm…trouble."

"You are."

"What? But I must go on the expedition!" she said.

Ah, yes, she must go. David was going.

"Could you get out of my bedroom, please? As you can see, I've not risen."

"You have to listen to me, please."

He stared at her. She wasn't going.

"Excuse me, then." He rose. He was glad to hear her gasp at his nakedness. He walked across the room to the bathroom, slamming the door.

He poured water and doused his face, needing the cold. He put on the bathrobe hanging on the door.

"Sir Hunter?"

He took his time, brushing his teeth.

At last, he threw open the bathroom door. "Coffee?" he asked.

"It's outside the door," she said, swallowing.

"Why don't you get it?"

"Right away."

Of course there was coffee. Emma had conspired with the girl. She hurried out, found the waiting tray on the floor and brought it in. "Cream, sugar?" she asked.

"Black."

She handed him a cup. Her hands were shaking, he noted.

He sipped it, sitting at the foot of the bed, staring at her. Then he shook his head. "What on earth can I do for you?"

She swallowed. "There is a way, I believe."

He arched a brow. "And that would be?"

"You...um...you'd have to become engaged to me."

Chapter 10

HE NEARLY CHOKED ON THE coffee; in fact, he did spit a mouthful across the room.

Kat stared at him with both alarm and a growing sense of anger.

"All right, all right, I understand that I have no title…that my home was less than elaborate!" she cried. "But…oh, Papa's picture is in the paper today. It's said that even the queen is anxious to look at his work. I will not be such an embarrassment, truly. And it need only be for the season! I only ask that you *pretend.*"

How she wished he were dressed! With his dark hair and far too many muscles visible, he seemed more imposing than she had imagined. And she was flushed and shaking, remembering last night, unable to believe herself that she had come here like this, and yet…

"Let me see if I really heard you correctly," he said. "You want me to pretend that we're engaged, so that you can go on a very long trip to pine after a man you can't have?"

"You have no intention of marrying anyone, anyway!" she said.

He leaned toward her. She nearly jumped back. "How do you know that?"

She waved a hand in the air. "Your affairs are notorious!"

"Perhaps I've changed."

She shook her head. He was making this very hard on her!

"What makes you think that this will help you any? I dragged you from the man's embrace when I wasn't your so-called intended!" His voice was like a growl. She was beginning to regret coming. He was just going to make her feel more and more like a fool. With ever less dignity.

"I'm not going to flirt with anyone," she said. "Or even try to influence David in any way."

"You're lying."

"No."

"Then why must you go?" he demanded.

She swallowed hard, certain that he was going to mock her yet again.

"I seriously think that his life is in danger."

Hunter groaned, rising. She did back away then. He stared at her, dark hair awry, his strong features set in a mask, like that of a bronze statue.

"Please, I don't understand why you won't believe me!" she cried.

He strode across the room, planting himself in front of the fireplace. She flushed again, wondering why her mind was wandering from the seriousness of her intent to the muscled outline of his body.

"Please!" she whispered.

He turned. "Miss Adair, this is the largest pile of manure I believe I have ever heard."

She forced her eyes to remain level with his. She tried hard to still the trembling that had seized her.

"But it's the truth."

He shook his head, staring at her. "And what? If there were really someone out there intent on killing David, just what do you think you could do?"

"I saved his life once."

"We're going to the desert. Not the water."

"Please. I…I swear I would make it up to you."

"How?" he demanded.

"I…I will be the best assistant you have ever had."

"Assistants are easy enough to come by."

She gritted her teeth. "I will listen to your every word, be at your beck and call. I will put pillows beneath your feet, fetch your drinks…cook, clean, anything!"

"You've yet to know the meaning of 'anything,'" he informed her harshly.

She flushed to the roots. "Sir Hunter—"

"If I agree to this insanity," he said, setting his cup on the mantel and moving before her, then making her most uneasy as he walked a slow circle around her, "and we are still on an enormous 'if'! If I agree to it, and you so much as go near the man, I'll drag you away by your hair. You'll rue the day you persuaded me to let you come."

She forced herself to remain very still. "That's cruel, but understandable."

"I am a man of many sins, and I assure you, pride is high among them," he told her.

"I've noticed," she said softly.

"And then again…how will it look if I find someone alluring along the way?"

"I'd simply look the other way," she said.

"What if I were to fall in love?"

"Then you would have to cast me aside."

"Oh, that would be a drama you would love, eh?"

"No!" Kat cried. "I'm just saying that…"

She broke off. He had returned to the mantel for his cup, and now thrust it toward her. "Coffee," he said simply.

She stared at him hatefully for a moment, then retrieved the cup to pour more coffee into it and hand it back to him.

"Ah, look at you! You'll do anything, eh? So far, we've only made it to coffee, and I can see you're ready to thrust a knife in my back."

"You are deliberately trying to irritate me," she accused him.

He took her by the chin, dark eyes, lips so close that she felt herself start to shake again, remembering.

"It will get much, much worse!" he warned.

"Then…you'll do it?"

He groaned again, deep and long. Then he waved a hand in the air.

"Get out."

"But, Hunter…Sir Hunter…"

"Out!"

"But—"

"Yes, yes, damn you! I'll do it." He spun around and looked at her. "I'll give you a performance this very evening that you will not believe. But you will, I swear, pay for it!"

"Thank you," she managed.

"Out!"

"I'm leaving!"

And she did. She ran out of the room as quickly as she could manage, nearly slamming into Emma in her haste. Of course, the housekeeping had been waiting just outside the door. She grasped Kat's arm, drawing her farther down the hall.

"He'll do it?" she said excitedly.

"Yes."

"I told you!"

"But he's so angry!" Kat said with a shiver.

"He'll calm down." Emma clasped her hands together happily. "Oh, this will be such fun! But everything must be done quickly, as well."

"Wait, wait, Emma! There's nothing to be done. It is a farce, a charade, nothing more."

"Good heavens, dear girl, don't you see? It must be a good charade. If Sir Hunter has agreed, he will know that my words are true."

"Emma!" Kat caught the woman's hands and stared into her eyes. "It's not real!"

"Miss Katherine, I helped you get in there and make it happen. Now you must humor me a bit, and also, believe this—if there is not some to-do about it, it won't be believed. Now, you go home and make the announcement to your father and sister. Trust me. Sir Hunter will be down shortly, and you will see. Oh, dear. There's today...tomorrow, and then it is time to sail. This will be wonderful!"

"Emma!" Kat tried to warn again.

"Go on, go on, now. I've a lot to do to plan the party by tonight."

"Party!"

"Naturally. Oh, a small one, in the best of taste. Go on! You must get busy, too!"

The entire idea had been insane. She hadn't formed it in her mind when she had come; she had simply hoped that

Hunter, being Hunter, and ever willing to watch her make a fool of herself, would have an idea.

But Emma had come up with this, assuring her that Sir Hunter may as well have a fiancée. He was, after all, ever being sought, and ever eluding those who would seek to claim his name. Now that it was done—and it had been such a rash ploy!—it seemed more insane than ever.

She was going to have to lie to her father. That was going to be very hard. Not so much now—she would make the announcement and sail away, and he would be happy and working, and delighted that she had done so well—but later…

When the engagement was broken.

"Go home! And be convincing!" Emma said. "Ethan will see that you get there safely."

"Emma, it is broad daylight. I will be all right."

"Sir Hunter would never send his intended out on an omnibus, dear, not when his carriage was waiting."

And so Ethan took her home, and somehow it seemed, he, too, was aware of the charade, because he was grinning from ear to ear.

When he helped her from the carriage, he said, "May, I, miss, give you my congratulations?"

She let out a sigh, shaking her head.

"Ethan!"

"Go in, miss. I'll come for you later."

When she went into the house, it was quiet. She thought perhaps that Eliza was still sleeping, but she knew that her father would be in the attic where the glass sheets on the eastward slant of the roof afforded him light.

And he was there, as she had expected, serious as he studied one of his ships at sea, weighing color and scheme.

He looked up as she came in, arching a brow. "Kat, what is it? You look so worried. Is something wrong?"

Oh, something was very, very wrong. She shook her head.

"My child, what is it that you can't speak to your father?" he asked gruffly, setting down his palette and coming to her.

"Papa, I need your blessing!" she said in a rush.

He frowned deeply. "For...?"

"I'm to become engaged."

"A man comes to a father when he would take a bride," her father said sternly.

She winced, having forgotten that he would feel this way. She opened her mouth, trying to think of the right thing to say.

"Indeed, he should!" she heard, and swirling around, she saw that Hunter was there, in the doorway of her father's workroom.

He was dressed in a handsome gray suit and crimson waistcoat, clean-shaven and smelling of soap and leather. His eyes dusted over hers, then focused on her father.

"Kat is a bit anxious. She loves you so. I have come to ask for your daughter's hand in marriage, Mr. Adair."

William's brows hiked as his jaw dropped. He stared for what seemed like eons.

Then his jaw snapped shut, and he grinned. "Well, well," he said to Hunter.

"She has enamored my heart and senses since I pulled her from the sea," Hunter said.

William was quiet again, then he started to laugh. He picked Kat up, holding her high above him, laughing. He lowered her, hugged her fiercely, set her down. Then he strode to Hunter and shook his hand. "Good heavens, yes, yes, yes! When Kat first walked in the room, I thought it was one of those boys...but, ah, yes. You and she. A perfect match. I saw it in my soul, but by God, it was never my place to speak, and if a parent were to point out such a perfect match to a child, well...daughters do not care to feel that they are being forced. After all, it is a new age." He was still pumping Hunter's hand. "This is quick, yes...but, you will have a voyage and more to know each other well before the marriage takes place."

He stopped shaking Hunter's hand at last, but only to pick Kat up again. Then he let out a bellow that brought Eliza, in a robe, and Maggie, covered in flour, up to the garret. "They're engaged!" William cried, hugging Eliza. "They're engaged."

"Engaged!" Eliza gasped, looking at them both.

"Lord above us!" Maggie breathed. "Ah, Kat, and would your sainted mother be glad and a-blessing you this day!"

Kat's cheeks burned. This, she knew, was the greatest guilt she had ever felt.

Eliza hugged her, and their eyes met, and Kat knew that her sister was well aware of the lie, and yet, apparently, understood it. Then Eliza gave Hunter a sisterly kiss. Maggie hugged Kat as boisterously as her father had done, though without the lift off the floor, hesitated in front of Hunter, then hugged him, as well.

When he was released at last, Hunter strode to Kat, taking her hand. "My dear," he said, and she was certain that only she caught the terribly droll note in his voice, "if you will be so kind as to wear this ring..."

She looked down at the item he slipped onto her finger, a gold ring with a yellow stone that shimmered in the light.

He stepped away from her, addressing her father. "I am loathe to run off, Mr. Adair, after dropping such a stunning announcement, but I believe I rather surprised myself in all the haste of this! I must be about… Please, all of you, Emma would like a small celebration at my town house tonight." He turned to Maggie, offering her a gallant little bow. "Miss Maggie, if you would be so good as to assist Emma, we'd both be most grateful!"

Maggie clapped her hands together, staring at him with wonder. "My dearest sir! With all the pleasure in the world. She need have no fear, I will follow her every dictate!"

"Good, then all is settled!"

He started out, then stopped, swinging back around, catching Kat's eye. "Good Lord! My beloved, in all the hurry, I forget the cause of all my joy!" He strode back to her. Then, as her father had, he picked her up and held her above him for a moment. Then he brought her slowly to the floor, letting her slide against the length of him. They, were, of course, both fully clad. And yet, as she slid down that length, she was vividly reminded of all that she had witnessed that morning. When she was solidly on her own feet again, he dipped his head to hers.

It was not a kiss such as the one they had shared the evening before. This one was light and tender, a lover's kiss, a promise. One that was entirely proper before a soon-to-be father-in-law. "Until tonight…"

The sensual rasp he could apparently set to his voice at will still caused tremors within her. When he walked away, she could still feel his touch.

And the mockery in his words.

"OH!" ELIZA CRIED IN HIS WAKE. "Oh!" She spun on her sister, cheeks flushed. "Oh, but, Kat, he is so *sumptuous!* So—"

Her words froze in her throat. "Um…so decent and kind," she said quietly.

"Sumptuous!" William roared. "Maggie, a wedding! There's to be a wedding!" And music or no, he grabbed Maggie's hands and began a jig about the attic.

LORD AVERY CAME STRIDING into the pseudo great hall of his town house where Hunter awaited him by the fire. He looked grave, and as he came forward, he was shaking his head. "I've heard! It seems every servant in the city is speaking of nothing else. Hunter, my boy! I have forced this on you!"

Hunter shook his head. "No, Lord Avery, and I am here because I was quite afraid you would think that the case. Perhaps you caused a quickening in my plan, but that is all."

"But, Hunter! You can't mean to marry! Why, the finest mothers in the land have cast their daughters before you, women of independent wealth and means have made it quite clear that they'd be delighted to bear your name. Sir, you have escaped matrimony these many years, and it was surely your intent!"

"Ah, but what man would escape forever, Lord Avery?"

"But, Hunter…"

"Lord Avery, yesterday you but pointed out to me the very assets Kat possesses that first stole my heart. She is a beauty beyond compare, but she is also courageous and bright, vivid, eager, young…tender, caring, loving. Dear friend, what was there *not* for me to fall in love with?"

"Oh!"

They both looked up, startled. Margaret was at the top of the stair, looking down, and of course, she had heard all.

She came sailing down the stairs and flew into Hunter's arms, hugging him, then kissing both cheeks. "Oh, forgive me, I'm so happy! Hunter, such beautiful words. Had you ever said such things about me, I'd have swooned at your feet!"

He laughed, gently setting her away, trying very hard not to grit his teeth.

This was definitely a lot of work to maintain a good secretary. Yet the lies fell from his lips so easily! Because, of course, they were all true, he thought bitterly. She had inflamed his senses from the start, and even as she firmly set him from her, she had beguiled him further. So careless was she! And, yet, perhaps, after these many years during which he had kept his distance, broken a heart here or there, it was perhaps only what he deserved. Had he known then…

"Lady Margaret, you are a golden angel, pure in heart and kindness and beauty, and some fellow out there will surely worship at your feet. In fact, I believe there are several."

Lord Avery let out a peculiar sound. "Yes, and she had best choose soon!"

"Had I even imagined that Sir Hunter's heart might be won, I'd have vied for it myself!" she said, smiling. "Oh, Hunter, seriously, I am thrilled for you both. We must throw a party, hastily, Father, since we're to leave—"

"There is a small get-together tonight, just our households, a few friends, at my town house," Hunter said, anxious to be on his way. "You'll come, please, say around eight?"

"Of course!" Margaret said.

"Indeed, Sir Hunter," Lord Avery said, staring at him anew. And obviously, now, believing the charade.

As he turned to leave, David Turnberry walked into the hall. The young man stopped short, seeing Hunter, and Hunter stopped, as well. "Good day, sir," David said.

"David," Hunter acknowledged.

Margaret floated across the floor, grasping David's hand. "David! He's to be married! Hunter is to be married."

David stared at him. "To…to…?"

"Silly goose!" Margaret laughed. "To his mermaid, Miss Adair!"

The color drained from the young man's face.

"David, you must congratulate Sir Hunter!" Margaret chided, obviously not noticing his sudden pallor.

Stiffly, David extended a hand. His Adam's apple bobbed. "Congratulations," he said.

"And we shall have a lovely party at his home tonight," Margaret said. "I must find something to wear!" She kissed Hunter's cheek and fled.

Lord Avery remained by the fire.

David spoke very softly. "I…don't believe…it can't be."

"Believe," Hunter said simply. He leaned close to David's ear and lowered his voice. "Touch her again, and I will break every bone in your body. I pray that I am understood."

With that, he walked around David and exited the house.

THE DOOR TO KAT'S ROOM burst open.

Isabella. She should have expected as much.

"Come in, please, do," Kat said.

The woman surveyed her coolly. "I don't believe it. Not for a minute. What is this new game you're playing?"

"There is no game," Kat lied boldly. "I am to be married."

She walked around to the wardrobe where Kat was busy trying to ascertain just which pieces of her clothing might in any way be utile for a trip into the desert. "You can lie to others, Katherine Adair, but I know the truth about you."

"And what truth would that be?"

"You covet another man."

Kat gave her attention to her clothing, picking up a cotton blouse here, a linen skirt there. "Well, Lady Daws, I *am* going to marry Sir Hunter MacDonald."

"I don't believe that you—even you, with your clever wiles—could have snared such a man as Sir Hunter!"

"Oh?" Kat turned to her, loathing her yet somehow afraid and unsure of the reason. "Why is that? Did you try for him yourself and fail?"

She was certain that the woman barely restrained herself from slapping her. Isabella's eyes were so cold, her mouth grim. Kat had never felt hatred so tangibly before.

"Do you mind?" she said. "I need to be packed."

"I will tell him the truth, girl. Mark my words. I will tell him the truth."

Kat couldn't help it; she started to laugh. "Tell him anything you please."

"You know, I warned you. You will pay for this."

"What are you talking about?"

"You cannot live this kind of lie and not pay, my dear. And you shall."

With that, Lady Daws spun around and departed.

Kat stared after her. "Well! You're not invited to my party!" she said softly. But then she bit her lower lip. The woman would be there. She would be there on her father's arm.

Kat sat on the foot of her bed, suddenly very scared. She'd be leaving her father to this woman.

The door burst open again. She started to jump up, ready to defend herself, as if there was a danger of being physically attacked.

But it was Eliza. "What's the matter?" she cried, seeing Kat's fear.

Kat shook her head, then ran to her sister and hugged her. "I can't do it! I can't go, Eliza, and leave father with her!"

"You can go because *I* am here!" Eliza said firmly.

"That is asking too much of you."

They sat together, holding each other. Eliza smoothed Kat's hair. "One day, you will be there when *I* need you. Now, I am here because you need me. Because Papa needs me. And we will be fine."

"She knows!" Kat said, shivering.

"She knows what?"

"That..."

"That it's a sham?"

Kat nodded.

"She can't really know anything, can she? I can promise you this, Hunter will never tell her the truth!"

And that was true, Kat thought. The only person who could really betray her would not do so.

She felt the ring on her finger. Eliza had told her that it was a yellow diamond, exceptionally beautiful, very rare with that depth of color.

Once again, another reason to be grateful to Hunter. No matter how he chose to make her pay.

The ring suddenly seemed to burn her finger. And suddenly, she felt as if she was burning all over.

She disentangled herself from her sister and forced a smile. "Well...if you need me when I am away, you must get word to me!"

Little good it would do; she would be so, so far away!

"AN ENGAGEMENT PARTY! You!" It was Camille who spoke, but both she and Brian were staring at him incredulously. Then Camille smiled slowly. "It's Miss Adair. It must be."

"It is."

"You're daft, man!" Brian exploded. "Sorry, but you've known the girl but a week."

Hunter laughed. "The two of you are going to preach to me?" he queried.

"Of course not," Camille said.

"Wouldn't think of it, old chap," Brian said. But they were both still staring at him. Brian cleared his throat. "Well, we should do a dinner or something, shouldn't we, Camille? There's not much time, but we could get something together at the castle for tomorrow night, perhaps."

"It's not necessary—there is a party at my town house tonight," Hunter said wearily.

"Then we must do something aboard ship," Camille said.

"Ah, there, a lovely idea! Or a party along the Italian shore! There will be lovely, balmy nights," Brian said.

"Again, it's not necessary."

"Well, we'll argue about this later," Brian said. "Camille, I have searched every file cabinet in the storage room and cannot find the map you're missing. I'll try the storage rooms."

"Which map?" Hunter asked.

"I had it on the floor the other day. We were both working with it, do you remember? Reading some of the papyri we had, and calculating. In fact, I had it out when I first met your lovely fiancée."

"Have you gone through my desk?" Hunter asked.

"I'd not have done such a thing."

"I'll look," Hunter said.

"I'm heading down," Brian said. "I think we've about finished...ah, and there's a good thing! We can quite enjoy the evening without worry." Brian winked at his wife. "I'm off."

As Brian headed downstairs, Camille followed Hunter into his office. "What kind of a game are you playing, Hunter?"

He groaned, sitting. Then he looked at her. "Would you be asking this because you played a few games of your own?"

"They were not of my making," she reminded him.

Head down, Hunter tapped a pencil on his desk, then looked up again at Camille, a woman he knew to be a true friend and confidante. "She believes that David Turnberry's life is in danger."

"And you don't?"

"I think he is spoiled and rich. He fell off a boat. He learned that it gained him concern. He claimed yesterday that he crashed into the door and hurt his head. Kat is convinced that he was attacked."

"Here, in the museum?" Camille asked, surprised.

He nodded grimly, then shook his head. "Lord Avery is afraid of her—afraid that she will lure the entire collection of Margaret's suitors from her side. Margaret, of course, is not so silly. I don't know, Camille. It seemed the right thing to do."

"Ah."

"You're not commenting."

"What would you have me say?"

"Something! That it's a wretched ruse, that we'll only hurt others...I don't know."

She smiled strangely. "Just take care that it's not yourself who's hurt. And, of course, if I didn't love you dearly, my friend, I would not be concerned, I would merely consider it your just due."

"Thank you. Have I really been such a roué, then?"

She laughed. "Just elusive." Her expression grew serious. "Hunter, about these disappearances, do you think that there is something going on?"

He took her hand gently. "Camille, we have all been looking forward to this expedition. It's never wise to forget to look over one's shoulder, but...nothing of great value has been taken. And we're leaving. If there is some foul plan afoot, we'll not be here. We'll be far away."

She stood and started to walk away, then hesitated. "Hunter."

"Yes?"

"What if whatever danger, real or imagined, follows us aboard the ship?" She sounded seriously worried, enough so that he felt a little chill of unease himself.

He smiled. "We will hunt down the culprit, skin him alive, and that will be that!"

"Ah, how assuring!" she said, and smiling, left him at last.

KAT DIDN'T THINK THAT SHE had ever been so nervous in her life.

They were to arrive early, she being the guest of honor, but from the time they stepped into the house, she could not sit still. And neither Emma nor Maggie would allow her to help in any way. Emma had brought in extra maids and servers for the day, and, of course, Ethan was there to see to whatever else might be needed.

Hunter was not even there when they first arrived.

"Kat, have some champagne," Emma advised.

"No!" she protested.

Lady Daws, of course, was there. "A sudden aversion to champagne, Kat? I've heard that it can get one into trouble," the woman said, eyes wide and innocent, even touched by concern. But, of course, William Adair was there, as well.

"Emma, I believe I would like some champagne," Kat said.

She nearly broke the stem of the delicate goblet in which it was served. But the champagne did indeed ease her nerves.

Emma asked Maggie to take over for a few minutes, then caught Kat's arm, urging her to follow. They ran upstairs. They went to the blue room, where she had first stayed. There were flowers in vases, brushes and combs, little touches that made it more personal. "It is yours, Kat, whenever you choose to be here, whenever you may choose to escape from downstairs."

"Thank you, Emma," she murmured. "But—"

"Sir Hunter said that it should be so," Emma stated firmly. "I must get back down. Take your time."

Kat lingered, but not long. Her father and sister were there, after all. She did not wish to desert them.

Then Hunter arrived. He greeted her father now as William, and kissed her sister with all affection. He pecked the cheek of Lady Daws.

The first of the guests to arrive were Lord and Lady Carlyle, announced by Ethan. Camille, in deep-mauve party attire, was beautiful, and yet, it was her smile that was most dazzling. Their arrival set Lady Daws on her best behavior, and she laughed with others and appeared quite human. Brian spoke with her father about the painting he had acquired, and Lady Daws held William's arm as if he were her own creation.

A few others from the Egyptology Department arrived, and then Lord Avery's household, the gentleman himself, Margaret and David. Soon after, Davis's cohorts were at the door—Robert Stewart, Allan Beckensdale and Alfred Daws.

As Alfred entered the room, Isabella stiffened. Kat could not help but watch the two. Catching his stepmother's eye at one point, Alfred acknowledged her, inclining his head. She returned the gesture, then gave her avid attention to William and Brian Stirling again.

At one point, Kat saw Alfred and Hunter talking. Alfred was a tall young man, but Hunter still towered over him. Hunter's words were low, but she had the feeling that they were tense. Alfred flushed and looked away, again catching the eye of his stepmother, who arched her chin and seemed quite pleased that he might be suffering in some way.

"A toast?" Kat turned. David was by her side. He had a fresh glass of champagne for her.

"Thank you, but I don't believe I shall have any more champagne."

"But you must!" he protested, and it seemed that he had been imbibing freely already. "You've become engaged. Who would have imagined?" He thrust the flute into her hand.

"The world is strange," she said simply. He was hurt, she knew. And yet she felt angry. "He wishes to marry me," she couldn't help but say, even if it was a lie.

His cheeks darkened. "His parents are long gone, and he has been off in the world on his own many years," he said, defending himself.

"Of course." Despite her words to the contrary, she took a sip of the champagne. Lady Margaret was watching them, she realized.

As was Isabella Daws.

She felt that she and David were standing too close. She backed up, nearly stepping on someone's feet—those of Alfred Daws, as it happened. She nearly lost her balance. "Whoa!" the young lord said, and rescued the champagne flute from her hand as David reached out to steady her. She quickly regained her balance and composure, thanking them both. "Your champagne," Alfred said.

"Thank you." She stepped back cleanly then. It might all be a charade to Hunter, but he was deadly serious when it came to David's keeping his distance from her.

And Hunter, too, was watching.

Margaret saved her, sailing in among them. "What fun! Honestly, Kat, this is just wonderful. I mean, of course, you'll still help Hunter, and you must have your art lessons, but we'll be more like a family now."

In other words, Kat wouldn't be a slightly elevated servant.

"Thank you, Margaret."

Margaret gave her a hug, and it seemed very warm and real. And once again, her champagne flute was nearly lost. Someone saved it, and it was back in her hands.

There was a delicate touch at the nape of her neck, sending frissons of heat shooting along her spine. Hunter was at her side. "Shall we eat, my dear?"

"Indeed, yes, I'm sure everyone is quite starving," she murmured. They were being watched, of course. He made a point of offering her a smile, catching the underside of her chin with his knuckle and raising her face to his. He smoothed back a strand of her hair with his free hand and placed a tender kiss on her lips.

She thought she heard a choking sound.

David.

The kiss seemed to linger a bit too long. He raised his face just slightly, his eyes touching hers. Only she could really see his eyes, both the challenge and amusement that burned within them.

"Dinner," she said, the word rather choked out.

"Oh, yes. Dinner," he said huskily. "I had quite forgotten."

Lord Avery cleared his throat. Hunter stepped away.

They were soon arranged around the table. Luckily, she was at one end, Hunter at the other. Alfred was to her side, while Lady Daws was seated down by Hunter.

Conversation began with current politics, then a champagne toast to the queen. It veered to the coming expedition, then a champagne toast to their voyage. Next, a toast was made to Eliza's fashion-design prowess, and then to Margaret's beauty. William's work was toasted. Then Brian Stirling rose to toast the newly engaged couple. "To Katherine Adair, far than a simple mortal beauty, to catch not just the heart but the hand of a man such as Hunter, and to Hunter himself, a lucky man in many ways, it's been said, but never so much as now! To long life, a successful marriage, a dozen children, and the best I could ever wish any man, the happiness I have found myself!"

"Santé!" William said, raising his glass, and the toast went round.

Once again, Kat realized, her head was swimming. Champagne, she decided, was an evil brew, sent to torment the senses rather than elate them. She was tired, not seeing clearly, and the night seemed endless. She had to keep smiling and chatting. She was quite afraid that she was going to pass out. At last, she was seriously so reeling that she escaped to the kitchen.

"Why, you're flushed!" Maggie said.

"Too warm," Emma agreed.

"We'll get you upstairs immediately."

They did so, bringing her up the servants' stairway. It had been impossible for Eliza not to have noted her disappearance, and she soon followed and was instantly concerned. Kat realized then that she was quite ill. Once they had gotten her dress over her shoulders, she tore into the bathroom, finding the commode in just the nick of time.

She was aware of the excited conversation as both Maggie and Emma rushed to help her. She closed the bathroom door, begging privacy. Agony ripped through her. She was violently sick once again, and then again. And when she was done, she nearly fainted. She wore a corset, and it was far too tight, and she couldn't find the strings.

"Kat!" It was Eliza at the door now. "You must let me in!"

She could barely reach the doorknob. Eliza rushed in, got a cloth, cooled her face and helped her rise.

"The stays!" Kat managed.

Eliza eased them. There was a robe on the back of the door, and she slipped it around her sister's shoulders, her eyes wide with concern. "Is it the excitement? The champagne? You're never sick!"

"Never," Kat agreed.

She was shaking, chilled, trembling again. But vomiting had been good. The agonizing pain was gone. She felt as weak as a kitten. "Come...let's get you into bed," Eliza said.

"Here?"

"Well, you are engaged to him now. This is your room now. And Emma is certainly proper!"

Kat let her sister get the door open and help her over to the bed. Maggie and Eliza were there, drawing down the sheets, drawing them up once again. Maggie worked the pins from her hair. "We'll not have them sticking into your pate, adding to your misery!" she vowed.

"I'm better…much, much better," Kat assured them. She tried to sit up but hadn't the strength.

"Tea!" Emma said. "I must make some tea."

And so she rushed away to do so. Kat closed her eyes. She opened them again. Her father was there, and his eyes were dark with worry. "I'm okay, Papa!" she assured him, and tried to smile. "Too many toasts!"

"Ah, darlin'!" he said, gently holding her.

Kat heard someone whispering, "She'll have to stay."

Then Emma was back with the tea. Eliza supported her, and she drank it, and the world seemed so much better. She closed her eyes. Drifted…

She dreamed of a rocking sensation, as if she were already at sea. Great waves swept by. They became sand. She was looking out over the desert. As she looked, a great black wing seemed to cover the sun, and the darkness boded a terrible evil. She fought it, trying to awaken….

She was awake. The room was very dim, and there was someone here with her. A figure, dark, and somehow menacing, staring at her.

She jerked up, crying out.

The figure disappeared. There were footsteps, running down the hallway. Emma burst in. She was in a nightgown now. She rushed to Kat and sat on the side of the bed. Kat almost smiled, the woman looked so funny in her nightcap. "What is it?"

Nothing, Kat realized. She had been dreaming, imagining giant wings, and she had dreamed a shadow. "I'm so sorry I woke you! I was dreaming."

Emma looked at her anxiously, smoothing her hair. "You're truly cool now, my dear. And not at all clammy. Do you feel better?"

"Much," Kat assured her. "The guests are all gone now, I imagine?"

Emma nodded. "Your father knew that you must stay here. Hunter insisted on the doctor coming, and he did, but you were sleeping quite peacefully by then. He believed it must have been the champagne and the excitement, and he said that he doubted you'd been eating nearly enough lately. So...apparently, he was right. You're much better."

"I never get sick!" Kat said.

Emma smiled. Obviously that wasn't quite true.

"Shall I make you something? Some tea, a bit of toast?"

Kat shook her head. "No...thank you. I'll just...sleep. I think that's what I need."

Emma left her. Kat plumped her pillow and closed her eyes. Again, she drifted. This time, she did not dream. When she awoke again, it was because soft light, barely more than darkness, was seeping in through the curtains.

Again, she knew there was a presence in the room. But this time, it was not malignant. She felt a touch, fingers on her cheek, catching the hair that had fallen over her face. Very, very gently moving it back.

Fingers, like a breath of air, on her head, and then again, testing the temperature of her cheek.

A knuckle, ever so light, like angel's wings, against her face. She breathed, and she knew the scent. Hunter.

After a moment, he was gone. She slept very deeply again. When she awoke, Emma was there to ask if she wanted to try to come down, or if her father and sister should come up. It was nearly night again.

Her last night in England.

Tomorrow, they sailed.

Chapter 11

KAT HAD NEVER IMAGINED that it would be so difficult to say goodbye to her father. She knew that she loved him with all her heart, but it was only when the last whistle blew and she knew that he, Eliza—and of course, Lady Daws—must leave the ship that she realized just how a part of her would be missing when she was no longer with her family.

Maggie and Emma had managed to become close friends in a short period of time, and so Maggie was a pile of tears, which didn't help Kat.

"Ah, luv, you can still come off the ship. But such a fine man will not come along again easily," her father said, a twinkle in his eye.

She clung to him. She shook her head against the broad expanse of his chest. "I'm all right. It's just that I love you so."

"But I will be well. Eliza and Isabella will be looking after me."

That, of course, was what she was afraid of—the Isabella part.

Then Eliza took her in a hug, squeezing her tightly. "I will look after Papa!" she whispered. "It will be fine!"

It must have been, Kat thought, that she was still simply so weak. When they walked away and she had to watch them standing, waving, on shore as they sailed at last, she knew that silent tears cascaded down her cheeks.

Hunter was behind her. They were in full view of many people, so it was natural that he took her in his arms. And it was most pleasant. She laid her head against his chest, and he put a hand on her head, soothing her. She realized for the first time that, somehow, he was truly her friend. Of course, that wouldn't mean that they would get along any better. But she had so much for which to be grateful to him. She vowed that she would never fail him in the work that he needed.

Many people stood on deck, watching as England disappeared. And then, as they moved away, groups began to splinter and to seek out their cabins.

This first ship would take them across to France, where supplies would be unloaded and then reloaded on the train. Their overland journey would take them as far south as Brindisi, Italy, where they were to board a second ship, which would take them to Alexandria, where again they would pick up a train. The train would deliver them to Cairo, and from there, the groups on expedition would set out for their respective digs. Most of those aboard were heading to Egypt, though certainly not all were planning on a season of expedition. Many went merely to flee the cold winter months.

Thanks to Lord Avery's title, esteem and money, their group had the best accommodations. Kat had a pleasant little room all her own, and there was space enough for a bed, dresser, slim wardrobe and small writing or dressing table. A door connected to Emma's room, which was smaller, and from there to a sitting room, which in turn connected to Lady Margaret's room. Lord Avery was across the hall with his valet, George, in the sitting room, and Hunter was down a few doors with a nicely elegant room of his own, which included a sitting room and an extra-small bedroom for Ethan. David, Alfred, Allan and Robert were on the opposite side of Lord Avery, each with a small cabin to call his own. There were minuscule baths for the ladies, while the men had to share. The Earl and Countess of Carlyle were at the far end of the hall, where they, too, had a suite of rooms. It was a ship, however, and space was tight, whatever one's position or wealth.

There were, Robert Stewart had assured her, far worse accommodations. She should see how they were below!

And, of course, she believed him and was grateful.

Their first day at sea, after the initial excitement and exploration of cabins, was one that saw many passengers keeping to their cabins. The channel was rough. The captain apologized and told them that he was sorry, but it was often so in the northern waters.

With everyone else apparently in their cabins, Kat chose to wander the deck. She loved the motion of the sea and the feel of the wind against her hair. She especially loved the strange feeling of power it gave her to stand topside and feel the lash of the elements.

She was leaning on the rail, enjoying the salt spray, when she noted another intrepid traveler who had not retreated to his cabin.

Hunter. He saw her at the same time and approached her. They were alone on deck, so there was no need for pretense of any kind.

"You're not feeling the pain of the motion?" he queried, taking a stance beside her at the rail.

She shook her head. "I love the sea. I am never sick."

He looked at her with a small smile on his lips. "Oh? Never?"

"Truly, I'm never— Oh. Well, once."

"I'm glad that you are better now."

She stared back at the water in irritation. "Perhaps… I must have eaten or drunk something bad," she said.

She was startled to see a frown form on his brow. He stared at her. "You couldn't have. There were many people there that night. No one else was ill."

"Well, in my life, that is possibly the first time I have ever been ill," she said. "So it must have been something I swallowed."

"There was a great deal of upheaval and excitement," he reminded her.

She groaned. "I have had worse days, I promise you."

He seemed thoughtful, and she wondered if he might possibly believe her. He leaned against the rail, no longer interested in the sea but watching her. "If not the champagne, the excitement or the food—consumed by everyone—what?"

"Nothing! I cannot explain it."

"You're not suggesting that…"

"What?" she demanded.

"That someone perhaps slipped something into your drink."

"I'd not have put it past Isabella!" Kat said.

"I had not even thought of such a possibility," Hunter murmured. He still watched her with such speculation that she was uneasy.

"I'm fine now," she said, looking away again.

"Yes, well, I should very much like it if you were to remain that way," he responded.

She shook her head. "I don't know what I am saying. Of course, it had to have been…a nervous disorder. There could be no one who would really wish me…dead," she said. Still, even saying the word gave her chills. She shrugged as if it had been a casual statement. But he still watched her, and she knew it. She turned her attention back to him. "Oh, seriously, Sir Hunter! I am not rich, I have no power, nor do I even possess any knowledge about anything. Why would anyone want to hurt me?"

"Jealousy, revenge."

"Jealousy?" She laughed.

He looked wryly amused. "Dear Miss Adair, I hate to shatter your total disregard, but there are those out there who just might envy your position as my fiancée."

"But that's preposterous. It's not even real!"

"But we've hardly announced that, have we?"

"Camille is happily married, my sister would never hurt me, Margaret could have any man she chooses. I hardly think anyone at the party would want me out of the way because of you. Lady Daws, of course, would certainly be interested— I'm sorry, I'm afraid that's not much of a compliment, for I believe she was interested at one time in any attractive man with any status whatsoever, though I do believe that she has set her talons on my father."

"True," he agreed.

"I did not mean to be offensive."

"I wasn't offended. It's just that, well, I am afraid I must be a bit skeptical. First, you believe that someone intends harm to David."

"Well, he *was* harmed! He was nearly killed."

"And then...well, is the person attempting to kill David the same person who's attempting to either kill you or make you deathly ill?" he inquired.

She shook her head, irritated anew that he was again mocking her. "I simply do not get sick, that is all. I will no longer say anything at all, since it seems that every word out of my mouth is an amusement to you."

He laughed, and she turned on him in something of a temper. But he was smiling still, and it seemed with good humor rather than mockery, and for a moment, she was caught by the light in his eyes, by the curve of his smile and by the realization that everyone else was really quite right; he was an extraordinary man, tall, powerful and handsome. Striking, really. And when his lips had touched hers, she had felt…

Her knees felt weak with the mere memory, and she looked away. Angry with herself, she rallied, but he had put an arm around her waist.

"Are you all right?" he asked.

"Yes…it was just a second of the ship's sway," she said.

"Ah."

"Tell me," she asked, glad of him next to her, aware that she had come to know his scent well—soap and shaving talc, mingled with the scent of skin beneath. "What will it be like when we get there?"

"Cairo, you mean? Well, I believe that you will find the hotel fascinating. It's the season, so I imagine there will be two or three hundred guests at Shepheard's now. And they all gather on the porch, the restaurant, facing the arriving travelers. They are rich and poor, many are British or American, some German…and French. Others, of course, but those are the main groups of tourists. Some have come because they are ill, sadly. Many, many who suffer from tuberculosis come to Egypt, and there are doctors who swear that the weather can prolong life. Every time a new party arrives, all the people at all the tables speculate on who they are, what they do and if they are in Egypt for vacation or for work, if they will go down the Nile or enjoy the sights of

Cairo. There are a number of new hotels, of course, and some very nice. But Shepheard's is where you go if you wish to know who else is around."

"It sounds...marvelous," she said.

"It is," he assured her.

She realized that his arm was still around her. And that she did not want it to move.

"Well, hello!" came a deep voice. Strangely, feeling an odd sense of guilt, Kat jerked away at the sound. "See, dear," Brian Stirling said to his wife as the pair strolled toward Hunter and Kat, "there are others up and about."

"Indeed, you two look hale and well!" Camille said, smiling.

Brian cleared his throat. "We did not mean to interrupt."

"You didn't," Hunter said. "In fact, Brian, I was about to go in search of you."

"Really?"

"I'd have a word with you."

"Excuse us?" Brian said politely, and the two men moved away down the deck.

"I am glad to see you so well," Camille told Kat. "There was quite a fright over you the other night. Hunter was frantic, riding for the doctor himself, dragging the poor man out of bed."

"I didn't know that," Kat said. Hunter had been frantic? "But I'm fine."

"Amazingly so. The others are mostly abed."

Camille was studying her strangely, but still smiling. Kat shook her head, shrugging. "I usually have a cast-iron stomach, so I'm very sorry to have ruined the party."

"It was *your* party, Kat."

"Yes, I suppose."

"Well, it's good to be started on this journey at last! Tomorrow, of course, will be quite a to-do, transferring from ship to train. And I believe, from all I've been told, that the train trip is long and tedious. But I understand that you will meet the art instructor tomorrow. You are still interested, aren't you?"

"In the art instructor? Or course. Why wouldn't I be?"

"Oh, well, with your upcoming marriage…"

Kat moistened her lips, then reminded Camille, "You became Lady Carlyle, and there you were, day after day, at the museum."

"Yes, well, it's a passion, I'm afraid. I imagine art can be the same."

"I have to admit, I did little more than sketch before. My father is the true artist."

"For you to be an excellent artist would take nothing away from his talent," Camille said.

The countess stretched, lifting her face to the wind. "There, the men are returning, filled with their secrets. Can you imagine? What do you think they were talking about?" she asked brightly.

"I don't know."

"Us!" Camille said with a laugh. "Or, I would hazard to guess, you. But then again, a fiancée can most likely wheedle such information from her intended."

"My stomach is quite indecently growling!" Camille announced as the men returned to them. "Do you think that any of the cooks are still standing?"

"Perhaps," Brian said. "Shall we see? Ah! Miss Adair. Perhaps we should not…"

"I'm quite starving myself," Kat said.

"Then we shall eat," Hunter declared.

OTHER THAN THE CREW, it seemed the people on board had retired. Hunter found that he could not do so. He prowled his cabin in his smoking jacket.

He wanted to dismiss Kat's words about why she fell ill, but he simply could not. Tonight, he had been tempted to taste each bit of her food before her, to sip from her glass, to stand guard by her side.

But they had dined alone tonight, or alone with Camille and Brian, and he was quite certain that none of the crew had evil intentions.

In his conversation with Brian, he had told him about the things David had said to Kat, and then about the words he himself had exchanged with her. Also, that she had thought she had heard menacing whispers at the museum.

"I would put nothing myself past Lady Daws," Brian had mused, "but she is not with us on the expedition, so how could she do either David or Kat harm? And as for David..." Brian had hesitated. "Interesting. If it were Alfred Daws, I would say easily, yes! If there were a plot afoot, it might well be instigated by his stepmother. His death would bring her the Daws wealth."

"True enough. But David is the youngest of four brothers," Hunter had pointed out. "Is this all silly imagination?"

"In the dark and in the desert, it is always wise to be forewarned. And so we shall be," Brian had assured him.

All very fine and good. But Kat was across a hallway now, and even with Emma in the next room, he didn't like it.

He stopped his pacing, aware of footsteps in the hall. He listened, assuring himself that what he heard was real. And it was.

He opened his door silently and looked out.

David Turnberry stood before Kat's door. He raised a hand as if to knock! Then his hand fell. Hunter was about to approach him in anger, but David turned away, walking slowly back to his own room.

Hunter frowned and waited. David did not return.

Hunter swore. He was to spend a sleepless night.

He swore again, then walked across the hall. He set a hand on her door handle. It was not locked. He cursed her in silence and stepped into the room.

She had been sleeping and his arrival awakened her. She jackknifed to a sitting position and was about to scream.

"It's me, so hush," he said, and she did.

Looking at her, he felt his body tense from head to toe. The light cotton gown clung to her form. The riot of hair that framed her face and fell in curls on her breast gleamed even in the dim glow from the night-light. He drew the chair from the dressing table or desk. Sliding it against the door, he took a seat.

"What are you doing?" she whispered.

"Sleeping," he told her. "And you should do the same."

He could see her frowning. "You must be wretchedly uncomfortable!"

"I am."

"Then—"

"You nearly had a night visitor."

"What?"

"David. You didn't invite him, did you?"

She stiffened indignantly.

"Then I'll see that he doesn't enter," Hunter told her.

She stared at him a long while. She eased her head down again. It didn't stay. She rose, taking the second pillow from the bed and giving it to him.

He wished she hadn't done. The cotton of her gown was so thin she might as well have been naked.

"Thank you."

She nodded, standing there, shivering.

"Go to bed!" he told her, and he was afraid that his voice was not in the least cordial.

She turned and did as he commanded.

The chair was uncomfortable. The pillow did help.

It was better than pacing his own cabin, listening through the night. At last, he slept.

THE MORNING BROUGHT UTTER chaos, or so it seemed, though Camille assured Kat that there was actually some organization somewhere. It seemed there were hundreds of boxes and trunks to be transferred from one conveyance to another, and the transfers had to be done by cart. It was all going to take some time.

They'd hired a number of carriages to take them from the docks to the train station, leaving the hands, French and English, to move the cargo. They stopped to eat at a lovely restaurant near the shore, and Kat realized that it was a meeting spot. A number of fashionably dressed people were at various tables, and one elegant, slim woman with silver hair and a lorgnette called out to Hunter.

"Why, as I live and breathe! Hunter, dear Hunter!"

Kat thought that he groaned. He lowered his head, then excused himself from their table and approached the other. The woman rose; he kissed her on the cheek. She seemed very anxious to give him some news, and after acknowledging the other women at the table, he sat for a moment.

"Princess Lavinia!" Camille whispered.

"Princess?" Kat echoed.

Camille nodded. "She married a Greek prince—she was born a MacDonald."

"So she's…"

"Hunter's great-aunt."

At that moment, Hunter arose, indicating their table with a sweep of his hand. Camille waved. Hunter beckoned.

"It seems she wishes to speak with you," Kat said.

"He's calling *you*, Kat," Camille told her.

"Ah." She rose, forcing a smile. Hunter reached out for her, drawing her near. "Lavinia, please meet Katherine Adair, my fiancée. Kat, I'm delighted that we've run into my great-aunt Lavinia, Princess of Ragh."

"My pleasure, Your Highness."

"Dear child!" Lavinia seemed thrilled, fascinated. "Good heavens, I was beginning to believe that the line would die out with Hunter. Too many girls, you see. You will have sons, won't you, dear?"

"Aunt Lavinia—" Hunter tried to stop her. To no avail.

"You're truly quite lovely. No title?"

"I'm afraid not."

"It's not what one might imagine, anyway," Lavinia said breezily. "Hunter, Jacob MacDonald died last week."

"Jacob!" Hunter seemed deeply disturbed. "How? The lad was only twenty!"

"The same disease that plagued him as a child. You do know what it means?" she asked gently.

"It means a young, gentle and very good man is dead," Hunter said.

Lavinia sighed. "And it is a tragedy. I had not seen him in forever, living in France as I was, and he and his mother up north of Edinburgh. Truly, it is sad, and I know that you'll mourn him." She looked at Kat. "What he isn't saying is that when my dear elder brother passes from the earth, the title will go to Hunter."

"What title?"

"Duke of Kenwillow. Not a large holding, but, nevertheless, quite respectable."

"My great-uncle Percy is in excellent health, and I believe he'll live to be 110. And I hope that he does," Hunter said.

"Bravo!" Lavinia said. "So, you're headed off to Egypt again?" she asked.

"Yes, Aunt Lavinia. The train leaves in just a few hours."

Lavinia grinned. "Perhaps I'll be on it. Go…shoo, have your luncheon, Hunter. I shall stop at the table and tell dear Lord Avery and young Carlyle hello just as soon as I've finished my tea. Fascinating. Yes, maybe I will head to Cairo, too!"

"Lovely," Hunter said, urging Kat back toward their own table.

"She's really your aunt?" Kat murmured.

"Great-aunt, yes. And quite a girl at that. She has traveled the globe. So it's likely that she will manage to be on the train. Let's order, shall we? We've some tedious time ahead."

The food was excellent, and Lavinia did join them, after saying ta-ta to her group of friends. She seemed to have known Lord Avery for quite some time, and delighted in baiting him. Margaret seemed to relish the interaction between the two, laughing each time Lavinia said something tart to her father. Everyone at the table, in fact, including Alfred, Robert, Allan and David, enjoyed the tartness of the conversation.

At last, the men left to see that the trunks and personal baggage had been loaded. Lavinia declared her pleasure with the lot of them. "I simply despise women who sit at home and believe the world will come to them! The world is out there and ours to take! So, we will all ride out on expedition."

"Actually, I'd intended to remain at the hotel," Margaret said.

"When there are discoveries to be made?" Lavinia demanded.

"Um, I prefer to discover being waited upon," Margaret admitted. But that seemed to please Lavinia, as well.

"And, of course, there is the fine art of watching those who come and go from the hotel," Lavinia said.

"Watching people?" Margaret asked.

"Oh, that is an expedition of discovery in itself," Lavinia assured her. "Well! I shall have to make arrangements. I don't want the train to leave without us. It is time to board."

THE TRAIN WAS QUITE ELEGANT, actually, but no matter how well appointed, it remained a train.

Hunter had seen to it that his compartment was next to Kat's. Camille and Brian had the sleeping compartment behind his, while Emma was just in front of Kat.

The men went to assure themselves that all was loaded properly, and Lavinia, who had indeed managed to join the group, seemed to be well aware of the arrangements. "Bless Lord Avery," she told the women, "because he hires his own cars, and we won't have to be transferring here and there and everywhere. It will still be tedious, children, but much nicer than if we were average tourists hoping to catch this train or that!"

Kat knew that she would have been happy to be an average tourist, for she had never been anywhere. Their compartments were small, but the car ahead, the club car—again, specifically hired for the comfort of Lord Avery—was quite pleasant, fitted out with sofas, a bar and beautiful little cherrywood tables, specifically for tea.

At last, they were off, and they gathered in the club car. Lavinia, who often did the season in Cairo, as it turned out, spoke about the wonders of the sights. "The trip down the Nile is exquisite. And the Valley of the Kings!"

"We won't be taking the trip down the Nile," Hunter said.

Lavinia's face fell. "Oh, dear, you can't combine work with a lovely vacation?"

"We're going to dig," Hunter reminded her.

"Perhaps there will be time somewhere for a few excursions," Lord Avery said, both amused and exasperated by the woman.

"For some of us, perhaps," Hunter said.

"We are students, after all," Robert Stewart said. "Shouldn't we be learning?"

"We learn as we dig!" Alfred Daws said seriously.

"And yet," David Turnberry said softly, looking at Kat, "every once in a while, there must be a break from work. And there must be a time of a day, and a time of truth."

He was looking at Kat. She felt extremely uncomfortable. And so she turned back to their bawdy, titled newcomer. "Lavinia, have you actually ever worked a dig?" she asked.

"Good heavens, yes! I have ridden camels across a sea of sands, delved into the dirt and the wind. It's magnificent!"

Tea was served by a Frenchman in resplendent attire, and suddenly, to Kat, this seemed like the greatest adventure in the world. And by day's end, there hardly appeared even so much as a note of discord among any of them.

The following afternoon, they stopped in Paris, and there were joined by the art instructor from Oxford, Mr. Thomas Atworthy. He was an elderly fellow, around Lord Avery's age, but sprightly and interested in everything around him. His tongue could be as tart as Lavinia's, and he was definitely Bohemian, having little regard for titles and wealth.

"So, you are my student!" he said to Kat, looking her up and down. "Your father is the fellow creating such a stir back home!" He peered more closely at her. "You will receive no pat on the back from me if you try to work off the laurels of another."

"I've no intention of doing so."

"And you're to be married. Does that mean that I am wasting my time?"

"I hope that marriage will not prevent me from seeing, or lifting a pencil or a brush," she replied. He seemed pleased with that. He wanted to take her walking in Paris, to see how she managed to sketch some of the sights. That wasn't possible, even though Margaret and Camille both brought up the possibility of a lovely afternoon in the glorious city before they moved on. But the men did not want to linger.

So Kat's only view of the exquisite city was from the station and through the windows of the train. Soon they were traveling again, and the countryside stretched before them.

In the first days, Hunter was at her side for all social occasions, and she wondered if he hadn't simply acquired such an acute distaste for David Turnberry that he had determined that she would not be anywhere near him. He played his part as her fiancé rather well, and as each day passed, she realized that it was not at all unpleasant to have such a man as Sir Hunter as her intended.

Several times, she found herself pressed between a hallway wall and David when they were headed in opposite directions. He would linger ever so slightly against her every time, his eyes speaking volumes of pain and accusation. They were still such beautiful eyes. She was so sorry to have hurt him.

The nights were quiet.

They had just crossed the border into Italy when the tutor, Thomas Atworthy, decided that Kat must begin lessons, something not particularly easy with the train in constant motion. But he sat with her in the club car, pencils and paper at hand, teaching her about shadow and shading, giving her his disgruntled approval when she produced sketches, telling her that art was not just what was seen in the one dimension, but what went on in the depths. She discovered that crusty as the fellow might appear on the surface, underneath he was very kind and knowledgeable, and she became most fond of him.

They were moving into Tuscany, with its glorious views, when she found herself sketching the scene she remembered from the station in Paris. Camille had come into the club car and watched with wonder.

"That's incredible!" Camille murmured.

"No, it's not," Thomas countered. "The shading here is lacking. And here! What have we spoken about all week, my dear Miss Adair! I wish to see depth. Life, the action that occurs beyond the obvious!"

"No, no!" Camille said. "That's... I looked out the window that day, and you have drawn what I saw. Quite perfectly, really. So much detail. How did you do that?"

Kat looked at her sheepishly and shrugged. "I have that sort of memory. Most often, for little snatches of things... I don't know. But what I remember, I usually do with accuracy."

Camille reached for her arm, drawing her to her feet. "Mr. Atworthy, forgive me. I'm going to steal your pupil for the afternoon."

"That's quite all right. I was ready for brandy and a cigar. Oh, dear Lord! Here comes Lavinia. Well, it will not be a peaceful cigar, that is all I have to say!"

Ignoring the professor, Camille dragged Kat through the cars and back to her compartment. It was the largest of the sleeping accommodations, naturally, for they were two, and also, they were the Earl and Countess of Carlyle. There was a large table to one side of the compartment, and all kinds of maps and papers were spread out on it. Camille produced a clean sketch pad and sat Kat down at the table.

Kat looked at her expectantly.

"Do you remember the day we met?" Camille asked.

"Of course," Kat said. "At the museum. You were working with a map."

"Yes, well, that map has quite disappeared. Do you think you could reproduce it?"

"You can't just acquire another?"

Camille shook her head. "That map was nearly a hundred years old. It was the work of one of the first eminent British Egyptologists to go into the country after Napoléon was defeated. He had access to documents we'll never see again. There were little landmarks sketched in on it. Would you see what you can remember of them? Oh, I know that I am asking the impossible. But would you try?"

Kat nodded. At first, her fingers hesitated on the paper. She felt that she wavered as she tried to draw coastlines and natural features. But then, when she had the base of the project sketched in, she began to remember. It was almost as if the map had been etched into a permanent place in her mind.

Camille stood silently by her side.

They were both so intent on the work that they jumped when the door to the compartment opened. Brian strode in, followed by Hunter.

Brian arched a brow. Camille's hand was at her throat.

"What on earth have we interrupted?" Hunter asked.

"Look!" Camille announced with pleasure. "Kat is recreating my map!"

Hunter crossed to Kat's side, studying what she had drawn. Their gazes met briefly, and she was pleased to see that he seemed to consider what she had done quite remarkable.

"I can't testify to any accuracy," she said.

She looked down quickly, saw his hands. He had wonderful hands. Ever so slightly bronzed, for he eschewed gloves when riding. His fingers were long, his nails clipped neatly. The clench of his fist was powerful, she was certain, and the touch of his fingertips could be...

She cleared her throat, looking over at Camille. "There may be more. I think I should stop now and take a look at it again in the morning."

"Fine. And actually, we'll be off the train tonight, in hotel rooms! The world will stand still for a bit," Camille said.

"Is this so important, then?" Kat asked.

"It may be," Camille said. She looked at Hunter. "Of course...it won't be perfectly accurate."

"We three know what we are looking for in the desert sands," Hunter said. "And we all know how hard it can be. Even if we had something that was perfectly accurate, it doesn't mean we would make a discovery."

"Well, with the loss of the map, it is the best that we have," Camille reminded them.

Hunter looked at Kat again. "Yes, it is."

There was a tap at the door. It was Lavinia, they quickly discovered, for she didn't wait to be invited in but opened the door. "Tea, children! Do come. We wile away the next few hours and then we'll have made Rome at last!"

BETWEEN THEM, LORD AVERY, Brian and Hunter had determined their course and decided that one night in Rome would do no harm, though the closer they came, the more eager they were to reach their destination.

There were elegant hotel rooms on the Via Veneto where the ladies might have time to enjoy long soaks in baths, and where they could sleep one good night before the rocking of the train and the motion of the ship on the journey to Brindisi and then to Alexandria. Kat's room was connected to a spacious, elegant parlor, with Hunter in a room across the parlor. Lavinia was at her other side, and Emma in the smaller quarters just beyond her, with the Avery and Carlyle suites just across and the others spread out beyond them. Though she had been raised listening to a great deal of French and had certainly been tutored in the language, Italian was new to her. How she loved the sound of the language! And Rome...Rome was magnificent, with so much that was ancient.

When everyone had taken time to rest, bathe and refresh, they were to meet in the elegant parlor between Kat and Hunter's rooms. Soaking in a long bath had been delicious, but Kat was not accustomed to too much creature comfort, and so she was quickly ready. She found that Camille had brought the sketch pad to the parlor, and she opened it, viewing her drawing of the map as she remembered it. Sitting there, contemplating, she remembered a series of little waving lines and put them in. There had been symbols in certain areas, and she began to recall more and more.

There was a tap at the door and she answered it. David, Alfred and Allan stood there. "Where is the fourth Musketeer?" she asked teasingly.

"Ah, gone to fetch Lady Margaret and her father," Alfred said, striding in, smiling. She still felt somewhat uneasy when he looked at her.

"There's coffee in that samovar," she said, directing them to a tray that had been set on the end of the piano. "Delicious. Actually, I don't think I've ever had anything quite so delicious as Italian coffee." She shut up, determined that she was not going to babble because they made her nervous. Pretending that they were all friends and nothing had ever happened, however, was very difficult.

David looked at her, trying to smile, offering his usual pained gaze. She smiled in return. Meanwhile, Alfred was standing before her sketch.

"What is this?" he asked.

She walked over to close the book. "Oh, just something I'm working on, not very good," she said.

"Oh, but it is!" Alfred reached for the book. She held tight, smiling through clenched teeth.

"Really, it's not!"

"But it is! Oh, please, Kat, let us see your work!"

"Yes, do, please!" David had come over, as well. Everyone, it seemed, had a hand on the book.

She could continue wrestling for it or simply let go. She chose the latter.

They set the book back down on the table, opening to the page of the map. They all stared at it for several long seconds, then back up at her.

"That's quite incredible. You can copy anything so?" Alfred asked. "What a talent."

"That's hardly talent, I'm just copying," she murmured.

"Where is the original?" Allen asked.

"Oh, lost in a pile of paperwork, I believe," she said lightly. There was a tapping on the door again. "Excuse me," she murmured. But the door had already opened. Lavinia, of course, in a lovely blue gown that complemented her silver hair. She carried a parasol and a light traveling cape.

"Are we off to see the sights?" she demanded.

"I believe so. We should all be gathered shortly."

Margaret entered next. She, too, was in blue, and this a very soft and true shade that matched her eyes. Kat studied the design of the gown; it was elegant yet utile, with a slight hike in the front of the skirt to afford easy walking on long treks. The bodice was quite decent, yet escalloped in a trim that emphasized the slim lines of her figure.

"How lovely!" Lavinia told her.

Margaret smiled, glancing at Kat, inclining her head. "I've a personal designer. An incredibly talented young woman."

Kat grinned, acknowledging with a nod the compliment on behalf of her sister, as Lavinia began insisting that she must know the designer's name.

"Ah, Jagger, what has taken you so long!" Lavinia demanded as Lord Avery walked into the room. "I, my friend, could have seen half of the country while you were still shaving!"

"Lavinia, the point is, could half the country take seeing you?" he retorted.

Hunter came in from the side door then, calling a greeting to them all. His gaze fell on the open sketchbook, then on Kat, and a frown briefly knit his brow. He walked to the sketchbook, closing it nonchalantly. "So, what treasure shall we view in the time we have?" he queried.

Camille and Brian arrived, and the latter informed them, "We've several carriages below, but it would be best if we chose an itinerary."

"I should so love to see the Forum and the Colosseum," Camille said.

"Then, if it is agreeable to everyone," Hunter said, "that is what we shall do."

They set off in the three carriages. Kat could not keep from continually staring out the window, amazed at the sights, arches and aqueducts, ruins here and there and everywhere dispersed between newer buildings, magnificent churches. And people! Italians bustling about, as busy as bees, ladies and gentlemen in fine clothing, gypsies approaching them, babes in arms. Cafés littered the walkways, and everywhere were shouts of *"Ciao, bella!"*

When they arrived at their destination, the mighty arena rising high, guides descended upon them. Hunter made the necessary deals.

"Lavinia, do take care," Lord Avery warned. "There are nooks and crannies and steep steps all about."

"Jagger," she complained, "I am not so old that I must be coddled. But I shall be happy to look after you!"

Allan and Robert managed to secure positions at Lady Margaret's side, and Kat found herself blushing when Hunter took her arm, his eyes on her possessing a strange light, a small smile on his face. "What is it?" she asked him.

He shook his head. "It is simply pleasurable to see your utter fascination," he told her.

There were groups all about, and here and there, they met Lady so-and-so or Lord so and so, Conte this or that, as it seemed that this was a popular spot for the elite of Europe to tarry on their journeys elsewhere, or to simply spend the winter months.

Once in the giant arena with their guide showing them where animals once were kept, where the caesars sat, how the masses were arrayed, they began to wander a bit. A friend of Hunter's hailed him, and Kat did a bit of roaming about on her own.

She wasn't quite sure where she was when she came to an area with rather treacherous footing that ended in a steep incline. Once, it had been steps, but they were broken and in disorder. She crawled atop one, trying to get her bearings. Taking another step, she found herself in one of the archways, where, she was certain the guide had said, those about to enter the arena gathered. She turned and realized that David had followed her, that he was staring at her—and that he barred her way.

"Kat!" He said her name like an adulation.

"David," she replied uneasily. "This is incredible, isn't it?"

"How can you live this lie?" he asked her reproachfully.

"David, we shouldn't be here," she said uncomfortably.

"I'll do it," he said.

"I beg your pardon?"

"I'll marry you. I'll defy my father. I'll marry you. With your talents..." He trailed off, as if not certain.

They were words she had longed to hear not so long ago. But now...they sounded strange. Out of place.

"David, this isn't the time—"

"Give me a chance!" He started toward her.

"David, are you mad? Hunter will tear you to pieces!"

David lifted his chin. "Hunter! The swaggering soldier, great man of the world! Well, he is forgetting that I am a Turnberry and that my father is one of the most powerful men in the country!"

"David, we're far from your father now," she told him softly.

"Kat, I know that this is a farce. There is nothing wrong in anything I have said or done. To be the mistress of such a man as myself is certainly respectable. But as I have said… Kat, you have so much strength, ability, and with you by my side… Oh, Kat, let me touch you, let me show you…"

Instinctively, she backed away. He followed. They were caught precariously on a step, with the incline just behind them. The sun was nearly gone, and the shadow of the archway left them in near darkness.

"David—" she began, looking into his eyes. She broke off, hearing a strange scraping sound. Looking up, she saw that one of the massive structural stones just above them seemed to be teetering.

It was going to fall!

"Watch out!" she screamed, clutching him, dragging him toward her. The effort caused her to topple backward. They both fell from the precarious step into the incline.

Chapter 12

BRIAN WAS HIGH ATOP ONE of the tiers with Hunter, watching as the Italian guides brought their caches of tourists about, when he asked, "Do you seriously think that there is far more than meets the eye going on here?"

Hunter shrugged. "I don't know. It would be quite bizarre. I can't imagine any reason that someone should want David Turnberry dead. But if it *is* so, would it likely be one of us? Still, Camille's map did disappear. I can't imagine that the map would do anyone any good if they weren't actually out in the desert." He shook his head. "And now, I'm afraid, everyone will know that Kat has managed to make a reproduction of it; the young men arrived this evening after she had been working, and they have all seen it. But to think that there is really something afoot here boggles the imagination."

"Mmm," Brian murmured. "I was speaking with Lavinia earlier, and she is really quite fascinating."

"Oh, she's a pip! But what does my dear great-aunt have to do with any of this? The only real possibility of anyone wanting anyone out of the way would be Lady Daws—she'd be glad to be rid herself of Lord Alfred. But she isn't with us. And there's been nothing in the years past to suggest that she might actually be a murderess. Besides, it's David being targeted, apparently. Where do we look? Lord Avery? Doubtful. Margaret? More than doubtful."

"I think that perhaps we should talk more with Lavinia. She knows everyone and everything," Brian said. "And she was telling me that it was, indeed, the scandal of the year when Isabella became Lady Daws. There were those who thought that she drugged the man to get him to marry her. And there were those, as well, who claimed that she had been his mistress for years, that she had known him before he married his first wife."

"But how would that put David Turnberry in danger?" Hunter said. "I see no logic."

"There must be logic somewhere. We simply haven't figured it out yet."

"If there is anything to figure out," Hunter reminded him.

It was then that they heard the scream.

"Kat!" Hunter cried, recognizing her voice immediately—and hearing the panic and desperation in it.

He began to run.

KAT AND DAVID TUMBLED over and over, and at last crashed into the wall at the base of the incline. He was on top of her, terror in his eyes.

But they were alive. And because they had rolled, rather than pitching straight down, they were mussed and bruised, but they were not, thank God, broken.

"Kat!" David held on to her, shaking.

He was heavy, pressing her down. And, surely, they made a less-than-innocent picture.

"David, off, please!" she begged, certain that her scream must have alerted the others. It had, indeed. Footsteps sounded above them.

Reaching the incline first, Camille called out a startled "Oh!" And came to a dead standstill.

Brian swept by his wife, carefully bending to walk down the steep incline, followed by Hunter. Luckily, Brian arrived first. He helped David up, and Hunter was free to grasp Kat's hands and pull her to her feet. She didn't at all like the look in his eyes when they met hers, but to his credit his first words were, "Are you all right?"

She nodded.

"What in God's name happened?" Brian demanded.

"A stone fell," Kat explained.

"Where were you when it fell?"

She pointed. The stone had broken into many pieces.

"We'll return to the hotel immediately," Hunter said.

"But there's so much more to see!" Kat protested.

Brian was already helping David up to the walkway. Hunter shook his head at Kat and said, "Not for you."

"But..."

Her protest was to no avail. She wasn't sure that her feet were on the ground at all as he brought her up to the walkway. Camille and Margaret made quite a fuss over her. Lavinia studied her and the structure where they had been, and the fallen stone. "How very, very odd!" she said.

"We'll be returning to the hotel," Hunter said flatly.

"Hunter, please," Kat said. "We have such a short time here. There are so many more wonders to behold."

"They're hard to behold at night, and it's nearly dark," Hunter said curtly.

"Perhaps the others would like to continue sightseeing," Kat suggested.

Again to no avail.

"Oh, there's been quite enough excitement for the day!" Margaret pointed out. She was at David's side, briskly slapping dust from his clothing. "Are you really both quite all right?" she asked anxiously.

"Fine," Kat said.

"Ever so slightly sore!" David said, offering Margaret one of his sweet smiles. Kat lowered her head, biting her lips.

He certainly knew how and when to smile, and just how to appear courageous and wounded at the same time.

"I have certainly had enough for the afternoon," Lavinia remarked. "But then again, children, I have seen these wonders many times. The world is such a truly magnificent place. Truly, I think that more travel should be required of children."

"Not all children can afford to travel, Vinnie," Lord Avery said, shaking his head.

"Then you should arrange for more to do so, Jagger!" Lavinia retorted.

"We can argue all night," Hunter said. "Kat needs to return to the hotel."

"We shall all go, and that is that!" Brian said. "Any objections?"

"Let's all go back together," Robert Stewart said. "Maybe we university men will step out on our own a bit later. Find Professor Atworthy—he's supposed to be out sketching somewhere."

"He won't be sketching in the dark," Hunter said.

"I believe he means that we free young gentlemen should do a bit of cutting up," Allan said, clearing his throat and laughing.

"You young gentlemen do as you wish!" Margaret told him. "I'm going to see to it that poor David has a lovely dinner and then is off to bed."

Kat caught a glance that David cast Allan's way.

There was a smug look of triumph to it. Something inside her made a little thud. She realized that she was coming to know him far better than she had dared hoped.

And that she was not at all sure she liked what she was learning. Still, she couldn't help but be worried for him.

"Let's move," Hunter said.

Minutes later they were back in the carriages. Back at the hotel, Emma, who had not been interested in the wonders of Rome, met them in the hallway and was aghast at the dust covering Kat. She took her under her wing, and once again, Kat had the luxury of a long soak in the bath. Emma's perfumed body salts smelled divine, and the suds were soft and luxurious on her flesh. She had to admit that the hot water felt wonderful, and that it did soothe the soreness in her muscles.

When she emerged, Emma was there, clucking with concern, ready to wrap her in a soft and elegant velvet robe. "Now, I've had a nice supper brought up for you, and after you have eaten, I want you to get some rest! Goodness, excitement does seem to follow you!" Emma declared, and left her.

After she had finished the delicious supper of pasta and veal, Kat lay down on the bed, but she hadn't the least desire to rest. She got up, still wearing the robe, paced the room a bit, nervous, wondering what Hunter thought, then she grew angry, aware that she had done nothing wrong, and she carefully cracked open the door that separated her room from the parlor and Hunter's quarters.

He was there, staring into the fire, sipping a brandy. He glanced up at her instantly. "Were you hoping I wasn't here?" he queried.

"Don't be ridiculous."

"Well, you opened the door. Come in."

"I think not."

"Are you now afraid of me?"

"No. I'm not afraid of you—or anyone."

"Maybe you should be."

"Afraid of you?"

He smiled slightly. "Maybe."

She stepped into the parlor, closing the door to her room behind her.

"Well, then," she said lightly, "let's have it out. With you, it seems, I am always at fault somehow."

"At fault? We had an agreement," he told her sharply.

"It was an accident!"

"Yes, but it's curious that you were involved in it."

She strode over to him. "I was exploring the ruin, and that was all."

"With David?" he asked politely.

"We were all at the ruins together."

"Odd, how you managed to be at the same place as he was."

"I was not arm in arm with him!"

"But you did just happen to be together."

"Yes! We just happened to be there together."

"Ah. And then a stone fell," Hunter said skeptically. "And once again, you were there, to rescue the love of your life. Or vice versa. And you managed to tumble to safety in each other's arms."

She ignored his tone as a sudden realization filled her. She gasped. Only just now did she see how close either she or David or both had come to dying.

She clutched Hunter's arm. "No...no! Stones don't just fall. Hunter, don't you see? I was right. David Turnberry is in danger!"

Hunter snorted with disgust, pulling his arm from her hold.

"Hunter, I am telling you—"

"Oh, yes, you've fallen out of your blind and absolute adoration for the man, and we're merely on a quest to keep him alive!"

She stared at him. "Think what you like!"

"He is still harboring delusions that you will sleep with him, become his mistress."

She kept silent for a moment, staring at him. He was definitely in a mood. And she surely did not want him finding out that he was very near the truth.

"You're not being at all cordial and I don't believe I care to speak with you anymore this evening," she told him.

She turned to walk back to her room. He caught her by the arm, swinging her hard against him, his grip firm on her arm, the length of her body pressed tightly to his. There was serious menace in his eyes, and a heated energy in his frame that seemed almost combustible.

"You don't care to speak to me?"

"Hunter...please!"

"How much of a fool do you take me for?" he demanded.

"Why must you ever assume the worst of me?" she cried in return.

"Because you are ready to sell yourself, body and soul, to a young fool who wouldn't know what to do with you if he had you!"

"Well, Sir Hunter, everyone cannot have your vast experience in life and love!" she mocked angrily.

"Perhaps it's not so much a matter of experience as it is a simple matter of real desire and passion in life," he returned.

"Ah, yes, you know life. There is no indecision for you, no uncertainty. There is nothing for you to fear, for your life is your own! There are not parents, loved ones, those who hold a hand in your future."

"The future, for any of us, is what we are willing to make of it!"

"Easy for you to say, and easy for you to do!"

"Easy? I had not his life of luxury. I was lucky to get into the queen's forces as an officer, and lucky to fight and survive, and indeed, yes, make of my life what I would!"

"With a princess for an aunt," she mocked.

"And you came from such a bitter place? A father who worked that you and your sister might do well?"

"That is no reason to mock David so!" she defended.

"Don't you see yet that you don't want him?"

"And I should want you?" she cried. Whatever anger or frustration was ruling her, she did not know. She sought only to make him understand, yet what, exactly, it was that she wanted him to understand, she wasn't entirely sure. She meant to be mocking only, to touch him, withdraw, to tell him that he was the only man a woman could want. "You!" she said scornfully again, and pressed herself harder against him, rising on her toes and pressing her lips to his.

At the very least, she took him completely by surprise.

But if she meant to play a dangerous game, he was willing to pick up the gauntlet.

She had begun the taunting kiss. He would see it through.

She had pressed herself against him; he put an arm around her back, fingers splaying across her spine. His left hand cupped the base of her skull, fingertips spread wide and caressing above her nape. His lips forced hers open, and when his tongue invaded the tender recesses of her mouth, it was as if a volcano had erupted within her, and she near melted with the heat. Her limbs seemed to grow weak, and she knew that what she had started was no longer something within her control at all, and that it should be stopped, had to be stopped....

Yet his tongue seemed to thrust deep into the core and essence of her being, and stopping was an impossibility.

And his hands were moving. She was still caught to his hard body, but his fingers caressed the length of her hair, teased along her shoulders, stroked her collarbone beneath the neckline of the robe. Brushed her flesh. A touch so light, she ached to feel it further, to know it better.

The robe parted, and the touch, so gentle, grew bolder, yet still at such a subtle tease that she ached to feel more of it. Then his fingers rounded over the swell of her breast, and thumbs played erotically on her nipples before he cupped the weight of them again. She was barely aware when his lips left hers, when they followed the trail of magic down her throat, pressed at her collarbone, formed over her breast, above and below, so erotic, his tongue then taunting, teasing, playing, where his fingertips had tread so lightly.

She gasped softly, fingers digging into his arms, body trembling throughout its length. She wasn't sure when the robe fell away, and she was barely aware that she was standing naked, that he had lowered himself, that his hands molded her buttocks and that his kiss then teased the flesh of her abdomen.

She could scarcely stand. It was an intoxication she had never imagined, never expected, and it felt simply as if she were on fire, seething....

And then, abruptly, he stood, bringing her robe with him and setting it loosely around her shoulders. "Miss Adair, either I am a better lover, or..."

It was the tone of the *or.* The implication. She flushed with humiliation, not even the great Hunter MacDonald could respond swiftly enough to stop her hand.

The slap of its impact against his cheek was loud, seeming to echo between them. He arched a brow.

"Since you do seem to run into the Right Honorable David Turnberry and accidents of the absurd at every turn," he said, "I believe you should stay in tonight—my *dear.*" And he left her standing there by the mantel, the luxurious robe that had given her such pleasure falling off her shoulders.

HIS BONES SEEMED TO HURT, his blood to boil, his muscles to burn, and there was nothing else to do but leave, escape, run away as fast as he could. He was furious with himself, furious with her, and so knotted and torn within that he was certain he would shortly explode.

He walked out to the street, down the Via Veneto, then walked and walked, and the next thing he knew, he was at the Spanish Steps. And he still kept walking.

At the next piazza, he noticed that one of the old, beautiful churches had a sign out front. "St. Philip's High Episcopal Church."

Interesting, he mused. The hordes of Englishmen and Americans had brought one Anglican house of worship to the very place of the pope's stronghold. As he walked by, a priest came hurrying out, preoccupied. He walked into Hunter.

"Scusi, scusi!"

"It's all right, Father."

The priest looked at him, frowned. "An Englishman."

"Yes."

"And you look in need of guidance."

Hunter shook his head. "I'm afraid guidance is not what I need at this moment."

The priest cocked his head. "You're Sir Hunter MacDonald."

"Yes. How did you know?"

"I've seen your picture in the papers. On your way to Egypt, are you, sir?"

"Yes."

"You look heavy laden. Confession is good for the soul, even though we be Anglicans."

"I think not, but I appreciate the offer."

The fellow offered his hand. "Father Philbin. Should you need anything, the rectory is the old building there." He pointed. "Say, even if you just wish a good pot of English tea, don't hesitate."

"Thank you, Father," Hunter said, and moved on. He was certain that in his current surly mood, no priest would want to hear anything he had to say. His long strides ate up the distance. Finally, at last, he stopped at a café, ordered a drink and took a seat at one of the sidewalk tables.

He had gone mad, he thought. He had simply gone mad. And now, with his blood cooling, he turned a bitter smile on himself. The situation with Kat was, truly, no less than he deserved, and if he was a madman now, well, the madness had begun the first moment he had seen her, and the insanity had grown slowly on a daily basis, especially since he had decided that he would give her every opportunity to go after what she wanted…

And what she wanted wasn't him. But she was as passionate and fierce as her fiery hair promised, and he could have completed what he'd started, seduced her, had all that he desired and won the game he hadn't even realized that he was playing.

And been no better than the college boys he mocked.

"Senor?"

He looked up. Ah, one of Rome's illustrious ladies of the night. More courtesan than prostitute, for she was elegantly dressed and her jewels looked real. She was young, he thought, but practiced. "*Per piacere… Oh! Mi dispiace*—you are Inglese!"

He nodded. How easy to smile, he thought, purchase drinks, bargain delicately and with innuendo, as one did with such a creature. How easy to drown oneself in alcohol, walk into the darkness, where one could with the mind's eye only.

"Yes, an Englishman, *signorina*."

She pouted, made the usual pretense at respectability. "I'm awaiting a friend. I thought I might join you at your table as I do so." Her eyes were endlessly dark, her hair lustrous, her lips colored a pure bloodred. She smiled, a pleasant smile, assessing him all the while, he thought, and determining that he would not be a bad trick at all, for he was assuredly with funds and possessed of all his teeth.

For a moment, he entertained the idea. Good God, if only not to feel so wretchedly frustrated!

But then something caused him to shake his head. "I should be happy to buy you a drink, and most assuredly, the table is yours. But I'm afraid I have to be going."

He rose, signaling to the waiter, drawing bills from his wallet.

"Must you leave, truly?" she implored.

Darkness would do him no good, he thought. Nothing could still what lay behind the facade.

"Yes, I must go," he said. He left the money and began his walk back. A long one, but reflexive.

The hotel was quiet when he returned, and he realized that the hour was very late. Nevertheless, he tapped on her door, ready to apologize.

The door swung open. She was clad to the throat in the most virginal nightgown imaginable, and over it was a concealing cotton robe.

"What?" she said.

"We'll be boarding the train around ten in the morning."

"I'm quite aware of that."

"As long as you are aware."

She closed the door in his face. He took a deep breath, tapped again.

The door flew open.

"I need to say—"

"No!" She was clearly furious. "There's nothing you need to say that I care to hear. You are the most despicable excuse for a human being ever to crawl up from the slime, and I loathe you, do you understand? The engagement can be off as of tomorrow!"

She was ready to slam the door again. He caught her arm, backing her into the room. Despite his plan to be a gentleman, he was glad at the alarm he saw in her eyes.

"No. I entered into this fiasco of a charade because you appeared in my bedroom—pleading! It does not end, and you will cope with what has occurred and learn from it!"

She glared at him, jaw locked, struggling to wrench free her arm.

It was then that he felt something odd, something that seemed to move over his feet. He went rigid, hardly daring to breathe.

"I—" she began.

"Shh!" he warned.

"But—"

"Stop, don't move. I beg of you."

He didn't look down. He simply knew.

It had passed him and was moving toward her. Her ankles and feet were bare.

She felt it when it touched her. Her eyes widened. Her lips parted just slightly. And she locked gazes with Hunter, fighting the urge to scream.

"Still," he mouthed. "Be still."

And so she was. Seconds seemed like eons.

She mouthed a single word to him, a question. "Snake?"

He nodded.

She swallowed hard, her eyes locked with his. Waiting.

More eons passed. And then, from the corner of his eyes, he could see the creature, slithering on across the room. He caught her up, swung her round, and made her stand on a chair. Then he strode toward the snake.

Snakes were certainly some of the quickest creatures he had come across in his life, but at least he had come to know them well. His feet were encased in leather, and he dared to slam his foot down hard right behind the head of the creature. He did so with all his weight and strength; a snake was powerful, sheer muscle, and if he didn't strike properly…

But he had. The creature couldn't rise, couldn't flare. It tried to open its jaw for an attack. The mouth worked. The eyes glazed. But then it died, the jaws still attempting to part.

"Oh!" He heard the expulsion of her breath.

She was about to climb down off the chair when he ordered, "No! Stay right there!" Silently, she obeyed.

Then, methodically, foot by foot, he went through the room. He tore through the bath things, towels, linens, soaps. At last, satisfied, he extended a hand to help her down from the chair, then they sat together on the foot of the bed. He didn't touch her.

She nodded to the place across the room. "It's…a cobra?" she asked. "But…we're still in Rome. Do they have such creatures here?"

He looked up at her. "No."

"Then…" Her voice faded. After a moment she said, "Brian Stirling's parents…were killed by asps, weren't they?"

She was trying very hard to sound matter-of-fact. There was a tremor in her voice nonetheless.

"Yes."

"But…the killer was discovered."

"Yes."

"So…you think that someone might be trying to…kill me? Why?"

"I don't know."

There was suddenly a firm knock at the door. Hunter got up, walked to open it.

In nightcap and robe, Lord Avery stood there, managing to look dignified and outraged despite his attire.

"Sir Hunter!" he said, his tone regal in its condemnation. "This, sir, this, I will not allow! The child's father has entrusted her to my care. You may have announced an engagement, sir, but that gives you no right—"

"Lord Avery, there was a snake in the room," Hunter explained.

"Bah! There are no snakes in such a fine hotel. Besides, this is Rome, not Cairo!"

Hunter walked over to the corpse of the asp, picked it up gingerly and presented it to Lord Avery. Lord Avery paled. "It…it should not be here," he sputtered.

"No," Hunter agreed.

"Why, Brian's father and mother…"

"Yes," Hunter said. "Lord Avery, I would deeply appreciate that you do not mention this to anyone."

"Sir Hunter! The only way a snake could have been in this room…"

"Yes."

"Then the girl is in danger!"

"I rather believe that," Hunter said.

"Excuse me!" Kat said softly. "I am here, and I am not deaf!"

Lord Avery turned to stare at Kat. "Forgive me, my dear." Then he looked at Hunter again. Lord Avery was simply not from a generation when young women made decisions on their own. "She must be sent packing on the first train home."

"No!" Kat protested.

Hunter didn't so much as look her way. He smiled at Lord Avery. "Let's sleep on it, shall we?" he asked. "There is little we can do right now."

"We should be calling the police!"

Hunter shook his head. "The police will not be able to solve this, and we both know it. There is nothing more we can do tonight."

"The situation must be handled," Lord Avery insisted.

"And so it shall be," Hunter promised.

At last, Lord Avery harrumphed and went out into the hall. Hunter closed the door behind him and leaned against it for a moment, then straightened. "Get dressed," he told Kat.

"Get dressed? But it's the middle of the night!" she said. "And...and I can't go home. Really. Please. I have to see this through."

"God knows, you're so charming to me, I'm sure I would cry every day if you left," he murmured dryly.

"I...oh, I can't say I'm sorry! You were wretched."

"Be that as it may, how far are you willing to go to stay on this expedition?"

"What do you mean?"

"Are you really ready to sell your soul?" he asked softly.

"But...I can't go home. I must go forward."

"Then you'll have to be willing to do as I say," he told her flatly. "So get dressed. I'll be back."

He left her room, then strode down the hall, hesitating before knocking at the door to Brian's suite. A few moments later, obviously awakened from a deep sleep, Brian answered.

"What is it?" he heard Camille ask sleepily from the bed.

Hunter looked straight at Brian. "There was a snake in Kat's room."

Brian stiffened as if he had turned to stone. Hunter saw the dark fury that crossed his face.

But Brian was controlled, exhaling on a long breath. "So. It begins again."

"I think it began before we left."

"The girl is so vulnerable!" Brian said softly. "Do you have a plan?"

"Well, not really a plan. But I believe there is something I can do. And I need your help."

Camille, hair wild about her lovely face, was at Brian's side then, wrapped in a robe. "We are ever here, Hunter, when you need us."

"I'm afraid it entails getting dressed and going out."

"Whatever for?" Camille asked.

"I believe I know," Brian murmured.

"Excuse me, then," Hunter said. "I have a lot of things to do with very little time." And he hurried away to make the necessary arrangements.

Chapter 13

AS COMMANDED, KAT dressed quickly. She was barely decent when he was back, rapping sharply on the door.

"I'm not quite—"

"Doesn't matter. Open up."

She did so, struggling with the back buttons on her shirt. "I told you—"

"Turn around."

She did so, standing very stiffly, aware of the brush of his fingers against her flesh as he finished the task for her.

He spun her around, giving her a critical appraisal.

"I haven't had time to do my hair," she said irritably.

"Just brush it. Have you a cloak or jacket handy?" She grabbed her cloak. "Let's go," he said.

She couldn't have protested. He was on a mission. He took her elbow, escorting her out. To her surprise, Brian and Camille met them in the hallway.

"Where is the snake?" Brian asked.

"In the bottom drawer of Kat's dresser," Hunter said.

Kat gave a start. She hadn't seen him put it there.

Hunter looked at her sharply. "There will be no further word about it, Kat, do you understand?"

"I live to obey," she murmured.

The gaze he cast her was anything but pleased.

A carriage was waiting for them at the doorway to the hotel. Hunter did not ride inside with the Stirlings and Kat, but hopped up with Ethan, saying that he was going to have to point out the route since he wasn't exactly sure where they were going.

When the doors were closed and she was in the carriage facing Camille and Brian, Kat asked softly, "Do you know what we're doing? Where we're going?"

"I'm afraid not," Camille said. "And you don't know, either?"

Kat shook her head.

The carriage came to a halt. The door opened. Hunter reached for Kat. Camille and Brian followed. Kat looked up, puzzled.

They had come to a church. To her amazement, Emma Johnson came running out the front door to greet them. "I woke Father Philbin, and he's waiting inside. And he's quite agreeable. He said he had a feeling that he'd be seeing you again, Sir Hunter."

"Um...are we *praying* for no more incidents along the way?" Kat inquired.

Hunter offered her a dark scowl. "We're getting married," he said impatiently.

She froze. The world around her seemed to spin, the air being filled with shards of glass.

Married!

She had been a dreamer all her life. Imagining scenes in her mind of what might be, seeing them as they should be. Married. Of course, she had always thought that she would be married. Not even because it was expected of a woman, and not because the role of wife was one she felt that she had to play. She had dreamed of marriage as the ultimate romance. Of being with someone day in and day out, loving, being loved, cherishing…

And a proposal! It should have come from a lover on bended knee, his eyes alight and on fire with love and desire, his words impassioned as he pleaded. Then again, she had started this charade. But it hadn't been real. It had been expedient. A means to an end.

She stared at Hunter, unable to move or to speak.

"We can't keep the fellow up all night," he said impatiently.

Expedient. A means to an end.

"We'll run on in, see what papers need to be signed," Brian said.

"Come, Emma, introduce us to the priest, please," Camille said.

Kat stood on the beautifully tiled walk before the church, still staring at Hunter. "You…you don't have to do this," she said.

He shrugged, impatient, if anything. "You pretty much agreed that you were willing to sell your soul to remain on this trip. So…here it is. I can't leave you alone because you seem to be in danger every time I turn my back. Even though he saw the snake, Lord Avery will soon have apoplexy from the thought of my rushing into your room time and time again. So I must be with you. This is the only solution I can find."

"Yes, but, Hunter…an engagement is one thing. It can be broken. I can't do this to you. I can't force you into such a sham!"

"Marriages end, as well, I'm afraid. I increasingly hear of couples divorcing. Not pleasant, I admit, but they do happen.

Of course, the scandal is terrible, but far less worrisome, I think, than the loss of one's life."

"But still...Hunter, honestly, I am not afraid for myself. I came from nothing...and, well, even if my father does become very famous, the daughter of an artist doing something slightly scandalous will be almost expected. But for you...well, I cannot, will not, ask you to live such a facade."

"When you walk into that church, it will not be a facade," he said starkly. "I will not risk your life, even if you are foolish enough to do so. There is no way I will return to England and your father without producing you, live and well."

She was not sure why she felt so ridiculously close to tears. It was just that she had simply...dreamed of so much more. He had proved himself to her in so many ways, so many times.

But...

She'd wanted love. Undying devotion. Tenderness, the loving, the cherishing. And he was so cold!

But then, so be it, she thought. And she shivered suddenly. She remembered too clearly his touch, the feel of him. And as she came to life and started down the path, anxious that he not see her face at that moment, she realized that she was truly in danger now. She had been so close to him, she had come to be so accustomed to him, that she hadn't realized that he had been stealing into her soul.

And if she became closer to him still, she was bound to lose her heart.

He would never believe that, even if she tried to articulate her feelings. She had set out on this journey to capture the heart and hand of David Turnberry. Hunter would never believe that she had come to know that she didn't love the man in the least, and that he had been right all along—if she could have David, she wouldn't want him.

He caught up to her in front of the church.

"I shall assume that this means you are agreeable to the plan?" he said.

"I will be an excellent wife," she assured him. "An excellent wife and a perfect assistant," she vowed.

To her horror, he laughed at her passionate avowal. "Ah, yes, Miss Adair. You will ride well, you will learn all about Egypt, you will be perfect. I have no doubt. Let's do this thing, shall we?"

She gritted her teeth, willing the tears that threatened not to sting her eyes. She walked into the church where the priest was chatting with Camille, Brian and Emma.

"Young people!" Emma said, shaking her head. "This should have been huge, Hunter! We should have planned the wedding, had a gorgeous dress for such a lovely bride."

"Emma, you can throw a huge reception once we are home," Hunter said, not unkindly. "Father Philbin, if you'll tell us where to stand, what to do?"

"Certainly. The two of you, here before me. Lord Carlyle, here, to the side, Lady Carlyle, by the bride. And, ah, there's your man! Ethan, good fellow, next to Emma there. Four witnesses on the license, lovely. Now…"

Father Philbin had a fine voice. The solemn words he spoke in the ceremony sounded utterly heartfelt. There was no music. No sound of tears from loved ones watching. There was no scent of flowers. Just the words. So well spoken. And to Kat and Hunter, so void of meaning!

She answered at the appropriate times. And so did Hunter. Her voice was as sure and strong as his.

As...cold and businesslike.

Another bargain struck!

A second ring slid onto her finger.

"And you may now kiss the bride!" Father Philbin announced, smiling.

Kat wasn't sure what she had expected. Another of Hunter's deep and reckless embraces, she supposed.

His lips barely brushed hers. "We need to sign the license," he said.

She nodded.

And it was done.

Perhaps no one else noted the almost hostile current between the bride and groom. Emma was still clucking over the lack of ceremony, Ethan was sighing as he listened. Father Philbin was cheerfully explaining to the Lord and Lady of Carlyle where certain wedding practices had originated. "You see, in the good old days, say, the time of Henry III and all his offspring, weddings were held in June—because baths were customarily taken in May. The bride and groom would not carry *too* great an odor! But that's where the bouquet came in. The bride carried flowers for the scent. The more flowers, the better their scent hid hers!" He yawned suddenly. "Ah, the hour! My blessings on your ventures, Sir Hunter, Lady Katherine."

Kat managed to thank the priest. When she was back in the carriage, she sat next to Hunter, aware of him, but silent, still in shock. Neither Brian nor Camille tried to make small talk. When they reached the hotel, Camille gave her a warm hug and a kiss on the cheek. "Best wishes, Kat!" she said.

Then she and Brian disappeared into their suite, and Hunter, key in hand, was opening the door to her room.

Their room?

She started to tremble, but had no intention of letting him see it. She slipped on in, but then stood in the center of the room, not at all sure what to do.

She was spared having to make any decision.

"Get some sleep," Hunter said curtly. He was striding about, once more, searching the room. He disappeared out into the parlor.

She bit her lip, then fled into the bathroom, changing into her nightgown. He had not returned to the room. She quickly slid beneath the covers.

He returned and doused the lights. He was still fully dressed. She felt his weight move the mattress as he lay down on the other side of the bed.

He was not touching her.

Nor did he touch her through what remained of the night.

THE NEXT MORNING, they boarded the train that would take them to Brindisi and the ship.

By noon, Kat was quite exhausted by the exclamations of surprise and congratulations that came her way.

Lord Avery seemed to think that Hunter had merely done the right thing, like a military man, followed the only option that made sense. Margaret was giddy, thinking it the most romantic thing in the world. Lavinia seemed to survey it all with a jaundiced eye. Allan, Robert and Alfred exchanged smirks and shrugged. David spent the day giving her sad glances and quite frankly managed to look as if he had eaten something bad. His look didn't impress her at all; she had seen his act for Lady Margaret the night before.

"Quite something, an elopement in the middle of the night," David said. She and Hunter were seated across from him and Margaret in the club car.

"Well," Hunter said, slipping his arm tightly around her and tangling his fingers suggestively by her throat, "I could bear it no longer. Night after night...so close."

"Oh, but it is so...romantic!" Margaret applauded for what seemed like the thousandth time.

"Don't even consider the same action, daughter!" her father warned from the next table.

From across the aisle, Professor Atworthy wagged a finger. "You will not forget your art or forget that art is work!"

"Imagine, Hunter married at last. And a good thing, since you might well be carrying the family title one day!" Lavinia noted.

"Aunt Lavinia, I have never believed that a title is what makes a man," Hunter said.

"No, but a title is most convenient!" Brian said, and his words were followed by laughter.

Kat merely wished that they would talk about something else. Anything else. But they didn't. By the time they reached Brindisi, she was ready to scream.

The ship did not leave until the following morning. Their accommodations for the night were at an old castle that had been renovated into an inn. The dining room was huge, an old great hall, and the food and service were excellent. But by dinner's end, Kat had a dull headache. She was nervous, waiting for Hunter to suggest that they go up to their room. But he seemed happy to linger where they were, sharing brandy with the men, listening to the trio that played.

When he was engaged in conversation, she made her escape. Their room, in one of the towers, was a suite, really, expansive and luxurious with a sitting room and bedroom. The bedroom had a massive canopied bed and an enormous fireplace. There was a bath, beautifully appointed, with gold fixtures. She decided to have a long, hot soak in it.

When she emerged, Hunter still had not returned. Exhausted and irritated, she climbed into bed. Hours later, she realized that she had dozed, and he was still not beside her. She rose and carefully tiptoed to the door leading to the parlor. He was there, standing tall and reflective by the fire, a snifter of brandy in his hand.

He looked up. "Did I wake you? I apologize."

"You didn't wake me."

"Well, then. Is there something else?"

"I feel that I am keeping you from your own place," she said.

"How is that?"

She waved a hand awkwardly. "I...well, I know we made a bargain. I just—"

He laughed suddenly. "I see. You lie there, nervous, not knowing just what is expected, is that it?"

She let out a long expulsion of air. "Yes. I have said that I will be a good wife."

He walked over to her. Something about his approach made her want to back away. "I know that you will be."

"There is no reason that you cannot sleep in the bed," she said.

"How very kind of you!" He touched her face with the palm of his hand, then tilted her chin upward. "Believe me, Kat, I did not marry you with any thought of a chaste life! Let me assure you that I have made you my wife in every sense of the word, and at my convenience and interest, I do intend to claim every right that is mine."

At his convenience and interest!

She did step away now, eyes flashing. "Indeed? Well, sir, I shall be happy to tell you if and when my 'convenience and interest' align with yours!"

He cocked his head slightly, his eyes like blue-black daggers of challenge. "Let's see…we're both aware of your infatuation with another man. We're both aware that you will avoid that man, because I could tear the two of you limb from limb and, mark you, find a way to get away with it. I am extremely proud, vain, even, sadly, possessive. There is no pretense between us. Do I want you, desire you? Yes. Do you want me, desire me? Well, I am not David Turnberry, but that doesn't matter. You will be a good wife. Will you be dreaming that I am him? Again, it doesn't matter. And so, these are the truths."

"Then why don't we just get it over with?" she demanded angrily.

He arched his brows, and she thought that he was angry, but he burst into laughter. "Whether you are in love or not, my dear, the act of love can be a rather beautiful thing. Not something that someone does as quickly as possible, like sweeping ashes from a grate!"

She bristled at his laughter. She wasn't sure what infuriated her more, his laughter or the fact that she never had the last word.

And so she merely lifted her head, giving him what she hoped was a completely disdainful gaze, then made an about-face and headed back to the bedroom.

He had seemed so lacking in interest that she was taken by surprise when he caught up with her, catching her arm, swinging her around to face him. His eyes were dark, soulless pits, it seemed, and she had never seen his jaw so rigid. A lock of dark hair hung low over his forehead and her heart skipped a beat. He was both exceedingly attractive and frightening.

"Now," he said.

"Now?"

"It seems a most convenient time and I am very interested!" His voice was low and husky, the heat of his breath warming her cheeks.

"It's not convenient for me and I am not interested!" she informed him regally.

He smiled. "And I am so sorry, because I don't give a damn," he said.

And then he kissed her again. There was no hesitance about him now, and the ravaging insinuation of his tongue gave no doubt of all that he intended to do with his body. She gasped softly beneath the assault, pressed her hands against him and felt the constriction of the muscles in his chest. The pressure of his lips lightened and coerced, seduced slowly, the tip of his tongue made a gentle loop over her lips. And then it plunged again, and she was aware that his hands had moved, that she was standing on her own, and that the white cotton and lace ribbons of her gown were being pulled and loosened. The great white sleeves slipped from her shoulders and his lips fell on the flesh there. She clung to him, feeling the sensation sweep into her again, weakness in her knees, the trembling of her body. His lips slid along her throat as his fingers manipulated the gown, sending it to the floor. She stood in the pool of white cotton and lace, and shivered, instinctively moving toward him for his warmth, aware of his hands then sliding erotically down the length of her back, curving over the bare flesh of her buttocks, rising again, pressing her hips ever closer to his own. He stepped back, inches from her, allowing his hands and lips to move and seek and touch. Her lungs failed to work when he teased her breasts, when his lips settled there, coaxing, caressing, his tongue wetting.

He turned her so that he was behind her. His mouth was at her nape, his fingers tangled into her hair, then his hands slid down, over her rib cage, then lower and lower on her abdomen. He had moved again, and she wasn't sure how or when, but his mouth with its tender caress eased along her hip, bathed her naval, plunged below. The shock of his next intimacy brought the breath she had held cascading from her body in a gasp; her fingers locked on to his shoulders, then his hair. The sensations that had stolen so swiftly and boldly into every cell of her body seemed to be swirling to an electric eddy. Words formed on her lips, faded without sound. She arched in a strange agony of sweet and scalding need, gasping still, desperate to move, afraid she would fall. At last she cried out, heedless of the sound, as it seemed that light exploded and pulsed throughout her, stealing strength, stealing sanity.

There was little time to begin to fathom the feeling, for he was up, and she was somehow limp in his arms, eyes closed. She was suddenly filled with the memory of what had been just *before.* He was a practiced lover. Excellent at this act that had brought her such sheer ecstasy. For her, there had been a change in the world, in the way the sun moved, that night came.

And for him? Was it just a diversion?

She watched him as he laid her down on the white expanse of the bed. She trembled as she remembered her one quick view of the man naked. He had removed his clothing with such haste and climbed so quickly on top of her that she had little for a second view. Yet in those brief moments her trembling was renewed and a single word ricocheted in her mind. *Magnificent.*

She felt the weight of his body on her, between her thighs, the burn of his mouth, hungry now, against her throat. And the first, hard thrust of him. Pain ripped through her, and she cried out, but he was quickly whispering to her, something, she knew not what, bathing her face and throat with gentle kisses...and then it seemed she was liquid again and there was a rampant force, and she was clinging desperately to him. She was aware of every constriction of his muscles, the force of his body in hers, and aware that she was again feeling the exquisite rise of something within herself. She couldn't breathe, then she breathed too quickly. Her heart stopped, then it thundered. His flesh against hers was damp, searing, the very world was rocking explosively, violently...

Again, she cried out in a gasp of ecstasy. She bit her lip quickly, gasping in a huge gulp of air, aware of him still inside her, the force of him, the weight of him...the sheets, the dim light in the room from the single lamp on the table, and from the dying fire in the hearth. She lay shaking, trembling, stunned by the cataclysmic nature of the night.

He eased his weight from her and lay at her side. She did not open her eyes. His arm came round her, cradling her to him. She thought he would speak, for the world had changed so that words must be said...

"Good night, my dear," he murmured.

And that was all.

She lay awake.

Diversion.

She had never felt such splendor. And yet...

Tears burned her eyes.

She tried very hard not to move, not once, during the long night. Though perhaps she inched against him. For she was half asleep when she realized that she was feeling that sweet, searing, molten sense of arousal again. His lips teased her back. Down her spine. He rolled her toward him. His mouth found hers. She was barely aware of what was happening until he was in her again, and then she was wide awake, filled with him, feeling as if she had been taken by a raging wave. And again, she rode the pinnacle of a searing wonder, breathless, heart thundering, the sensation so powerful it burst with light.

Afterward, she played possum so long that she drifted. When she opened her eyes at last, he was gone.

IT WAS A BUSY MORNING AGAIN. Loading the ship, finding the cabins, seeing to the last details. The men were up and at the docks first.

Hunter should have felt on top of the world. It was not that he lacked a certain swaggering pleasure in the night. It was just that David Turnberry's face seemed to be before him at every turn. The man was doing nothing wrong. He was checking off boxes as they came, making the right inquiries, doing his work. Yet Hunter couldn't so much as pass him by without thinking that he would gladly rip the fellow's throat out were he to go near his *wife* ever again.

The ship was crowded and cramped for space, but they would not be aboard long. And when they disembarked this time, they would be nearly at their final destination.

"That's the last of it," Brian said. "Shall we join the ladies?"

"A drink, dear Lord, a drink! I'm expiring!" Robert said teasingly.

"I'm sure we can find a drink," Hunter said dryly. "They will be serving aboard."

"But that, my thirsty young fellows, is one of the reasons it's so important no box be left behind."

"Wine, whiskey, beer, water," Alfred Daws checked off.

"Women and song!" David finished, teasing.

Innocent words. Hunter longed to give him a left cut to the jaw.

He refrained and looked up at the sky. "Fierce weather ahead," he said to Brian.

"Do you believe so?" Allan asked, looking at the sky and frowning. "It looks good to me!"

Two hours later, out at sea, Hunter's forecast was proved correct. The ship was being tossed about in the sea as if it were a toy of the gods. Again, everyone retreated to a cabin.

Except Kat and him.

She stood on deck by the rail. Watching her, arms hugged about her waist, hair flying wickedly in the wind, he was tempted to leave her alone in what seemed like a moment of true happiness.

He could not. He approached her and said, "It's too rough out here today, even for a mermaid." He took her arm gently.

She looked as if she would argue, then seemed to realize that he was not trying to ruin her pleasure, but was sincere.

She nodded.

They went below decks to their room. Apparently, in the crowded ship, they had the only parlor. Princess Lavinia and Lord Avery were there, playing gin. "Children, sit down, join us!" Lavinia commanded. "We've ordered a meal. You can eat, can't you?" she demanded of Kat.

"Actually, I'm quite hungry."

"Thank the Lord! Hunter should never have a mealy-squealy bride," she announced. "Gin!"

"Lavinia, I daresay—"

"Jagger, don't you dare say! I do not cheat at cards!"

Lord Avery gazed at Hunter. "Have you checked the cabin thoroughly?"

"I have, sir."

"Interesting crew we have here," Lavinia said, shuffling the cards.

"Oh?" Kat said.

"Mmm. Jagger, do you remember all that went on with young Daws? No, no, before that. With old Daws! I am trying to remember. Isabella came from a good-enough family… grandfather had some sort of a title. But she was a rash young thing, and it was suspected that she was after Daws, despite the fact that he was years older. She would have been barely out of her teens then! And, of course, he didn't marry her. He married Lady Shelby, daughter of that French count, didn't he, Jagger?"

"Um…I'm sure I don't remember all this, Lavinia."

"Lady Shelby gave Lord Daws his heir, Alfred, and they thought he would lose her then. She managed to kick around for several years, though! Then, of course, she did die, and Daws married Isabella…and died soon after!"

"Then, of course, we've young master Robert Stewart!" Lavinia murmured, passing out the cards, picking up her hand. "Do pay attention to the game, Jagger!" she admonished.

"Any skeletons in his closet?" Hunter asked lightly.

"Um…well, he's from an illegitimate branch of the family, but he is related to the royal Stewarts, of course. There was some minor nonsense about him at school. Nothing much. Oh, there's our dear young David. The fourth son! Not much promise there, I'm afraid, Jagger, since your daughter is so fond of the lad. Then again, it would be harder to find a more prestigious or influential peer than his father. The man quite has the queen's ear, and has Parliament and the prime minister twisted round his finger. And as to money…well, his father could bathe in the stuff on an hourly basis."

"That's crass, Lavinia."

"Do forgive me, Lord Avery!" she sniffed, using his formal title. "We are among friends and family. I'm but stating the truth."

"There's Allan. Allan Beckensdale," Kat said.

"Allan, of course. Good fellow. I heard from a little bird that he's helped many a friend out of gambling debts. A hard worker at university, excellent reports from all his professors."

"Would you say that any of the others had a grudge against David for any reason?" Hunter asked her.

Lavinia looked down her nose and past her spectacles at him. "Jealousy? He is the leading contender for Margaret's hand, is he not, Jagger?"

"I had thought so," Lord Avery said, looking at his hand. "Aha! Gin!" he cried.

"Are you sure, Jagger. Can you even see your cards?"

"Good Lord, woman!"

"Ah," Lavinia said, looking up. "I believe supper has arrived."

Supper had indeed arrived. Chicken in herbs, winter vegetables, fresh-baked bread. The meal was excellent. They were barely through it when he noticed Kat trying to contain a yawn. His heart went out to her. It didn't harden with the anger he was all too quick to feel.

"My love," he murmured, touching her arm. "I'm sure our guests will not mind if you retire early."

Startled, she sat up straighter, looked around and then admitted, "I am exhausted."

Lord Avery stood instantly. "Young woman, get to bed."

"Good night, dear!" Lavinia told her. She didn't rise. Kat bent to kiss her cheek. Lavinia hugged her warmly.

Hunter had stood, naturally. He walked to her side, kissed her cheek. "Good night, my love," he murmured.

She stared at him, and he knew that she considered his use of the word *love* to be pure mockery. He met her eyes, refusing to look away. She nodded and departed through the connecting door.

When the door was closed behind her, Lavinia leaned toward him, tapping him on the hand with her perfectly manicured nails. "You don't deserve her!"

He ignored that, leaning close to his great-aunt. "Lavinia, can you think of any reason anyone would want to hurt Kat?"

She arched a brow, then sat back, thoughtful. "She has no great riches of her own...although, of course, she is now married to you!"

"Other than that," he said dryly.

"Perhaps she knows something...can do something...oh, good heavens! I don't know, Hunter. Why? What is going on with this expedition? Rocks falling when they haven't moved for centuries!"

"I don't know," Hunter said.

"And an Egyptian asp in a room in Rome!" Lavinia said.

Hunter stared at Lord Avery. "I have only spoken to Lavinia," Lord Avery said defensively. "And she is your great-aunt!"

Hunter sat back, shaking his head. A decanter of brandy had been delivered with the meal. He poured a measure for himself and Lord Avery.

Lavinia cleared her throat.

"Aunt Lavinia! I do beg pardon!" he said, and poured her a measure, as well. She sipped the brandy, nodding at him. "Nephew, I will keep my eyes open. And my sight, at a distance, is most excellent. And even up close...well, I do have my spectacles! There is little that I ever miss."

"I'm sure," Hunter said.

Not long after, they all departed for their respective cabins.

Hunter locked the door to the hallway, then entered the bedroom. The darkness was almost complete. He let his eyes adjust.

He walked to the bed and looked down. His heart caught somewhere in his chest, ceased to beat. She was beautiful, and so vulnerable as she lay there. Her eyes were closed, and her breathing even. She slept, and seemed to do so with peace and ease.

Even in the darkness, the burst of hair that splayed over her pillow burned with deep radiance. He suffered, watching her, and for a moment, wondered what he had done.

How hard was it to love someone, as he loved her, and know each day that he was only a substitute for what she wanted?

How hard to hide the truth of his feelings, for pride would never allow him to show them.

Then he exhaled, turning away.

And what would it matter if he could not keep her safe from whatever danger threatened?

No. That was not a question. He would give his life to keep harm from befalling her.

So thinking, he disrobed silently and slid in beside her, keeping his distance, staring at the ceiling, praying that the rocking of the ship would soon allow him the mercy of sleep.

Chapter 14

"MY DEAR LORD! IT IS EGYPT!"

Kat stood on deck, her happiness at their arrival so complete that she smiled at Hunter with pure joy. There was nothing of any other emotion.

He smiled back, enjoying her enthusiasm. Camille, too, was thrilled. She looked at Kat, wide-eyed, exuberant. "I'm here, we're here!"

"Let's hope you're both so pleased when we're sweltering in the desert and the sand is whipping into your eyes," Brian said laconically.

"Oh! I shall love the sand and every minute of it!" Camille returned.

They all stood about talking, pointing, excited, as they came nearer and nearer the shore.

Kat noted, however, that David seemed thoughtful and silent. His mood seemed quite strange to her. But it was no act, for he had kept a distance from the others, just watching.

At last they were alighting on Egyptian soil, and soon they were all excitedly, buying little pieces of fabric, fruit, bangles, various little pieces of art, fake and real, from the vendors who thronged the area where the ships came in. There were people everywhere.

"Wait until you see Cairo," Hunter said, smiling, his hand on her shoulder.

"Well, I must wait, I suppose. We have another train ride."

"Indeed, we do."

And on the train to Cairo, there was more excited talk, everyone expressing amazement that they had finally reached their destination. The train brought them to the station where again, there were vendors everywhere, but carriages awaited them, and soon, they arrived at Shepheard's Hotel.

Nothing could have prepared Kat for their arrival. Many others besides their group had arrived on the train, too, though she knew that Lord Avery, Brian and Camille, and Hunter would draw the most speculation, the greatest flurry of whispers.

Staff came running out to assist them as they arrived, a general manager bowed over and over again to the group, welcoming Hunter, Brian and Lord Avery back, welcoming the others for the first time. Their boxes, trunks and multitude of crates were gathered from the cart that had followed their coaches, and they had to move past the hundred or so curious onlookers who dined on the patio so that they might settle into their rooms.

Before they could pass completely, though, someone called Hunter's name.

"Why, Sir Hunter MacDonald! You've made it."

Hunter stopped. Kat's arm had been looped through his, and she naturally stopped, as well. "Arthur!" Hunter exclaimed. He turned to Kat. "Come, dear, meet a friend. We'll be right along!" Hunter called to the others.

"I'll see to your paperwork," Brian called back.

Curious, Kat accompanied Hunter. The table they approached was in the shade, and the fellow at it was wearing a white casual suit and hat. He was middle-aged, a trifle stout, and wore a mustache. There was something familiar about him.

He rose. "Why, Hunter! Who is this?" the man asked.

"Arthur, my wife, Katherine. Kat, Mr. Arthur Conan Doyle."

She gasped and was instantly horrified at her lack of propriety. She quickly closed her mouth and stared at Hunter. "Seriously. I told you, we are old friends. I have written a few books myself," he said.

She looked from him to the man who had invented her favorite character and written so many excellent stories. "Forgive me!" she said softly. "I simply cannot tell you what an honor it is to meet you!"

He smiled, a pleasant fellow, and indicated that they take seats. "My dear, I'm flattered. And thrilled. Just don't tell me that you are lamenting the death of Holmes, or I think I shall scream."

She shook her head. "I have no intention of telling you anything. You are the writer."

"I like this girl!" he told Hunter.

"I'm rather fond of her, as well," Hunter murmured dryly.

Kat didn't care. She was sitting at a table in Cairo with Arthur Conan Doyle.

"I'd heard you were down here," Hunter said. "And your wife?"

Doyle sighed softly. "The weather is better here. You'll see the dear girl soon enough. How long are you in the hotel?"

"Lord Avery is staying on here the whole time. We'll keep our rooms throughout, but I'd like to set up at the dig site by tomorrow."

"Then you must join us for dinner tonight," Doyle said.

"Oh, yes!" Kat exclaimed.

Hunter smiled. "I believe my wife has spoken. Since that is to be the case, let's please do get into the rooms now, Kat. We'll have to spend some time preparing for the move tomorrow."

"Of course," Kat said.

Arthur Conan Doyle stood as they departed, arranging to meet at eight. There was a restaurant where the view of the pyramids at night was incredible, and they would go there.

She was walking on air as they made their way into the lobby, where their keys were waiting. The pleasant man behind the desk stopped them when they would have continued on.

"Sir Hunter, there is a telegram for a Miss Adair."

"That is me!" Kat said, awed. "I mean, it was me," she said quickly.

"We're newlyweds," Hunter explained.

The man nodded, smiling, and passed over the telegram. She looked at Hunter, her eyes wide. "I've never received a telegram before!"

"You should read it," he suggested.

Her fingers shaking, she opened the envelop. "It's from my father! He misses me but wants me to know that he and Eliza are doing very well... Oh! And they're on their own," she said, flushing with pleasure. "Apparently, Lady Daws went to France to transact some business." She sighed with relief.

"You apparently don't care much for her."

Kat couldn't help but smile. All of the threats that Lady Daws had heaped on her meant nothing now. Thanks to Hunter.

"She assured me that—" Kat hesitated "—as soon as I was home from this journey, she'd see that I was sent to a strict school on the continent!"

"Well, she has no power over you now," Hunter said.

"No, but...I am terrified that she will marry my father!"

Hunter was silent. They were both aware that could still happen. He didn't try to tell her otherwise. "I don't believe she would have done so before," Kat murmured. "Not when he was poor. But his world has changed so since you introduced him to Lord Avery."

"There is always a price to pay," Hunter said softly.

"Well, at least, for the time being, she is in France. And Papa is working on commissions—he has too much work, actually. Of course, he can't finish the portrait of Lady Margaret for Lord Avery until we return. Oh, Hunter! He must be doing very well. We never could have afforded to send a telegraph before!"

"He deserves the recognition," Hunter said. "But, now, if you wish to accompany the Doyles to dinner, I have much to do."

Their rooms were just a half flight up from the lobby level and down a hallway. Their luggage had been delivered and neatly aligned. Emma had been there briefly, for some things were already unpacked.

Inside the room, Kat turned to him again. "Arthur Conan Doyle!"

"Would that I were he!" Hunter murmured. "I have never seen such excitement from you."

"Oh, but you don't understand. Sometimes I would be with my father when he was working, and I would lose myself in the stories. I think he is brilliant!"

"He is a fine man."

Hunter reached out and touched her face, wiping something from it. "Soot of some kind," he told her. "Well, we'll be in sand to our ears by tomorrow."

"It has been a long trip, leaving the ship…the hours on the train. A bath would be lovely."

"Take a look in the bedroom, dear. This is Shepheard's, after all."

There was a lovely bathtub. Kat filled it, anxious to wash away the grime of travel. She should have felt tired, but she did not. In fact, she had never felt so alive as she had in the past few days.

As she lay in the tub, she couldn't help but wonder if the timing right then was convenient, and if her husband might be interested…

But then she heard commotion from the outer room and knew that he was busy. She could only pick up bits and pieces of what was being said, but apparently, Brian was with him, and they were arranging for camels and horses for the next day. She stepped from the tub. Tomorrow, she would turn into the best assistant and secretary.

Wrapped in a huge snow-white towel, she walked to the window. A sense of wonder filled her again.

There, on the horizon, were the three great pyramids. She was really in Egypt.

And she would be happy to pay the price of being here. Tomorrow.

Tonight, she was dining with Arthur Conan Doyle.

There was a soft tap at the door to the hallway. Curious, Kat walked to it. "Yes?"

"It is Françoise, from housekeeping, my lady."

She opened the door. The girl who stood beyond was beautiful. She had the exotic look of an Egyptian, with her black hair and dark eyes. Her dress was English, a simple blue-gray gown adorned with an apron. She carried a handful of white towels.

"Please, come in," Kat said.

The girl entered, heading into the bathroom. When she came out, Kat was by the window again.

"Good evening," she said, ready to exit. "And if you need anything..."

She was behaving, certainly, as she had been taught. Not to annoy the guests, simply to serve them.

"Actually," Kat said, "I would like some help." She pointed out the window. "Which is which, please. I'm on expedition, but I'm really frightfully ignorant of so very much. Would you be so kind?"

The girl moved to the window to join her. She was shy, it seemed, but seeing that Kat was serious, she pointed. "There...as you can see, the largest, that is the Great Pyramid of Khufu, or Cheops. There, and there, the pyramids of Khafre and Menkaure. Khufu ruled about twenty-five hundred years ago, at the pinnacle of power during the time of Egypt's Old Kingdom. Some believe that the Sphinx was part of his complex, but—" she shrugged "—the scholars remain in debate about that."

Kat stared at her. The girl seemed especially articulate and well educated.

"You should be a guide," she said softly.

"I'm a woman," she murmured. "The hotel is good work. Thank you, Lady MacDonald." She bowed, ready to leave again.

"Wait, I'm so sorry, but...are you Egyptian?"

"My father was French," she said simply, "but I am Egyptian, yes."

"My father would love to paint you!" Kat said, smiling, shaking her head. "You truly have one of the most beautiful faces I have ever seen."

The girl blushed, then obviously uncomfortable with the compliment, gestured out the window. "The pyramid is something that came about because of the platform, or mastaba, that covered tombs before. The Step Pyramid of King Djoser at Saqqara shows how the steps were achieved, mastaba over mastaba. Of course, the Pyramid of Cheops is the crowning glory of such building. And yet, they say, our desert is riddled with treasures yet to be found. And so...that is why you're here."

"Yes, I am on expedition," Kat said.

The girl offered her a smile then. "You and your husband are with the Earl of Carlyle. Your husband has come many times before, and there is always speculation about what he will find. You will not be so far away. When the desert sands threaten to swallow you, the hotel will be within reach. I pray that you like my country."

"I already love your country," Kat assured her, and let the girl go at last.

Later, when she had finished dressing and still awaited Hunter, she found herself standing at the window again.

Looking below, she saw two figures in the shadows between walls of the building. They seemed to be meeting furtively. One looked anxiously around.

It was Françoise, Kat realized.

She tried to make out the other figure. It was that of a man. The two came very close, whispering. The man was obviously angry.

Kat gasped when she saw him strike the girl.

She couldn't possibly have been heard, but it seemed that the two looked up. She stepped back from the window.

When she looked down again, they were both gone.

She wanted to find a way to talk to the girl again. Her heart bled for the young woman who appeared to be so cruelly abused.

FROM THEIR TABLE, they could see the pyramids rising from the sand, and Arthur Conan Doyle was quick to point out to Kat that tourists were climbing them.

"I cannot wait to do so!" Kat breathed.

"Well, we shall have to wait a bit; there's a lot to be done," Hunter said. He saw Kat's face fall.

Louisa, Arthur's wife, laughed softly. "Hunter! You have seen the pyramids too many times. You surely remember how magnificent they were at first sight, how overwhelming in size and shape and simple existence!"

The woman looked well enough, Hunter thought, but she was dying. He knew that Arthur had taken her to more than one doctor. The diagnosis was always the same. Tuberculosis. But Arthur was not one to accept any such diagnosis without fighting back. He and Louisa, and the children, at times—daughter Mary, son Kingsley—had moved about, seeking the best climates, and she had already outlived the doctors' predictions. She was a wonderful, sweet-natured woman, and she and Arthur suited each other very well. Arthur had once told Hunter that he had been fortunate in his family life, and even fortunate to have suffered the illness himself, for it had taught him he did not need to maintain both a medical career and a writing career. He was bitter now, however, because the public was actually hounding him to bring Sherlock Holmes back to life.

That, when he was facing a real life tragedy.

But tonight, Louisa looked well. And Kat's pleasure in everything about her was so contagious that everyone felt merry.

In fact, he had almost forgotten that he needed to be worried.

"Tell me, are you as great a detective as your creation?" Kat said teasingly to Arthur.

Hunter winced slightly, knowing how Arthur felt now about his famous character. Holmes was driving him mad.

But to his surprise, Arthur had an answer for Kat.

"My dear, all the credit goes to an old professor, Dr. Joseph Bell. He was amazing. A patient would walk in, and he would know by the fellow's clothing and shoes what he did for a living and where he had been. He could look at a man's hands and know immediately a great deal about him. Thus, he could diagnose his patients more readily. He was a brilliant fellow. I, in turn, am often tempted to write Watson when I am to sign my name! At any rate, like Dr. Bell, I have learned to look at the world and those around me in a different way." He glanced at Hunter. "Have you been experiencing some mysterious happenings of late?"

"Yes, I would say so," Hunter replied.

"Do tell!" Louisa encouraged.

"Shall I start at the beginning?" he asked, glancing at Kat.

She looked back at him uncertainly.

"We're not at all really sure if we've had mysterious happenings," he said, "or a series of truly remarkable coincidences."

"Very curious, Hunter. We've had a few around here, too.

You tell me yours, then I shall share what I fear is rather common knowledge."

Hunter glanced at Kat again, then began speaking. "You see, I met my wife because a young fellow—a son of Lord Turnberry—tumbled into the Thames. Kat, who was on her father's vessel, dove in to save him. I dove in, as well. Later, the young fellow confided to Kat that he believed he'd been pushed. Then after that, let's see... A map has disappeared, Kat was possibly given something to make her deathly ill the night of our engagement party, a huge stone fell from the Colosseum where Kat and David happened to be, and last but surely not least, their was a cobra in Kat's room in Rome."

"Goodness!" Louisa exclaimed. "I see your dilemma. Accident...or coincidence?"

"At first," Hunter said, "I didn't believe that there could be a reason for anyone to harm David Turnberry. I can't even begin to think of a reason anyone would want to harm my wife."

Arthur was looking at him, frowning gravely. "I believe you do have quite a mystery on your hands. Who was with the lad on the boat the day he was sailing? Anyone with you now?"

"His friends, school chums," Hunter said. " Robert Stewart, Allan Beckensdale and Alfred, Lord Daws. His stepmother, by the way, happens to be a friend of Kat's father."

"Mmm," Arthur murmured.

"It's ridiculous to think that any of those men, college companions, would be dangerous to one another!" Kat said.

"My dear," Arthur said. "You claim to be my ardent reader. What you must do, always, is eliminate the impossible. What is left, no matter how improbable, is true."

Kat looked at Hunter. "I'm afraid we're still at a loss."

"Then you need more clues. And you will have to find them. And, most important, you must be observant of all things at all times." He looked at Hunter. "Keep me posted, eh?"

"Naturally. Of course, some of what I've told you is well known, but..."

"We shall keep your confidence, of course," Arthur assured him.

"So! What gossip and mystery goes on here this season?" Hunter asked.

"Well, sadly, some of the usual. But it seems that many treasures have gone missing from digs in the general area of the Giza Plateau. There are rumors that the digs are cursed. A few workers have actually disappeared, and a few have returned to Cairo, anxious to beg, borrow or steal, rather than go back out on the sands. One poor fellow, seemingly half mad, claimed that chanting rises from the sand." He smiled ruefully at Kat. "It was during the Old Kingdom era, the time of Khufu, that the kings started to emphasize their godliness, or their associations with the gods. Afterward, pharaohs were also claimed to be the sons of the great sun god, Re. At his death, a pharaoh became one with Osiris, the father of Horus, and the great god of the underworld. Priests became powerful by seeing to it that common people were duly awed by the godlike men who ruled them. So, it's easy to see how today's people might believe that somehow, there are those about still chanting, still worshipping their mighty ruler-gods."

"It's just desert winds," Louisa said softly, then squeezed her husband's hand. He cast her a bittersweet smile.

Louisa cleared her throat and winked at Kat. "Mesmerists are all the rage in London now, aren't they?"

Arthur stiffened. "All hoaxes—yet quite fascinating."

"He has taken an interest," Louisa said with a good-humored sigh. She looked at her husband again. *Please, don't miss me too much. Don't seek me when I am gone!* she might have said aloud.

"Well," Hunter murmured, "you are both welcome at the site at any time."

"And if I can do anything..." Kat began, looking at Louisa.

"You are here and it's a lovely dinner," Louisa said. "A beautiful night. So, dear Lady Katherine, how do you find the hotel?"

"Fascinating!" Kat said, then she grew troubled. "I talked with one of the hotel maids this afternoon. She was quite fascinating, as well. A beautiful woman, Egyptian, but she said that her father was French. She was so well spoken."

"Ah, yes, I've seen the girl," Arthur said.

"Yes," his wife agreed. "And she is quite lovely. Impossible to miss."

Kat hesitated. Hunter was looking at her curiously.

"I saw her later, too, when I happened to look out my window. She was down in a shadowy area between the buildings talking with a man. He struck her. I...I wish there was something that I could do."

There was silence for a second. "Sadly, my dear, there are men in England who think nothing of striking their wives. There is little you can do here."

She flushed, because Hunter was still looking at her. "It's just...wrong," she murmured. She looked up and met his eyes. "It is wrong for anyone to strike another person."

A touch of amusement lit the deep blue of his eyes. "Indeed. But then again, we can be cruel in many ways, such is the nature of the human beast," he said.

She thought that it might be the closest they would ever come to apologizing to each other.

And still, the thought of the girl troubled her. But it was true. There was little she could do.

IT WAS LATE WHEN THEY finally returned to the hotel. Still, Hunter had a few notes to go over, and as he was anxious to get to the site, they could not be forgotten. He was at the desk in the parlor when Kat came out. She was in a robe, her hair freshly brushed and burning radiantly down her back.

He arched a brow at her.

He was startled when she moved before him, hesitated, then took the pencil from him, sat on his lap and threaded her fingers through his hair.

He was so startled, in fact, that he nearly dropped her.

She pressed her lips to his. Teased and played, running the tip of her tongue over his mouth in seductive circles. His desire came like a bolt of lightning.

"What is this for?" he whispered.

"I am so grateful!" she said. "You...Mr. Arthur Conan Doyle..."

He might have been mad, but he felt stricken to the core. Angered. He stood, setting her on her feet.

"Madam, I do not want your gratitude!"

"I...I..." she stuttered, then stared at him with fury. "Trust me! You shall never receive it again!"

She left him, hair flying behind her as she strode to the dividing door.

It slammed in her wake. Loudly.

He stared back at the paper. Then he rose, walking to the door, opening it, closing it. She was on the bed, as far to the one side as it was humanly possible to be without sliding onto the floor.

He doused the light and disrobed in the dark. He crawled in beside her and reached for her. She was as stiff as a two-by-four, but nonetheless he climbed on top of her. "Never come to me," he said, unable to read her face in the dark, "for anything other than the reason that you want me. Ah, but I am not the man you love and desire, you would say? Still...come to me because you want me, not because you want to thank me or you want something from me, do you understand?"

"Is that all?" she queried.

"No."

He leaned down, seeking her lips. She tried to twist from his hold.

"Sir, I am not interested, and this is not convenient."

"You do not forget or forgive, do you, my love?"

"It's extremely rude for you to come to me now!"

"No, it's not. I'm here because I do want you," he said very softly.

She let out a soft breath. And when he wrapped her in his arms again, she braced against him at first, then relaxed.

When he made love to her, she began to make love in return. Her fingers, so delicate, over his back. Her lips, utter nirvana on his flesh.

And each moment, a little bolder...

Later, he lay by her side, holding her against him. In silence.

Good Lord, how he loved his wife!

Chapter 15

THE MORNING WAS FILLED with chaos. The Egyptian guides and workers were there, a dozen of them. The camels were letting out long braying noises, obviously distressed at the commotion.

"Eh! Watch the big one!" Allan cried out in warning as Kat walked by. "He keeps trying to bite me."

"Allan, talk nicely to it, and you'll get along," Camille advised. She was dressed in a white shirt and a khaki-colored garment that looked like a skirt but was, in fact, wide, flaring pants. Kat's own outfit was similar; her blouse, however, was cream, and her legs were clad in a shade of brown. She had on men's socks and very ugly boots, but they were perfect for the desert, so she had been told. She also had a hat, another must, Hunter had assured her.

"Kat!" David called.

He was with the horses, and she walked over to him. "Hunter has said that she is to be yours," he told her, indicating a bay mare. "She's a beauty!" he said, and offered her a smile.

She smiled in return. Not even David could bother her today. "She is lovely. And nicely small."

"Arabian horses do not tend to be as large as our English breeds," David informed her.

"That one is fairly large," she said, pointing out another of the horses, a beautiful animal with a dish-shaped nose, taut muscles and a dark coat that glistened in the sun.

"Yes, of course. Hunter's mount," he murmured. He stared at her. "Hunter always gets the best, doesn't he?"

She didn't like the innuendo in his words. It was sexual, somehow. "It appears that every horse here is exceptionally fine. It also seems to me that you have to choose one horse and not be looking for a different animal every other minute. What is the mare's name?"

"Alya," he said, seeming annoyed. He looked away. "There is Abdul. He is leading the caravan."

A handsome Arab was atop a camel, calling instructions to his turbaned workers. Camels were loaded heavily with all manner of boxes and trunks. They seemed well equipped, however, to withstand the weight.

Her attention was suddenly drawn to an argument going on between a local man and Lord Avery. Lord Avery appeared perplexed; the local man kept bowing and apologizing, but he was insistent on something, as well.

As she watched, Lord Avery produced a wad of bills and gave them to the man. He in turn began bowing again, thanking Lord Avery.

One of the guides was mounted near Kat. He was young, with a quite beautiful face and almond eyes. He saw Kat glancing his way.

"Do you know what that was about?" she queried.

He only inclined his head toward her, and she knew that either he hadn't understood her or didn't intend to answer her, since it would not be his place.

"I'm Kat," she said, nudging her horse closer.

He stared at her uneasily for a moment, but then accepted her introduction. "Lady MacDonald, I know who you are. I am Ali. At your service."

"Please...I'm very new at this!"

He sighed. "Just a misunderstanding. Young men sometimes forget to pay the bills for their entertainment," he told her. "Some of your party were out last night at Rashid's...restaurant. Rashid asked Lord Avery for payment. There was nothing wrong. Everything here is a negotiation, you see."

"Thank you," Kat told him.

He nodded, smiling slightly. She liked him immediately.

"Mount up!" Hunter called suddenly.

"Wait!" came a cry from the front steps of the hotel. Margaret, in a pink dress, her blond hair almost white in the sun, was there, a picture of pure feminine beauty.

She hurried over and hugged Kat first. "I will come out in a few days' time!" she promised. She wrinkled her nose. "Once you're all set up!"

Lord Avery had followed, Lavinia on his arm, ready to wish them all luck and godspeed.

"If anything!" he warned Hunter and Brian.

"We are but a day's ride," Hunter assured him.

Lord Avery nodded. Kat saw that Margaret had given the others a brief kiss and hug. She remained with David. His head was lowered close to hers. She kissed his cheek, then hurried back.

Kat was proud to be able to swing unassisted onto her mare's back. Hunter swung up onto the large Arabian stallion like one born to the saddle, which, of course, he had been. Then, with the camels still noisy and sand flying about, they were on their way.

The mare was wonderful, just the right size for Kat. Her gaits were as smooth as silk. The view! First, the city streets, people going about their business, so many of them, women balancing water jugs on their heads, children, goats, chickens.

They left the city behind and were out on the sand. It was golden, shimmering. The pyramids rose majestically, the Sphinx sat in royal splendor. It was impossibly magnificent. The sun played one way on the pyramids, then another. The colors changed subtly.

And for the first two hours, the journey was magical. Perhaps even the first three hours.

And then the heat began to seem oppressive. The sand seemed constantly in her eyes. It was no longer golden or shimmering.

Just...sandy.

The mare was perfect, but Kat's legs were aching.

The pyramids were no longer gleaming. They were just... there.

But she was determined not to complain. So her throat was as dry as a rusty razor. So she might never walk again. So she was parboiled, inside and out.

"Brian! Hunter!"

Thank God! It was Camille, several horses ahead of her, who cried out.

"We must stop...we must break for just a minute, I beg you!"

"Camille, there's a little watering hole, not even a true oasis, but it's just ahead. Can you hang on for five minutes?"

"Five minutes! Indeed."

Of course, five minutes was really half an hour. As she rode up to the small spot of water in the ground, surrounded by a few scraggly date palms, Kat feared that she would not be able to get off her horse without falling. Hunter was up front with the guide Abdul and Brian, studying a sheet. She realized with some trepidation that it was the sketch she had made of Camille's missing map.

"May I help you dismount?"

She looked down. David was there.

She doubted she could make it on her own. "Yes, thank you," she said.

He was circumspect, gripping her by the waist, giving her a chance for balance, then releasing her. He offered her one of his smiles.

"Thank you," she told him.

He offered her his canteen. Again, she thanked him. At the first touch of the water on her lips, she longed to drink until the canteen was drained.

"Slow, steady!" he warned softly.

"I'm so sorry!" she said, and returned it.

He grinned. "I can refill it here. You just have to be careful. You can get very sick, gulping water out here!"

"I'll remember that."

She wobbled slightly as she made her way to the water hole, anxious to douse her face in it. Camille was there, perched on the trunk of a fallen palm. She had her hat in her hand and was waving it to cool her face. She offered Kat a sheepish smile. "It is very hot."

"And it's winter," Kat added.

"It won't be so bad once we make camp," Camille said, and Kat had to laugh, wondering which of them she was trying to assure.

"Camille, are we looking for a location on the basis of what I drew?" Kat asked worriedly.

"Not exactly."

"What exactly?"

"We knew approximately where we were digging. But that map gave clues that we could find nowhere else. Look. Look over the sand. What do you see?"

"Sand."

Camille shook her head. "See how it undulates?"

"I believe that is heat rising."

"No, no, the waves of sand itself. When you see those rises, no matter how slight, it means that something is probably buried beneath. Take the Sphinx—they don't really know yet just how deep it actually goes. Desert sands are merciless. They can cover whole cities, rises, cliffs, all but the greatest of buildings. You see, there is an area, this we know, where there were cliff formations. Not true cliffs, but formations caused by changes over thousands of years. They made a natural cover for certain graves, just as the Valley of Kings was a natural site, due to the terrain. What we're seeking is completely covered, but once discovered, it should be a complex, with rooms leading to shafts leading to more rooms."

"I see. And we can find it by looking at the land."

"Well...that's where the map comes in. There were clues due to angles of the pyramids and more natural boundaries. That's where your sketches come in."

"Mount up!" Brian called. "Time to move on!"

Kat wasn't certain she could so easily mount this second time. She was in far too much pain.

She looked at the mare, then felt that she was being watched. She turned around. Abdul, the handsome guide, his dark eyes gleaming, was there. He nodded to her, then the horse, then, in one smooth motion, picked her up and sat her on the horse. She thanked him and he nodded.

Off they rode. Sand flew, and a minute later, she saw that Professor Atworthy had come to her side.

He rode with his sketchbook in hand.

"Kat, you should be capturing these images."

"Professor, I'm sorry. I am catching nothing but sand at the moment. I swear, tomorrow."

He shook his head, tsking. "Ah, there is so much, so much!" He rode on ahead.

Somewhere along the line, they stopped for lunch—sweet cheese, bread and more water.

She stood by her mare, Alya, staring at her that third time. She knew there was no way she could leap atop her.

But once again, when she turned, Abdul was there. She offered him a rueful grimace. He nodded and set her on the saddle. Once again, she thanked him.

It began to grow dark. Amazingly, she was no longer hot. She was chilled. That morning, she hadn't begun to see how she was going to need the canvas jacket Hunter had insisted she carry in her pack. Now she was most grateful for it.

At last, Abdul cried something to Brian and Hunter, and they came to a halt. The workers began to hurriedly dismount. Shouts rang in the dark, and the pack animals went down on their knees.

She sat on the mare, unable to do anything.

This time, Hunter came to her. He grinned up at her, but it was a gentle grin. "I did tell you that you needed the riding lessons," he reminded her.

She nodded. "You did."

"Don't you want to get down?"

"I can't!"

He laughed, reaching up for her. He steadied her against his own hard form. He started to move, and she clutched him again.

"Just...just one more moment!" she pleaded. "Hunter...I'm sorry! I'm in such wretched shape. I won't be able to help with the tents, with unpacking, with preparations, with—"

He caught her chin, moving her face, directing her vision. Her eyes widened. She had never seen such efficiency!

They had come to something like the small oasis they had stopped at that morning. Here, there were more trees. And there was a strange rising slope in the sand, something that almost formed a natural barrier. A dozen tents were already pitched, sheltered by the wall, and around the tiny spring of water.

"Oh!" she said.

"We'll just get something to eat, and then to bed," he said.

"Lovely! Which is our tent?"

He pointed to the far end, where two larger tents were pitched. They were connected by a stretch of canvas on the ground and another above, which formed a roof. No walls. It was like a porch or a garden, in a way, a spot shared by tenants of a town house.

She started to stumble away from him, wanting nothing but to lie down and sleep. He pulled her back.

"No. Supper first."

There were fires lit, and soon, the smell of something delicious cooking. She hadn't realized just how hungry she was. One of their workers was trying to turn meat over a spit and stir a pot at the same time.

She approached the man. "May I?" She wasn't sure that he understood her, and so she reached for the spoon. The man frowned. "Please, I'm hungry," she said. "Let me help!"

She offered him a broad smile and took the spoon. He frowned, but allowed her to do so and gave his attention to the spit.

Abdul crossed to them and began speaking heatedly to the man, who in turn lifted his shoulders. "Abdul! I want to help. We're all out here together," she said, not knowing if he understood.

She heard laughter, then a few words in Arabic. She turned. Hunter was there, talking to Abdul. He looked at Kat and shrugged. Abdul looked at Kat and shrugged.

She shrugged and kept stirring. Again, Abdul shrugged to Hunter, then moved on, apparently looking for the serving utensils.

"What was that all about?" Kat asked Hunter.

"They aren't used to help, that's all."

"Is it all right? Am I offending anyone?"

Hunter laughed. "Not so long as you keep your help to stirring! But come on, Camille wants to see if you can add anything to the map at all."

He helped Kat to her feet. Another of the Arabs came forward, having finished with whatever his last task had been, and took over the stirring. A fire burned by the tents. Chairs had been set out on the stretch of canvas.

Camille had the sketchbook, and she was studying it. Seeing Kat, she thrust it toward her. "Do what you can."

"All right," Kat murmured. She sat, and suddenly realized what she had seen on the lost map, something she hadn't understood till today.

The little watering holes. Such as they were at now. Such as they had stopped at earlier.

"Ah!" she said, filling them in and remembering others. She thought of what Camille had told her earlier about the undulating sand, and she sketched in the ripples.

"My God," Camille said. "Better and better."

"Uncanny," Brian said, shaking his head.

Kat added a few finishing touches, seeing the original in her mind's eye almost as if it were directly before her.

She gazed up. Over her head, Hunter was looking at Brian.

"A hundred yards dead east!" Hunter said.

"A hundred yards dead east," Brian agreed.

Kat never knew exactly what was in the pot she'd been stirring. She didn't care. It was delicious, as was the lamb cooked on the spit and the bread she was given. She drank water and a cup of wine, and when she was done, she didn't care about anything else.

Not the lack of facilities, not a long hot bath, not fresh, crisp sheets.

She went into the tent she shared with Hunter, climbed beneath the blankets fully clothed, and was asleep in a matter of minutes.

Nothing evil touched her dreams. They weren't even about the endless sand in the desert, or the sound the camels made, or the way they smelled.

She dreamed that she was at the restaurant again, under the stars, with the view of the pyramids. And Arthur Conan Doyle was there. He was smiling, yet looking very grave at once.

Eliminate the impossible.

And then the possible, however improbable, is what is left.

So...just what were the actual possibilities?

KAT AWOKE TO MUCH CLANKING and commotion. The sound seemed far away, and she didn't really want to be bothered by it.

"Up! Up!" A firm shake on her shoulder. She grudgingly opened her eyes.

Hunter was there. He seemed refreshed, had changed and, bizarrely, was smelling quite nicely. She felt the grit of the day before covering every inch of her.

"We're moving," he said.

"Moving?"

"The first bit of uncovering we did led to a structure below. It will make excellent housing."

"A tomb!" she said, amazed.

He laughed, his eyes excited. "No, but, surely, once a storeroom of some kind. It's perfect. And it means that we are on the right track! Come, come, up. One must on expedition."

She rose, dusting herself off, tasting the sand and wishing, for that moment, that she were back at Shepheard's Hotel.

He noted her discomfort and smiled. "It's not so horrible, really. We're fairly well set. There is the very small pool just beyond, and Abdul has managed to rig something of an enclosure. Go, take your leisure. You'll see that the new circumstances are better."

Their guides were magicians, it seemed. A series of canvas flaps had been arranged around a very small section of their precious little pool of fresh water. Camille was just emerging when Kat arrived on the scene, her face bright and clean, her hair loose and down her shoulders. She was in a pair of trousers and a simple shirt, ready to become thoroughly involved in the dig.

"Good morning!" she cried jubilantly. "We're to start. Well, actually, they've started, as you can see. We'll become involved in a bit of the lighter work, right away." She frowned. "Trousers. You need plain and simple trousers. I have plenty. Wait, and I will get them for you."

Fifteen minutes later, Kat was refreshed and redressed. Again, she was amazed at the speed with which the workers could move. The canvas tents had disappeared. Not far from where they had been, was a deep, newly dug crevice in the desert floor. Age- and sand-worn steps led down to an opening.

Following Camille, Kat looked around skeptically. "How do they know what this was?" she asked. "And that it wasn't a tomb?"

"There are no paintings on the wall, no record of a great and glorious life or the afterlife to come," Camille said. She pointed to symbols, vague and fading above the door. "That is the sign of the worker, the digger, the builder. Supplies were kept here. But, you see, supplies must be kept for something, so I believe that we are really just right where we should be!"

"That's wonderful."

"Come along now, let's get up to the work zone!"

Before she could follow Camille to the area where the men were working, Hunter appeared, Thomas Atworthy at his side. The instructor pressed a sketchbook into her hands. "We record every step we take," he said.

"Kat," Hunter said, "if you will please work on the opening here, the entrance to the building we have found? Pay special attention to the symbols above the door."

She nodded, then Atworthy spoke again. "Come, come. There's a slight ledge where they were digging, a perfect place to sit!"

And so, her first morning was spent sketching, and with Atworthy at her side, making suggestions, she found that she was very pleased with all that she did. She became so involved that she forgot time and place until the professor at last tapped her on the shoulder. "They are breaking for tea," he told her. He passed her a canteen and she thanked him, realizing that she was very thirsty. The sun had risen high. Thankfully, Hunter had insisted on the hat.

It was so much cooler down in the ancient storeroom, away from the sun. Cots, bedding and canvas tents had all been arranged within; it was almost as if they had separate rooms, for the area was expansive.

"There might even be a series of tunnels down here," Hunter remarked as they gathered below, taking up camp chairs, passing out teacups, bread and cheese, and amazingly fresh and very English scones. But then, of course, they hadn't been gone that long, nor had they gone that far; it just *seemed* as if they had traveled forever. "Definitely something we need to explore," he said to Brian.

David came down the steps, removing his hat, wiping sweat from his brow, followed by Alfred Daws. "Good God!" Alfred exclaimed. "I must say, I'm impressed, Sir Hunter, Lord Carlyle, that you have done this so very often! It's quite exhausting."

"It's just the sun, the heat. We're not accustomed to it," David said, offering a sheepish smile.

"Where are Robert and Allan?" Camille asked.

"Ah, coming. Robert is convinced that he need dig just a little farther and he'll come upon something."

"We could dig for days, weeks...months," Brian warned softly.

"And once we make a discovery, we must dig even more slowly," Hunter said.

"And we're looking for the tomb of this priest…this Hath-sheth?" Kat said.

"Exactly," Hunter said.

"Aren't we in a strange place for such a burial?" she asked.

"No." Camille rose and went over to the little camp desk set up just inside the entry. She found the translation Kat had done back at the museum. "'He who will sit among them.' I believe that refers to the pharaohs who lie in the great pyramids, because it continues with 'he will lie in the gentle shade of those who built the kingdom.'"

"And then, you see, we had the map," Brian said. He looked around as he spoke, his tone casual. Kat had the feeling that he wasn't really quite so casual, and she was certain that he and Hunter exchanged glances.

She remembered their conversation with Arthur Conan Doyle and his wife. Eliminate the impossible.

But…where did it really all start?

Had someone tried to push David off the sailboat that day, hoping that he would die?

And then…

None of it made sense. The only ones aboard the sailboat had been Robert, Allan, Alfred and David. They were all students and the best of friends! They might well seek to seduce a young woman and aid in such indiscretions for one another, but that was a long way from attempted murder!

"Goodness!" Alfred Daws said suddenly, looking at the sketches that had been done that morning. He looked at the professor and then at Kat. "These—"

"Ah, my protégée's work!" Atworthy said with pride.

Alfred Daws gave Kat a sharp look and shook his head with admiration and surprise. "It's so lifelike!"

"It's exactly what your father captures, Kat," Hunter said. "Something of another dimension. Life."

"Thank you," she murmured.

"And you managed to create a map that you'd seen…but a few times?" David asked.

"Sometimes, I remember exactly what I've seen. Not always, I'm afraid."

"Still!"

Robert and Allan came in then, arguing lightly. "I told you that you'd not find a door waiting for you if you did just a few more feet!" Allan said, sighing. "Now they'll all be done with tea and we'll get no break!"

"You didn't have to stay! You were just afraid that I was right!" Robert argued back.

"You may have a good fifteen minutes, lads," Brian said, laughing. "And you are missing the point of the expedition. We are a team."

"Exactly!" Allan said.

Robert shook his head, laughing. "Can't help it. I want to make the great discovery!"

"Well, then, there's opening the tomb, and then discovering what's in it, isn't there?" David asked. He looked at Kat. "I think I will it expedient to follow Sir Hunter's lovely new bride. She seems to have powers that none of the rest of us possess."

Kat couldn't help but cast a quick glance Hunter's way. His face was cast in shadow. "Kat, I believe, will be sketching as we go. Not digging."

He set down his cup and headed for the stairs.

Later that day, when much of the work was ending, Kat went over to the area where the horses and camels were kept, not far from their small pool, or oasis. She found her mare and was stroking the animal's nose, when she saw Ali not far away.

"Hello!" she called to him.

He nodded. She realized that he was there strictly to guard their livestock. She walked over to where he stood in the shade of a palm. "So far out here, are we really in danger from thieves?"

"Lady MacDonald, the poor will always envy the rich. And likewise, there are those who long to cash in on the work that others do." He hesitated. "Each season, you know, there are a number of digs. Small tombs found, many that were robbed centuries, even millennia, ago. But this has been a rough season thus far. Articles found by day disappear by night."

"Well," she replied uncomfortably, "even we are robbing the tombs of the ancients, in a way."

He looked at her with his dark almond eyes, as if hesitating to speak. Then he did so, and a certain contempt was naked in his voice. "I have seen, Lady MacDonald, landed Englishmen send out invitations, that they have acquired a mummy, that there will be a party for the unwrapping! The bodies have been used for fuel for fires. That brand of robbery disturbs me. But we are a poor country. There are those who come here seeking our treasures, yes, but determined that the important ones stay here and that the people are compensated for anything taken from the country. Should the treasures all remain? Yes, they belong to my country, to my people. Can we afford for them all to stay? No. And therefore, I am happy to serve such men as your husband and Lord Carlyle, for they do not seek to rape a land and a people. Will I guard this place with all the power and strength in me? Yes, for the thieves—be they my own people or alien—do not just rob from the English, the French or the Germans, they take from my country."

He stopped speaking and flushed. "I'm sorry."

"No, no! Please. I am so grateful that you speak to me!"

"It's not my place."

She shook her head. "Ali…I…I don't really believe in separation by status or class or…" She stopped, flushing. "Let me just say that I think you are my friend, and I thank you for your friendship."

He bowed his head. "I work for your husband with the greatest pleasure."

"Thank you," she told him, and with a wave, headed back for the camp.

Camille was alone in the little area in the front of the building they had uncovered, reading, sipping tea. "You look all in!" she told Kat. "You're down that hall—" She pointed. "Actually, this has been an amazing discovery already, though the walls offer little and there are certainly no treasures. I have sat here trying to imagine just what this place was used for…I mean, exactly. What equipment did they keep here? Did the architects work at a desk here, as we've done? Were the rooms lined with containers for the treasures, or the treasures themselves? Perhaps it was even used as housing for some of the more elite workers."

"I'm afraid you know volumes more than I on this subject," Kat said.

"Ah, but without you, Kat, we might have been stumbling around forever. You cannot imagine what an asset you have been. I remembered the map, of course—I was the one who discovered its meaning at the museum. And who could have imagined that it would disappear? But I haven't your perfection of memory. And I do believe that the discovery will be incredibly important and that, indeed, it will be made. I'm sorry, I'm keeping you, and you look absolutely exhausted!"

"Oh, I believe I will become accustomed to this soon enough," Kat assured her. She smiled and started for the hall Camille had indicated, wondering now, as Camille had, just what the structure had once been used for. She hesitated in the darkness of the hallway and looked back. "Thank you, by the way. Thank you very much."

"For?"

"You have made me feel not only welcome, but useful."

"Oh, my dear! Don't you see, you're perfect for our work. And for Hunter."

Kat's smile faded slightly. She was glad of the darkness. "Thank you," she murmured again, and went on.

For a moment, the hallway was dark and she felt uneasy. She treaded where the ancients had, and it was a little unnerving. A lamp, however, was burning from a room ahead, and she hurried toward it.

Nearing it, however, she stopped. She heard Hunter's voice, but he wasn't alone. She realized that he was speaking with Ali.

"Sir, I do believe it is the exact piece," Ali was saying.

"The pawnbroker was found dead, so the paper says. You know, of course, that we are getting this news quite late?"

"Yes. But it seems that they believe the pieces have been in a private collection, and that they recently came into the hands of the dead man. I believe that the scarab shown in the sketch was found earlier this year, near Dashoor."

"Well, as you have said, we must keep our guard up."

"My men are well trained," Ali assured him.

"I know. You and your father are some of the best men I know. We are very grateful to have you with us."

Ali said something, his voice very low. Kat realized that she had been eavesdropping. She hurried the rest of the way down the dark hall, anxious that she not be caught doing so.

The light seeped through a piece of canvas that had been rigged as a doorway. Kat opened the canvas and saw the two men, and the arrangement of the bedding and belongings within the area. A crude mattress of blankets and pillows had been set against one wall, while the trunk with her clothing and that which contained Hunter's were set against the opposite wall. There was a camp desk with an oil lamp where Hunter and Ali stood, and camp chairs had been set around it.

"Hello," she said to the men, smiling.

Ali bowed his head to her. "Good evening, lady. Forgive the intrusion. I will leave you now."

"Good night, Ali," she said.

And he was gone. "What was that all about?" she asked Hunter.

"The usual. One must always be careful. But then, we are aware of that already. Excuse me, I must see Brian."

He left. Kat hesitated, then tore off the heavy boots and the trousers and the shirt she'd been wearing, folding them neatly, since they would have to serve again. In her trunk, she found a simple cotton shift and slipped it on.

Hunter did not return. At last, she crawled into the bed on the floor and closed her eyes. She opened them again. Last night, in the canvas cover beneath the stars, she had been exhausted, and she had slept easily. Tonight, she was chilled.

What had the ancient Egyptians done within these walls?

At last, Hunter returned. She kept her eyes closed, and yet, felt a deep chill when he doused the lamp. It was better when she felt the vital warmth of him beside her.

Moments later, she felt the touch of his fingers, moving lightly down her back. She inched closer to him, grateful for the touch.

Eager.

He turned her toward him. She radiated in the feel of his kiss, and even in the slightly awkward motions taken to dissolve clothing. It was amazing, in the pitch darkness, that she felt so cherished. Not just desired, cherished. But then again, she knew that he was well practiced at this art. Still, in the night, she felt only the delicious rise of sensation, so sweet, then so desperate. She heard his breathing, the pounding of hearts. Felt the slick dampness of his flesh moving against hers. The force of him within her…the burst of sensation that climaxed between them, a wonder all its own.

It was only as she drifted toward sleep that she realized that she'd been hearing bits of conversation from beyond the entry of their lair, where the desks were set, tea served and all gathered. Several of their party were still awake, talking about the day's dig.

Robert…and then she heard Ethan's voice, asking if the young men needed anything before he retired for the night.

David's voice sounded, thanking the man, telling him no.

She was startled when Hunter spoke. "Does that bother you?" he inquired. There seemed to be nothing more in his voice than polite curiosity.

"No," she said flatly, and turned from him, curling toward the wall.

She didn't know how she could possibly know such a thing, but she was certain that he thought she was lying. She wished that she could tell him that she was not, that she hadn't even known that people were beyond their little inner sanctum.

But more words wouldn't have changed anything. He still wouldn't have believed her.

Besides, she was certain that he didn't really care.

Chapter 16

IT WAS NEARING DUSK on their third day when the riders appeared on the horizon.

Camille and Kat had both just emerged from the "desert bath," as they had come to call their little watering hole, and the horses were just visible on the horizon. It seemed to be a large party, at least ten riders.

They came to stand on the little rise above their camp building where Brian and Hunter stood, both looking to the horizon, as well.

"Who is it?" Camille asked.

Brian turned to her. "I believe it is the Lady Margaret," he said.

"There are so many!" Kat gasped.

Hunter said, "Lord Avery would never allow her out into the desert unescorted. Most of the riders will be guards."

His words proved to be true. Soon, the riders reached their location, and most were men, armed and wearing their flowing head scarves and desert caftans.

Emma, distraught and uncomfortable, had accompanied Lady Margaret.

As had Arthur Conan Doyle.

There was a flurry of excitement over her arrival, all the young men trying to outdo themselves in an effort to see that she had everything she needed. Emma, of course, was moaning, and it was Ali who quietly went about seeing that she was given a chair and a strong shot of whiskey first thing.

Kat, after hugging Margaret, was delighted to greet Arthur Conan Doyle. He was joyous to be out in the desert on the dig and seemed pleased, as well, to see her again.

"Fascinating! Simply fascinating!" he told Hunter and Brian once they had walked him through the structure they had discovered.

"I can see, my friend, that you are already writing a book in your mind!" Hunter told him with a laugh.

"Well, the mind is like a storage facility itself, eh?" Arthur said.

With the visitors came fresh supplies, though they were hardly down on their own. Lamb, which was cooked over the open fire, and several pies that still had a just-out-of-the-oven taste. It was a pleasant evening, almost a party.

The workers, ever vigilant, arranged for Lady Margaret to have a section in the building with a cot and every nicety they could manage. Arthur would join the men, and Emma was given a little space just beyond the ancient doorway of Lady Margaret's sector. That night, Kat fell asleep the minute she lay down on her bedding on the hard floor. When, or even if, Hunter came in, she didn't know.

The next morning, Lady Margaret was sitting on the sand in a camp chair with a canvas roof rigged over her head. A little table was set at her side, along with a pitcher of water. She watched the proceedings.

Kat, nearby, sketched, discovering each day that she was more and more fascinated by the art of drawing people, just as her father was. The workers had such wonderful faces! Ali's, so proud and beautiful, and others, work-worn and yet so noble!

And then, of course, those with them.

She drew a sketch of Camille, digging in the sand, looking up just as her husband came to her, smiling as he bent toward her. There was so much tenderness between the two! Kat looked critically at her work and was delighted to see that she had captured the mood with her pencil.

"Kat, may I see?" Margaret begged.

"Of course!"

"Lovely, so lovely!" Margaret said. Then she sighed. "How do you do it?" she whispered.

"Do what?"

"Stay out here! It's wretched."

Kat was startled. "Actually, it is not so bad."

"The cot is horrible."

"At least you're on a cot," Kat said with a laugh.

Yards over, where the workers had been digging, there was suddenly a shout. Kat leapt to her feet. "They've found something!" she cried.

With Margaret at her heels, she began to run.

It was one of the workers who had hit something. He was shouting excitedly in Arabic, and both Hunter and Brian were at his side, then down on the ground, hands in the sand as they kept sweeping the desert away.

"It is! It's...well, it's something!" Brian cried.

"Perhaps only an empty shell, such as we have already discovered," Hunter murmured, "but then again, perhaps more. Margaret, you have been good luck for us!"

"How wonderful!" Margaret said. She looked at her shoes and the hem of her skirt. They were covered with sand. "I will get out of the way then, so that you may continue."

"We'll take tea now, I think, and then continue," Hunter suggested.

"Break?" Robert Stewart cried. "Ah, Sir Hunter! We are on the brink of discovery!"

"And there is a lot of desert on whatever we have found. It will not go away without us."

And so they took their break. Returning to the camp ahead of the workers, Kat found Arthur seated by the campfire, where a kettle heated continually. He was busy scribbling away in one of his notebooks.

"They've found something," Kat told him.

He looked up cheerfully. "I heard the commotion."

"You didn't come out!"

"I daresay, they've a long way to go before they've anything to show for themselves." He smiled, then a slight frown creased his brow. "Have you seen any of the newspapers lately?"

"I heard that there has been a rare scarab found, and that a pawnbroker was killed," Kat told him.

"Oh?"

"That's not what you were referring to?"

He shook his head and reached to his side, producing a paper that was in English, but printed, apparently, for the tourists in Egypt. "They have put a name to a local mystery," he said.

"And that is…?" She accepted the paper.

As her eyes scanned the article, Arthur summed it up. "It all has to do with the very priest you're seeking. The fellow who talked to the gods. Police in Cairo suspect that a cult has risen. They call themselves Hathshethians. They believe, supposedly, that his spirit lives in the desert sands and that he is calling them together to be the protectors of Egypt. A fellow was caught stealing from a crate at the museum—the Cairo museum. As he fought off the police, he yelled something about the revenge of the Hathshethians. Sadly, he was shot in the struggle, and so little is known about this society."

"How very strange," Kat said. She shook her head. "As you said, why steal from the Cairo museum if you are trying to preserve Egypt for the Egyptians?"

The others were coming close behind. Arthur lowered his head toward Kat. "Exactly. So if that isn't the case…"

"One can assume the cult isn't really out to save Egypt?"

"My thought exactly," he said. He spoke more quickly. "Therefore, I would think that someone, at least, the organizer, high priest, whatever, is in it for gain."

"A group to steal treasures and sell them to the black market," Kat said.

"That would be a logical solution," he told her.

Then he fell silent. Allan Beckensdale, shaking the dust from his hair, was entering. "Ah, the thrill! It's great, outstanding!" he said. "But, ah, for tea, yes, amazing. I realized, after Sir Hunter spoke, that one does need nourishment to endure the sun and sand and wind and keep digging!"

The conversation during their meal was lighthearted, everyone guessing what they had come upon, exactly.

"Remember, we thought that we had made a find immediately, when we came upon this place," Hunter said.

"But it was scarcely buried!" David said. "And absolutely empty."

"It must have been storage," Camille insisted. "What else could it have been?"

"A morgue?" Arthur suggested.

"Oh!" Lady Margaret cried.

"No, no, Arthur, I don't think so, truly," Camille said.

"Think, Lady Camille! All these little rooms, the hallway? Where better place to store bodies after the removal of brains and—" he caught Margaret's shocked countenance and amended whatever he'd been about to add "—store them in the various salts they used. Sorry, my dear. They didn't simply wrap the dead, you know. They dried them first, and it took about three months."

"So…you think that each of these little rooms was…was a place for a body to be preserved?" Margaret gasped.

"Arthur," Camille interjected softly, "if that were so, I believe that the walls would have been lined with prayers and depictions of Horus and others."

"I believe that Camille is right," Hunter said. "Lady Margaret, we are surely living in old storage space, nothing else."

Margaret seemed somewhat appeased. David rose at some point and came around to her chair. He spoke to her softly, holding her hand, seeming to assure her of something. Kat was curious regarding his words, and nothing else.

But when she turned her gaze from the pair, she saw Hunter regarding her, his expression unreadable, and her heart sank. She turned her gaze from him, as well.

When tea was over, Kat took up a position again with Lady Margaret. Trying to cheer her, she did a drawing of her. Watching her own work, she thought of how lovely Margaret really was. Born to wealth and position, she had nonetheless always been kind. She was sincerely concerned for the welfare of others. Delicate, like a rose in the desert. That was Kat's thought as she sketched, shading as Atworthy had taught her, for depth.

She thought her finished project one of the best she had done. Margaret was delighted with it, smiling broadly.

"Kat, how lovely, how kind! Why, you have made me quite beautiful!"

"But you *are* beautiful. Surely, you know that."

Margaret smiled. "I am rich. And I would not be loved for my money."

"Margaret, I swear, you are beautiful!"

"Thank you. But...see those fellows out there?"

"The workers?"

Margaret laughed. "No, our student workers! Allan, Robert, Alfred...and David. Can you sketch them? Sketch them as you see them now—and as you see them in your mind's eye? And with your soul."

Kat looked at her, afraid that she might have known what feelings she had once harbored for David. But then she realized that Margaret had asked her for a far different reason. Her father was pressuring her. And she truly didn't know if she would be making the right decision.

"As you wish," Kat murmured, frowning as she thought how to tackle the concept.

"Here, if you would...draw on the horizontal, one face after the other," Margaret said.

Kat began to do so.

Robert Stewart first. Fine face, wide eyes, slightly narrow lips, a bit of arrogance, but an open smile. Allan next. Perhaps the least classically handsome of the group, but with honest eyes and a real enthusiasm for life, pleasure in what was around him. Then Alfred, Lord Daws. Again, some arrogance. Lean face, strong cheekbones, a challenge, a devil-may-care, I-am-who-I-am, I-own-the-world look about him. Then David. Beautiful David.

But as she sketched him, Kat realized that she was drawing a chin that was slightly weak, eyes that hid a constant fear, a manner that was uncertain, seeking.

She handed the book to Margaret when she was done.

Margaret studied the sketches carefully.

"Thank you," she said.

Kat looked at the sketches over Margaret's shoulder. There was something that disturbed her about her own work, though exactly what, she didn't know.

David? She had drawn what she had begun to see.

Allan. Perhaps she had done the same. She liked Allan best.

Robert Stewart? Well, he did think himself akin to royalty.

And Alfred. Again, the fellow *was* Lord Daws.

It was his picture, however, that bothered her most. Strange, she should have liked the fellow, should have felt a real kinship with him. They both despised his stepmother so!

She didn't hate him, any more than she hated David. She believed in her heart that, even if Hunter hadn't arrived that night, they would have let her go. David would have accepted the fact that she couldn't be his mistress. They had been behaving like very spoiled schoolboys.

And that, basically, was what they were.

"Hmm," Margaret murmured. She glanced at Kat. "Have you sketched your husband?" she asked.

"No."

Margaret laughed. "You must!"

"I—"

"For me, please. I had such an infatuation for him for so many years!" Margaret admitted. "Of course, I never dared tell my father! And, of course, to him, I was never more than Lord Avery's precious little blond daughter. He was polite, tender, caring...but, oh, I envied those women he looked at with that certain glint in his eye. Oh, I am sorry, I'm talking about your husband. Of course, I've never seen him with anyone as he is with you. Except, of course..."

"Who?"

"Oh, nothing, never mind."

"Margaret! That is not fair!"

"Yes, and I'm sorry, truly sorry. Young women of good breeding do not sit around and gossip thus!"

"I'm not, in truth, a young woman of good breeding, not in the sense that you mean, and therefore, it's quite all right for you to finish that thought!"

Margaret started to giggle again. "You are so determined, and passionate, and surely, that is why he loves you so."

"Margaret!"

"Oh, surely, you've heard some rumor. Luckily, rumor doesn't mean a thing to any of them. All of England knows that Brian Stirling turned into a hermit, a so-called monster, after his parents' deaths. And that was when Camille met him. But at the time, Hunter thought that Brian had really lost his mind. And he was so afraid for Camille. He tried to scare her away from Brian—he was really worried. Strange, of course, because he—Hunter—was instrumental in helping Brian when the truth was finally known. And the two of them quickly became the best of friends. They have so very much in common. But, truly, I have never seen Hunter with anyone else as he is with you. He and Camille are wonderful friends, and I believe that Brian and Hunter would second each other at any turn. So...what I've said is really idle gossip, and that is all. He does love you so, Kat!"

Kat kept silent. She couldn't tell Margaret how very wrong she was.

"Thank you. That is a lovely thing to say to me."

"Do a sketch of Hunter. Do it for me. You see, now, to me, he is my very good friend, as well. I would cherish a drawing of him."

And so Kat sketched Hunter. And she sketched all that she had come to see in him. The light in his eyes that sometimes mocked himself. The set of the chin that promised he would see every vow through. The cheekbones, the brow, the slight smile. And in his likeness, there was both arrogance and humility, pride, passion and strength. He was strikingly handsome, and perhaps she hadn't even realized that until she had fashioned the truth of his face with her own fingers.

"It's wonderful!" Margaret said. "Truly wonderful. You must show him."

"No!"

"Please? He will love it!"

"No, Margaret, I beg you! You mustn't show it to him!"

And then Margaret stunned her with her wisdom, saying softly, "Kat, you did have that very silly affection for David going, but...well, anyone can see that you have moved far beyond it!" She looked away. "David sees it, and I believe he is quite heartbroken. Because David can't quite decide his heart." She sighed. "I would be loved, Kat, for me. Not for money. And I would never have a husband who chose me because I was Lord Avery's daughter, because I was wealthy."

Kat gazed at her, so touched and truly admiring all that she saw in the young woman whom she had judged to be so light of heart and mind. She put down her sketch pad and hugged Margaret warmly.

"Well, this life may be for you, but it isn't for me!" Margaret claimed. "Tomorrow, I'm going back to the hotel. And that is that."

"But, Margaret..."

"I really do enjoy Shepheard's. And there are so many visitors. Lovely, enchanting people to meet," Margaret said. She shivered.

It was growing colder, Kat thought. It was amazing to go from such heat to such chill. But on the desert, it happened often enough.

The light was beginning to fade, and it was time to pack up her pencils and pads for the day. Margaret helped her, and together, they headed back to camp.

KAT HADN'T REALIZED THAT Ali had left them until she saw him riding back across the desert just as the sun was setting in earnest. Margaret had gone to her quarters.

Hunter was still on top of the hard stone slab they had uncovered earlier, and Ali rode straight to him. He dismounted with the expertise of the desert horseman, and she thought that he, too, was someone she must draw.

Her brow furrowed as she watched the two. Whatever he was telling Hunter must have been worrisome, for Hunter listened to him with grave attention. When he had finished speaking, Hunter set an arm around the fellow and they started walking in together.

"Kat!"

She turned. Camille was there, soap and towels in her hand. "We've a guard around the watering hole. Can I interest you in a dispersal of desert dust?"

"I... Yes!" she said, always glad to be something less than completely coated in sand.

She glanced at Hunter and Ali. Hunter was the one doing the talking then, Ali nodding as he listened. She turned and followed Camille.

"I saw the sketches," Camille said. "The portraits. That's a lovely one you did of Brian and me. I should very much like to have it."

"Of course!"

Camille shook her head. "You never knew before that you were as good as you are?"

"My father is the artist."

"Yes, a wonderful artist. But so are you."

"Professor Atworthy has certainly taught me a great deal."

"I'm sure he has. But your skill, your talent, they were always there."

"I always enjoyed drawing, and watching my father. He is far better with oils than I am."

"Well, I think that everyone has something unique. With you, perhaps, it's your ability to remember so well. To put on paper what you've seen before."

Kat chuckled ruefully. "Like today. I was supposed to be sketching more of the dig and I wound up doing sketch after sketch of faces."

"I'm sure that will be fine," Camille said. She thanked the workers who were standing guard around the canvas screen of their "bath." In the shallow but clear, cool water, she shed her trousers and shirt and ducked down, soaking her body and hair. Kat followed suit.

"Ah!" Camille said rising. "Can you imagine! Brian has told me about digs he has been on when there is no water, none at all, and every drop must be saved for drinking. I suppose I would endure it, though. I do love all this so very much!"

"It is exciting," Kat agreed.

"Not to everyone. Lady Margaret is unhappy."

"She plans to return to the hotel."

"It's best. We'll go back now and then ourselves, you know. This is slow work. Very hard, very tedious."

They lingered in the water until the last of the light, then rose, dressed and returned. By then, supper had been prepared, the others were all about eating or finishing up, returning the utensils. Although their workers were able and adept at every mode of service, Brian and Hunter ran the kind of camp where everyone pitched in, and therefore, most often, everyone tended to his or her plate and utensils.

Kat and Camille had just finished eating and were cleaning up when Hunter made a surprising announcement.

"There will be a party heading back to the hotel tomorrow," he said. "Lady Margaret is returning to her father with a full report of all that has happened thus far. Mr. Doyle is returning to his wife, and our young men will be heading in as well, with several of the workers as escort. Oh, Kat, you will be joining them, too."

"What?" She was so startled that she voiced her incredulity in front of everyone.

"You're going back," he repeated.

"But...why would I be going back?" she demanded.

A hush had fallen over the group. She realized that everyone was watching the two of them. Camille was pretending to pick a piece of lint from her skirt. Arthur was scratching his head, looking at the fire. The others made no pretense of doing anything but watching.

"Because I have said so," Hunter told her.

She didn't care to have an argument in front of the entire company, but neither did she simply intend to back down and meekly obey.

She stood, straightening her hair. "We shall discuss it later," she said, and walked out of the tent.

She was stunned. Why on earth was he so eager to get rid of her? So eager, in fact, that he would send her back with David.

She should have known that he would be right behind her. She had cleared the area of their camp by no more than a hundred feet when she felt his hand on her arm, stopping her, spinning her around.

And he was angry.

"Do not defy my authority in front of the entire company," he said sharply.

"Then don't send out shocking edicts in such a manner!" she countered. "I have no desire to go back. Margaret may be uncomfortable out here, I am not!"

"I want you back at the hotel."

"Why? I've done nothing wrong out here, I've I've settled well, I think," she said, faltering a bit. She had thought that he had enjoyed the fact that there was a body awaiting him at night. She had thought that...well, if he didn't really care for her, at least he enjoyed her!

"I will explain to you. Apparently, there is a cult out here, and it is growing increasingly bolder. Ali has been out, gathering information. There was an attack on a camp just south of here, nearer the Nile. That group had been working in the tombs of some lesser queens. Two men were killed."

She shook her head. "But you're here. And Brian is here. And we have Abdul and Ali...and if you don't send them back, Robert, Allan, Alfred and David!"

"You're going back," he repeated stubbornly. "As are they."

"Is Camille going back?"

"No."

"Then why must I?"

He let out a massive sigh of exasperation. "Because I have said so!"

"But—"

"Kat! You seem to be a magnet for trouble. I want you back at the hotel."

She was shocked by his words. She swallowed hard. "I will not go back."

"Believe me, you will. One way or the other."

He meant it. She could imagine the rich humiliation of being bound and tossed over her horse's back to be forcibly removed from the desert. It would make Ali unhappy to perform such a service, but he would do it. And none would protest Hunter's authority.

She was angry and close to tears. Oh, yes, sending her away would doubtless keep her safe from attack, but she was convinced that the real reason was that he was tired of her, that she had, indeed, proved troublesome. She wondered what she had done to make him feel that way.

"You would *force* me out of here?" she asked.

"Absolutely."

She started past him, then. She stopped, tossing words over her shoulder, not at all sure why she was saying them, except that she was so very hurt. "You are loathsome, you know!"

"You should be happy.You'll be off with your ever precious David. And I will not even be with you."

"Yes, but I'm sure I will be under guard."

"You may guarantee that. Ali would kill without a qualm in his heart. They are very strict about such matters here."

She hissed out an oath and started back for the camp, still wondering what transgression had so turned him against her.

She paused, staring out at the rows of tents, at the moon, shining down with all its glory, in the distance, touching the enchanting rise of the great pyramids. The common area was empty now; perhaps everyone was packing. Everyone but Hunter and his chosen few.

She hurried down the dark hallway to their private area. She, too, should pack.

She chose not to.

She wanted to throw something. There was nothing to throw but the lamp, and she didn't want to be cast into pitch darkness, not when she was alone. She threw herself down instead, curling close to the wall on the bedding, her face to the wall.

She lay awake, eyes staring at nothing, seething inside. He was not that far behind her. She heard him shed his clothing, douse the light and lie beside her. She felt his hands on her back. She stiffened, trying to inch away from him. There was not far to go before being entirely smashed against the wall.

"Kat...you will be gone," he said, and despite her last words to him, he did not sound unkind.

But then, why should he? He was the one doing the dictating!

"I will be gone because you are sending me away. And that is your choice," she said.

"You little fool. I am afraid for your life."

"What about Camille?"

"Camille has not been involved in nearly so many dangerous situations of late as you have been. And she is Brian's concern. You are mine."

"And I don't care to go."

"But you will."

"Then you will kindly take your hands off me."

She was startled by the sound of his laugh, ever so slightly arrogant, and yet even more bitter. "So all the world is a bargain with you, is it?" he demanded.

"No! Yes! Maybe...I don't know. What do you want it to be?" she demanded angrily.

He rolled her to face him. She was dimly aware of the power in his voice when he said softly, "The truth? I'd never risk the truth, my love. But we will not part like this."

She was stunned, then, to learn that anger could be such a staggering aphrodisiac. There had been nothing she'd wanted more than to be cold to his touch, pretend that his touch was nothing to her. She was becoming known for the precision of her memory, and now she wanted their lovemaking etched indelibly there, every detail—the scent of his naked flesh, the slick feel of it rubbing against her, friction, heat, the slightest brush of his fingers, his every kiss and caress. She didn't think that she had ever responded with such searing passion herself, clinging, arching, moving, touching tasting...shoulders, chest, beyond, for it suddenly seemed that it had never been more important to seduce and arouse.

She could only pray that some small piece of herself would be caught in his mind, in his soul, and even, if naught else, in the carnal memory of the flesh...

And still, in the end, there was nothing but the wall. No words. He did not intend to relent. She was vaguely aware that he lay awake just as she did. But with passion spent, he was distant. He did not even draw her against him.

Eventually, morning came, and quickly, he was gone.

KAT WOULD NEVER KNOW how very sorry he was to see her seated on the mare, chin high, refusing to so much as glance his way.

Nor would she ever know just how worried he was, heart and soul. He had told her about the cult attack at the other dig.

He had not told her the worst.

That Françoise, the French-Egyptian girl, had been discovered out in the desert, her throat slit, her blood drenching the sands. Kat would find out soon enough. The news was being shouted throughout Cairo. But by then, she would be at the hotel. Lord Avery had sent messages, and he had returned them, asking Lord Avery to see that Kat was as protected as his own daughter. And Ethan would stay at her side, as well.

He still didn't trust David and his cohorts, but those young men were being sent back, too, something he had determined with Abdul, Ali and Brian. The only certainty they had was that the young men had not been the culprits who had attacked and killed the two men at the other camp. He was sending the women off with an escort of half the workers, David and his cohorts, as well as Ethan and Ali. It would take a horde to stop them.

Kat would not look at him. He walked to her, anyway, taking her hand where it rested on the saddle as she waited.

"I'll be there in a week or so myself," he said.

"Will you?" she inquired with a complete lack of interest, moving her hand.

"Kat, this is necessary."

"No, it is not."

"Well, then, my love, take care, and good journey."

He didn't try to kiss her goodbye, and merely signaled Ali. The caravan set off.

As the last of the horses disappeared from sight, Brian came to stand by his side. "This cult is serious," he said. "Not something that we only have to wonder about. People are being openly slain."

"Do you really believe that these people think that an ancient priest is calling to them?"

"No, do you?"

"Absolutely not. I think that it's organized. And I think that..." He hesitated.

"That what?"

"That someone British has created this Egyptian cult."

"Yes, perhaps, but what bothers me is this... How does it connect with what has been happening in our journey? The stone at the Colosseum, the snake in the room in Rome...even what took place before?"

"I don't know. Pity Arthur left with the others. His powers of deduction might have been of tremendous use!"

"YOU MUSTN'T BE ANGRY," Margaret said, riding alongside Kat. "This is for the best."

"I'm not angry."

"Oh, but you are! You're absolutely furious."

"There's no reason for this."

"There is. Hunter believes that you're in real danger."

Kat shook her head. She started to speak, then closed her mouth. Margaret just didn't really understand the truth of any of it.

Ali was riding at the front, and each time they neared a dune or the smallest obstruction in their path, even so much as a tree, he called a halt, sending out riders. Kat was certain that it would make the endless ride even longer, but Margaret had told her that it was not nearly as far as she had thought—when she had ridden out, she had done so with camels carrying tons of supplies. They were just a group on horseback now, and they were moving much more quickly.

"Well, I think the fellows, with the possible exception of Allan, will be glad to be back for a night," Margaret mused. "I think they far prefer the nightlife in Cairo to the loneliness of the sands."

"I'm sure," Kat murmured, wishing she wanted to take part in a conversation. Margaret was truly nice. And she was trying very hard to make Kat feel better.

She had just turned toward Margaret, ready to smile, when she heard the high-pitched cries from across the sand. There was a dune to their left, and it must have been higher than it appeared, for suddenly, there were riders coming over it.

They were dressed completely in black, turbans loosened to shield their faces. Nothing but their eyes were visible as they swooped down on the caravan. For a moment, Kat was stunned and frozen by the awful majesty of the attack, the thunderous horsemen, perfect in their precision, bearing down on them.

Ali roared out some kind of an order. His men began to circle around Margaret, Arthur and herself.

"Dear God!" David breathed from behind her. He was fumbling to draw his weapon, a pistol. He had a second weapon, that one strapped to his saddle. Kat urged her horse closer to his.

"Give me the gun."

"No, no. I will shoot. I will protect us. I am the man."

"Give me the gun!" she shouted, and reaching over, she snatched it from the holster on his saddle.

But by then, though she was surrounded by Ali's men, the fighting was upon them. The sand blinded her. She heard Margaret scream, and she turned her horse in that direction.

She was stunned when a noose came around her, dragging her from the mare and depositing her hard on the sand. The stuff filled her eyes and mouth, and she coughed and rolled, entangled in the rope. It jerked, and she rolled again, and saw the fellow encased in black as he walked menacingly toward her, ready to collect what he had snared.

She raised the pistol and fired.

The man fell.

For a moment, she stared at him, shocked that she'd had the presence of mind to shoot, and also, that she had killed a man. But she didn't dare linger in the sand. She would die by being trodden to pieces by one of the horses, which now were everywhere, if she didn't move quickly.

She staggered to her feet, trying to see through the terrible fog of sand. Out of it all a man came rushing at her, his sword raised.

She screamed and tried to shoot again.

Her gun had jammed.

She looked up. The fellow had lowered the sword and was coming toward her. In his free hand, he carried a rope.

She turned to run.

For the second time, a noose flew.

And she stumbled into the sand. Rolled. And he was there, all in black, reaching down for her.

Chapter 17

CAMILLE SAT IN THE DOORWAY of the camp area, studying the sketches that Kat had done. She thought that the girl might do excellent satires in any magazine, for her quick portraits certainly captured very apt little essences about people. She was glad to see that both she and Brian had been seen as nothing more than kind and gentle, and she was touched at the way that Kat had somehow managed to put onto the page the depth of their relationship.

She had to smile. The fellows, the students! Rich, elite young men all. And that so evident. She paused, frowning, something about the sketch of Alfred Daws nagging at her. She frowned, trying to fathom what it was. It didn't register. It would pray on her mind, she thought, for quite some time. She sighed, ready to go on to the next.

"Camille, what on earth are you scowling at?"

She looked up. Hunter and Brian, both looking tired and dusty, were coming in. "Oh, maybe you can help! See this, that Kat has done?"

"Interesting. Amazing likenesses," Brian said.

"Strange," Hunter murmured.

"What?" Camille asked quickly.

"I...don't know exactly," he said, then shrugged. "There's something about the sketch of Alfred Daws."

"I agree!" Camille said. "But what?"

"Something familiar..." Hunter shook his head. "Of course, it's familiar. The fellow just left."

"Yes, yes, but that's not it," Camille said. She looked at Hunter. "It bothers you, too."

"We'll think of it, whatever it is," he said. "May I?"

He took the pile of sketches from her. She noted that he studied the sketches of the students just as she had. "There is the touch of the quixotic about David," he said.

"She's caught that rather weak chin admirably," Camille said a bit tartly.

"Mmm," Hunter allowed. He turned the page. "That's really beautiful," he said, indicating the likenesses of Camille and Brian.

"I thought so, too."

"Go on. She's done one of you."

"Oh?"

She thought that he turned the next page with some trepidation. And that he was startled to see the excellent and compelling portrait she had done of him.

"Maybe she doesn't hate me so very much," he murmured. "Or didn't." He tensed, realizing that he had spoken aloud.

"Oh, she's just angry that you've sent her back," Camille said.

"Mmm." He snapped the book shut and handed it back to Camille. "We thought we might do a bit of exploring in here," he told her, gesturing within.

"This place, whatever it was," Brian explained, "might be part of a complex. We've found all these room and hallways, so we're going to go about tapping walls and see if we can't find where there might be a false wall."

"Excellent idea!" Camille said, rising, dropping the sketchbook, forgetting it for the moment. "Since there has been another something discovered just yards away, it's more than possible that they all connect!"

"Let's get to it," Brian said.

KAT FELT THE SAND BENEATH her fingers. She grasped a handful of it and threw it into the eyes of her attacker.

He cried out, staggering back.

She fought the rope that entangled her. Struggling, she rolled onto a dead man. The fingers of the corpse still clutched a sword. Without the least hesitation, she wrenched it free. When her attacker stumbled toward her again, she lashed out with the weapon. She might not have known just how to use it, but it had a deadly blade that found its mark.

She heard a cry and spun around. There was a rider bearing down on David. She swung the blade again. Perhaps her opponent didn't dare chance the fact that she had no idea what she was doing. He veered away.

A moment later, there was someone behind her. She spun around, swinging the blade. She heard a scream.

She had been lucky again.

But the next mounted man who came racing at her caught the blade with his own; hers went flying over the sand.

She was defenseless. A man on foot let out a cry and rushed toward her.

She heard someone riding hard behind her and then strong arms snatched her up. A gun exploded. The fellow who had been rushing toward her fell, and she realized that she had been saved.

Ali had come for her. His horse reared; he was turning back.

But already, horses were thundering away. Their attackers had struck with lightning speed; now they were departing with equal haste. In seconds, they had disappeared. It was as if they had never been.

Except for the chaos left behind. Bodies littered the sand. Ali eased Kat down, and she rushed to a man who lay groaning in the sand. Allan. He pushed up, wincing. She saw that blood was oozing from a wound at his side.

"My God, Allan!" she murmured. She wished then for a petticoat, but a piece of her trousers would have to do. She ripped the hem out and hastily fashioned a bandage to tie around his midriff.

"I'm all right. I think," he said.

Someone was at her side. She looked up. It was Ali. "Two of my men are dead. This fellow is wounded. We've got to move, get to Cairo, and quickly."

Arthur Doyle, a sword still gripped tightly in his hand, walked up. "Lady Margaret! Where is Lady Margaret?"

"Oh, no!" Kat cried, jumping to her feet. Around her, those who could were rising. Margaret's name was shouted over and over. Kat, losing all thought of squeamishness, began running from fallen body to fallen body, desperately searching the sand.

There was no sign of Margaret.

"We must find her!" Kat told Ali. Yet she knew, even as she stared at him and he looked back at her, that they would not. Allan was bleeding. Others were injured. Their pathetic little party would not make it.

"In Cairo, we will get help," he told her.

She lowered her head but nodded. She tried to take hope. They had kidnapped Margaret; they hadn't killed her. They must have known that she was worth a good deal of money—a far greater sum than might be brought from the sale of a trinket. There would be a ransom demand, and Lord Avery would pay it.

She had to believe that! She had to.

There was a sudden wailing sound. "Margaret!"

David. And the wail was pathetic.

Kat looked at him with no feeling. And wondered how she had ever been so hopelessly attracted to the man.

"Come," Ali told her softly.

She nodded.

HUNTER USED ONE OF THE HUGE cast-iron frying pans as he methodically knocked on the stone, searching for a hollow sound. It was important that he keep moving, that he keep doing something. For his thoughts were making him quite insane.

Perhaps there had been no reason to send her home. She had been right; if ever there was a group that might have formed something of a bastion against attack, it had been here. But she was so stubborn. She might have walked off in quest of something one day. She might have found a tunnel, or good God, she might have fallen into a hole.

Had he been wrong? And why couldn't he figure out if there was a menace among them, a viper within their own nest....

He slammed the pan against the stone.

He could not forget her, could not get her out of his mind now for even a minute. Last night...a man could live a thousand lifetimes, and not have a night such as that. The feel of silk about him, the silk of her hair, the whisper of her breath against his flesh, the way she touched him…

Slam!

Clunk.

He stood still, listening. He slammed again. The sound that sprang back at him definitely suggested that there was air beyond the stone.

Brian and Camille both came running. Brian walked up, took the frying pan from him and tried again.

They stared at one another.

Then Camille let out a cry of joy and triumph. "I'll call the workers!" she said.

"Picks, we need picks!" Brian declared.

"We've found something, old chap, we've done it!" Brian said, shaking his shoulder. At best, Hunter could manage a nod.

They had found something. Indeed, perhaps a great discovery.

But what had he lost in the finding?

LORD AVERY COULD NOT to be consoled. Yes, perhaps the men who had seized Margaret were keeping her alive, for she was worth a small fortune. Perhaps they were. But perhaps they were not.

Kat tried to help him, to think of something to say. But there was nothing. Emma kept crying, believing she had failed. Ethan, who had been wounded, was stitched up and put to bed. Allan, too, had been patched up and put to bed. Professor Atworthy had received the worst of the wounds, and the doctor was with him, staying at his side.

There were so many tears, such wild remonstrances, and yet, it seemed to Kat, that though the police had been brought in, no one was really doing anything. At least, with Ethan put to bed, she was not being followed about every second. Ali was heading back to the camp, the only one who seemed determined to do something.

The following morning Kat quickly bathed, found appropriate clothing and determined that there must be something that she could do. She hurried down to the desk, thinking that she would ask to see the girl Françoise. She was also determined, although she hadn't asked Hunter, to offer the girl a job back in the United Kingdom.

It had to be better than being slapped about!

The young man at the desk looked stricken when she asked about Françoise.

He cleared his throat. "You haven't heard?" he asked, not unkindly.

"Heard what?"

"She…she is dead. Slain. Left in the desert," he said sadly.

She gaped at him, stunned.

"I saw her…there was a man…he slapped her!" she managed at last. "Did she have a husband…a lover, someone who would do such a thing?"

The desk clerk shook his head and his face reddened. "She had…customers," he said at last. "The management had threatened to let her go. Here, well, our people our respectable!"

"So, you believe that she was a prostitute, and that one of her clients killed her?"

"I don't believe anything, Lady MacDonald. I don't know."

Kat turned away from the desk, deeply hurt and troubled by the murder of one so young, beautiful and sweet.

She wandered toward the patio café, not really thinking at all, not sure where she was going. But as she passed the bar, she saw that David was there alone, drinking. As she stared at him, his head fell flat on the bar.

She shook her head and walked in, tapping him on the shoulder. "David."

He jerked up and winced, apparently having twisted his neck. "Katherine...Kat, Kat, Kat! Ah, what a fool I have been!" His head plopped down again.

"David, you're drunk. What's the matter with you? You need to clean up and get it together, and get out with the men who are searching for Margaret!"

He started to laugh, and his laughter scared her. "They have her. Don't you see that yet? *They* have her. I'll die, I'll die. Haven't you realized that yet?"

"David, what are talking about?"

"Kat, help me, take me to bed." He gave her a foolish grin. "Oh, that's right. You don't want to take me to bed. You have *him*. The all powerful. Tell me, Kat, he's legendary. Is he really that good?"

"David, if you weren't so pathetic, I'd blacken your eye. Please, tell me what you're talking about. Who has Margaret? Do you know?"

"Over the dunes!" he muttered. "How did they know? How did they know that they should come over the dunes?"

He was making no sense. She motioned to one of the waiters, gave him some coins and asked that he see the Englishman up to his room. That done, she returned to her own for a moment.

Over the dunes.

Whoever the horsemen had been, she was suddenly certain that their headquarters, or whatever they might call their base, had to be just on the other side of the sand dune over which they had come to make their vicious attack.

There was a noise in the hall. She hesitated, then cracked open her door slightly. Someone, a man, was walking along the hall dressed in European attire, but carrying a bundle of cloth in his hand.

A burnoose?

She watched the way he moved, noted his height and frowned.

Then she froze. She realized just what she had seen in the picture she had drawn that had so teased at her mind.

The sound of Princess Lavinia's words slipped in and out of her memory.

Scandal...

She knew him before...

Kat flew into action. If she didn't, he would be gone. And if she didn't find a way to stop him...well, who knew? The pieces weren't all together yet, but as Arthur Conan Doyle had said, *Eliminate the impossible. Whatever is left, however improbable, must be true.*

There were too many coincidences. And then there was what they had seen, what they knew.

She was out the door and following him. She couldn't simply try to explain what she believed for that would take too long. Margaret might be lost!

He was just disappearing down the stairs.

She hastened her steps.

THE WALL BROKEN, HUNTER and Brian entered the shaft, lanterns held high. Camille tried to scurry behind her husband.

He stopped her. "Dear, we don't know what we'll find."

"But I wish to find it, too!"

"Please," Brian said very softly. "Let us just see where it leads."

She sighed deeply.

"Camille, we need you out here. What if someone comes?"

She looked at Abdul, standing next to her, a very capable man. He grimaced at her.

"You will come back and tell me the minute—no, the very second!—you find anything."

"Of course!" Brian said.

And so Camille stayed behind.

The two men moved slowly. Here, the walls were covered with paintings. Brian paused, lifting his lantern. Symbols streamed over the walls. Hunter followed the light, frowning as he tried to make out the patterns and translate in his head.

And there he saw it. The hieroglyph that stood for the name Hathsheth.

"We're here," he murmured.

"The temple?" Brian asked.

"I believe that's what it says. Let's keep going."

Ahead of them was darkness and behind them was darkness.

Brian swore suddenly.

"What?"

"Another wall!" he said with a sigh.

And it was then that they heard Camille scream their names.

AS HE HURRIED DOWN the stairs, the man bundled his satchel of cloth tighter, likely trying to hide exactly what it was, Kat thought. On his tail, Kat followed carefully, keeping her distance, not wanting to be seen.

He paused to give a cheery hello to someone just outside. Whom, Kat didn't know, because she'd flattened herself against the building. As he moved on, she dared slip out of hiding again.

He was heading for the stables.

Again, she followed.

His voice, once more, was level and steady. Concerned as he spoke to one of the grooms. "I must ride out myself, see what can be done, what can be found!"

With both men busy acquiring his mount, she slipped through the door. And once they began leading his horse out, she ran hurriedly along the many stalls, looking for Alya, her mare. At last, she found her. No time for a saddle; her hands shook as she tried to put the bridle on the horse.

He was leaving.

She grabbed a handful of mane and leapt upon the horse's back, heedless that she wore skirts and they now bundled less than decently around her thighs. She let the mare press open the stall door, and she ignored the groom as she rode by him.

Outside, it was growing dark, but the lights in the busy street revealed him just up ahead. His pace was quick, but not heedless. He looked like a fine young Englishman on a mission, careful of the women and children in his way.

And then he was out of the city, loping across the sand.

It was dark, she could hardly see, and her own mission was quite insane. But she no longer believed that Margaret was being only held for ransom. And if she didn't follow, the young woman well might die.

And if I do follow, we'll probably both die! she mocked herself. *And yet…*

There was really no choice.

ALI WAS THERE. Despite the fact that he was greatly disturbed and blamed himself, he was coherent, telling them all exactly what had happened.

"Oh, my God, poor Margaret!" Camille breathed.

Hunter couldn't help but clutch Ali's arm. "My wife...Kat?"

"She fought with us, Sir Hunter." He spat on the ground. "Better than the men. And she is well. Safe at the hotel. I saw her there myself. And the man, Doyle, he is fine. Your fellow, Ethan, is hurt, but there is a doctor. Others are hurt. Two men dead. And Lady Margaret, a shame that I must bear forever, taken."

"Ali, you fought. Men died. There is no shame in your fight," Brian said.

Hunter was already moving.

"I must see Kat," he said when Brian would have stopped him. "Ali will come with me. Tomorrow, first light, you, Abdul and the rest of the men must start searching."

Hunter was grateful for Ali. The man could see in the dark.

KAT WASN'T AT ALL CERTAIN how she managed to follow the rider in the darkness. Partially, perhaps, she knew that he was retracing ground that she had already ridden that day. And, thankfully, the moon rose full and high that night, bathing the landscape with a pale glow.

She decided, after the first few minutes, that riding bareback might be easier than with a saddle. Definitely easier than with a sidesaddle!

Still...her legs ached. She thanked God for the little mare, who had the ability to move at an even lope, swift and never rough.

But dear God, how hard and long he rode!

At last they came to the dune she recalled. She dared to ride to the crest of it, but then she reined in the mare, slid off and carefully trod through the sand, leading the horse, so that she might stop and see where the man was going.

But he had vanished into thin air.

She hurried over the dune then, completely baffled. But then she saw it. An area with scraggly pines, dead palm fronds strewn about, and a very small, depleted water hole. Far too sad to be called an oasis.

She hurried to the area, then desperately began pulling at the fronds. To her amazement, as she did so, a door opened in the sand.

Ancient ingenuity? No, the door was new, wood, and the contraption had been so cleverly built that one could enter and bring the camouflage back down upon the closed door.

She hesitated, then gave the mare a swat on the rump. "Go home, girl!" she whispered. She was far more afraid of someone suspecting her presence if he saw the horse than being caught once she was within.

The hole gaped before her. The steps leading downward were ancient. She hesitated again. Too late to change her mind. The mare was gone.

She started down into the black hole in the earth.

HUNTER WAS CERTAIN THAT they reached Cairo in record time. His mount was lathered and he feared that he had nearly killed the creature, but left with the finest of grooms, he would surely survive.

He needed to see Lord Avery, but first, Kat.

He burst into their suite, shouting her name. No answer. Damn her! She was angry with him, and surely feeling justified now, but he was going to shake her from now until doomsday if she didn't answer him soon.

"Kat!"

But tearing through the rooms, he realized that she wasn't there.

He crashed into Arthur in the hallway. "Sir!" Arthur exclaimed.

"My wife…is she with you?"

"Obviously not. No great powers of deduction needed there."

"Where is she?"

"I've no idea."

"She must be with Lord Avery."

"I have just left him. She is not there."

He was afraid he was about to do bodily harm to someone when Ali came striding tensely toward him.

"She left! Hassam said that he saw her tearing out of the stables, bareback!"

"What?" Hunter said, an icy hand about his heart.

"One of the English fellows had gone to the stable, told Hassam he was going to ride out, see what he could do. He had barely left before Lady MacDonald tore out after him," Ali explained quickly.

Hunter looked from him to Arthur. And then, absurdly, what he'd seen earlier in Kat's sketches suddenly clicked in his mind.

"Which fellow?" Arthur demanded.

"Never mind! I know!" Hunter said, and ran down the hall for the stairs, Ali on his heels.

"Wait! I am coming, too!" Arthur thundered. "I have sailed to the ice caps, attended in the service. I am a doctor. I am strong and able!"

"Come, then! But I'm waiting for no one!" Hunter shouted back.

SHE WAS NO LONGER BEING kept out of the latest exploration. Her husband needed her to hold the lantern.

"Brian, there is no more avid enthusiast than I, which is something you know very well," she said. "But there *is* tomorrow!"

He was tapping walls again.

"Have you ever just had a feeling, my dear?"

"What?"

"A feeling, an urge within. Call Abdul again—I'll need help with the picks."

"Brian, please, what are you talking about?"

"We need to break this wall now. Tonight!"

She shook her head. She was worried sick herself. Not for her own safety. Abdul had set every man about the camp with a rifle, and his fellows knew how to shoot. They were prepared for trouble.

But she felt ill. Margaret! Poor, delicate Margaret. And Lord Avery. He must surely be losing his mind. How could Brian be so obtuse?

"Abdul!"

The man was already there with the picks.

She held the lantern.

Then she wished that she was wielding one of the picks herself. She watched Brian's face and knew that he was suffering, too. And beating up an ancient wall must have felt very good.

"My turn!" she cried after a moment, and Abdul was forced to relinquish his tool and hold the lantern while she went to work.

The wall began to crumble.

THE STEPS LED DOWN to an anteroom. Sconces held burning lanterns on the walls, and when Kat first came down to the level, it was silent but bright. She quickly tried to ascertain some sort of layout for the tomb or temple and noted instantly the many giant, floor-to-ceiling pillars. Because she happened to have read the papyrus regarding Hathsheth, she knew that she was seeing his name, his sacred scarab, everywhere she looked. Other gods were depicted, but the priest himself was depicted as a god. She heard movement, the shuffle of feet, the sound of voices, and she scurried quickly to the left into a narrow hallway. It was rather ill lit, with only two lanterns, and it was a perfect place in the shadows to try to observe.

Three men, clad in red cloaks, walked through the center where the pillars rose so high. They were heading westward along another hallway.

She realized then that the hallway led straight west beneath the desert. There were no massive rises and falls of the sand and the dunes beneath the ground. Straight west would lead to Hunter's encampment. How far it was, with no natural obstructions, she didn't know.

It would be foolish to walk straight into the open. Instead, she sidled along the narrow, dark hallway. There was a dim light at the end of it. She came upon another room. There was a door—once again, a modern addition—at the rear of the room.

Someone in one of the red cloaks was striding up and down in front of it.

As she stood there, debating, she heard the soft sound of sobbing.

Margaret.

The fellow in the red cloak paid no heed. He just kept up his pacing.

Kat realized that she had no weapon. And she probably had very little time. But she knew that it was Margaret crying from behind the door, and she couldn't just sneak out. She would never be able to get help in time.

After a few seconds of pondering, she realized that the fellow in the cloak was a man of habit. Ten steps forward, ten steps back. Ten forward, ten back.

She hesitated just a second longer, then tore back down the narrow hallway. It was still quiet. She grabbed one of the torches from its sconce and stared at it. She'd never be able to douse the flame; it had been soaked in something to keep it burning through the night.

She raced back along the hall to the room—and kept her distance. The fellow was coming forward.

Ten paces.

He turned.

She ran.

She prayed that she had the strength to hit hard enough. Perhaps her desperate plea was heard. She slammed the torch down on the fellow's head with all her might, and he went down.

His cowl caught on fire. Desperately, she grabbed the flaps of his cloak and buried the flame. She turned to the door, terrified that there would be a lock—and no key. But the door wasn't locked, only bolted. She slid the heavy wooden bolt slowly, praying that it would make no noise. There was a slight creaking sound—enough to solicit a gasp of fear from within.

She dragged the door open, the torch high in her hand.

It had been dark within. Margaret, apparently, had been thrown in there and simply left. She was on the floor as close to the door as she could get.

Kat had expected to find her covered in the desert sand, a result of the fighting earlier. To her amazement, Margaret was dressed in a golden collar and chemise, sheer trousers, anklets and a headdress.

She looked at Kat, her mouth opening to form a scream.

"Shh!" Kat hissed. Seeing her, Margaret started to cry again. Kat lifted the torch higher, trying to assess the room where Margaret had been held.

Her breath ceased. Her heart caught in her throat.

Rows and rows of the dead lined niches in the walls. She remembered what she had read, and she felt ill. There were dozens of dead women here. They had not been mummified. They had been the wives of the great priest, and at his death, had been locked in here. Buried alive. They had taken their assigned pallets, lain down upon them and awaited the next life.

Margaret turned, seeing her face. Apparently, she'd never had a look at the dark chamber where she'd been kept prisoner.

Now she saw it all too well.

She clapped her hand over her mouth, but not in time to stop the beginning of a terrified scream.

Inwardly, Kat swore. *We might have had a real chance!*

Too late. She had to salvage what she could.

"Help me!" she commanded Margaret fiercely.

She thrust the torch into the other woman's hands and began tugging the cloak off the man who lay on the floor. Apparently, as frightened as she might have been, Margaret also had an instinct for survival. She started to help Kat, working with her free hand. She was feverish in her desperation. Kat could only imagine what she had suffered in the time elapsed.

Kat was certain that she heard distant footsteps. "Hurry, hurry, hurry!" she urged Margaret. She got the cloak off the man and dragged the body into the mausoleum. She reached for the cloak, ready to put it on, ready to start pacing, ten forward and ten back.

"I've got to shut the door again. It will only be for a minute."

"No!" Margaret clung to her.

"Margaret, I'm going to pretend to be him—"

"You can't shut me in here, you can't!" She was in a raw panic. Her grip was like steel. Her terror was so great that Kat realized that any urging would be useless.

"All right," she said, her heart sinking. "Put this cape on. Walk calmly along the hall. You'll come to an open area and you must go up the steps at the end of it. Push when you reach the top. It's a door."

"They'll follow me."

"No, they won't. Come on, I'm right in front of you, I'll lead you to the steps, then you must go, do you understand?"

Margaret nodded. Kat pushed her down the hall, to the stairs, and for a moment, she dared pray that they both had time to make it.

Then she heard footsteps. Turning, she could see the men coming. She shoved Margaret. "Go, and so help me God, you figure out a way to get help!"

Margaret was gone. Kat let out a scream and went tearing past the figures coming their way. As she had expected, they turned, anxious to capture her.

The hall was vast. She was young and swift, but eventually, she knew, the room must come to an end.

It did. At a wall. A high wall. And before it was a chair fit for the gods. No, not gods. A god. A god to be worshipped.

Little did those who were seduced to pay homage here really realize that the god they worshipped was money. That hardly mattered.

The cloaked figures were coming fast behind her. In seconds, they would be upon her. They would tackle her to the ground, if they had to.

Kat didn't have to be stopped. There was nowhere else to go, not from where she now stood. She simply came to a halt and stared at the seated figure, now divinely dressed, eyes done up in charcoal, gold on his chest, a staff in his hand.

Naturally, he inclined his head and smiled.

"Welcome, Kat."

The god began to laugh.

Chapter 18

THE FULL MOON BATHED the landscape in a glow that allowed them to follow the two sets of tracks.

The desert, however, was ever shifting. There were several times when they had to retrace their steps, search again.

As time ticked by, a greater fear seared Hunter's heart. He thought of the girl, Françoise, and the fact that she had been so swiftly and brutally eliminated, just because she had…what? Failed in some way? Seen something? Threatened someone?

Beyond a doubt, Kat was a threat.

He began to wonder, for as he rode his mind was tormented with a never-ending swirl of thoughts and emotions, if David Turnberry was really supposed to have died the day he went off the sailboat, of if that had only been a warning. He was certain that, by the time the massive stone fell in Rome, Kat was the target.

She must have been an amazing thorn in their sides from the moment she had dived into the river. And then, when he had come up with his plan that had so appealed to Lord Avery, they must have been incredulous and then perhaps even hopeful that it might aid their cause.

They simply hadn't counted on her talents. Hadn't realized how artistic she was or how remarkable her memory.

"The dunes!" Ali shouted.

And there they were, caught in the moonlight.

His pulse quickened. He had thought the full moon a godsend. Now he realized that it was a curse. For the full moon, traditionally, throughout the history of mankind, was a time of sacrifice.

He swore softly and dismounted, searching the ground.

The tracks continued up the dune. He followed them first with his eyes. And then he gasped.

For a moment, he felt the breeze, the chill of night, and it was almost as if he had gone back in time. There was a woman on the crest of the dune. She was adorned in ancient costume, clad in jewels and gold, and as she lifted her arms, the cloak cast around her fell away, and she stretched out her arms to the heavens, a priestess greeting her god.

Then she fell. And as she began to roll down the dune, he ran toward her, catching her halfway, lifting her into his arms.

Her eyes opened wide as Ali ran up quickly behind him. "Oh, Hunter! They have her, they have her and...oh, my God!"

THE GOD WAVED HIS HAND, and the cloaked figures went away. He was amused then, smiling at Kat, as if she had caught him at some college prank that he thought incredibly clever, and he certainly did want her to know how he had gotten away with it.

"So. You weren't surprised to see me. When did you figure it out?" he asked her.

"When I realized that you looked just like your mother," Kat told him.

"Amazing. No one ever saw it before. Of course, you realize, I didn't know that she was my mother until a few years ago," Alfred said with a shrug.

"What I don't understand," Kat said, desperate to keep casual conversation going because she was so terrified of what would come after, "is why all the subterfuge between you and her. Obviously, you've been working together. And how...how did your mother—your father's first wife, I mean—accept your father's mistress's child as her own?"

"That, well...my father was Lord Daws. Just as I am Lord Daws. She enjoyed being Lady Daws. When she couldn't produce a child, I suppose she was given an ultimatum. And when you have power and position and money, well...there's no end to the way records can be changed and what people will do. Now, of course, you! Ah, Kat—Lady MacDonald, sorry! Let's see, how you stumbled into this is quite amazing. I figured that someone would save good old David that day—he was beginning to suspect too much about me, so I had to give him a really good warning. You see, all he was really supposed to do from the beginning was steal the blasted map. But you dived in and saved him! When my mother found out who had done it, and that Lord Avery wanted to see that you were rewarded, well! I thought she would have apoplexy on the spot. She was doing so well, working so hard to sell your father's work—and, of course, in the meantime seeing that all our Egyptian treasures were sold!—and there you were, ruining the whole thing, making your father's work known! Personally, at first, I found it exceedingly amusing. Naturally, too, if you were willing to sell your soul for David, I was happy to help send you on the road to hell, and give David another reason to remember what he owed me. Ah, Kat. We were aware, immediately, of course, that the expedition Lord Avery, Lord Carlyle and Sir Hunter were planning would bring them dangerously close to our operation. We did, at last, manage to steal the wretched map. And they might have stumbled around a great deal more... Who in God's name ever would have imagined that you could recreate something so ridiculously well?" He sighed. "I am sorry. You are a most unusual young woman. Pity that your life will have to end as it will."

"Why?" Kat demanded. "You were your father's only heir!"

"Alas! I do love to gamble. Sadly, I went through that first fortune rather quickly. But my mother...um, well, she's been involved in a few slightly illegal affairs before. And, as long as the world didn't know our real relationship and believed that we despised each other, most of the time things went very well."

"How long has your mother been involved in the Egyptian black market?"

"This, all this? Well, it's really been a lovely setup. We only started last season. The point of it is, you see, you have to share. Now, mind you, you don't have to spend a fortune, you just have to keep the money flowing. There are so many poor people, Kat! And when you make them believe that you are turning the world over to them, well...you become a god. Oh, and it is much more fun being a god than a mere lord, by the way." He laughed, pleased with himself.

"And Margaret?" she whispered.

"Margaret. Ah, she is a creature of sweetness and beauty. Innocent, pure! Loved by all. And that's exactly why she'll make such a lovely sacrifice."

Kat's heart skipped a beat. She realized that he didn't know yet that he no longer had Margaret.

"You would really murder Lady Margaret? Lord Avery would tear the world to pieces to find you. He wouldn't rest until you were…drawn and quartered."

"That punishment was outlawed eons ago, Kat!"

"He would see it reinstated. Hunter will kill you, you know," she told him.

"How? I was attacked today, just the same as all of you."

It was her turn to laugh, and he didn't like it, but she couldn't help it. "Alfred, do you really think that others won't see what I saw?"

His expression turned surly. "So what?"

"She's here, isn't she?" Kat asked. "She's not is France. She pretends to be abroad selling art, but she comes here."

"Clever girl, Kat, so very clever!"

The words were spoken from behind her. She knew the voice. She spun around.

"Lady Daws," she said. The woman was there. Like her son, she was dressed in white. She wore a headdress adorned with gold, taken straight from a likeness of Nefertiti, Kat was certain. She was stunning and elegant in her attire.

Regal.

Deadly.

"You know," Kat said, still trying for a casual tone, "Eliza is the one who is very clever. She has known that you are truly pure evil from the start."

"Eliza!" Lady Daws said with disgust. "Well, poor girl! She'll be so distraught when she hears about your death in the desert that she'll probably have some terrible accident herself. I really don't want her around when I marry your father! Oh, look, Alfred! She's so red, so angry, about to combust! Oh, this is better than any physical torture I could devise! Yes, my dear, I think I will marry your father. He's going to be quite famous. Who knows? Had I realized that he might have become such a wealthy man, I might not have needed to throw myself into this elaborate scheme. But then, well...actually, it *is* fun out here. Having people *worship* you. And the money that comes in for the pieces...it's simply astounding."

Kat knew that she had to control her temper. "Isabella, I never thought that you were actually in your right mind, but I hadn't thought you to be insane."

"Insane? Do you realize what I have managed to do?"

"Do you realize that your little pyramid is toppling, that you have taken this all too far?" Kat said softly. "You're going to get caught."

"And how is that, dear? Do you think that your bumbling archeologist friends are really going to find this place?"

She was so smug. Just then, several hooded figures streamed into the room. They fell on their knees before Isabella.

Kat didn't understand what was being said, but she did get the gist of it. They had discovered, at last, that Lady Margaret was gone.

Isabella spun round in a rage. She strode toward Kat, seizing her throat. "Where is she?" she shrieked. "Where is she?"

Kat caught the woman's wrists and sent her knee into her abdomen. She knew she was going to pay for it, but fighting back for that brief moment was sweet. Cloaked figures rushed forward. A hand swung, catching her on the cheek, hard. So hard that she stumbled to her knees.

Someone caught her arms. She was dragged up and then struck again.

The world swam...

She was vaguely aware of Isabella screaming that they must find Margaret.

Her hair was caught, her head dragged up. She saw Isabella's furious eyes.

"Hardly pure, and certainly, a wretched little witch," the woman hissed. "But you'll make a fine enough sacrifice! In fact—" she brought her face close "—I shall revel in the killing!"

MARGARET WAS SCARCELY coherent, but eventually, Hunter was able to understand that she had been beneath the earth.

"There are dead people…corpses, bones…"

"Margaret! Where?"

She waved a hand over the dune.

Hunter stood, looking at Ali. "There's a hidden entrance to…something! I've got to find it."

"By the trees, Hunter," Margaret said. "There's a palm… I tripped on the fronds, coming out. It's there, I—I think you lift the palm fronds."

He started to walk away, but Margaret roused herself again, this time to grab his arm. "No! They'll kill you before you get to her…there are scores of them. They're at some kind of prayer and…I think…soon…I was to be killed. Hunter! You can't just walk in there. You can't fight that many people!"

He looked at Ali, knowing that she was right, that he couldn't save his wife if he was dead.

Time was ticking away.

He saw the cloak she had cast aside. "This is what they wear?"

She nodded. "I have to get in there," he said, kneeling down by Margaret. "And Ali has to get to the camp, to get help. Margaret, you've got to have courage. We must find a safe place to leave you."

"No!" she cried, grabbing him.

Ali looked at Hunter. "She can ride with me."

"She'll slow you down."

It was true. But it was true, as well, that he was afraid to leave her.

Just when he thought there was no option, another horse appeared coming over the sands. A single rider.

"Who the devil...?" he murmured. And then he smiled. "It's Arthur! Ali, I'm going in. You must have Margaret ride with Arthur and you get to the camp first. Bring Brian, Abdul and the others. Make sure they're armed. And get back as fast as you can!"

He ran up the dune, swept up the red cloak and hurried across the sand once again. There! The palms...and in the sand, just as nature would have left them, the fronds.

SHE AWOKE IN DARKNESS. Trying to move, she felt something heavy on her wrist. She touched it, puzzled.

Then the world seemed clear. She had taken Margaret's place in the tomb with the corpses of the priest Hathsheth's many wives.

The thought, in the darkness, washed over her like a wave of black panic. She fought it, gasping for breath, desperate to calm herself. Carefully, she rose. She was clad in something sheer, with metal everywhere, and something on her head. She touched the heavy door and pressed. It was bolted. And she knew that it was a heavy bolt.

She started to turn around, hoping that there was another way out. Yet she was loathe to leave the door, knowing what lay in the room.

Again, she found that she was desperate to catch her breath. And for a brief moment, she was afraid that she, like Margaret, would dissolve in tears and fall to the floor.

She had never found life so precious, so miraculous, as it had been in the weeks past. All because of...Hunter. And because, in his arms, she had discovered what it really was to know love.

Hunter. Good thought, solid thought. He would come after her.

He had no idea where she was!

Ah, but Margaret was out roaming somewhere in the desert. Unless, of course, they had found her again.

Someone will come! she thought desperately.

But then again, someone might not. She had to find her own way out of this situation. And if that meant walking to the back of a pitch-black room filled with ancient corpses, then so be it!

And so she started back. She had to set her hands before her and feel her way. Her skin crawled. She wavered, touched something. It crumbled beneath her fingers.

Bone.

She paused, inhaling and exhaling slowly. She came to a wall. A dead end.

"No!" she half whispered, half moaned, aloud. She became desperate, following the wall, banging along it. Nothing.

Then, suddenly, the door opened.

None other than Isabella Daws herself had come for her. "Kat, it's time. Think of it this way—all the people here believe that you will join the gods, that you'll be a wife to them. I mean, that's a rather lovely way to look at it, don't you think?"

The woman was framed in the doorway. Kat imagined that at the least, they might have another really fine fight before it all ended. She moved forward again, reaching to her side for one of the bones, a solid one, she hoped. She meant to smash it right across Isabella's face.

But two heavyset men stepped before Isabella just as she grabbed up the femur her fingers fell upon. And though she crashed it against a male arm with all her strength, she did little harm. The bone crumpled to dust on contact.

She was rewarded with Isabella's delighted laughter.

The fellows dived for her, one on each side, going for her arms. She struggled insanely. And she began to scream.

KAT!

The sound of her scream nearly caused Hunter to give himself away. He had to keep calm, had to wait until he could see her, get to her. And then...

He had to fight. And pray.

There were dozens of them now, men dressed in the red capes and cowls, and all of them chanting ridiculously. They were swaying and chanting, heads bowed, before the great chair, where Alfred, looking like a ridiculous boy dressed up for a masquerade, was sitting.

Before him, on a slightly lower dais, was an altar. Ancient white stone, set with restraints at top and bottom. Hunter had been working his way up to the front since he had slipped in with the group, but now, with Kat screaming and being dragged in, wriggling and writhing and fighting like a tigress, he knew he had to make his move more quickly.

Past body after body. They seemed to have put themselves into some mesmerized state. No one seemed to notice as he inched closer and closer to the front.

Lady Daws, head high, slight smile in place, as if she truly believed herself to be the reincarnation of an Egyptian queen or, indeed, a goddess, led the way. However, Kat was not lending sanctity to the proceedings.

She was resplendent, as well, with a brilliant gold corset covering her breasts, a narrow, white gauze skirt held to her hips with gold, and gold entwined into her hair. Bracelets adorned her wrists and ankles.

"Are you all insane?" she shrieked. "This is murder, not a sacrifice!"

Her words were powerful and strong, but unheeded. The chanting did not miss a single beat.

"Omm..."

He pressed past the last of the fellows—zombies!—standing before him. As he did, Kat was dragged up onto the dais. It did take two of the men, one on each side, to get her there, he noted, and since her legs were flailing—and she was managing to throw a few good kicks into the faces of the men who would restrain her—a sharp command was called out. Instantly, the fellow by Hunter's side jumped to the fore, grabbing a shapely, flailing leg.

Hunter sprang quickly to his side. He caught the other leg.

He needed her to see his face. He captured her ankle and pretended to slide it into the restraint, praying that no one would notice—and that she wouldn't kick anyone else until he was ready.

The sound of the chanting suddenly changed.

The first two men who had secured her wrists moved back.

Kat madly worked at the restraints, still screaming, calling them all blind fools, idiots, murderers and worse.

Then there was a drumbeat.

Alfred stepped from his god's chair. Isabella approached him, holding a pillow high. There was a long-bladed knife shimmering in the torchlight upon it.

Alfred swept up the knife. Isabella stepped back regally.

Alfred approached the table. He raised his arm.

And Hunter could wait no longer.

SHE WAS ABOUT TO DIE, and she had never known that such hatred could seethe in her heart. So many things should have touched her mind with greater fervor! Her love for her dear father, and fear for him in the future. Eliza! Lord Avery, who had been so good, Camille, Brian…

Hunter.

And it did seem that his face swam before her eyes, that the ache in her heart was largest because she loved him so very much, because…

We should have had a life. I should have had a chance to tell him that I have been falling in love with him bit by bit since we met, that I realized far too quickly that it was he I loved, wanted…

Another drumbeat!

Alfred was smiling and ready to kill, to delight in stabbing the knife straight into her heart!

Then…

She realized that a foot was free just as one of the figures cast aside his cloak.

Hunter.

Alfred half turned. Hunter slammed his fist into his face so swiftly that Kat could hear the snap of the bone in his nose. He went down.

A roar went up.

Instantly, Hunter moved to free her from the restraints.

"Hunter!"

She screamed his name in warning as Lady Daws, snarling in fury, threw herself at him. He turned, slamming her with an elbow that sent her flying back against the wall.

"Hurry, hurry!" she pleaded, one wrist free, one foot free, desperately working at the knot.

A huge fellow bellowed and started for Hunter. He reached into his waistband, produced a pistol and shot him.

Silence reigned for a second, long enough for Hunter to free her of all the restraints at last.

She jumped up behind the dais, ready to face the oncoming crowd.

Hunter had his hands full. He emptied the pistol and drew a sword. She saw the sacrificial knife fallen by the side of the altar and made a dive for it. She came up to find a massive man about to strangle her.

She winced as she drove the blade home.

Men were falling before Hunter and her, one after another. She was back to back with him, ready to defend herself, to fight with him.

But no matter how they fell, more came. Bleakly, she realized that they were going to die.

"Hunter!" she cried softly.

"What? I'm a little busy!"

"I..." Her knife was stuck in an arm! She threw a punch. She heard an *oomph*.

"You what?"

"I love you!"

"What?"

His sword made a wild swing and he turned toward her.

"Hunter, watch out!"

He swung back just in time.

"I'm serious. I've known it a very long time…I… Oh!"

Someone grabbed her from behind. Burly hands came around her.

A gun exploded. Then more shots were fired. A cry sounded, loud and clear.

"Stop or die!"

She knew the voice that had stilled the room. It was Brian Stirling, Earl of Carlyle.

The fellow was wrenched away from her. Strong arms were reaching for her.

Hunter's.

And, streaming in from everywhere, so it seemed, were their friends. To her left, Ali had a man at sword point. Before her, wielding a walking stick with an expertise that would have done Holmes proud, was Arthur Conan Doyle. Abdul had a group at gunpoint.

Allan, barely standing, still held a pistol. Robert Stewart, looking fierce, was at his side.

David was there. His face was ashen, his hand was quivering.

The workers who had been with them, all of them, were there. And then, coming in from behind Lord Carlyle, a slew of men in uniforms—Egyptian police.

She looked up at Hunter, who held her in a tense, trembling grip as he stared at the scene around them.

Suddenly, she felt incredibly weak. "We're going to live!" she whispered.

And then she passed out.

SOMEWHERE ALONG THE LINE, someone had supplied her with a cloak.

A black one, not one of those worn by the cult! And they had gotten back to the hotel, though she didn't remember the ride. There was a brandy in her hand, and they were all gathered—except, of course, Lady Daws and her son, Alfred.

Lady Daws, so she'd heard, had lived, and was ranting insanely in a cell somewhere in Cairo. Alfred was dead. He'd been trampled to death.

Emma had finally stopped clucking over Kat, and Margaret had stopped touching her face and crying, and Camille—who had said that the brandy would be the best thing at the moment—sat across from her, calmly smiling.

"How did you get there so fast?" Kat whispered at last, bringing a halt to all the other voices in the room.

"We might well have ridden our horses to death," Robert said, "but we weren't there first. Hunter must have been riding like a maniac."

"Yes, but..."

"May I give this a try?" Arthur asked. He addressed Kat. "Lady Katherine, you followed Alfred Daws. Hunter and Ali followed you. They stumbled upon Lady Margaret. Hunter took the cape and cowl and went down the stairs while Ali rushed to the camp. I came a bit more slowly, bringing along Lady Margaret. While all this was going on, two things were happening. Lord and Lady Carlyle had broken through the walls—and the underground passage did lead to the temple.

They were able to stream in from that end. However—the police arrived because David Turnberry went to Lord Avery with his belief that Lord Alfred Daws was involved in all that had gone on and told him why. Robert and Allan were roused—no one told Ethan, the man is still too badly injured—and the police were notified. Then a massive assault moved through the desert. There!"

Kat turned to Camille. "You broke through the walls."

"Yes, ironic, isn't it? Our great discovery led to a temple that Lady Daws had not only stumbled upon—through some of her contacts in the black market—but made use of. However, she did not find the tomb of the high priest. I believe we will have that left for us!"

"Bah! Tombs!" Lord Avery declared. "I'm taking Margaret and sailing for home!"

"Oh, Father!" Margaret protested. "I wish to stay!"

"Why on earth!" he exclaimed.

"Because my friends are here," Margaret said. She reached out a hand to Kat. "True friends!"

"And what makes you think that Kat would want to remain here after all that happened tonight?" Lord Avery demanded.

"Well," Kat told him softly, "the danger is gone."

"Humph! Humph!" he repeated, looking at them both as if they were crazy. "Do you two think that Lady Daws and that wretched boy managed this all on their own? There are other evil entities in on this, I assure you. And how do you know if we rounded up all those people in the ridiculous red capes?"

"I believe that the Egyptian police will be able to handle it from here, Jagger," Lavinia said, shaking her head. "They are very fine people."

"But, but..."

"Oh, Jagger, do stop blathering!" Lavinia commanded. "Simply ask the children, all of them, what they want to do! It seems to me that the season has actually been helped along, now that the menace is gone. If they all want to stay, I say, let them do it!"

"Well," Camille said, her eyes sparkling, "I do believe we're on the verge of a truly great discovery."

"My love, we will do as you wish," Brian told her.

"My lord Carlyle," Robert said, "I am delighted to stay on as planned."

"I, too," David said, and his words were firm.

"I would stay," Allan Beckensdale said, and looked at Kat ruefully. "Perhaps...perhaps your sister and father could be coaxed into joining us."

"My sister?" she repeated.

"It would be such a pleasure," Allan said politely.

"Hunter?" Kat said.

"You truly wish to stay?" he asked Kat.

"I do, if you do."

"I'm asking you."

"But—"

"Oh, good heavens!" Lavinia said, rising. "It's time we all got out of this room. Jagger, I believe we're staying. Besides, Ethan is in no shape to travel. This is not a cowardly group. We are subjects of Queen Victoria. But now, all of you, out, out!"

"I still don't understand how..." Robert began.

"Come, then, my boy," Arthur told him. "Out, and I will explain it all again."

One by one, they began to file out. And at last, Hunter and Kat were alone.

She was in a chair near the hearth. He stood by it. There was a moment's awkward silence. Then they both spoke at the same time.

"Hunter, I—"

"Did you—"

"It wasn't just because—"

"Say it again."

"I know you won't really believe—"

"Say it again! Please."

"I love you!" she said.

He left the hearth to drop to his knees before her. And his eyes, wickedly deep and dark, seemed to devour her. He caught her hands and kissed them. She shook her head, not knowing the right words. "I believe I began falling in love with you the minute I met you," she added softly. "And I fell out of whatever I felt for David very long ago. I kept comparing him to you. I know…I don't believe that you'd just cast me out—but you did send me away!"

"I was terrified for your life. You are sadly reckless."

"Hunter, I merely do what makes the most sense at the moment."

"Well, we could argue that forever. And we probably will. No, I can promise that we will argue endlessly over it, but…that is for the future. So…say it again."

"What?"

"'I love you. I want to be with you forever. I couldn't bear it when you pushed me away. I had to pretend that…I didn't love you.'"

She winced, then said, "I don't know exactly what you feel for me—"

"You must be joking, my dear. Apparently, I have worn my heart on my sleeve before everyone else."

"You could say it, too," she suggested.

He smiled, cupped her cheek, lifted her head.

"I love you. No, adore you. And I will happily be anywhere in the world, home or abroad, anywhere, if you are there."

"Oh, Hunter!" She threw herself into his arms. He backed away slightly, clearing his throat. "Ahem. This is certainly an...interesting outfit!"

"Interesting?" she said.

"Indeed."

She laughed, savoring the freedom to touch his face, smooth his hair.

"Well...we are here. In this lovely room. This lovely, very *convenient* room."

"Ah!"

He rose and gently picked her up, cradling her into his arms. And when he kissed her that time, she knew that she had never before known such a kiss.

DAWN WAS BREAKING and they still lay awake, and she knew even more.

"Hunter."

"My dear?"

"You told me once that I should only come to you because I wanted you. That should be the only reason, ever."

"And?"

She rolled to him, leaning on his chest. "There is an even better reason."

And he laughed, pressing his lips to hers. "I am the one who has learned that lesson," he told her. "It is love," he said softly.

The sun rose over the desert as he took her in his arms again.